THE
MIRROR'S
EDGE

Also by Steven Sidor

Skin River

Bone Factory

THE MIRROR'S EDGE

STEVEN SIDOR

THE
MIRROR'S
EDGE

STEVEN SIDOR

St. Martin's Minotaur

New York

THE MIRROR'S EDGE. Copyright © 2008 by Steven Sidor. All rights reserved. Printed in the United States of America. No part of this book may be used or reproduced in any manner whatsoever without written permission except in the case of brief quotations embodied in critical articles or reviews. For information, address St. Martin's Press, 175 Fifth Avenue, New York, N.Y. 10010.

www.minotaurbooks.com

Library of Congress Cataloging-in-Publication Data

Sidor, Steven.
    The mirror's edge / Steve Sidor.—1st ed.
        p. cm.
    ISBN-13: 978-0-312-35413-8
    ISBN-10: 0-312-35413-4
    1. Journalists—Fiction.   2. Missing children—Fiction.   3. Brothers—Fiction.
4. Cold cases (Criminal Investigation)—Fiction.   5. Domestic fiction.   I. Title.

PS3619.I36M57 2008
813'.6—dc22   2007051830

First Edition: April 2008

10 9 8 7 6 5 4 3 2 1

To those bodies dumped in the woods, and never found.

I think about you.

Acknowledgments

The road to the end of this book was a long and tortuous one. I have some people to thank for seeing me through. My agent, Ann Collette, performed above and beyond her duties, and always at the highest level of excellence. Ben Sevier and Keith Kahla provided support, patience, and brilliance. Brian Padjen, Bob Tuszynski, Ross Molho, and Jamie Howard are the best friends a guy could have. My parents helped me when I needed them. Congratulations to Jennifer and Tim Szopa. Erika DuPlantis and Tom Anvin were good company. Lisa, Emma, and Quinn are my reasons to believe. Special thanks are due to my pal, Gary Heinz, who gave me the desk and the title.

THE
MIRROR'S
EDGE

I came to Egypt to find them.

This morning, in the lobby of the Hotel _____, I had an incident. I accosted a Belgian businessman and his son. Grabbing for his hand, I knocked a cup of hot black coffee to the floor. White china shattered on scarlet marble tiles. Brown splashes stained the cuffs of his linen slacks. My apologies came in another language. The concierge summoned the police. They led me away.

I have some money, still, from the book. I have my old press credentials.

The Egyptian officer flips through my passport.

"Your name is Jase Deering?"

"Yes."

"You are journalist?"

I mumble a response.

"Pardon?"

"Yes, I am."

They're letting me leave the country. I must go immediately. The next plane. I should be thankful. My situation is precarious. I had a double-edged razor blade taped to my thigh and the bottom of my trouser pocket cut away to give me access. The police confiscated the razor along with a number of my thigh hairs when they jerked the tape free. They suspected drugs, or worse.

After an awkward escort to my departure gate, I get on the plane. We're in the air now, landing gear safely stowed for the transatlantic crossing. A window seat, the first row of coach. Emergency row. Extra legroom. Amazingly, the space next to me is unoccupied. Perhaps I will try sleeping, but later.

I look out at an uncluttered sky.

I study the buildings, ancient and modern, on the ground as they get smaller. I see the tips of minarets. When the plane banks hard left, I observe a transition to vast stretches of sand. We climb to our cruising altitude, and as soon as the flight attendant gets up from her jump seat, I order a drink.

She leaves me. Thinks I'm a nervous flier. In her haste, she bumps the long leg of a passenger in first class.

His eyes—they follow her.

Is it him?

Sitting there, relaxed, in the second row of first class across the aisle.

I have his profile in view. A bright oval of evening sunlight burns on his *Times of London*. Dyed his hair red and cut it short; it's almost shaved to the skull. He has gained weight over the years, softness around the middle, and he wears glasses, though they may be cosmetic and not prescription. Round lens tinted lavender, pewter wire frames.

Are they part of his disguise?

Because it *is* him. He's grown a laughable mustache too.

When the attendant brings it, I gulp my Chivas and swallow another Percodan. The Egyptians didn't touch my pills. Small miracle. They acted as though they felt sorry for me more than anything. I'll wait to build up my courage.

No, it's not him. No ring.

Ten intact fingers.

I ask him to stand, helping him rise because he's befuddled by my approach, the smell of Scotch lacquered on my breath. It shocks him.

How tense I am, how close. He's too short, by six inches at least. I simply walk back to my seat, saying nothing.

The flight attendant has checked me three times in the last ten minutes. My altercation with the Englishman from first class is over, but she pegs me as a psychotic. It's a long flight to take without a companion, without sleep—because who am I kidding, I haven't slept well in ten years; and if I do fall asleep, there's a good chance I'll wake up screaming. *Wouldn't that be wonderful?* I hold on tight and let the booze and pills work their minor magic.

Magic.

How odd it is I choose that word.

I took out this pen and tablet of paper to distract myself. I'll write until we land. An eternity in my present state of mind. The hours creep when you can't think about the future. My future is nonexistent at this point. Or at least it feels better to think about it that way. I can't afford a cold self-assessment. My career has smoldered. I dwell entirely in the past. My memories, the only ones real to me, are of a singular and prolonged nightmare. I find a story of pain, madness, perverted sex, torture, greed, fear, murder, family secrets, breathtaking loss, lies, pure evil, and ultimately . . . *magic.*

The word feels stupid and childish in my mouth.

But I know what happened, or, at the very least, I thought I knew what happened then, and how to tell the story. I wrote about it, earning enough fame to trigger the jealousy of my peers. That was long ago.

I stare out my portal at the moon, the stars. I ignore my reflection in the glass. I watch the black ocean gliding beneath me. Settling across the two seats, an airline blanket covering my lap, I get ready to write it down for the thousandth time. I'm shaky. A little more Chivas steadies the nerves.

Putting pen to paper.

I let the memories come.

Chapter 1

I will start my story in a place I shouldn't. My beginning won't involve the woman I once loved, my writing partner, Robyn Matchfrost. No, and the Boyle children, those two perfect little two-year-olds who went missing and whose disappearance sent me on my darkest journey— they are not present here.

This is something that happened when I was a child.

My brother, Matthias, walked into the woods one winter's day when he was twelve.

He never came out.

We play soldier in the pines.

A broken transistor radio serves as a walkie-talkie, a natty bedsheet—my parachute—trails behind me filling with dead leaves. I've tied two corners together; there's a hard, little knot rubbing under my chin. The enemy stronghold is a bombed-out convent in the forests of France. Barbwire hoops spiral through the courtyard. A machine gunner's nest deals murder from the bell-tower shadows. My mission: destroy the nest.

I walk on the homeward side of a shallow stream. The stream cuts across my grandparents' Michigan property like a mirror crack. My older brother holds down the tree fort, no more than a hundred yards away, armed with pinecone grenades and a plastic Tommy gun. Even poorly equipped, Matthias always makes the better Nazi. Maybe it's because he's two years older and a head taller, or it might be his shock of white-blond hair, so fair that in a certain light his eyebrows disappear. My brown curls match our father's in his childhood albums on top of the piano. Donna Cirincione—Grandma C or sometimes we say Mama's mama—she calls them my pelt.

Matthias is good at giving orders. That's why he's in the fort and I stumble on the ground. Burrs hook to my pants. Dampness seeps through the sides of my boots. I tell myself not to be surprised if, instead of the pinecones, Matthias throws rocks.

I gather the knot in my fist and, using my Swiss Army knife, cut. I watch my men slicing their chute cords. Good men, and many will die today. Never see home again. So much sacrificed to save an unpronounceable French hamlet and a dozen nameless, frightened nuns. I stuff the bedsheet into the hollow of a tree. We rendezvous at the water crossing. Silent, smoking—their heads cool as statues—my men fix their minds on killing Germans. After five minutes, we saddle up.

The winter has been mild, and the stream can't stay frozen. I cross on loose gray slates tilting in the current. A few old patches of snow persist in the deepest shade. They're like bones floating on a sea of rusty pins.

I remember the wood smell, an odor of freshly sawn boards, and I remember leaning into a tree trunk and coming away with sap on my shirt, stickiness at the back of my neck. I remember my eye catching the liquid red of a fox slipping through the underbrush.

I pick up a log to protect myself. The day keeps quiet, holding its breath. Pines everywhere. There is a crow marching through a zigzag of sunlight. I swat at him. The branch whistles, missing. His wings open— feathers fanning out like a hand of black playing cards—he flaps once, hopping sideways, aloft for a single windy beat. He lands and cocks his head for a better look at me. His eye is like a bubble of oil. He opens his beaked mouth without a sound. He flies.

Overheated in my new blue sweater, the wool itchy as ants, I unbutton my grandfather's hunting jacket—I'm wearing it because Mama says mine is too thin for the woods. As if the woods are a colder place. I decide to take the jacket off. I hang it on the sharp remains of a tree that has split in half and been fed upon by something. The pulpwood transformed to a corky orange.

Mama is right about the woods.

The cold is scooping under my clothes. My sweat cools to glass. I put the jacket on again, stubbornly leaving it unbuttoned. I roll back the sleeves.

I've been getting over the flu. The light-headedness of being sick is still with me. I'm fogged in by over-the-counter decongestants. When I swing my arms, the sea-salt tang of my grandfather's aftershave puffs into my face. I feel a little like throwing up. Acid spiders in my throat. I swallow down saliva, winter air tasting like stones.

The fort.

I duckwalk through underbrush. Needles soften my footfalls. I think I hear Matthias, his voice hushed and deep from the belly. Giving commands.

Constructing the fort was simple. Scrap wood from our Grandpa C's workshop, nails from his Folgers coffee can. He lent us two hammers and a hacksaw to do the job. Grandpa C liked that we were builders. Told us to take his wheelbarrow for hauling the boards. Dad would've helped us, except he's at home. I gave him my flu.

The fort is like a shoebox—top off and tipped sideways. We put it up between two trees growing close together. We pounded in braces. We made a five-step ladder, nailing two-by-fours crosswise up one pine. We have to swing ourselves to get in, but a man can reach. He can reach inside and a boy will have no place to hide.

The sergeant paces along scarlet arches of thorns. This spot, in the country of my imagination, was Nazi barbwire. But here and now is no game. We are searching for Matthias. My mother and grandfather have gone off. They picked a direction. My grandmother and a deputy named Cady have taken the opposite. I remain under the fort with the sergeant, whose name is Billy Dean Gatlin. We are within a small oval clearing directly beneath a tree. The fort is empty, the way I found it four hours ago.

The sergeant fingers a carved trunk. "You boys do this?"

I inch up. Stand tiptoe. "No, sir."

"Possibility?"

"What?"

"I said is there any possibility Matthias could've done it?"

"He didn't have a knife."

"Right. That's good to know," he says, finger brushing the spot of bald chipped wood and the slit. "This mark here might be a clue."

"I know what a clue is."

"Yeah?"

"It's a mistake."

"There you go, partner." The sergeant meets my gaze. No nod, no additional words. Eyes gray as a bucket. Smooth chest visible inside the unbuttoned collar of his shirt. His neck is golden. He's chewing on something. Sunflower seed. He spits the husk.

Mama finds Matthias's stocking cap. Inside out. Blond hairs pulled at the roots.

The gathering at the Cirincione farm swells. My father arrives. Bleary, coughing into his fist. He has his weekend eyeglasses on. They're speckled with paint. Duct tape holds the frames together. Looking like he skipped his shower this morning. I'm embarrassed to see him in public unkempt.

I tug his coat.

"What is it?" he asks.

"You forgot to switch your glasses."

"Go inside the house," he says.

People jostle me. Ignore me altogether. Then they realize I might be the key. I'm brought front and center. They take turns squatting down to my level. Going eyeball-to-eyeball with the kid.

The only witness.

Except I didn't see anything.

That's not what they want to hear. They're too freaked out about the prospect of a missing boy to put on their happy faces for my sake. I see anger brewing. They need to locate my brother. I'm a path, but I'm also an obstacle. The sheriff's men seek my full cooperation. When that yields little, they convey disappointment. All the attention is yanked from me. I'm demoted to a chair next to the fridge. Under a clock that uses birds instead of numbers. Tick-tick-tick. It sounds like a baby bird, hungry for a beak filled with red worms. If they could send me away, they would.

You aren't supposed to lose your brother in the woods. Even if he's your older brother, and he's the one who should be keeping an eye on you. *Nice going, Matthias. Look at the jam I'm in. Where are you?*

The window above the sink has a spiderweb in it. I don't see any spider. The web trembles. When I switch to looking at the glass, I expect to see the sky slowly getting darker. But it's black.

Where are you, Matthias?

I have a thought: what if they can't find him forever? That thought is electricity. Pure fear. I'm vibrating in my seat. Hairs on my arm prickle. Static crunches my ear. My bowels go shifty and growl.

I'm scared. A brand-new scared I've never been before.

Midnight.

The clock birds go nuts.

A t dawn, they start to find my brother. Piece by piece.

The trail of body parts runs north.

Up near the interstate there's a van. My dear brother's abused torso is inside.

The family hears the news together. My coldcocked parents hit the floor. They claw each other. Moaning. Screaming names. Like the others in the farmhouse, I am a spectator to their grief. We watch them wrestle more than themselves. Strangers I've never met are crying at the sight of my parents and their pain. The farm empties. Snot teases in and out of Grandpa C's left nostril like a party whistle and Grandma C topples over. Ambulances are parked in the yard. We ride one into town. Oxygen is leaking under the mask into my grandmother's blank, wrinkled face.

The siren calls out.

Traffic stops for us on a beautiful Monday afternoon.

I wade through this viscous dreamworld.

I feel a quivering. Crush before it spreads. Take a Perc if they're handy. Pour liquid courage on top.

Life is a mystery.

That's barroom philosophy, but it's also true.

Death is a riddle. We get the answer too late. No way around it. Call your answer God or Allah or Oneness. Just remember to call.

Worship.

Make sacrifices. Do the rituals.

Obey.

But you never really know, do you? How it's going to end.

I don't believe in a divine order anymore. But I believe in devils. Because devils have bitten at my heels and run me through the woods of my brother's slaughter. For thirty years, they've treed me. Hounded and haunted. They've twisted me up and burnt me down. I'm walking, talking charred remains. I inhabit the wreckage of myself.

He's the lucky one, they'll say.

The boy not chosen.

On the third anniversary of the disappearance, Dad falls from the twelfth-floor balcony (Matthias will always be on twelve) of a single room at the Holiday Inn in San Diego. His hometown. He pays for the room with cash. He brings no luggage. The girl at the desk remembers this: he requests a view of the bay. Alcohol pervades his system. But any blood sample drawn after his boy went missing would've come back looking like wine.

My parents had divorced. He'd lost his modest law practice. Alienated his friends. Moved away as he slid precipitously down the social ladder. Self-destruction, by the time he reached the physical stage, was well learned.

Mama and I get a phone call. We are still living in the Midwest, not the family house but an apartment in the same part of a different town. We don't get many calls. Once in a blue moon, it will be him. Late-nights jolts are his specialty, and it's always still early from where he's calling. The bars have let out. He's about to punch through into 100-proof oblivion. But then a little space, a bubble, must open around him where he can pretend nothing ever happened and he's feeling okay, even cheery, and he calls Mama. She listens. She doesn't scream at him. No, she eases him off to bed. I never get waved to the phone. He never asks for me, or maybe she gives him excuses if he does. He's in no condition to talk to a child. But I'm guessing he never asks.

Before he headed for the coast, he'd ignored me to the point I felt nonexistent. I don't remember actually seeing him during that time. I remember, instead, the locked door to the den and my misshapen face reflected back at me—a dwarf's head and nubbin fingers—by the doorknob. We go this way and that. A carny game. Always rigged. How I boiled with hatred while staring at myself in curved brass. Dad launched into full retreat. Peered through me as if I were a creature of fog. I loved him. He loved me. But it was impossible. He seemed so afraid. He couldn't touch or talk or be alone in a room with his surviving son. Me, the live ghost. My mother hated him for the way he shivered in my presence. He did worse to her. Accusations. *You're a goddamned liar. How could you?* Facets of betrayal explored. Adultery. Stealing his money. His pills. He never blamed her outright for Matt's death. But, please. He took many, many pills. It seemed like an overdose every morning. *Down the hatch!* Chased with his dram of pulp-free orange juice and cup of French roast. Time for his daily walk. And then slugs of whatever filled the flask he sank deep into the stinking pocket of his leather coat. He'd stagger home after sunset. Void, brush his teeth, and go out again. He didn't eat anymore. He'd become a chemical and liquid man.

It is a chemical and liquid man that goes over the top rail, accelerates to a blur, and breaks open on the sidewalk below. He leaves no note. People suggest this means the act was not deliberate but an accident. I can't say. He'd emptied the minibar. His shoes and socks were left on the balcony. He was too hammered to hold a pen. He'd never been a letter writer. The police find a photo inside his shirt. Matthias. Little League. He's wearing his BIG TONE'S AUTO PARTS ASTROS uniform and showing off his batting stance. Back in the hotel room, Dad's empty money clip is on the television. Wallet too. Another photo, and this one's been slipped out of a frame—too large to carry in a billfold. The edges are unbent, the backing stiff. Their wedding day.

I am nowhere to be found.

Mama and I get the ashes mailed to us in a contraption resembling a cake box, tied with yellow string, dangling from a little plastic handle and two metal hooks. Inside is a smaller box sealed with reinforced tape. Then, finally, a copper canister with a key attached to its side, like on shoe polish. I was curious. Turn. Quick peek. An eyeful of soot and nothing more. What did I expect? Cuff links? A smutty incisor half-buried in the Sahara of dust that once was my father? We put Dad next to Matthias's stocking hat on the mantel. The apartment complex doesn't allow fireplaces. But ours came with a phony setup that burns natural gas and has a wall switch. Blue tongues appear dancing behind the grate. We don't enjoy fake fires. Hardly enter the living room except when company stops by. Almost never, you could say.

You wouldn't be wrong.

Where's Mattie?"
Her darkened bedroom is right down the hall from mine. We leave our doors open. The question wakes me up. She's not hysterical. She's not awake either. I learn this from repeated experience. She never says it twice. I lie back. Pull the covers taut with my toes. Seek the moon,

if it's there. Full tonight. Cornered and shredding through the blinds. Daylight hours, Mama would never ask me about my brother.

Last time she did, I had no answer. That utterance defined the end of her happiness. My lack of response was the start of everything after. Incompleteness. Loose ends. The fun-house floor drops. Her question becomes a hole she can't climb out of. She doesn't need to hear another echo to know she's underground.

But thoughts, dreams, and prayers she devotes to an ongoing interrogation. She is continuously asking. Directing inquiries to God or the universe. I never find out which, or if there's a difference. She does not recover. Even decades later, playing with her grandchildren on a beach in South Carolina, wearing a straw hat with a paper gardenia stuck to the crown—her body language speaks.

This is wrong. We need to go back. Look again.

"Don't you dare ask me to smile. Go on. Take your silly picture. You never listen to me anyway." Her hand flicks up into the view of my camera as I press the button. We can always say she's waving. At least the girls are having fun. Oblivious. Hopscotching the blobs of dead jellyfish stranded by the tide. Shrieking. The girls run. Stop. Are transfixed. Reach their wrinkly fingers into the sea. On hands and knees they pluck a fiddler crab from the roiling surf. Laugh as he snips the air.

But I am listening, Mama.

It should have been you, Jase. Why not you?

Chapter 2

It happened ten years before my Egyptian plane ride. I was a regularly working freelancer then, living in Chicago. Talented but difficult—that's how people in the magazine business described me. I was divorced but in love with another. In love with Robyn.

The story found me. Claimed me.

Abduction.

Twin boys. Shane and Liam Boyle. The tender age of two. Adorable children with feathery brown hair and huge smiles for the world. Chubby, healthy juggernauts. Identical bookends. The spooky doubling directors exploit in B-grade horror flicks. Low-budget special effect. It works because the routine of trusting your eyes gets overturned. But they're cute too. If you'd seen them, at the zoo say, or being hauled through a snowy park on a sled, you would've been tempted to snap a picture.

But people can't do that, not the way things are. Every adult cast as a potential pervert, complete with a ring of turgid, sticky-handed friends. Stranger dangers. Look out and tremble. Parents are required to be forever suspicious. I'm a parent and I'm the same way. If I don't know you, STAY THE HELL AWAY from my kids.

These boys have handsome parents. Tad and Una Boyle. Traumatized beyond comprehension. Sickened. Wrenched apart. Or so it would seem. No one knew then how bad the scenario would play out for those two. Astonishing pain. I couldn't have guessed and I'm a good guesser when it comes to worst-case scenarios. I'm versed in the practice of pain management too. But Tad and Una I couldn't help.

Trials lay in wait. Exposure. Betrayals.

You hear horror stories, but never like this.

It starts, innocently enough, in their living room.

November 1.

High noon. All Saints' Day. Alignments of factors both astrological and mundane come into play.

Tad and his wife aren't home. The boys are. It's their birthday. A day of destiny, of appointments both missed and kept. A red-letter day. The boys have a nanny, Regina Hoffman, who is, by all accounts, a real-life Mary Poppins—practically perfect in every way. But this is the day she makes a terrible mistake.

Today a nightmare comes alive.

She will be the first person it grabs.

Doorbell.

Good girl Regina checks the peep.

Guy in a gray uniform, charcoal jacket, and a matching milkman's cap. He's not a milkman. He carries a clear blue jug hoisted on his shoulder. He's throttling the neck with one gloved hand. In the other hand, he holds a pink Plexi clipboard. His appearance is neat. Bushy mustache and big aviator sunglasses. Hair a little long, stiff and unnaturally black, but that may be an effect of the thick plug of peephole glass. It bends him. Colors aren't really the same. Regina opens the door—a hand's width because there is a security chain, and she is a careful girl, a trustworthy girl. An Alberta clipper lashes south from Canada. It is the coldest day so far this season. Looking at him, she's staring into a deep freezer. She squints. Crosses her arms.

"Howdy," he says. He sticks out the clipboard. He rotates it vertically to fit in the door opening. "Initials are fine."

The Boyles don't have a watercooler. Regina knows this for a fact. Shares it. But the deliveryman says, "New customer."

She asks him to confirm the address.

He nods, says, "I brought in their setup last month. The lady of the house has long hair. Am I right? She wore dangly silver earrings. Dressed all black. Had a funny name too. I remember her. Eula?"

"Una," Regina says without thinking. She has to admit the description is right on. But where's the cooler? In the basement? Did they put it upstairs in Tad's office?

The deliveryman says, "I can't check the address."

"Why not?"

"You've got my clipboard." He's smiling.

Well, that much is correct: 3033 Goethe. The name *Boyle* scrawled at the top. The signature on the order looks like Una's. Regina skims the slips underneath. She sees initials, names she doesn't recognize, although the streets are from the neighborhood.

She prints *RH* next to the Accepted box. She passes the clipboard back to him.

He shifts under the weight he's shouldering. "Thank you, miss."

Regina thinks he doesn't seem that much older than she is. He's not thirty. Midtwenties maybe? He's got a long jaw and a sharp chin. Boyish complexion. The mustache covers his upper lip, ages him. What's the deal with him calling her "miss" anyway? Maybe that's how they're trained to talk at the water company headquarters. Can't be too polite.

"Leave it on the stoop, please," she tells him.

"You sure?"

"Yes." She watches him frown. "Why?"

"You'll have yourself a big ice cube. In a few hours, anyway."

"I'll get it later, thanks."

"Okay." He lowers the jug to the porch stoop, up against the railing. His back is to her. She's closing the door. His head snaps left. She can see the corner of his eye move beneath the dark lens. He holds up a finger. "Hey, any empties inside?"

"No. I don't think so."

"Okay then." He waves. "Have a good day. It's a cold one, that's for sure. Bye."

Regina wants to shut the door, but he's standing there. His head's cocked and his mouth is pinched up like he's sucking a lemon drop.

"You want me to put the water around back?" he asks. "In the garage?"

"Um . . ."

"It's no problem. Seriously." He picks up the jug again. Her eyes follow the capped spout, shiny and blue, embossed with an ocean wave—as it's bobbing in the air. His gray-gloved hand is snug below. Sideways he goes, one foot taking the first step down. Adding, "Course, they'll have to walk it in. It's a heavy bugger. But that's better than sitting out here. I don't want to say anything, you know? Folks are crazy. Believe it or not, miss, I've had bottles stolen before. Not this street but one over. Those mansions on the lakefront. Let me set this in the garage for you. Quick."

"I suppose that's safer. I'll get the key." She closes the door. Engages the dead bolt. She grabs the house keys from a wall peg. The boys are shouting. They're in the living room, tearing out the couch cushions, jumping in the pile. Being what they are—boys. Regina doesn't want to give the deliveryman a set of keys. She can give him a single key though; take it off the ring. Only the garage key. What's the harm in doing that? She pries the closed circle on the ring. Splits it. The keys jingle. The ring snaps shut. Why do they make these things so difficult? Shane hits. Liam cries. Shane cries. Regina shushes them. Hugs them. She puts the cushions back in place. There's a gentle knock on the door. The cushions are flying again. Regina unlocks the door. The deliveryman is waiting, smiling.

Regina says, "Know what? Here, just put it here by the door."

She unhooks the chain.

He's in.

Then she notices the jug is empty. Droplets running down inside and a loop of water coiled at the bottom. A hollow thump when the jug hits the tiles. He knocks it over with the toe of his shoe. She's watching it fall. Roll across the foyer. She doesn't see his hand sweep behind his back, under the jacket. He straightens.

He lays the muzzle of a SIG-Sauer 9mm automatic between her breasts.

"Oh my God."

"Not hardly, miss." He presents handcuffs. She's told to turn around. Put her arms back. Keep her pretty trap shut.

"Please don't hurt me," she says.

The cuffs bite.

"Where are those lovely, lovely boys?" he asks.

No. 3033 Goethe is a hot crime scene.

The boys have vanished.

A wine bottle lies broken. Sweet, spicy odor permeates the air. Glass fragments have exploded, fan-patterned, into the living room. One of the boys may be bleeding on his way out the door. *Pending further lab tests based on the initial evidence*, the police are careful to stipulate.

We don't have much more we can state at this time.

But there is more.

The small, bloody footprint, exact enough to have been intentional, is that of a toddler. The shattered bottle was a wedding gift to the Boyles. It contained snake wine from Vietnam. Rice liquor poured over a cobra's body. Herbs mixed in prior to fermentation. It is a healthful drink said to enhance virility. For special occasions only. This cobra's hood is stretched open as if he went into the bottle alive. He's dead—long dead, of course—pickled and sealed off with wax. But free again. Landing beside the couch with his menace intact. The police step around his corpse tenderly. As if he might be resurrected only to sink his fangs into their ankles. He has lived for four years on the summit of a bookcase. Well beyond the boys' reach . . .

What's this now? A body rolled out on a stretcher. IV bags. Female. Young, semiconscious. Regina, the nanny. They're steering her curbside, to the idling ambulance.

Our lovely, high-minded, dutiful press closes the gap. A wooden barricade falls over. Everyone takes a second to determine if the sound he or she heard was actually wood slapping concrete and not gunfire.

We are in the preliminary stages of this investigation.
Please stand back.
Move back.
Get that camera out of my face now, sport.

The scene is bubbling chaos. A TV anchorman lives nearby. His wife saw the first squads pull up to the house and double-park. The paramedics' truck cruises to a stop. It doesn't take long for news to spread. *Catching fire* is an apt phrase.

"*Detective? Excuse me, Detective?*"

"*Was there a note?*"

"*Any note?*"

"*Did the kidnapper leave a ransom note?*"

"*Is it true the parents received a call?*"

"*What can you tell us about the kidnapper's demands?*"

"*Are the boys alive?*"

I'm not there, but Detective Brendan Fennessy is. He and his partner, Detective Maria San Filippo—they catch the call.

"Everything about the grab was systematic," she says.

Unlike most crime scenes, it's hard to imagine anything bad happening inside the Boyle residence. Of course there's no white picket fence surrounding the premises. An iron gate swings inward at the sidewalk. Never locked, merely latched. On the stoop, you face a hundred-year-old wooden door. It's thick. You can tell by the sound of your fist knocking. The grain has pin-sized wormholes. They paid a grand for it. A trapezoid of stained glass held in a frame tilts against the bay window, paving candy-colored light across the floor—a happy road to nowhere. You smell sandalwood leeched into the furniture fabrics because the mother is a habitual burner of incense. The twins' toys are scattered, educational. This isn't a too pretty house. It's even better. When people fantasize about family life, this is the house living in their dream. If they dream city dreams, that is. Because the Boyles are city dwellers. Their happiness is a small, expensive, treasured item. Barbarians lurk at their gate, haunt the very streets. To visit the Boyle house is to visit safety. Refuge. A haven.

Illusions we create for ourselves.

Like I said, I'm a freelancer; I'm not a street-beat reporter. At the time of the Boyle abductions, I was lucky enough to have a regular gig. *Chi-Town Monthly*, a local slick with the largest circulation in metro Chicagoland. I was a contributor. You'd find my bio listed under that title on the second page of the magazine. Seeing my name there made me feel good. As a rule, I don't show up with pen in hand and lean over the yellow police tape trying to get somebody to talk to me. No, I get there much later. After the hoopla, the staccato of flashbulbs, the buzz. I go in-depth. Time is usually on my side. I pick up all the chewed bones, sift the cold ashes, and start over. I collect facts and opinions. Contemplate photos. I digest. I have the luxury of reflection, my own and others', and nobody rushes me into anywhere I don't want to go. But I'm saddled with the penalty of old news. Rehash. I need to find the germ, nugget, or little diamond—a good reason to tell the whole story again. Stretch the tale to the best length.

Then clip and polish.

Print.

When the Boyle case was glowing cherry red, I wasn't in the picture yet. But Fennessy and San Filippo fill me in. I listen. They tell a good story. As most cops do.

"Like the thing with the camera," Fennessy says.

"That was beyond systematic," San Filippo says. "The camera bit showed foreknowledge. But the floating arm . . ."

I can't resist the bait. "What camera? What arm?"

Fennessy swallows a forkful of Denver omelet. He wipes his lips with a paper napkin. We're eating at Pan's diner. There's a mural on the wall above the service window: crudely drawn knockoffs of the Boy Who Never Grew Up, Hook, and Tinker Bell. If Disney ever finds out, the owner will be smacked with a lawsuit. Fennessy's partner has her nose in a coffee cup, but her eyes peek over the rim, not looking at me but straight at Fennessy. It isn't the first time I wonder if they've ever slept together. They'd make a cute couple. He's handsome in a preppy, condescending sort of way. She's a classic Italian beauty: dark hair, crème-caramel skin, a smoky liquid gaze that makes a man wish he were in better shape. The gaze is focused squarely on Brendan Fennessy, but he doesn't seem aware. He spends so much time with Maria they're like a pair of veteran marrieds. Finishing one another's thoughts and sentences. They have a comfort zone established. Know how to act together in public. Her look sends him clear messages. *You be the one to tell Deering this story.* But Fennessy's taking his time. Going to give it to me slow.

"Tad Boyle is a womanizer," Fennessy begins, "but he's also a manizer. That's not a word, is it? What would they call him?"

"I think they'd say slut," San Filippo suggests.

"Tad Boyle is a slut. He beds his students. Male. Female. Yin and yang. But Tad likes them on the cusp."

"Of eighteen," San Filippo says.

"How does he keep his job?" I ask.

"He doesn't. They were drumming him out when the kids were taken. The process to remove him was in motion. He'd been censured. The university's conduct committee reached the limit of their patience. They were leaving a paper trail for themselves. His file is Dickens thick." Fennessy spreads index finger and thumb apart to show me, like he's asking for a slice of cheesecake—*This much, please.* "Nothing the committee couldn't sideline temporarily. They put him into professorial limbo. He'd been a bad boy. But he's published regularly and spectacularly."

"In the past," San Filippo says.

Fennessy nods. "Those days are apparently over. Still, he has a reputation. Good and bad. Most of his sexual conquests didn't complain either."

"That's in the past too."

I'm moving a cut-up syrupy pancake around my plate. I hear the pause. So I know I should ask. "There was a student complaint prior to the boys' disappearance?"

"Three days before," she says.

"What does this have to with a camera?"

"Nothing," he says. He's spooling the air with his finger. "Tad had video cameras hidden inside the house. They were linked to motion detectors. If a person entered Room A, the camera started rolling film. When they left, it snapped off. And so on throughout the house."

"Every room?"

Fennessy shakes his head. "Selective rooms."

"Did you ever think he was an overly protective father? Keeping tabs on the babysitter? From the photos I've seen, those kids look pretty precious. Maybe he was making sure the twins were cared for properly."

"I have no doubt he was keeping tabs on Miss Hoffman. He had cameras in her bedroom, her bathroom, and the living room."

"Those were aimed cameras," San Filippo says.

"I see."

"And Mrs. Boyle tells us she knew nothing about them," he says.

"But the kidnapper did?"

"Not exactly," San Filippo says. She pushes her coffee cup away. I am captivated by her sculpted chin, her dented pillow lips. I see we've arrived at the point where she'll be taking over. "The sound on the tape is worthless. You hear the boys fighting. But the microphone isn't sensitive enough to pick up the supposed conversation Regina Hoffman has with the kidnapper before, and after, he gets inside."

"You believe her statement?"

Detective San Filippo shrugs. "She came off as genuine. Said she felt guilty and stupid. When we got to her—she was still in shock. Talked about what happened very matter-of-factly. She wasn't selling it. No theatrics. And the guy hurt her . . ."

"How did he do that exactly?" I have a minirecorder in my pocket, but I'm not using it. I'm filing every word away into my memory banks. Fennessy knows me. He exchanges a glance with San Filippo that indicates she should withhold details. The main detail being *mirrorrorrim*. A palindrome. Nonsense word. Mirror, mirror. The deliveryman who snatched the Boyles cuffed Regina to a standing radiator in the kitchen. Then he rummaged through the drawers until he decided upon an instrument. He chose a pair of rubber-handled shears. Opened them as wide as they would go. He slipped the SIG from his belt, pointed it, and told Regina he'd shoot her in the face if she moved. He wrote on her. *Into* her. She bled. She'd have some scarring. But that morning, eating at a booth in Pan's diner, I don't know any of these facts yet. I'm in the dark. The deliveryman is a mystery man to me. Mysterious also are his methods.

"I can't tell you the nature of her injuries," San Filippo says. "She'll be okay. But it was not pleasant."

"Vagueness wastes my time. Go on."

The detective winces at my prodding and I know I've annoyed her, probably dropped a notch on her respect scale. More exactly, I've been recategorized as just another asshole journalist. Our previous good vibrations are lost in the chill. I'll win her back later. Here and now, I need to know what I need to know. "We don't have any usable sound on the tape," she says, "only a stationary visual recording."

"Maybe if the tape was cleaned up, you might isolate—"

"We had an expert take a crack at it," Fennessy says, interrupting.

"No luck?"

"Nada," he says.

San Filippo glares, tight-lipped. She nudges Fennessy and he slides out of the booth, lets her brush past—guys would pay for the privilege— then he sits again. I watch the lady move. I'm not alone. Heads are popping. Fennessy tells me what any idiot would've already guessed.

"Powdering her nose," he says.

I don't believe him. Oh, I'm sure she's in the restroom, doing what people do in restrooms, but her temporary departure isn't about touching up eyeliner. It's a reset. She's giving me a chance to improve my manners. I appreciate subtleties. And San Filippo is subtly telling me to zip it.

Fennessy motions for the check.

"I'll get this," I say.

"You're too kind." He doesn't have to put away his wallet. It was never leaving his pocket. We're bargainers. We practice multilevel give-and take.

I settle into the butt-grooved vinyl. Cool my jets. There's an imbalance I'm up against. Two-on-one, which is something I can handle fine. Our rhythm was sputtering before. They're not fighting me, but I feel resistance. I can tussle and scrap with the best on the block. Hit me. I enjoy it. Really, I'm inspired by pain. But in my business you have to understand pressure. Who's under it? Who's exerting it? How hard to squeeze, how often, and when it's best to sit on your hands and then—okay, hands out again—take what's being offered. Be thankful. I called the detectives. They didn't have to agree to this breakfast. I'll get what I want from them unless I blow it. Friendly is easier. It can be more productive too.

I blunt my edge. Light up a smoke.

When San Filippo returns, Fennessy doesn't bother getting up. He eases himself to the wall. She takes his warmed spot on the end. This way, if she decides to cut me off and walk . . . it's done.

Subtleties. They make the writer's, and the cop's, world go round. But the obvious has an important role as well. Never underrate the obvious.

"I'm listening to you," I tell her. "Detective San Filippo . . . Maria, I don't know where you're taking me. Or why. But believe me when I say, I want to go there. So please continue."

She knows bullshit. Nothing's special about mine. But I've said the right thing.

"Tad hid the living-room camera in a bookcase. The top shelf is cluttered with figurines. The Boyles don't strike me as 'figurine' folks. But these are handmade totems from Asia, South America, Africa, etc. . . . places the Boyles have traveled. Anyway, they're up high and pushed to the front of the shelf. Lots of dust and shadows behind them. One figurine has feathers and a hole cut in the back. No dust. Tad removed a book, slipped in his camera, and put this feathery lump of clay with the open mouth—that's where he gets extra points for being clever; the lens is shooting *through* the figurine, out the mouth—and the feathers provide a distracting camouflage . . . I couldn't spot the setup even when I was staring right at the thing. And I knew what to look for."

"What's on the tape?"

"Prior to the afternoon in question, not much. Babysitting 101."

"Regina doesn't have a boyfriend who pops in for a quickie at nap time?"

"Tad Boyle's fantasy. Yours too, Jase?" Fennessy asks.

"I was wondering why he went to the trouble of setting up this surveillance if all he's going to get is crackers and juice."

"We asked him that too," San Filippo says.

"Did he squirm?"

"Surprisingly, no. He copped to being a garden-variety voyeur. Likes to watch people in secret. Naked people are better. Therefore, he installs the cameras in the bathroom and bedroom. But it's not a must. He enjoys a panorama."

"Interesting."

"What? You think he's lying?"

"No. I think he's telling you the truth about being a voyeur. But I suspect he's got a good reason for the camera in the living room."

"Like what?"

"I don't know. I merely *suspect*." I kill the last of my coffee. "Tad volunteered the tape?"

"No."

"How did you get it?"

"You heard about the, ah, viper?" she asks.

I nod, very nonchalant. *Who hasn't?*

"It came from the same bookcase. One of our crime techs climbed a ladder to measure from where the wine bottle fell. He found wires . . . and the camera in the living room. We confronted Tad. He stared at the wall for minute. No excuses. He went into the hall closet where he stashed his stuff, came back, and handed us the tape."

You need to remember that this was happening in the mid-eighties. Before everybody was busy getting busy by watching themselves. Before Soderbergh's *Sex, Lies, and Videotape*. Before Rob Lowe got caught logging his own underage adventures at the '88 Democratic National Convention. This was a nanny cam in the pre-nanny-cam era. Tad was ahead of the curve.

"Can I watch the video?"

Tennessy and San Filippo are amused. "We knew you'd ask," she says. "Though I'm rather inclined to make you beg."

I've never been teased by thirteen-year-old girls. Never have I paid a dominatrix to torture me. This thrill with San Filippo is as close as I want to get.

Folding my hands like the altar boy I once was, I humble myself.

"Pretty please, Detective?"

San Filippo carries a cardboard box filled with videotapes. The tapes are for a VHS player, which isn't a gimme during the days when Betamax still fights a losing battle on the shelves of mom-and-pop video stores. The machine we're using at the station is bulky, a top-loader. Looks like it should have a coin slot for quarters built into the side.

"We shouldn't be doing this. Allowing you to see it," San Filippo says. The tape in question—she's plucked it from the box and clutches it in her hand. I'm seated in a medieval plastic chair, my legs already going numb. The television sits across from me, switched off, like a rippled tank of oily smoke in which I see my reflection growing anxious. For a horrible interval, I'm convinced she's changed her mind. That I'm out. Out. Opportunity lost. She can't keep the smile from her lips. Okay, I get it. More torment. I'll not screw with the diva in the future. She has my respect. She has the story I want.

Fennessy enters the room. Shuts the door. Roll film.

The perspective is odd. Fish-eye, I realize. And, at the moment, the room is empty except for the twins, who aren't moving. I'm thinking the tape must be stuck, but then there's activity at the edge of the screen. The deliveryman crouches in the doorway, trying to persuade the boys to come closer. *Come hither.* The boys are frozen. Not in fear. They're curious. Curiosity might've killed the cat, but it paralyzed him first. The deliveryman speaks into a walkie-talkie. He holds it toward the boys. *See my toy. Want to play?* I can't see his lips moving. Can't read lips either. But I imagine. I'm sure the good detectives know a reliable lip-reader. No matter. The distance, image quality, and his mustache obscure his mouth. He does it again.

Talks, turns the handheld unit to face the boys.

Again.

Longer this time.

Waits. Waves, like a clown, wiggling his gloved fingers.

Hiya. How you doing? Are you ready to go for a ride?

A moment arrives when the available light seems to change. Pale gray leaking around the deliveryman's shoes. He steps back into the vestibule. You can't see him there. The dark gray returns. Something's happening. The boys are animated. On the move.

Then up floats this arm.

There's a person standing out of the shot. Behind where the delivery-man was crouched a moment ago. Is it him? No way of telling. This person extends his, or her, bare unisex arm. Points a finger at the location of the hidden camera. The arm comes up buoyantly, languidly, as if it is—yes, San Filippo definitely had it right—floating.

"Somebody else is there? In the house?" I ask, whispering for no good reason.

The arm sinks down. Disappears. The deliveryman never comes back into view. The boys have gone out the door with him. With *them.*

No motion to detect. The camera snaps off.

"That's certainly—" I begin to say.

Fennessy traffic-cops me. STOP. He says, "It's not finished."

Quick shot, camera on and off, a matter of seconds—the passing blur of a shoulder. Then the recording starts again, fuzzy, operating under a major electrical snowstorm. An object passes in front of the lens. Very near, out of focus. The camera begins shaking. The object again, in passing. Small, gnarled, and resembling a chunk of coal. Oh, it's a shrunken asteroid that's all. Simple enough. Are there hands guiding it? You can't tell, really. The snowstorm is a full blizzard. The object, when it's in view, crowds the screen. Snow and the mini-UFO. I can sell this story big-time, to the *Weekly World News.* What is that thing?

Eclipse.

"It's time to put down your pencils," Fennessy says.

"What happened?"

"The video crapped out." He punches a button on the remote control and tosses it on the table. The TV gives off a bitchy static crackle.

"Did the tape run to the end?"

"No, there was plenty of unused space. Another hour available, at least."

"But it's blank?"

"Blank."

"Then Ted erased it."

"It's not erased. This part where it goes out is a total mess. But not what comes immediately after. That's blank. Never been taped over."

"The deliveryman did something . . . mechanical? . . . to break it."

"Maybe he did," San Filippo says.

"What did he do?"

Unsure ground for the detective, but she wants to be persuasive. "Strong disturbance of the electrical fields might cause . . ."

"Did you spot him in that last bit?" Fennessy asks me. "Because seriously, Jase, if you did, you've got way better eyes than I have."

"Well, he or his accomplice . . ." I tap out a smoke. They help me to think. "That flying rock, what was it?"

"We don't know," San Filippo says.

"What caused the weird shaking?"

"The camera malfunctioned." With this pronouncement, Fennessy stops any further discussion. He seems as though he's about to summarily dismiss me as well. So I throw him a question, change directions.

"Could the accomplice be one of the Boyles?"

"Why would Tad give the cassette to us if it's one of them? He's not stupid. He could've destroyed it."

"Not the nanny?"

Fennessy rewinds the tape. Stops at the departure scene. The boys are about to walk off. This video snippet is, I later realize, the final confirmed glimpse the world will have of them. Wherever they are today, they're boys no more. Fennessy jabs the arrowed remote keys, forwarding frame by frame. Pause tape. He touches his pinkie to the television screen.

"See there?"

"What is that?"

The screen image is unstable, jittering. He's pointing into a slice of speckled background: the Boyles' kitchen. He brings his face right next to the screen. "Her foot. The heel of Regina Hoffman's right foot."

Afterward, sitting in my station wagon, I never consciously decide to commit myself to the story. But I do. I'm too fired up to write much down. It's all in my head though. I still have the lined steno pad I used for taking notes that day. The lonely date scrawled at the top. No notes.

Just like the alleged kidnappers.

No calls either.

That's what finally sold the story for me.

Whoever took the Boyle twins didn't show any interest in giving them back.

I have a small confession to make. I skipped over it, but I want to disclose my version of events with accuracy, shortcomings included.

Back inside the station—Fennessy has just shown me the nanny's foot, then he snaps off the TV. Whether in confusion or frustration, the detectives walk out of the viewing room, leaving me alone with the box of Boyle videos. The tape showing the abduction is inside the machine. I would never steal that tape. But I feel temptation.

Like the Boyle twins, curiosity complicates my life. I poke around the other tapes in the cardboard box. These all came from the Boyle house. Some of the tapes have labels, others don't. I see a label that reads *B-day Party (1 year)*. Stealing evidence from the police is no way to win friends. It's a crime. I've never stolen from the cops.

But I figure these can't be *that* important to the case. Certainly, *B-day Party (1 year)* won't be missed. Watching it will give me an insight into the Boyle family I wouldn't otherwise have. Here's my chance to spy through the keyhole. I'm compelled to look. I might notice something everyone else glossed over. Observing a slice of the Boyles' life in the *Before* phase might offer me a better understanding of the *After*.

If I ask for the tape, they're bound to say no. I tell myself I can always mail it back anonymously or slip it into Fennessy's desk at a later date without hurting anyone. I can make a duplicate. Cops bend the rules for themselves all the time.

The more I say here the worse I sound. Noble intentions aside, I'm guilty. I have no excuses because no one forces my hand. I'm aware that if I take the tape, then it's because I want to and nothing else. I also know it's probably going to be too risky to return the thing. Taking it would be wrong. That's exactly how it is. And I know it.

I fold the pages of my notepad around the tape.

San Filippo opens the door. "You ready to go?"

"My work here is done." I smile at her. She points her thumb at the door.

If I get up and go, then I'm stealing the tape. Or I could dump it on the table and play the dummy. Shuffle my papers.

I've never been good at playing the dummy.

I steal it.

Chapter 3

R obyn Matchfrost was my lover and my writing partner. I can't remember which came first, love or work. It was simultaneous. We melded. Our lives, our work, everything came together at once. I won't say our relationship was symbiotic. But it was close. She was my counterweight. What I lacked, she had in spades. She was another blonde, like Matthias, though her color was a shade warmer. I never tired of watching her. When I lost her in the labyrinth of the Boyle story, my life flew out of balance. An honest talk, early on, might have saved us.

I'll never know.

Robyn is legally blind. She wears sunglasses. Not cheap ones, mind you, but Versace. Black frames with a little polished Medusa logo. She wears them for the comfort of others. It is her one concession to the cliché. She disdains the white stick and prefers a friend's arm when out walking. Robyn can see light. Not much else. She carries a loupe magnifier in her purse. If an object is large enough, bold in detail, and if it interests her beyond the tracing of her fingertips, she may employ the illuminated lens. She doesn't do this often. I don't fault her range of interests. To be honest, her eyesight is worsening and I think the loupe does little good.

Late one evening, after a raft of Chinese food and too many Tsing Tsao beers, I broach the subject of a guide dog. She stabs her chopsticks into the back of my slow-moving hand. She doesn't speak to me for a week. How she knew where my hand was, I can't answer. I think that may be her point.

Robyn rarely leaves the building alone. Her condo is on thirty-four, we have our office on twenty. We overpaid. But the office has a view I enjoy—a clear shot above congested Lake Shore Drive and the table of gray-green waves breaking off Lake Michigan. In the northwest corner of the ground floor—twenty-two Robyn steps and a hard left from the elevator bank—there's a bistro with an excellent wine list. They also serve by the glass. Robyn finds her way to the tiny zinc bar most afternoons. She flirts with a bartender named Hernando. She allots herself a single drink for these visits. White or red? Her choice clues me to her mood. I like red-drinking Robyn. Red Robyn buys us dinner and nightcaps, leaves the calls on the answering machine unanswered, and bounces jovially atop her king-size bed. White Robyn puts me on notice.

I'm late. Her wineglass has been emptied. Hernando's pouring a coffee. I sit near the bar, at a granite table the size of an old LP. Hernando ignores my presence. That's okay. He's not a favorite of mine. I don't know what Robyn tells him. I assume only the worst. His failure to acknowledge me ticks my blood pressure up a few points.

Don Cheeseball, I want to say, *why donna you go jerka me a soda?*

For Robyn's sake I let the urge pass.

She's magnificent. Watching her leaning sideways against the bar, her silk blouse blousing—she breaks my heart. Makes me feel like a peasant, tasting my own cigarette breath, burping the Scotch I had instead of lunch. I search my pockets for a mint. Robyn laughs at something Hernando has said, and it's a hearty sound full of promises. I catch a whiff of the dried sweat inside my collar. She makes my life easy. I'm not accustomed to easy. As a defense against the everyday rudeness of our chosen field, Robyn has learned to affect a degree of callousness and worldly boredom. She's not very convincing. Hah! I find a ginger chew in my inside pocket. Indonesian characters printed on the waxy paper.

When was the last time I ate Indonesian?

I switch seats. Occupy a stool at the far end of the bar. The seltzer button of Hernando's gun stops blowing bubbles midway through an order of cran-raspberry fizzes. He pardons himself, descends a stairwell posted Staff Only. I guess into the basement where he can change whatever needs changing. The exciting, privileged life of Hernando.

I hate to see him go.

Jump two stools.

Robyn's neck has a great curve. Female Matchfrosts share this physical trait. I've studied photos of her mother and grandmother. Same curve. Funny how an assemblage of muscle and bone can be passed down like an heirloom. On Robyn, it's perfection.

While I'm indulging my apparently bottomless capacity for voyeurism, she picks up my scent. Though she's pretending she hasn't. I'm always happy playing along.

"Anyone sitting here?"

"Can't a girl drink her coffee in peace?"

"You're not at peace."

"Well, then here's to the war." She offers to clink her cup with mine, only I haven't been served.

"To the war." I kiss her on the cheek.

"What were you eating?"

"Why?"

"You smell like stale Christmas cookies."

I straddle my stool, stand up on the crossbars, and snatch a maraschino from Hernando's arsenal.

"Well?" she asks.

"Well what?"

"Breakfast with the detectives? How'd it go?"

"Illuminating."

"You're being cryptic. I hate you cryptic."

"It's a go. Something very bad went down in that posh two-story brownstone by the lake. I haven't gotten a handle on exactly what. But they—the detectives, I mean—for whatever reason, they showed me a videotape. Sick vibes aplenty. I don't know who to trust, which is always positive."

"Uh-huh. I presume you're talking to the parents next."

"I haven't thought about it."

"Liar, liar." Her right hand snakes under the edge of the bar top and catches the button fly of my jeans. Stays there. Tight. "Pants on fire as usual," she says. Her fingers are nimble. Two buttons open.

Red Robyn. My kinky brilliant girlfriend.

"I want to interview the nanny first," I say. Moments like this, Robyn relishes my ignoring her. When I don't react, in her murky world, a light flashes to green. Or she sees a solid red staring her in the face and decides to run it. Robyn finds power in the flagrant defiance of visual cautions. What are *you* looking at, pal? Maybe Hernando's prepped her with his smooth accent. She's acting awfully juicy. Hernando's back at his station and she's highly aware. She's the most private exhibitionist I've ever known. It's one reason we work so well together.

Her finger. She gets a lot of traction. From the elbow up, you'd guess nothing was happening. Her bare shoulder tenses. I notice the strips of muscle standing out, a blue vein like dribbled ink running to the underside. If I glance around to check who's watching, she's likely to flop me out for a nice public airing.

Finger*nail.*

Robyn can be merciless. I love her for it.

"She was there, saw the kidnapper, she'll have the most to tell me about him. Her direct experience of him is important." My voice all husk.

With her free hand, Robyn opens up her shoulder bag and passes me a black binder. Inside are the addresses and phone numbers for all the principals in the Boyle case. She's typed quick reference biographies onto index cards (I can slip these in my pocket). There's a two-page list of contacts—friends, neighbors, colleagues, etc.—spokes around the wheel, the Boyle twins at the hub. Paper-clipped stacks of Xeroxes printed from microfiche files: Chicago Public Library, University of Chicago course catalog, ALA conferences, *American Theatre* magazine . . . all my background materials presorted. Highs and lows of the lives I'm about to enter. *Regina Hoffman's high school yearbook senior portrait. Tad Boyle's Nebraska DUI. Una was in an all-female theater group called The Black Mollies; she played a few lead roles. The Boyles' wedding announcement as it appeared in* The New York Times. Here, under a second clip, articles about recent unsolved child abductions, broken out geographically—

Chicago, Midwest, U.S., international—color-coded for age, sex, and family income/education levels. Robyn has a wide circle of people she employs as resources. She sends cases of champagne to the reference departments of at least three major libraries. Her Rolodex shames mine. She can work a phone like nobody else. But still, I can't explain how she does it. I've seen it happen time and again. I depend on it as I do the sunrise. But I don't understand it.

"Let's get a table," she says.

They have long, white tablecloths at the bistro. Robyn can absolutely flay me between courses. I wave for the hostess—a smiley college girl earning her coin dealing menus to the upwardly mobile. Which she, no doubt, aspires to be—and is. Wholesome, bred Midwestern, business-school-bound—I deduce these things instantly, unfairly, and with no evidence or chance at rebuttal. We do this to each other, don't we? Social triage. The snap judgments designed to keep us among our own kind. Unless we have needs that require a short-term dip into the quick and dirty strata layered below. Or maybe, like Ms. Hostess, we're pushing higher. She pats the hips of her blackbird velvet skirt, adjusts her abbreviated jacket. I'm so right about her. Eager to please. Cute.

Not my type in myriad ways.

"How are we this evening?" she asks.

I clear my throat. Try removing Robyn's vise grip before we rise together. I'm rewarded with cat scratches. She's brutal. Unpredictable. Guilty and blasted by the world.

"Just fine," I say.

Later, when Robyn's asleep, I watch the birthday tape for the first time. No real surprises jump out at me. Other than the party is not at the Boyles' house. It looks like a pizzeria. Low lighting, a long wooden table sporting a red-and-white-checkered tablecloth. Pitchers of soda and beer, pizza pans, and half of the pizza slices are already gone. The flag of Italy hangs in the background. Young adults and small children mill around—I'm guessing these are the Boyles' friends, and their offspring are the ones crawling under the table.

The twins are dressed alike, yellow shirts and brown overalls. I've never been keen on the idea of matching outfits. Brothers should have the chance to be individuals. But Shane and Liam are enchanting. They are *identical*. Their appearance makes a case for special indulgence. The adults in the room can't keep their eyes off them.

We witness the opening of presents. The boys are more excited by the boxes, bows, and wrapping paper than they are by the gifts inside. It makes me laugh. My girls were the same way. It drove my ex-wife nuts, as if they conspired to embarrass her in front of our guests. As if their lack of interest were planned. But Una Boyle looks happy. We don't see much of her because she's operating the camera.

Tad's there. Fidgeting, almost grumpy. I notice every time the camera settles on him, he's checking his watch. His body language says he'd rather be elsewhere. In the company of his nubile students? I'll reserve judgment for the moment. But he doesn't come off well. Perhaps he and Una were fighting before the party. I can certainly relate. When my children were that age, the marriage was tense. We weren't sleeping enough. We weren't sleeping *together* enough either. The memories are flooding back. I'd quit smoking as a concession to my wife's vanity. I say vanity because she never had a problem with my habit until the kids arrived. She didn't care about my health. What she cared about was appearances. Dads shouldn't smoke. So I didn't. I wanted to be a healthy, happy, non-smoking father. And I was, for a time.

All toddler birthdays have six stages: Greeting, Eating, Gifts, Cake, Crying, and Departure. I fast-forward through the tape. Here we go. One of the boys is crying. His bottle has rolled way. He's pulling on his ear. Maybe he's got a bit of infection starting in there. I don't know. But the weird thing is that his brother's not crying. This incongruity seems to piss off the one who's upset. The boys are sitting side by side. The little guy with the tears on his face, he grabs his brother by the elbow and tugs hard, like, *Hey, can't you see what's going on here? Can't you show me some sympathy?* His ploy works. Now both boys wail. A swirl of frosting licked off mom's finger soothes them.

Now we're at Departure. Una pans the restaurant. One last look before the lights dim. I give Una credit. The birthday party has no theme.

I'm old-fashioned that way. I don't think a kid's party needs any theme other than It's Your Birthday. She's not giving much of a voice-over to the taped proceedings, which is, as far as I'm concerned, another bonus. Her camera drifts. Picks up a couple of the pizzeria drivers sucking on Pepsis, waiting for calls. At the far end of the restaurant, there's a pinball machine. It's too far away to see any details. Una resumes documentation of the partygoers packing up and saying good-bye. I don't see Tad anywhere. He might've bugged out.

Una swings her lens around the room. The drivers are gone now. But somebody's playing pinball. A man. He blocks out the machine, but we know it's in the corner from the previous scan. She keeps the camera focused on him. Maybe Mommy's bored too. The back of this guy captivates her. He must feel her gaze. He twists around, his hands still on the sides of the machine, working the flippers. You can't see his face. The lights from the game glare into the void between him and the camera. They're oranges, reds, purples. You see the slanted face of the game shine like a mirror.

The boys cling to their mom. They're stretching out their arms. Ready to go home.

"Okay, you guys. Want to take a ride?"

The camera cants off to one side, but she's still aiming it at the guy.

Una chuckles.

That guy playing pinball?

He's waving.

The tape ends and I feel guilty for stealing it. It means nothing to the police. But to the Boyles, who may never see their sons again, it's irreplaceable. I'm going to return it to them no matter what it costs me.

I'm tired and sore. Red Robyn wears me out. But I feel great as I switch the television off. I sit there on the carpet for a minute, not thinking about anything in particular. At least I don't remember having thoughts. I turn the television on. Rewind the tape and watch it again.

Chapter 4

The next morning, Regina Hoffman surprises me. I'm in manipulator mode when I place the call. But there's no hesitation on her part. A nervous tremolo quivers her voice. Yet she agrees to meet me. Knowing full well I intend to pick at whatever scab has formed over the last year. Underneath lies the most wounding experience of her life. But she sounds giddy. As if she'd expected me to call, then couldn't believe I really did.

She asks if it's okay to meet in the South Garden of the Art Institute. The lunch crowd's not bad, not with the hint of winter blowing off the lake. Nobody will eavesdrop on us. Plus, it's convenient. Her husband is an assistant curator. With an exhibition in the pipeline, he's spending long hours uncrating canvases. To break up the afternoon, she usually brings him his lunch. How about noon?

Cement walls with heavy patchwork, silvery stone planters, and steps. Orange gravel slushing underfoot. Mighty Chicago looms above. The trees in the garden are mostly hawthorns. I'm walking north. Our meeting place is sunken down to my left. Behind the museum, billboard blue letters spell out the Prudential buildings.

I've not led a prudential life.

A smell of lake water, bus exhaust, a lit cigarette.

Now I know why she asked to meet outdoors. Regina's chain-smoking, sitting on the edge of a planter. I'm guessing it's a new hobby by the way she's pulling in these nervous mouthfuls. Tongue burners. Keeps glancing at her hand, puzzled. The wind cuts the smoke away from her face. She's *thin* thin. Her hair is chopped, colored midnight blue, a sure standout even among her new goth friends. Assuming she's made new friends. This is not the young woman of a year ago. Today she's dressed in blacks and grays, a long, frayed skirt. East Indian scarf, red as sin, lashed at her throat. Still a Mary Poppins—but with a razor in her boot. I've been watching for a while. Done a discreet vulture circle to make certain it's her.

"Ms. Hoffman," I say, offering my hand.

Startled, she fumbles the lit cigarette and it lands—a single spark—on my shoe.

"God, I'm sorry," she says.

"My fault," I say. "Think I can save it."

Move to pick up the smoldering butt.

"Don't bother," she says.

Pall Malls, unfiltered. Doing serious bodily self-harm. I turn my Florsheim edgewise and crush.

The susurrus of the fountain—funny, I hadn't noticed it before—fills my ears. Regina tells me something. I miss it.

"What?"

"Filthy habit," she says, another nail stuck between her grim lips. Fingers attacking the wheel of a flip-top lighter.

"Filthier the better," I say.

Nervous laughter. Snick as the lighter closes.

I get a quick peek into her purse. See the gun. A pistol. Nothing big, nothing fancy. I'm no gun expert. But I've seen these before. Smith & Wesson Bodyguard AirWeight, if you want to be technical. J-frame. A .38 snubbie. Has a shrouded hammer so the carrier doesn't snag things. You don't want to blow away the maid sitting next to you on the el. It's a concealment weapon. And, okay, I can understand why Regina would feel the need for protection. She's picked it out in stainless, which is cool, shows a touch of class. Yet . . . when someone is coming out of the house with the purpose of meeting me, I don't expect them to be packing.

With cops it's different. A plumber lugging around a plunger, that's normal. To be expected. But if I'm out for a nice evening walk in Grant Park, say, or the lakefront, and a young lady saunters by with a plunger sticking out of her purse . . . it's unusual. I'm curious. Maybe disconcerted. *Is she sane?* I might ask.

Is she sane?

I'm going to find out.

Take out my pad of paper and pen, very professional. Not using the minirecorder here, because first, the wind, and second, I don't want to spook her. We make it past the preliminaries no problem. Who I am, who I write for. Who she is, how she came to work as a nanny for the Boyles. Stuff we both knew before we arrived in this garden. I have to begin somewhere. Lob a few safe questions before I bring the heat. My patience is quickly spent.

"Did Mr. Boyle ever come on to you?"

She tries to read something in my face. "You've met him, right?"

"Not yet."

"Oh. You'll see how he is. Attractive in a brutish way. If he didn't open his mouth, you'd never guess he was an intellectual. Looks like he digs in the ground for a living. Huge, rough hands, dirty creases. Built like a bloody bull." Regina holds her nose. "He plays up his primitivism. Stands too close. Eyeballing. Literally sniffs you out. To answer your question. Of course he came on to me. My first day on the job. During breakfast, as the boys were eating their Cream of Wheat."

"Where was Mrs. Boyle?"

"I don't remember. In the shower? Getting dressed? She was home. I know that much. Upstairs. Because I was like, 'Wow, is he really doing this?' She could walk down the stairs any second."

"How'd you deal with him?"

She shrugged. "Tad comes on to everyone. Seriously. It's like, 'Hello, shall we tango?' "

"I'd heard that."

Regina's running through some memory in her mind's eye. Her face cycles emotions as she talks. Embarrassed, flattered, sad. Bemused. "He didn't *do* anything. I laughed at him. Gave a shove. Told him to behave or I'd quit on the spot. His effort was halfhearted. I was too old for him, if you can believe it. The boys needed a new nanny more than he did. Una would've positively shredded him if he chased me away. She watched over the whole family like a hawk."

"Was she an okay boss?"

No answer.

Not okay.

"Una has problems." Regina sighs. "You're a reporter. You'll find out."

"Why don't you tell me? That's how reporters get answers—people tell them."

"Not from me, not about *her*. These aren't buried secrets. You shouldn't need to look too hard. Fact is—you'd have to be pretty stupid to miss it. Una can't hide. Not even from Una herself. Maybe that's why she needs to write everything down, making lists and keeping track. Imposing order on the world. That's my clue, Jase, all I'm giving up."

If you lose a woman's only children, you cut her a bit of slack. Despite her having been a slave driver and lorded over you. That's the lesson. You don't drag that woman's name in the dirt. You owe her this at least. That is if you're telling the truth and whatever tragedy transpired was not your fault. Loud, clear: Una is strictly off-limits.

Move on, I say to myself. Curiosity drives me like a drug. I want to know more about Una. But I can't ask for any more. Shake hands with my info jones.

Keep Regina talking. The interviewer needs to push forward before the interviewee starts thinking too much about whom she's talking to. But she already has. Part of her is closing off. Drifting downstream into the quicksilver future. And I'm past. I'm history. Journalistic dead meat.

I go open-ended.

"Tell me about that day," I say.

She does. I don't learn anything new. I hear it from Regina's perspective, sure. She's told her version many times. There's a rote quality, a detachment that clicks into place. I watch her mentally checking off the high points as she walks me through it. First this, then that. This, this, that. But the facts are the same as Fennessy and San Filippo conveyed. I need more. I need better from Regina. She has it inside. I know where to look. I'm not proud of the fact. My instincts are right. I have a job. She has a story.

My story.

Want to know something? Most people, no matter how bad it is—*diddled by a fat uncle ... drowned my babies ... too stoned to put the bolts back into the jet's tail cone*—they want to tell you.

Six a day, picked 'em right off the street. Men or women, I didn't care. They was money. I spent it on freebase ... She fit in two suitcases ... I never saw the guy who snatched my brother—

That's the truth.

Getting there is simple but unpleasant: you have to come right out and ask.

Say the words. Don't listen to yourself asking, listen to them.

I'm gearing up for the big invasion of privacy. The whole conversation's invasive, actually, but we're at the spearhead moment.

"What did the deliveryman do to you?"

"I'm not supposed to tell."

"Says who?"

"The police."

"Well, I can understand—"

She lifts her skirt.

At the flash of white thighs, I turn away.

"No, look at it," she says. "I've never let anyone see before, not in the daylight."

I tilt my head. To passersby—I don't know if there are any because I'm momentarily transfixed—it must seem here's an awful dirty old man, paying a punk girl to ogle her panties.

I'm reading pink scars.

Regina runs her palm across raised, shiny tissue. Revealing one crude letter at a time. "*M-I-R-R-O-R*, then backwards again on this leg. See? That's how he said it: 'Mirrorrorrim.'"

"What's it mean?"

"Haven't a clue. He spread the scissors and cut me on both sides. They match up." She crosses her wrists, fingers bent to show me how the blades moved against her. "Afterward, he had me close my legs tight. 'So they bleed together,' he said."

"Nightmarish." I shake my head. The cruel doubter in me prods, *Wonder if she's lying? We've visited nightmare country, right, Jase? Never seen this girl there.*

She drops her skirt. "It burned, really burned. God, but I couldn't move. The worst thing, though, was losing Shane and Liam. They were great boys. I think they must know I tried. But I'm only—"

Stop.

They were great boys. She's given up on them. Like the detectives, perhaps? Why else would they let me inside their case? Waving their evidence under my nose to give me the scent? Am I their cadaver dog? Howl when I find the graves, is that it?

A tear scrolls down Regina's cheek.

Plummets.

"Know what's weird?" she asks. She flaps at the smoke. Jumps down. Stubs her cigarette out on the planter.

"What?"

"Everything is." She laughs. Covers her mouth with her hand. Face flushed. Alert shark eyes frightening me. She picks up her purse, rummages inside. My chest pulls tight. I'm at point-blank range. Breathe out my relief when she palms the red Pall Mall pack. The sturdy lighter in action again. She stares off. Her quiet voice: "My life is good. I shouldn't be worried. The worm has, as they say, turned. I met Nathan, my husband. We got married, found a cute apartment, bought a puppy—"

"But . . . ?"

Her laugh. Smoke pencils through her eyebrow. Her eye squeezes shut. "I've been thinking. What if the good in life doesn't matter? What if the worst thing that happens to us makes us who we really are?"

I don't know what to say.

"The attack—I'm stronger for it," she says. Shows me her biceps, chuckling. "And I'm meeting new and exciting people every day." Her smile makes me wonder.

I think about the gun as we're saying our good-byes.

She reaches out for a handshake.

Grasp.

She says, "Hug me."

I'm resistant for a variety of reasons. Not least of which is Regina Hoffman might be off the deep end blowing bubbles.

Her arms fall around mine. She is madly strong. I'm doing nothing in response. Go slack, submit. On tiptoes, she's pressing her soft, black-lipsticked mouth to my ear.

"We're being watched," she says.

Paranoids with guns in their purses are best entertained.

I return the hug and ask, "Where is he?"

"Not a he, a she. Throwing pennies into the fountain. Let's walk." Regina puts her arm through mine, turns me, just as Robyn does. Strolling. We walk the same way, pretending I'm in charge.

"Where are we going?" I ask.

"Inside the museum. Quickly. She's following us."

Michigan Avenue. Pass the iconic bronze lions—man-eaters. Up the steps to the museum's west entrance, I steal a glance backward. There is a young woman, yes, with a backpack and Chinese Red Army cap. No different from a thousand posers milling in a hundred major cities around the globe.

"I think you're mistaken," I say.

"I am not." She releases me and pushes through the revolving glass doorway. I ought to let her go.

Ought to, but I don't.

I follow.

"You want more of this story?" Regina's voice rings out in the lobby.

"I wish you'd tell me."

She digs for her museum pass. People are bustling in, buying tickets, and checking their coats. Her cheeks suck hollow as she puffs away.

"Mirrorrorrim? Do you want to know more, yes or no? You have to say it."

"I want to know everything."

She snatches the pad of paper sticking up from my pocket. "Give me your pen."

A guard is approaching us, speaking in a clipped British accent.

"Smoking is not allowed in the building. Please." She's Indian. With enormous glaring eyes, a wrinkle-free uniform, and a tiny diamond stud sparkling in her nose.

Regina is unfazed. "Go here. A bookstore. Talk to Father Byron."

"Should I say you sent me?"

"Doesn't matter. He'll figure it out."

We are three. The guard smells of champac flowers. Her voice is level and controlled. She does not raise it above polite conversational volume. "Please extinguish your cigarette. You may not enter the museum."

Regina doesn't look at her. She drops her cigarette, lets it burn on the floor.

"Be careful, Jase," she says.

I glance down at her chicken-scratch note. It's an address I see, the name of the bookstore. Regina is walking backward. Away from me. Smoke leaks from her nose.

"Wait," I say.

"Don't trust anyone," she says.

Regina stops. Her tears are back.

There's space between us. The crowd fills it in. The guard bends to retrieve the cigarette. Noisy—it's difficult to hear. I have Regina's face in full view. I can't hear her, but I can read her lips clearly.

"Don't even trust me," she says.

She turns on her heels. At once she's lost among the horde.

Chapter 5

ather Byron Timmerman," Robyn informs me. Opening the heavy
phone book on my chest. Her cooling sweat slicks my rib cage.

"Sounds Jewish," I say. "Except for that *father* part."

"Not Jewish, Jesuit."

"Fantastic. I love a good Jesuit. Ever since the vomiting scenes in *The Exorcist*."

"But not Jesuit anymore. He's defrocked."

"Do we know why?"

"We do not."

"Can't be he's a buggerer. That's allowed. Must be a heretic."

"Let's keep an open mind."

"You're betting on buggerer?" I ask.

"I'd like to give the man a chance."

"Just don't give him your backside. That's mine." I give her hindquarters a gentle slap. "Nevertheless, I say heretic. And heretics are okay in my book."

"Never heard of this bookstore he runs."

"Where is it?" I don't need maps when Robyn's around.

"Up on Ashland and Foster."

"And did Regina get the name correct?"

"Unimaginable Vortices, right here in the yellow pages." Her face presses close to the cheap newsprint, using her lens snatched from the nightstand.

"I'm stopping at home first. Change my shirt. This one smells like parts of you."

"Let me have a whiff."

"You are so twisted and wrong. Afternoon delight is over. Get off me. Where're my shoes? Hey, ease up. The thing is attached, you know? I can't leave it here."

"Pity."

Father Byron is potbellied, bird-legged. Besides a chestnut soul patch under his carplike mouth, he's virtually chinless in his turtleneck. He's insulated by a trampled-looking down vest and a knit cap with a short leather bill. The salesroom is drafty. Somewhere in the back a window must be wedged open, or a door. Gray streaks of rainwater mar the aisles.

I step into permanent dampness, a ghostly fingering of my skin. Spy a mummified mouse sticking to a glue trap among the stacks of books. Musty volumes line the walls, giving host to mold colonies. Spores scuffle up my nostrils. My nose drips. Father Byron, seated in a chair—the kind used to umpire tennis matches—he's busy reading a magazine.

He shifts. Pages turn.

Fishing Facts.

This man looks like a seller of minnows, not occult books.

I negotiate a maze of folding tables, Pisa towers of secondhand paperbacks. Reach the foot of the guru. He's wearing black Chuck Taylors.

"Do much fishing?"

"I am a former fisherman," he says. His voice is baritone, a 1950s TV dad's voice. Like root beer pouring down into a frosty dimpled mug.

Corner of my eye, I catch a glimpse of brittle, feeble lights. My vision stretches into a tunnel of gloom. No one home but the mice. There's a bad connection in the wires. The lights dim and reignite.

"Father Byron. That's you?"

"Yes, my child."

"Quite a collection you have here."

"We offer an array of occult studies, as well as radical politics. Are you looking for anything in particular?"

"I'm into the darker sort of stuff. Cults and sects. Practices involving kidnapping children and, ah, flesh cutting?" Wonderful. My verbal skills are sharp as a spoon.

"Do you mean ritualistic human sacrifice?" He smiles, showing me bridgework and bumpy purple gums. A sinister Velcro crackling as he slips a pipe and pouch from his vest. He thumbs tobacco into the bowl. His thumbnail is overgrown, curved and stained. It's been filed to a point.

"I've got a confession, Father. My name is Jase Deering. I'm a freelance writer working on a story. Someone sent me to you."

"The girl with the orange hair sent you?"

"Girl with blue hair, actually."

"One and the same, no doubt."

"What's *mirrorrorrim*?" I try to make the question sound casual.

He stares down at me. He still has priestly eyes.

The pin-drop quietness grows more palpable by the moment. *What a small, cramped store this is.* Claustrophobic. A tinderbox—I mean the sheer volume of paper, the lack of sprinklers, and the narrowness. *Those bad wires.* Pulsing air blows through like a bellows. I have an idea of fire. Yes, fire would be thrilled to pay a visit.

From the alley beyond the backroom comes the sizzle of rain falling on bricks.

"Who did you say you are?"

"Jase Deering. Regina Hoffman said you could help." I have an urgent need to flee this space. "Father, do you fancy a drink?"

"I enjoy a whiskey now and then."

"Bad weather hampers a business like yours. There's a tavern around the corner. Do they serve whiskey?"

"They do."

"Can we take our conversation down the block?"

"You're buying?"

"That I am."

He scrambles down from his perch with surprising alacrity.

Into the obscure barroom we go. Father Byron Timmerman is a well-known patron. The bartender states up front he's not allowed to run a tab. I show cash. We're served.

Father Byron smacks his lips and holds his Irish whiskey carefully. He touches the glass with every finger of both hands. He drains and pushes it forward, a look of expectation in his eyes. I summon the bartender. I haven't touched my whiskey. I usually follow this rule that says, don't drink whiskey. Especially with strangers. It's a good rule. When I break it, I end up in regrettable situations.

The ex-priest takes a deep breath. His hands ring a full shot, and I see the tremors kicking in. I escort him to a booth for privacy. I push him to speak.

"You used to be a priest?"

"Once a priest, always a priest. I am no longer sanctioned by the Church. I have been thrown out of the gates. The gates are locked behind me."

"Why?"

"I was present at the strangulation of a girl."

"You need to tell me more than that."

"Her mother believed her to be possessed by a demon. Her mother killed her. I did nothing to stop it. I was under the influence at the time."

"Alcohol? You went into that girl's house drunk?" Scoffing, I shake my head.

"I was under the influence of the demon."

The terrible truth is I smile. But he is not joking, and I put away the smile quickly, though not quickly enough. I've passed judgment; now he's suspicious. "You say you're a writer. Exactly what is it you want from me, Mr. Deering?"

"Explain *mirrorrorrim*."

The word is a trigger. He shudders like a gun-shy dog.

"We live in constant danger," he says.

"You mean Regina is in danger?"

"Regina, you, me . . . especially Regina. They're not finished with her. One way or another, they'll have her. She must remain watchful. I told her so. I told her not to trust anyone. You could be an agent, Mr. Deering. Though, I think not. They wouldn't send someone posing as a journalist. It's not their style. They hate the truth."

"Who are they?"

"Why, the cult that stole those twin boys."

"Give me some facts."

"Facts, eh?" He snorts.

"What's funny about facts?"

"You are not operating in a realm of facts, Mr. Deering. If you want to get at what happened to those children, you'll need to lose some baggage. Lose it fast. Let Fortune's whims carry it away. You'll need to free your mind. Facts, I'm afraid, are chains. Tell me you want Truth, and I'll do everything in my ability to aid you. But, for God's sake, don't ask me for fucking facts." Tiny froths of spittle whiten the corners of his mouth.

"Sorry. Sometimes I get—"

"It's okay."

"I can spot it on you a mile away, you know?"

"What's that?"

"You're a dreamer. You see past the illusions of so-called reality. But you've been having the dark ones. Correct?"

I sip my whiskey. I think about leaving. Remain seated. My skin feels warm and itchy. I lift the edge of my sweater and scratch my belly. I've sprouted a rash at my beltline. Some category of mite, no doubt, is thriving in Father Byron's store, or perhaps on Father Byron himself. I'm glad we are sitting with a table between us.

"Do you have any familiarity with the black arts?" Father Byron asks.

"Ask my demons."

Father Byron sniffs. "Forces assemble throughout the world. They always have. Whole cultures design themselves around magical concepts. They call it religion."

"Religions don't kidnap children from their homes."

"Some would disagree." Father Byron appraises me. I feel like a student. He's preparing to give me a lesson. Or maybe I'm a congregation of one. He wants another shot at delivering a sermon. "You've heard of Aubrey Hart Morick?"

"The satanist?"

"That's the one. What is your knowledge of him?"

"He was a con man, sideshow barker, failed absurdist playwright, and charlatan. He wrote lyrics for heavy metal bands in the late seventies."

"You missed the key accomplishments."

"Which are?"

"Lose the baggage, Jase." Father Byron stands. He pantomimes lifting two heavy suitcases. Then he jettisons them to Fortune's whims. Which lie, apparently, in the direction of the restrooms.

"Am I being too factual?"

"You've regurgitated the digest version of the man, the who's who entry."

"So?"

"Are you the digest version of you?"

"What is it you have to share with me, Father? Tell me or I'm leaving."

"You may be better off not knowing."

"I'll be the judge of that."

He sits.

And so begins the unraveling of his story and of my life as I knew it.

Chapter 6

The Serpent of the Plains. That's how he would come to be known. But Aubrey Hart Morick, Morick the Elder, the Black Blood Druid—call him what you will—he was born into a hardworking Belfast family during the turn of the century. His father helped to build the *Titanic*. You didn't know that, did you?"

"Hardly auspicious."

"But perhaps prophetic?"

I cock an eyebrow.

"He had a hand in creating two of the great disasters of the modern era."

I become acutely aware of Father Timmerman's tongue. It seems peculiar and active. Protruding here, lapping there. The fleshy quality is lost. It appears instead to be a rough, raspy lump of foreign matter—a nub of coral, maybe.

"He died nevertheless of consumption. That's when Aubrey's mother moved the family to America. They joined her brother's brood in Connecticut. Later, she remarried. A German she met in Milwaukee. Aubrey hated him. The man was an ogre. Silent for days, weeks. He beat the boy mercilessly. With no cause, or so said Aubrey. Are you feeling all right?"

Like a gaudy, plastic strawberry worked between his teeth, or, more dreadful—something once living and now turned inside out. I've started drinking and I'm nauseated. The whiskey in me is already at work. No worry. A bit of poison cleans the pipes. Strip off my wet jacket and roll my sleeves. Improvements. The crisis may have passed, and I may be coming around. I'm still queasy. Dizzy too. My ears ringing as if a high-pitched tuning fork were wavering behind my head. Fading and returning.

"The immigrant Moricks lived in a small apartment," Byron says. "His stepfather's surname was Rheingold. Like the old New York beer."

I shake my head.

"You're too young. Too much a Chicagoan. Have you ever lived anywhere else?"

I haven't.

"Well, it's trivial and coincidental. But his stepfather, who shared a name with a beer company, lived in the Beer City of Milwaukee and worked in a brewery. Drove a beer truck. I'm sure they moved the beer barrels by hand. After bottling became popular, they loaded cases on trucks. Either way, he was a big bastard. Scary drunk. During one drunken beating, Aubrey, then a lanky teenager, fell down a flight of stairs. Rheingold probably threw him. Young Aubrey liked to draw and kept a neat row of sharpened pencils in his shirt. His spill down the staircase lodged a pencil in his left orbit. The eye could not be saved. He wore a patch for most of his adult years."

This talk jars my memory bank of album covers, a file box of skimmed articles printed in *Rolling Stone*. "I remember photos of him with a glass eye."

"Black glass, yes, he was quite the showman. His fame, notoriety, came late in life. After the incident with his eye, he ran away from home. He became a drifter. Rode the rails some and experienced the underbelly of the USA firsthand. A period he never wrote about, never talked about in public. But he emerged from it as a different man. The assumption is he turned to petty crime. Ran cons. Grifting. He'd been jailed. Never for long though. Gregarious and convivial on the outside, as con men must be, but he grew icy innards. Then he went into the theater business."

"How do you know so much about him?"

"I met the man. Don't look shocked. I was at seminary and questioning my vocation. For the weekend, at least. I visited the city. Got drunk. Did everything I could to get laid. Short of paying for it. I went to a concert. Someone gave me a backstage pass. Morick was there. We talked until sunrise. He talked, I should say. We all—the band and their roadies, the groupies, and I—sat around him like children and soaked up his words." Father Byron removes his cap and finger-combs the thin hairs over his skull. "He was a madman, of course. Or he played the madman role to the hilt. It's entertaining hearing the mad tell their stories."

A glint flashes in the good father's eye, and a chuckle erupts. We both know my thoughts. Cold air blows over my shoulders. The honk of a car horn, loud, then muffled.

The bar is filling up with men: laborers, retirees, and a sprinkling of bohemian types. The last group is identifiable by their ominous overcoats. Check out the retro eyewear and lack of basic hygiene. These are smoking men. For the first time in hours, I light a cigarette.

"I'm not making a connection here, between your brushing up against Aubrey Hart Morick and the disappearance of the Boyle twins."

"I wanted to illustrate the man's charisma. Of greater importance is his writing. The lyrics and stuff, that was for money. Most of his evil act was simply for the money. But he did, in fact, become knowledgeable about satanism. He did become a believer. Beyond question, he was the most powerful mage of his time."

"A magician like Houdini you mean?"

Envision the televised stagecraft of my youth. A white dove reborn from a silk handkerchief, the chime of steel blades, and women floating on air. Best of all is the escape artist. One memory sticks. He's padlocked, then submerged and crammed—his body displacing water—into an overflowing milk can. I hold my breath at the thought. The lid locked down. Black water. Brrrr.

Father Byron puffs with frustration. "How can I put this? During Morick's middle phase, he first became convinced magic was real. He wrote complex magical rituals or workings. His practices were recorded. On film. He was obsessed with preservation. This might interest you— the disposition of those films remains unknown. Rumors were he ordered them destroyed upon his death. I doubt that. Morick the Elder was an egomaniac. Very likely, a psychopath. He would want his work to survive. He would want himself to go on."

"Who doesn't?"

"Yes, but we accept out fate, don't we? Morick did not. He designed a sacrifice to ensure his power continued. The incantation associated with this sacrifice uses the word *mirrorrorrim*. Worlds occur simultaneous and parallel to ours. Some lighter, some darker. Some very much darker. *Mirrorrorrim* is a password. It allows blending of the shadow world and ours. Secrets words for secret worlds, you understand. Occultists love secrets. So do magicians. Without them they're impotent. *Mirrorrorrim* is uttered during a sacrificial ritual."

"This ritual has a name?"

"The Cloven Print," the old priest whispers.

"Cloven? Like a hoof?"

"And like a throat." Father Byron runs his thumbnail under his turtleneck. "It's a blood rite. Quick and dirty explanation? Twins, identical twins, are merged into a single being. This new being catches fire with the power of the mage, like a wick held to a flame."

"He burns with it." I flick my lighter.

Father Byron grabs my hand. The flame blows out.

"The mage's power is nourished and sustained. Key to it is—at the moment of the merging, one twin will die. In flesh only, that's important. But the other—the stronger of the two—survives both in body and spirit. Why would this interest the Black Blood Druid, you ask? Morick the Elder was a powerful mage. Yet never powerful enough. As death claims one twin, there's a chance for someone else to slip into the living twin."

"Sort of a piggyback ride?"

"A ride with a steep cost," Bryon says. "The mage must be strangled to release his spirit. So it's murder and suicide. The act is about timing. One twin dead, the other is in spiritual suspension. The mage cuts the deck and shuffles in. He *prints* himself onto the flux of spirits. If it's done correctly, you get a trinity. Three into one." Father Byron claps his hands sharply.

People seated around us turn.

I smile at them politely.

"I do like the symmetry of that," he says.

"It's all about building a supermage?"

The erstwhile priest exposes a rictus of tawny teeth. The grin dissolves. His face is heavy. His back draws upright as if a cord jerked him toward the ceiling. "He'd be unstoppable. According to Morick, he'd also likely be immortal. At the very least this supermage would live hundreds of years. Morick posited that his power would be enormous. He would, among other things, have the ability to exert his Will over others psychically. He would play chess with real-life pawns."

The lure of turning life into a rigged game is tempting. It appeals on a gut level. What about chaos? What happens, I wonder, when chaos enters the mix?

"Tough luck for the twins," I say.

"Yes and no. He who's chosen to live *lives*, if only as a host for the mage's Will."

"Frankly, I wouldn't want to be host to a psychoparasite. This Cloven Print leaves everybody worse off than they started."

"Not the Will of the mage."

"You're right. For the Will of the mage, it works out rather nicely."

Touching base with Robyn. Subterranean pay phone—I find it after staggering down a long flight of cement steps. City codes don't apply at this establishment, I guess. No Exit signs. No railing. I'm going to place my call. But first—nature and a chance to behold the grim Spackle work of the johns. An oldster in the stalls invokes Mother Mary as he horks up his dinner. I've pissed and I'm out in the—I don't know what to call it—the lounge area? Nice place for a knifing. My ass leveraged against a cigarette machine. I'm buying and talking. Quarters have a pleasant weight. Listen to them tumble into the machine. I pull the big release plunger.

No Lights. Marlboro Red box.

"What?" I say for the third time into the phone.

Robyn is telling me to come home.

I can barely hear her. The bar is full of mannish noise. Haven't seen a woman yet, other than the barmaid. If somebody unplugs the cig machine, I'll be in total darkness.

I promise to call it a night.

I hang up.

I return to the table and survey the damage. Phalanx of shot glasses— that's why I feel so drunk. As a preamble to wrapping up, I say to my companion, "Morick killed himself. I read about it."

"You're in error. His suicide was a rumor. It sprang from an incident, an attempt at the Cloven Print. Aubrey Morick hanged. He was attempting the rite. But he bailed. Or something went wrong. They cut him down."

"Who cut him down?"

"His followers. This was a private ritual but not an exclusive one. There was an audience. Morick had a scar around his throat from the rope until the day he perished."

"How did he die?"

"He died in a fire. In his own kitchen. He'd been drinking—not unusual, the man was a drunkard—but supposedly he'd also been trying to sober up. He put a kettle on. Tea bag waiting in the cup. Cookie and a napkin. Perhaps he had a visitor stop by unexpectedly. The front door was wide-open when the housekeeper arrived the next morning. Water spilled everywhere, as if Aubrey were throwing it around. The authorities are not certain of particulars. His sweater caught fire and went up in a flash."

The ex-priest makes a flourish with his hands.

Unspeakable—I can't find words.

"When they found him, Morick was, rather incredibly, still alive. The police were aghast. He was airlifted to a specialized unit here in Chicago. Second- and third-degree burns over ninety percent of his body. Oh, my dear child, he was a charred rack of bones. The flames burned themselves *out* on him and he laid there melted to the kitchen floor—all through the night! Can you imagine? He died without ever regaining consciousness."

All religion viewed from without seems hogwash. Resurrection, nirvana, enlightenment, even the very concept of Godhead . . . well, the list goes on. Since prehistory we humans have obsessed on the thought of becoming a meal for birds and foxes, beetles and grubs. Death the Leveler blows his breath on our spiritual templates and they flutter away like scoops of confetti. I tell this to Father Byron.

"To the outsider, what you say is entirely true."

"But not to the believers."

"*Et voilà.*" Father Byron grabs me by the shoulder. That sharpened thumbnail of his digging like a talon.

"Morick has believers?"

"Oh, yes, I'm afraid he has grown his base in recent years. Underground. Quietly, steadily, like a trickling of rain into a great blackhearted pool."

"You said he was dead."

"Not the father, the son. Graham. Aubrey had a son."

"Graham Morick kidnapped the Boyle boys?"

"Obviously he did. But he doesn't go about his tasks without significant help. He needs worshippers. He needs funding. The elements of his father's cult, the new recruits—they are behind this too. Graham's here. He's in the city."

"Aren't you afraid of him?"

"If he kills me, and he might, then everyone would know. I've talked to the police. I've made it plain to them. Graham deems me unworthy of confrontation. He thinks my blathering inoculates him against any real investigation. He's wrong. I think he fears me on a certain level. I was a consecrated priest. In this game of ours, that still signifies."

The priest and I are drunk.

"Graham is his father's son," he says. "I'm convinced he snatched those boys and he will kill one of them. He's planning to execute the Cloven Print ritual. I know it."

The bar is almost empty. Lights are on.

Words are afloat.

"In his heart, Aubrey Morick believed in the Cloven Print." The priest is slurring.

I stand up. My ability to balance encourages me to move out of the booth.

"How do you know that?"

"Because, dear child." The old priest rises, unsteady. I put a hand under his arm. He shuffles closer. He takes my face in his hands. "Once upon a time, Graham Morick had a twin brother, named Griffin."

That night I dreamed a nightmare. Reaching back for the last tidbits— it was a drunken dream, a swirling collage of tail ends grasped from the edge of wakefulness. All I sense is a flickering. Then, like a poorly edited clip of amateur film, like the grainy video I'd watched of the Boyle abductions and the birthday tape—I remember, quite vividly, fluidly, viewing myself reciting incantations in one of Aubrey Hart Morick's mysterious lost recordings. This was dreamworld, dreamtime. I'm kneeling. The forest floor smoothed but packed hard beneath me. The insect noise is huge. Maybe it's the jungle? Corpses arranged on the ground. Blood is shining. Throats hacked. I'm drinking from a gourd.

Father Byron squeezes my shoulder. His face tilts into mine.

"Jase, Jase! Where do you want to go?"

I'm at the curbside. Traffic zips by.

The dream is over. A taxi door opens. The dream is over.

Where do you want to go?

The dream is . . .

Chapter 7

Robyn hums. She's a morning person. Fresh from the shower, her rosy white rump passes the gap in the doorway. I am not yet reconstituted. I am a gluey eye checking out the scene. The chatter of NPR drifts from the kitchen radio, the sense of it indecipherable in my state.

Brushing her teeth. The water running. Her hair, braided, is a softly swinging rope. I only glimpse her. The bathroom lights are switched off. My Renaissance blind woman, she can do this—shower, fix her hair, and make her toilet in the dark. She walks into the bedroom. The sole of her upturned foot arches before me.

I've slept on the floor, it appears.

A silver tea service—wheel lines tracked into the thick, snowy carpeting. Is that rye toast I smell? An uncapped jar of fig preserves floats above, and a knife. Clank and scrape.

She stands over me naked, eating.

Her golden bush toweled into a wild state. I smell her sea tang.

The curtains are pulled open. Sunlight hammering into my eyes.

"You up?" she asks.

"Huh."

"Are you awake?"

My ears stuffed with cotton, her voice traveling underwater.

"Feeling a bit deaf," I say. I struggle upright and receive a stone dagger of pain for my efforts. "God, I'm not doing well."

"You were perfectly shitfaced. Lucky for you Johnny was downstairs. He knew to call me and not the police."

Johnny is a doorman who works in the building. Usually, he's on days. But he works overtime before the holidays. Big family. Lots of Christmas presents.

"How bad was I really?"

"Pretty bad."

"Did I get sick?"

"In the cab you did."

"No."

"I paid the driver off. Guy wanted to behead you." She laughs curtly, without merriment. Walks into the walk-in closet. Eating toast with her left hand, picking an outfit with her right.

"Look, I'm sorry," I say.

"No need."

This tactic of tolerance is worse than outright screaming. She's not my wife. Why do I feel so unhusbandly?

"Robyn, don't be this way."

"What way?"

"You're trying to make me feel guilty by not reacting." I cough into my fist and taste the acidic remnants of the night. On my knees I quake at the bedside, like a sinful boy at prayers. This posture is familiar. How often I've ministered to Robyn while she lies on a talus of pillows and cracks herself wide open.

"Your guilt is your own responsibility. I have work today," she says.

Puritanical pain in the ass.

"Where . . . where are you going?" My interest piques. I have to say that Robyn's recent tendency to stay close to home is both a worry for me and a comfort. The lakefront properties are so convenient. I worry she's becoming reclusive. Office space and hearth lodged under the same roof; an outstation where she conducts her business, our business, remotely if well. No reason to ever leave. She's dependent on me for contact. Face-to-face. I'm talking about the human touch. The comfort being: I know where my woman is.

Yet I roam.

"I'm doing an interview," she says.

"With whom are you conducting an interview?" When I'm hungover, proper English steadies me like a rental crutch. I'll lose it when I'm feeling better.

"Secret," she says.

I'm in no mood for secrets.

Quick peek in the mirror. Worse than I thought—my bleary, unshaven doppelgänger returns. Owlish patches around my—are those eyes? Okay, I'm a mess. Dying for a hit of nicotine, I defeat the arcane mechanism on the sliding glass door. I'm out on the balcony standing in the crosswinds. Shirtless, but wearing my vomit-streaked trousers and thin, brown socks. Not daring to sit in the metal patio chair for fear of losing skin upon departure. It is frigging cold. I do a shivery two-step and smoke. Pick apart the city views to distract myself. Here's the noxious green taint of the Chicago River below us. South of the river, mountains of real estate I'll never be able to afford. Left, you see flinty Lake Michigan. Damn, I'm freezing to death. I abandon the cigarette in a flowerpot. Go inside. To warmth. Robyn.

Despite my debauched condition, I'm aroused. A little encouragement and I'll be ready for action. Posttraumatic sexual vigor raises its ugly head, or wants to. Robyn knows me. My patterns of behavior are well-established. She loves me, right? I drape an arm around her. Enjoy the friction of her champagne slip.

She shrugs me off. "You've got time for a cold shower. Move it."

"I need about fourteen recuperative hours in bed."

"I'm interviewing the Boyles," she says.

I can feel my jaw hanging.

"Want to come?" Her chin pushes out, the cocky little wag. She's aiming slightly to my left because she can't see me. Not wholly. I'm a walking shroud in a room full of shrouds. Sometimes I'd like to slap her. That's right. Slap a blind girl. But I plant a hard kiss instead.

And grab the soap.

H ow did you manage to arrange this?"

"By accident, really. I was calling around the English department trying to get colleagues to cough up a bit of dirt on Tad's extracurricular love life. Mum's the word, as you'd expect. Even though they hate him, they're loyal. To a point. Prof in the comparative-lit wing tells me ra-ther mysteriously to call this number. It's a campus extension, to a locked faculty carrel over in the Humanities Research library. Who'd think they'd put phones in there? They must flash or something. Anyway, it's Tad's old carrel. His stabbin' cabin pied-à-terre . . ."

"Who answers? Tad?"

"No. Una. She's packing up his stuff."

"Dutiful."

"Pathetic, if you ask me. But she says they're leaving the country."

"What?"

"It's been almost a year."

"Don't play coldhearted. You're appalled too."

"Yes, of course." By her tone, I'm thinking maybe she isn't so appalled. Robyn's maternal instincts are hidden. To the point they might be snuffed out. I can't imagine her mothering anyone—except me.

We're stuck at a stoplight. The manhole at the intersection is open, and a Streets and San crew has pitched their tent. A grizzled city worker waves cars through. Individually, it seems.

"You're taking Lake Shore Drive, aren't you?"

"No, I'm not. Will you just sit back?"

"Turn around. This is my last official suggestion."

Traffic, to Robyn, is pachydermal fields of stop-'n'-go color. But she has an uncanny sense of direction—my trusty bush guide and interpreter. I reverse and bump up over the curb, hang a U-turn. Then it's zigzagging Ms. Pac-Man style through the one-ways and alleys. We pop out on Clark. Tunnel a path into the Gold Coast. As I drive, I tell Robyn about my night with Father Byron. I mention the Morick clan and their entanglement in the black arts.

"What black arts?"

"Oh, the usual ones—calling up demons, and worshipping old, neglected gods, witchcraft, sorcery, spells, mind control, sex magic, human sacrifice . . ."

"The Morick family is here? In Chicago?"

"Aubrey's surviving son, Graham, has been sighted. At least the ex-priest thinks so."

"That's disturbing."

"If it's true," I say. I'm still on the fence about Byron's tale.

I'm suspicious by nature. But I love a gruesome story. *And, if it's true, we have ourselves a fantastic gruesome story.*

The neighborhood has seriously improved. You can almost hear the riffling of hundred-dollar bills. "Which Boyle has the bucks? They're not getting by on a teacher's salary."

"Tad's family. Una was an orphan, as far as I can tell. The paperwork is sketchy. I've got one of my mole people working on it. Her adoptive parents weren't poor, but they weren't the Pritzkers either."

"Where did Granddaddy Boyle get his bankroll?"

"Banking."

"That's handy."

From the outside, the home is gorgeous in an understated, no-need-to-prove-anything sort of way. I don't have an *Amityville* moment. No flies. No walls oozing blood. Haven't been inside yet, but more than any sense of dread I get a pang of envy. Wish these were my digs.

Robyn lays into the buzzer. She slips her glove off and knocks, bare-knuckled.

Not a stir. We decide to head around the back.

"She knows we have an appointment," Robyn says. I detect her excitement, fluster is more like it; she doesn't do interviews in person. I do. No-shows don't surprise me. Neither does hostility or boredom.

Surprises don't surprise me. But Robyn volunteering herself for an interview is most unusual. I take it she's tired of her cloister. It strikes me, now that I see her in a new setting, just how shut-in she's become. This outing will do her good. I'm happy she's expanding her limits.

The Boyle yard is a narrow patch of yellowed crabgrass abutting a vegetable garden. Two parallel privacy fences separate the neighbors. The garden is large, half again the size of the ill-kept lawn. Pumpkins bulge on the vine, shading orange to speckled green, and flowerless sunflower stalks lurch against the garage like madwomen. I see the planted rows picked clean of lettuce, cucumber, zucchini, and maybe Italian parsley. Little faded markers stuck in the dirt. Someone is a family gardener, like my mother was. They've slacked off their recent duties. Tomato vines have shriveled and drooped to the ground taking their stakes with them; bound together, as they are, by strips of old nylons. I touch one, unknot the hosiery. Slip it into my pocket.

"Hello?" Robyn, edging forward, makes herself known.

"I'm in the garage. I've lost the key to the side door. Come through the alley."

Una's voice startles me. I hadn't expected her to be nearby—only a thin, uninsulated wall between us. There's no window on this side. She hasn't witnessed my small theft. Yet I gaze over my shoulder at the rear of the house, checking the curtains for spies.

We fumble at the gate. Nudge aside a garbage bin.

The garage is a wooden, one-car affair from the late forties. A door made of planks swings upward, the top half driven into shadow. Inside are moving boxes by the dozen. A Volvo buried beneath trash bags full of clothes. I want to peek, to see if they're children's clothes, but I don't. She'll see me and know my line of mental inquiry. Through the dusty windshield of the Volvo, I spot two car seats still strapped in place. I feel guilty.

Una had been beautiful. You can tell that the minute she stands up, walks over to shake hands. She's tall, nearly my height, and square-shouldered. She retains a beauty's carriage. Coltish—a sloppy angularity that's never been polished out. Conducting herself as if her handsomeness were a burden she's learned to cope with, rather than a genetic prize. Only the posture doesn't quite fit anymore. She's distant. Her facial expressions arrive chilled. Black-haired, dark-eyed, under thirty; every woman she has met from her girlhood on has hated her, just a tiny bit, in her heart of hearts. Men think foremost of bedding her. And she knows.

She seals a box top with shiny packing tape. The roll shrieks under her hand.

Whatever else grief, or guilt, has done, it has ravaged her physical charms. Mined them out. But the larger structure survives intact. Watching her talk and sort through boxes—between sips from a smudgy wineglass—is a sad spectacle, like standing amid ancient ruins. I keep looking away. Staring at her again. My mouth sucked dry.

Here's a mother.

If the story's to be believed, some creep has her children. Or he did for a time.

I want to take away her pain. But I am a realist too, knowing the likely outcome of my endeavors will be to twang the knife buried in her heart.

I steel myself.

People play dangerous games," she says to us. The conversation shifts from perfunctory politeness to thornier matters. "They think because they're smart—they've got a blue-chip education and a few bucks in the bank—they think nothing can hurt them. Savvy operators. They'll know when to back off, get out of Dodge."

"You and Tad were like that?" I ask.

"Were we assholes?" Una stops rummaging. "Don't worry. You can say it. We've certainly been accused of much worse."

"Were you?"

She doesn't answer. I spot the bottle of chardonnay she's stowed behind some paint cans, probably as we were skirting the garage. Her shame has evaporated. Or her need is too great. Una hoists the bottle and fills her glass. *Fills* it.

"Where is your husband?" Robyn asks.

"Good question. Always a good question." Una nodding as she speaks, absently tucking her long, black strands behind her ears; she squints at Robyn in the somber one-bulb garage. Sunglasses—the oddity of them here. But sunlight slants across our backs, the alleyway and its lunar surface cast under a smoky glare. "Is there something wrong with your eyes? Why are you . . . ? Look, sorry, I'm an idiot."

"When do you go abroad?" Robyn changes subjects.

"Sunday night. Fly in to London Heathrow. Spend a week, then by train and ferry over to Dublin. We've sublet an apartment near Trinity College. Tad's researching a new book. He won't talk to me about it. Tad can be horribly cloak-and-dagger concerning his writing."

Dublin. Where did I just hear about Dublin? Not Dublin, but somewhere on the same island. Up north. Belfast. Father Byron. Aubrey Hart Morick's childhood home was in Northern Ireland. The words spill out before I do any thinking.

"Do you know who Graham Morick is?"

"No." Then a frown. Puzzlement? The name, the name. Liquor warring against her wits. Or are these second thoughts? "Yes. I've only talked to him once. Why?"

"You've spoken with Graham Morick?" I step nearer. My shadow enfolds her and causes confusion, discomfort. She repositions.

"At a dinner party, I think. No, it was a campus picnic. Fourth of July? You know I may be wrong. The name just sounded familiar." She shakes her head. "I don't think I ever met him. I'm certain I haven't. It's just the name . . ."

From the cobwebby recess behind the Volvo's bumper, she hauls a sawhorse.

She puts it between us.

"Were the boys with you?"

"On the Fourth last year? I don't remember. We never take the boys to faculty events."

"Graham never met the boys?"

"I told you *I* never met him. Even if he was on campus for a party . . . it was a departmental function. The boys would've been home with Regina."

"Does Tad, by chance, know Graham? Are they acquainted?"

"You'll need to ask Tad. Is Graham . . . does he have a predatory history or something?" Her visage twists up like a rag. I'm afraid she'll wail. She's expecting new blows, and the heaviest.

I've led her into a dark wood with my questions. Now I'm leaving her there.

"Not to my knowledge," I say. My coyness is torture, and I regret it. The cruelty was accidental. But I'm not going to tell her any more. Not going to bring up devil worshippers and inchoate rituals dependent on the killing of a twin child. "His name turned up when I was talking to other people."

"Turned up?"

"It's nothing."

"Tell me. What do you know?"

"Nothing," I say. "Really, like you said, just a name."

Her fear is resolving. I don't know what precisely to expect out of her—but it is fast approaching and probably not good for the two people standing opposite. I notice myself backing up. I hook on to Robyn's sleeve and tug her along.

Una's forearms are ropy muscle. She's wearing a flannel shirt rolled to the elbows. Her right hand hasn't given up its glass. But the left is free. My eyes are drawn to the fist.

She is around the barricade. Tearful.

They are tears of fury. A growl building in her throat escapes.

"Get out."

I realize she's drunk, but not only drunk. There are pills in that head of hers, and despair. I'm hoping to forgive her weaknesses, hoping she'll forgive us ours. It's not going to happen today. Una's face contorts with hatred.

She throws her glass.

The shattering registers as a close, brittle explosion on the telephone pole behind my ducking head. Crystal slivers land in my hair. The garage door comes down hard. I have to grab Robyn to keep her toes from getting snapped off.

"That went well," I say.

R obyn is shaken. She regrets our excursion. Me? I know better than to take insults and hurled glassware personally. Una's rage wasn't about me. I feel shitty that we aggravated her pain. But we didn't cause it.

In the passenger seat, Robyn is ruminating. She needs a distraction to cure her disappointment. Her defense mechanisms are fully engaging. Pretty soon she'll start flirting with me. Thinking she's been swatted down for leaving her eagle's nest. Superstitious lady. The minute she meets resistance, the scenery thickens with portents. Chalk it up to her deep New England ancestry, this daughter of a Daughter of the American Revolution; her highbred anxieties are stitched into the bone. Madly organized, logical tending toward aloof, and a stickler for details—but still she's searching the skies for witches. Everything under the sun becomes imbued with meaning, our pilgrim souls suffering constant perils, the universe divided into black and white. She loves the idea of order and the inherent drama when order is upset. She loves to control.

I'm different. Give me my chaos. What I know best.

The world isn't about you.

It isn't about being *about* anything.

Robyn wants to go home. Maybe my sudden sweet tooth is nothing but a delaying tactic. But she gives in. We stop for two gelatos on Michigan Avenue, within a rifle shot of the Art Institute, where punky Regina warned me not to trust.

"I'm going back to Unimaginable Vortices," I say.

Only Robyn can make a plastic spoon look sexy. She panther-licks the back of it and chews her coconut nougat cream. Watching her makes my teeth sore.

"Why go there again?"

I have no immediate answer.

She says, "I want to kick off these heels and listen to my Piaf records. Get a foot massage in front of the fireplace. How does that sound? I'll wear the mink bikini you brought from San Francisco."

"Father Byron talked a lot last night. But he didn't tell me what I really needed to know. He wasn't getting drunk just because I was paying.

He was scared. In his mind, he was taking a big risk. I think he has first-hand knowledge of Graham Morick."

"You're going to choose some funky old padre over me?"

My pager is vibrating.

I check the number. It's Fennessy. And there's a 9-1-1 attached.

"I've got to find a phone."

"Call me a cab while you're at it. I'm not going to any damn bookstore."

R obyn catches her cab. I'm driving north to the bookstore. My conversation with Fennessy convinced me. He told me not to go. But first he told me Regina Hoffman's husband had reported her missing an hour ago.

"Man was agitated," says Fennessy. "He spent the night trying to track her down."

"I'll talk to him."

"I wouldn't do that."

"Why?"

"He was, like I said, agitated. *Angry* is probably a better description."

"Well, I think I can handle an angry curator."

"He's a big guy. I would not piss in his Cheerios. Oh, and he seems to think you're responsible for his wife's sudden disappearance."

"It's my fault? Regina isn't the picture of stability."

"The husband says you were the reason she took off. Your interview upset her."

"I upset a lot of people."

"No kidding."

I run down the basics on my encounter with Father Byron Timmerman, then the Una fiasco. Fennessy holds his comments to the end. One of the traits I like about him, that and his subtlety. Turns out he knows the proprietor of Unimaginable Vortices and his theories on the Boyle case.

"C'mon, I can't believe *you* of all people were sucked in. That fringe lunatic Timmerman peddling his hoodoo-voodoo bullshit."

"I wasn't sucked in."

"You were."

"He was somewhat convincing, I thought. I didn't think so last night, but I'm starting to think that now."

"He's a fucking NutterButter."

"Did you look into Graham Morick?"

"We did."

"The Boyles might've met him. At a university get-together. Did you know that?"

"News to me. But Morick lives near the campus. They might've crossed paths. Wise up, okay? We checked him out. He's a normal guy who illustrates books for a living. I didn't notice any pentagrams or horns. He wears a cape, but a person is allowed a fashion statement."

"He wears a cape?"

"See what I mean? Right there is a perfect example. You shouldn't believe everything you hear."

"But if one of the Boyles met Morick . . ."

"Graham Morick is a dead end. Now tell me why Regina would run away. And if she did—she left behind her car and her clothes. Did she say anything out of the ordinary? Let me turn that around. What did you say to her? I know your reputation. But, seriously, she's only a kid."

"A messed-up kid," I say. "I don't think she said anything I'd classify as *ordinary*. She acted paranoid. Thought strangers were following her."

I feel bad she's lit out. But I don't feel responsible.

"Confess, Jasc. The girl has a certain allure. Did you make a run at her?"

"Detective, Detective . . . you shouldn't believe everything you hear."

"I hope she turns up. I'm getting a gut feeling that I don't like."

"Give her a little time. Sounds to me like she got excited and took to the hills. For the record, I'm worried about her too. Keep me posted."

"Will do."

The bookshop is closed. I cup my eyes from the street. Look in. Dimly blue, like the electrical haze inside an appliance. Backing away, I sense a slippery chill, almost wetness where I've touched the window. Rub my hands together. The sign's flipped. The hours posted, nine to nine daily. No answer after rapping the glass. Mail spillage on the doormat under the slot: envelopes leaning against the other side of the door. Nobody's come through this way, not since the delivery. I walk to the bar.

A bad-dye-job blonde, her roots muddy as an ax wound, tends the bar. I don't see anyone I recognize from last night.

I'm turning to leave, then figure what the hell. Nothing ventured. Turn back.

"Hey, you know the place down the block, the bookstore? I needed to buy a book from there, but the store is closed. Does that happen a lot?"

"Some days it's open. Some days it's closed."

I open up my wallet and give her a twenty.

"What'll you have?"

"I'm not thirsty. I want to know about that guy who runs the store."

"He's a weirdo." She takes the bill.

I hold her wrist. "C'mon, try harder."

"Sometimes he has meetings there. Late meetings. Nights. People come and he locks them in."

"What kind of meetings?"

"I don't know."

"Anything you might tell me would be helpful."

She shakes off my hand. "I'll tell you something about the weirdo. When he has these meetings of his? After everybody's inside? He pours holy water on the door. I've seen him do it. He has this squeeze bottle with a cross on it. He squirts it on the glass."

Chapter 8

I should go and spend the evening with Robyn. My hangover has only now lifted. My motor's running. I come home to my bachelor's cave—to my home away from Robyn. Heat up soup. Clam chowder. Oyster crackers and white pepper, a jolt of Tabasco. I pace the studio in my underwear, spooning from the mug. Music plays from my boom box. Joy Division, "Love Will Tear Us Apart." The only songs that excite me are the desperate ones. When it's over, I snap off the tuner. My gears are meshing neatly.

I moved into the Chaucer Arms after my divorce. It's a shithole, basically. Bath, kitchenette, closet. A worktable, a couch, and a Depression-era Murphy bed. These drab rooms—they look like the places where men die alone. I try not to dwell on that. You can't beat the location if sleep has never been a major part of your life and if carousing is. The bars and dance clubs along Rush and Division are legend. On the week end nights, the cops barricade a stretch of Division. They pull up a paddy wagon. They wait. Drunks are dependable. If what you're depending on is their getting drunk. There are whores inside the bars, pros and amateurs. Most of the action is of the one-night-stand variety, attracting singles or married players. I have been both.

Prior to Robyn.

My pager's humming on the table. I know it's her. I know she's lonely, in danger, torn from her social moorings and dragging anchor out to sea.

She'll take me with her if I'm not careful.

The trip won't be bad. It will feel wonderful. She makes me feel wonderful. A two-person universe with Robyn—I suppose I can live with that. But I'm not ready to settle for a relationship sewn up airtight. I know that's what she wants. Horizons trimmed away so only two faces fit. I'm not ready. Not yet.

Blame Isabella, my first and only wife according to the law. What can I say about Isabella and not sound unfair? I fell for her. She had an evil little grin and a chubby bottom and was everywhere else very, very sleek. I should have paid more attention to the rest of her. The reason the marriage, our marriage—no distancing here—came unglued was I didn't show enough attention. So said Isabella. I don't disagree entirely. I need my women to have an extra helping of brains. Isabella was, and is, smart—a graphic designer with a thriving business fiefdom. But her interests ran to shopping and visiting European cities trounced during the Second World War and no more. She is a good mother to our daughters. I like her new husband, Dieter, despite my best efforts.

When my ex-wife's around, it's a collective state of perpetual mourning. We regret what we did to each other, what we said and meant—everything ugly into which we evolved. Together we were rotten. We can't help picking through the aftermath, but we summon our strength to be cordial. We do it for our children. They mistake politeness for love. They still think there's a chance for reconciliation. Despite Dieter. Despite Robyn. Our two girls are holding out hope. Nobody likes to deny their kids' hopes. But Isabella and I back together? It's never going to happen.

I try to be the best dad. My trouble is I can't view childhood in an idealistic way. I see it as a perilous ride. I'm fully prepared to discuss the journey. But I'm not going to lie. Life hurts. Being a kid is tough. I see their vulnerability and innocence. They're so wide-open to heartache it makes me grab my chest. I don't want to be overprotective. *You get knocked around,* I always say, *but you move forward and pretty soon you're fine.*

Or you aren't.

I don't tell them that last part. I don't want them to know. Some people get stuck. Reality is too much for them. I'll feel safer once the girls have reached the other side of adolescence. A lot of the hardest knocks come early. We Deerings are not fragile. We rack up our fair share of traumas. Innocence looks better the farther you travel from it. Eventually, I plan to tell them that.

For now, I don't know what to say.

Be glad you're alive. Make a few friends. Write things down. Read.

The girls love Robyn. Robyn does this amazing trick when she's with them—she becomes a girl herself. It's no game, no playacting. She reaches back in time and transforms herself. Her body language changes, her vocabulary; she is exuberant. She gives the girls what I can't—a no-strings-attached adult playmate without the biological baggage.

Let her have the girls and the girls have her. I want them all to be happy. I want the girls to experience something they never did in the presence of their mother and me. Ease. Relaxation. A comfort zone that mimics family. Therefore, I sit in the corner while Robyn and the girls play house. I partake by proxy. I am the father who keeps watch and never interferes. When they want me, I'm here. One day I'll have a whole family again. I'm not sure how. Yet here I am, fingers crossed.

The pager buzzes.

My eyes sweep over to the tabletop—snag upon the creamy white rectangle waiting quietly beside the noisy electronics—and I remember the envelope.

I left it there, unopened.

I'd almost forgotten about it.

Dysart gave it to me when I came home.

If Robyn and I mutually enjoy the loyalty and soundness of having Johnny the doorman—with his six or more kids to feed and clothe and keep in toys—ever vigilant behind the marbleized reception counter at the lakefront properties, where Robyn's name appears solitary on the leases, then I alone appreciate Dysart the second-rate deskman (he's never at the door or outside his glassed-in office) at the Chaucer Arms.

I maul the paper corner with my teeth. Rip away and discard. No letter inside but a folded news clipping. Shake it out.

New Jersey *Star-Ledger,* undated.
A follow-up article by the looks of it. No photos either.

Plucky's Massacre Death Toll Mounts

The death today of Sea Girt resident Gretchen Lagerman brings to a total of eleven the fatalities resulting from a shooting spree last Saturday night at Plucky's Beachside Bar-O-Rama. Sixteen other bar occupants (two employees and fourteen patrons) were also injured in the midnight melee. Nine remain hospitalized, three in critical condition. Suspected in the shooting are six alleged members of the Blood Hogz outlaw motorcycle gang. According to an FBI spokesman, the Hogz are a national crime organization with two local chapters in New Jersey. Eastern NJ chapter president Denis DeFrancesco, killed in a fiery exchange with sheriff's police, was born and raised in Belmar. County records list him as the owner of a small farm in rural Monmouth County. Dubbed the Hogz Pen, the farm has reputedly served as the gang's headquarters and a distribution point for illegal drug and gun trafficking. Five of the six heavily armed assailants were shot and killed following a brief hostage standoff. The survivor, Alejandro "Bag" Martinez, remains in serious condition after receiving a gunshot wound to the neck. Police and local FBI are still searching for a motive in the attack. *Talk to Martinez!!!*

The last bit of urgency scrawled in red pen.

I turn the clipping over. On the reverse is a gray advertisement for radial tires. Middle of the page, same red ink—a block of tight script so regular and neat it could be mistaken for a stamp. These three phrases:

Defile the Flesh
Feast on the Living
Love the Dead

People send me stuff.

Every now and then, it's weird stuff. And they want me to have it.

Not as frequently, I'll grant, as they make offerings to television news anchors or columnists. They're big targets. I don't attract too many freaks. But I get my share. Every journalist in the public eye does. Ninety-nine percent of the unsolicited oddities funnel through the office address, through a postal box rented for just these purposes. We dump everything we don't recognize into a laundry basket. We keep the basket in the closet, next to the water pipes. Anything blows up, the whole building will be missing their showers.

When the basket can't hold anything more, not even postcards, I sort though the junk. The letters go fast. Most are boring or sad, or boring and sad. Parcels take longer. I have a couple rules. If it drips or squishes, out it goes. If it's heavier than a bowling ball, I open it in the tub with the door closed. I've only had to do this once, when an intrepid beach-lover mailed me a box of toxic sand. Last rule: if there's money inside, I keep half and donate half to charity. This rule has been applied twice. Neither the Lighthouse for the Blind nor I have since changed the way we do business.

I can't remember the last time I got a mystery delivery here at the Chaucer Arms.

I'm sure it's happened. But rarely.

D ysart?"

He lifts his face from the book.

"This letter you handed to me before, it didn't come through the mail. There's no address, no postmark. It had to be hand-delivered. Do you remember who gave it to you?"

Momentary silence, as Dysart's fleshy eyelids are lowered. They reopen. "Messianic-pope type," he says. The pane of thick safety glass separating us garbles his voice.

"Excuse me?"

"Messy and smoked a pipe. White guy." Dysart touches his chin. "Little beard." He descends into his reading, and although he hasn't moved an inch, I feel his departure.

The note has to be from Father Byron.

He fits the description. Both in garbled form and clarified. He seems the kind to pass secret messages.

"Dysart? Hey, buddy." I tap on the divider.

"Yes. What is it?"

"Do you remember when the guy was here?"

"Regular mail delivery is about eleven. Your man gave me the envelope before the mail arrived. But not by much."

"Thanks."

"Don't mention it."

Ride the elevator back upstairs. I close the cage. Press my number. Damn if the sepulchral elevator hasn't trapped the perfume of French cigarettes. Gitanes. Faint, but undeniable. Maybe we have a new tenant from the Continent. Maybe she doesn't understand the danger of mixing fire and elevators.

When the elevator stops at my floor, I dash out.

My studio is the first unit on the left.

I leave my door unlocked if I'm roaming within the building—doing laundry, running to the vending machines for a Pepsi or a bag of chips, etc. Bad habit, I know.

Just how bad? I'm about to find out.

My door's half-open.

A man wearing a black raincoat stands with one foot over my threshold. I startle him. He backs into the hallway. He alarms me as well. I'm frozen. He's at least a head taller than I am. His dome is razor-smooth. Collar unbuttoned to accommodate a massive neck. He has a bull's ring pierced through his nose.

This is the Gitanes smoker. A lit specimen chinked between his knuckles.

"Are you Deering?"

I'm uncertain how to answer.

Try nodding.

He moves closer. The hall lamps throw honeyed light. His skull shines.

"Don't give me trouble," I say.

He's trembling, the front of his coat grayed with ashes. "You've given me plenty."

To whom have I given trouble lately? He's too young to be Tad Boyle.

I don't know what Graham Morick looks like. How would he even know about me? Then it clicks. What name did Regina say in the gardens? Nathan?

"Nathan?"

"Mentioned me, did she?" He's snuffling back tears.

This pierced ox is Regina Hoffman's husband, the assistant curator.

"Would you like to come in?"

"I guess so. Sure."

C an I get you a drink?"

"I don't drink alcohol."

There's no place to sit and have a conversation in my room. I offer Nathan the desk chair. The temptation arises to pull out my bed, if only for an extra seat. That would be too odd. I park myself on the edge of the desk instead.

"You've been following me?"

"I waited in the coffee shop across the street. I lost patience. I had to talk to you."

"How did you get past Dysart?"

He shows bewilderment.

"The doorman," I say. "He's always down there."

"I didn't see anybody."

"The lobby entrance is usually locked."

"It wasn't."

Dysart has to use the bathroom sometime.

Nathan coughs. He asks me for a glass of ice water. I bring him an ashtray too.

"No word from your wife?"

"No. And I'm . . . I'm losing it." He pounds his fist into the outer muscle of his thigh, gives it a good, meaty thumping.

Getting punched, generally speaking, is something I avoid. Nathan here figures I caused his wife to disappear. I want to clear that up. I notice he wears a bulbous ring shaped like a lion's head, his middle finger being swallowed. That ring would hurt.

"I'm sorry to hear she's gone," I say.

"You should be." Glaring up at me. The chair legs creak.

"During our interview, toward the end, she did seem upset. Thought we were spied on. We weren't. Sorry I can't offer more help than that. Was Regina . . . had she been seeing a doctor or anything?"

"She's not mentally ill."

"Of course not. But the stress of her attack—"

"I told you she's not crazy."

"What do you think happened?"

"It's obvious, isn't it?"

"Honestly, no."

"She's been taken."

I consider the possibility. Maybe Nathan is right to worry.

"This may seem strange, but here. Read this clipping." I pass him the "Plucky's Massacre" article. Immediately, he brightens.

Quick stab into his pocket for a pair of reading glasses. They're collapsible, spidery. I watch him open them so delicately. Imagine them perched on the bridge of his nose in the pin-drop hush of the museum. He finishes and his shoulders slump. He tries to return the cut-up newspaper.

"Does that have significance?" I ask.

"Not to me."

"Turn it over."

He follows my instructions.

"In the red—see right there? Those phrases ring any bells?"

He shakes his head.

"Are you familiar with a man named Graham Morick?"

"He's the one."

"What one?"

"Regina . . . that old priest at the bookstore convinced her. He sold her on the fact this Morick was, I don't know, demonic or something. He claimed Morick kidnapped the Boyles. She was petrified. He asked her to join his group."

"We're talking about Father Byron? It's his group?"

Nathan nods. "He wanted her to meet with them at the bookstore. He said they could train her. Give her protection from Morick. They were organizing a plan to confront him. Seemed more like an assassination plot to me. I made her stop going. I thought everything had settled down. We were living like normal everyday people."

I tried not to stare at the steel ring, big as a padlock, speared through his septum.

Normal everyday people.

Why would you want to be one of *those*?

Poor Nathan seems lost, but I'm not the man to put him on the right path. I send him home instead. With assurances that Regina will likely call, Fennessy and San Filippo are fine detectives, no situation is as bad as it appears. The last is a lie. He seems aware but comforted. That which I perceived to be his anger was in reality frustration. I promise to follow the Boyle story wherever it may lead. I will call him, yes, if I discover anything at all, yes, and will you please call me if Regina makes contact. Yes, yes, yes.

My hand in the center of his expansive back, I'm practically pushing him out the door. But a question nags. Do you know any journalist who doesn't have a *final* final question? I ask mine.

"Nathan? How did you know where I live?"

"Regina had your address written on a scrap of paper."

"I never gave her my address."

The curator ox shrugs.

Next time I will remember to lock my door.

Paranoia can be a wonderful gift. The world takes on tremendous meaning. Any minute, the smallest detail might spell lurking danger. Senses are heightened. But also there's the urge to run away. Go and live on an island under a coconut tree.

From a street-corner pay phone, I call Robyn. She picks up first ring. I hear the Piaf record playing loudly in the background, even before I hear my lover's voice.

"Jase. What took you so long? I've been calling and calling."

"I know. Sorry about that. I was busy. Look, I think we should dig up background on Graham Morick. I need—"

"He's here."

I stand there on the pavement. The wind blows leaves around my feet.

"Jase?"

"It's windy. I thought you said—"

"Graham Morick is here right now. I looked up his number and he lives not too far away. I called him because I just couldn't believe the story you told me. That old priest said such awful—"

"He's in the apartment?"

"We were talking on the phone. Then he offered to stop in."

"I'll be there. Stay put."

I break into a run. Leave the phone dangling by its cord, twisting in the breeze.

When I arrive at Robyn's—Morick is gone. Holding the door for me, Robyn beams joviality. I might guess she's tipsy, but there's no real evidence to suggest that. Her attire—she's wearing a string tank top, no bra, a pair of tight jeans. Barefoot. A fire's blazing in the fireplace. Although Morick was an invited guest and not an intruder, I search the rooms. The apartment is scorchingly hot. Logs in the fireplace, twice the number I would use, spit sparks onto the edge of the carpet.

"You made the fire too big."

"Graham did it for me. I couldn't ask him to put it out."

Graham is it now?

I'm infuriated. For God's sake, how long has she lived in the big city? Inviting strangers into the apartment. But Robyn seems fine. No physical harm done.

"I hope you weren't dressed like that."

"What?"

"That T-shirt is practically transparent. I can see your nipples. I mean, Jesus, it's—at the very least, unprofessional. You're the one lecturing me all the time."

"I thought you liked my nipples." She giggles.

I grab her by the elbows. Her smile disappears. I'd like to shake her senseless.

"Don't let strange men into the apartment," I say.

"I let you in all the time."

"I'm not joking. Graham may be involved in a cult that kidnaps children."

"Are you going to tell me he's the devil next?"

I pull her arms back. "I mean it. Don't let him in again."

Her throat is flushed pink. I notice her reddened lips, though she's wearing no lipstick. It's amazing how quickly we're naked and on the floor. Rug-burned, spent. I'm tracing the handprints I've left on Robyn's sweet, pear-shaped bottom. Joined—her haunches rest on mine. She's bitten my thumb. Hard enough I cried out. Deep indentations—they'll bruise and turn blue by morning. This isn't the first time.

Not for anything, I'm afraid.

What was he like?"

"Tall."

"Don't say dark and handsome."

"That I wouldn't know, would I?" Robyn leans her head against my chest. She closes her eyes. Her hair fans out and the strands are whiter than my skin. "He took up the entire doorway. Though I think he must be slender. He wore a long leather coat. I could smell it. When he took the coat off, he didn't seem nearly as big."

"What did you discuss?"

"He couldn't stay long. But he wanted me to know Byron Timmerman has been stalking him for years. That man thinks Graham is demon spawn or some other nonsense. He's had to file harassment charges. There's a restraining order against Timmerman. Sorry, but your priest friend is crazy. Talking to me, Graham was sophisticated and rational. He has a reassuring voice. He spoke with confidence, not like some slinking child-nabber. I'd say he was irritated by the situation more than anything. He works as an illustrator of children's books. In person, he's exactly what you'd expect."

"I wouldn't know what to expect."

"He's sensitive. Timmerman has made his life hellish. The thought of you writing an article—he's panicked that people will take the allegations seriously. If they do, he'll be ruined. Prejudged and preconvicted. Anything involving the abuse of children puts the townfolk in the mood for a lynching. You know that."

"It sounds like you're defending him."

"I can see his point of view. He illustrates *children's* books."

"Can he live on that?"

"He obviously does. He didn't walk in off the streets."

We're silent for a moment. Robyn is sighing and snuggling down for a quick catnap. While in my head I'm tabulating the earning power of a book illustrator whose unlikely father was a renowned and prolific satanist.

This I now know: Aubrey Hart Morick's impenetrable exegeses of black magical practices remain in print decades after his death. Sales are brisk. Their popularity reaches worldwide. Graham is his father's literary executor and sole beneficiary. This entitles him to a labor-free stream of cash estimated at an annual rate in the low six figures.

How fortunate to have an inheritance.

Lying in front of the fire, I worry. Robyn fades, drowsy in my arms. I think I'll show her the birthday tape of the Boyle twins. Let her listen in. I want her to understand what's at stake here. She'll experience the tape and have the same reaction I did. She'll want the kids found. She'll want the person who took them to pay a dear price. I don't know if Graham took Shane and Liam. But he's a suspect in the minds of some people. That should be enough to rule out any private chitchats with him.

I peel myself from her. She grumbles and crawls over to the couch. Her arm drapes across her face. Deep breaths. She isn't stirring.

I'm on my knees searching for the tape. The other night, after I watched it, I slipped the tape behind Robyn's video player. I'm sure that's what I did. I was careful. I took the time to *hide* it.

Now it's missing. I get down lower. Sweep my hand under the entertainment center. My face is in the carpet. I'm eyeballing the wires hanging down the back of the electronics.

No tape.

Robyn has these bouts of compulsive cleaning. I've learned to live with them. When she starts in—her hair pulled back in a ponytail, wearing an old shirt of mine, bucket and broom in hand—I head out the door.

But if Robyn found the tape, she'd tell me.

Wouldn't she?

I don't say anything. Maybe I stuck the tape with my jacket. I'll check the studio back at the Arms. But I'm not crazy. The tape was right here. Tapes don't spontaneously combust.

I wander into the kitchen. I'm looking over the counters, quietly opening drawers.

"What are you doing?" Robyn asks.

Oh, looking for the tape you found and failed to mention? "Getting a glass of orange juice," I say.

"Let me have a sip."

I open the refrigerator. "We're out of juice."

"Forget it. Just come here."

We kiss. She makes room for me on the cushions. I wedge myself beside her.

"Someone left an envelope for me at the Arms."

"Someone like . . . ?"

"Anonymous."

Robyn sits up, yawns. I explain about the article I found inside the envelope, about Nathan haunting my building, and our subsequent conversation.

"I want to go out to Jersey and interview this Martinez," I say.

The fire flickers. A log crumbles and smoke spirals into the room.

"When?"

"As soon as possible. Tomorrow. I'll drive. Be gone three, four days, tops."

"That's nuts. All you have is a clipping. Sent to you anonymously? You said that, didn't you? Nothing connects this clipping to the Boyles."

85

"Timmerman left me that letter. I know he did."

"Even so, he's a questionable source. I told you what Graham said—"

"I'm going."

Robyn stands up. She grabs her underwear to catch my runny seed. She dries herself. Unlike me, she hates to argue. She won't go toe-to-toe. Other, more serpentine methods of persuasion are her forte. "Then I'll buy you an airline ticket. You can rent a car at the airport."

"I don't want your money, Robyn."

"Of course you do, silly. My money and body keep you interested."

The body, yes. Even her postcoital regime intrigues me. But I won't be distracted.

"We can't afford it," I say.

"I'm rich, remember? And you're not doing badly for a divorced guy who types for a living. Let me get the ticket, a commuter flight from Midway. This time tomorrow you'll be in a sleazy motel watching porno and thinking about how much you miss me."

Chapter 9

Robyn is two-thirds correct. The TV doesn't work. So I'm left to my
own devices. The motel is a standard one-level strip; sets of blue
doors in pairs facing the highway. Air conditioners hanging outside the
front windows, and blackout drapes so the parties inside can forget the
hour of the day, do whatever it is they are there to do.

In darkness and in peace.

My room smells like a urinal cake. Once I get a cigarette going, I
don't care. There's no need for me to stay in places like this. I like to.
Keeps me sharp. Makes me feel stealthy, flying into town under everybody's radar. Quiet in, quick out. I rented a Ford Escort at the Newark
airport. I could be a salesman, a frugal tourist, a guy passing through on
his way to a funeral. Nobody.

New Jersey is enjoying an Indian summer. By the time I reached the
motel, the heat started to bother me. I popped out of the driver's seat,
twisted, and felt the knots rearrange in my lower back. My soles ticked
on the blacktop. SANDCASTLE MOTOR LODGE raged pink at the noon-
day sun. I shed the jacket and sniffed. I needed a fresh shirt. Above the
office doorbell—RING FOR SERVICE!—somebody had punctured the
vinyl siding with a nail and hung a thermometer. Its black needle spiked
eighty.

I got a key to room 33 and felt very biblical.

Moved my rental car to my rental bedroom.

I retrieved my bag from the trunk. Threw cold water in my face, put the phone on the round table under the lampshade, and started making calls.

B reak time.

Switch on the TV. That's when I discover it's fried.

For the last ten minutes, I've been trying, without luck, to reach Fennessy.

The afternoon phonathon went well. Good news. I've already discussed arrangements with Bag Martinez's lawyer. He's pulling strings to avoid the usual red tape involved with putting my name on the approved visitors' list. Bag will talk to me. No problem. Martinez attends weekly rehab therapy at a YMCA near the prison. Tomorrow, I'll meet with him there, before he goes into the pool. This saves me a day or more. I guess they bend the rules for prisoners like Martinez. He's no risk for escape. Locked up for life, and a quadriplegic to boot.

I ring the squad room in Chicago again. Different number.

"San Filippo here, how can I help you?"

"Detective, you're so polite."

"I do my best. Who is this I'm talking to?"

"Jase Deering."

"Had I only known, I would've dropped an F-bomb on you first thing."

"We all have regrets."

"If you're calling about Regina, she's still missing. If you're calling about the Boyles, they're still missing. If you're looking for my partner—"

"Among the missing?"

"He's home, sick in bed. I think he gave me the plague too. I'm not feeling so hot. This coffee's going down like I haven't seen the last of it."

"You should come to New Jersey. The sun's shining, nary a toxic cloud in the sky."

"What are you doing in Jersey?"

"That's why I'm calling. Tomorrow I have an interview with a banged-up biker named Martinez. He was involved in a shooting spree five years ago. All the other shooters are dead. I wanted Fennessy to see if he could contact the locals. I'd like to get their take on, as we say, the night in question. I tried them this morning, but they ran me around. I need help. Maybe you could melt the ice. Tell me who I should be talking to."

I hear a drawer opening. If you want an ice melter, you can do worse than a Mediterranean princess with a gun and an attitude problem. I give San Filippo a shorthand version of what went down that night at Plucky's. She's jotting notes, not blowing me off. I take that as progress.

"What's his name again?" she asks.

"Bag Martinez."

"Bag?"

"That's right."

"Why do they call him Bag?"

"How should I know? Bikers have nicknames. His real name is Alejandro, but if I call him that, he'll probably spit in my eye."

"I'll pass along the message." Quick intake of breath. She stifles a moan.

"You okay?"

"Not really."

"Go home. Get some sleep."

"Stay out of trouble, Deering. We can't help you out there on the shore."

"Trouble's where the fun is. Wouldn't you agree, Detective?"

But I'm talking to a dead line. Maybe she was right about the coffee. I feel a touch unwell myself. That time of year. This field of subhuman endeavors too.

Sleep doesn't sound bad.

I lay back, stretching out above the covers. The mattress is soft. Thoughts arrive of those who have gone before me. The Sandcastle maids— I hope they're thorough. Ah, maids in their uniforms. Close my eyes.

That's when I first hear the children singing in a strange language. I step out to see if they're in the playground across the street. While I was unpacking my car, I noticed it—a cloverleaf of pea gravel loaded up with tubular park equipment. A short cross street bordering it ends at the water. My initial thought: *What kid is going to hang out on a jungle gym with the ocean yards away?* The voices could be coming from there. Far away, but close enough.

Empty.

The swing-set chains are moving, but I can't hear *them*.

My eardrums hurt. I'm also picking up this high whine like a circular saw.

Maybe the ocean does it. Being so close, the watery element affects the sound waves. Plays tricks. I walk to the edge of the parking lot. The land behind the motel stretches back for a mile of big, sandy flats, and in the distance, sketchy green hatching delineates a marsh; a silver salt creek snaking to the beachfront. Perpendicular to the beach goes a rock jetty, its staggered white geometry ensnarled by the pummeling sea.

Sound has nothing to echo off in this panorama.

Where is it coming from?

The volume lifts a notch in open defiance. Reading my thoughts. The children are singing a song about laughter. Every refrain contains a snippet of mimicry.

Ha ha ha!

Ha ha ha!

Hahahaha! Ha!

Coming from inside my room? Stand in the room and the sound is clearly outside. Stand outside . . .

Okay, I'm losing it. Really now, and getting pissed off.

I *hear* them.

Faintly.

Step back inside 33.

Press my ear to an interior wall. The music grows louder. But there is no music, no instrumental accompaniment, only a choir of childlike human voices. Are they human? Well, they have to be. Don't they?

I keep my ear there.

Maybe 34's TV works. Maybe the occupants of 34 like listening to foreign children ululating hour upon hour with no commercial breaks. What language is that? I'm no polyglot, but I can tell Italian from Cantonese. What I'm hearing sounds like German run through a reel-to-reel at half speed. With hissing and animal growls chopped into the mix. The result is lo-fi derangement. They're working off a song list of Gregorian chants leavened with preschool rhymes. I stuff my face in a pillow. The sounds are getting under my skin, making it crawl. I call the motel office and complain. Bang my fist against the wall. The singing never stops.

Ha ha ha!
Ha ha ha!
Hahahaha! Ha!

I'm not going to sleep. I lock up. Drop the motel key in my pocket. Take a walk on the beach. I slip off my shoes and my socks. Roll my pants. The sand feels good, not too hot. Underneath the top layer, if I dig my toes down hard, it's quite cool, pleasant. I have my sunglasses on, so the ocean isn't the right color. Grayer, less sparkling. Shells somersault in the surf, crabs skitter and rebury themselves. The waves wash over my ankles. They pull the tension right out of my body. I unbutton my shirt.

Nothing like an ocean for vastness. Your being beside it and feeling so small, it makes your problems shrink too. These powerful engines of salt water and wind—their edges are just enough for mortals. We get a taste and a cleansing. After which we're sent home. Because a part of us knows, doubtless, that oceans are great black-hearted maws capable of chewing us up and grinding our bones quicker than any fairy-tale giant.

My father taught me that.

I can't walk a beach without thinking of him. San Diego boy, he loved to sail and shared his love with me. Given a good map and a compass, I'll navigate any skiff respectably. I learned on Lake Michigan. The islands, not the big water, were always my favorite—Washington and its rocky sisters near Green Bay; then toward the Straits of Mackinac, finding the archipelago: South Fox, High, Beaver, Garden, and Hog (I'm forgetting some, I know); southward home (my mother's parents' land), and the Manitou Islands and Grand Traverse Bay. These were the fantastical kingdoms of my youth, and still are, though I haven't captained a boat in years.

The tide's coming in. I step too close and soak my legs.

I'd almost forgotten about the disturbance in my motel room when, farther up the beach, below the dunes, I spot two children—a brother and sister?—staring into a pit dug in the sand. Are they the elusive singers? No. I'm too far from the motel, and these children aren't singing at all. They're silent, crouched. Fixated on whatever's inside the pit. The boy, who's older, aged nine or ten, wears a Cub Scout neckerchief tied like a bandit, covering his face. I wonder why, until I draw closer. The rich stink is enough to knock me back and raise my gorge. I cover my nose with my hand. As I'm edging nearer to see what's down there, the boy jumps into the hole and disappears.

The pit is shallow, boat-shaped.

The boy kneels as he works pliers into a corpse's open mouth.

The corpse—a bull shark, maybe six feet long—is brown, bloated, rotting. A huge, mangled wound is oozing yellow on the fish's back, where someone—I'm guessing our Scout here—hacked away the dorsal fin. The boy pulls on the shark's teeth. His pliers snap, hard and empty. The boy swears. His little sister swears. He has a saw, a hammer, and a large flathead screwdriver on the sand beside him. How he can work in that stomach-churning stench, I don't know, but he is determined to get another souvenir. His sister seems content, lazily probing the shark's wound with a wooden stake.

"Did you catch this shark?"

The children don't reply, don't even acknowledge my presence.

"You know," I say, "you're not setting a good example for your sister by not answering me. It's rude."

The boy grabs hold of a tooth and waggles it side to side. "She's not my sister."

"She's your friend, then?"

"I'm not his friend." The girl scowls at me, flicks sand pebbles in my direction.

"What did this shark ever do to you?" I ask.

The boy says, "He ate my dog."

His answer stops me.

"Really?"

The boy's eyes crinkle; he's smiling under his mask. (I think both of them, this boy and this girl, have old eyes. I don't like them.)

The girl thinks his joke is funny. She's been lying in the sand on her belly. Now she rolls over onto her back. I see a small pile of shark teeth. She was hiding them from me. She sees that I've noticed and she scoops them into her brown hand.

"I want a necklace," she says. Sand sticks to her like sugar.

"And what do you want?" I ask the boy.

He's sweating. Tiny bits from the shark's damaged mouth fleck his arms. He investigates deeper with the screwdriver; the point of his tool crunches.

No response. The smell is more than I can take. I'm light-headed. I turn, heading back to the motel. Then he answers me.

"I want my dog back."

They're laughing.

I wake during the night. A child climbing into my motel bed sinks the mattress and pulls the blanket taut. Another child, or maybe the same, sits in the chair where I made my phone calls. I fumble for the lamp. Lights on. I am alone. I don't believe in dreams. Refuse to put any stock into the meaning of them—that's a better way to explain it, I suppose. The singers, the weird interlude on the beach, my thoughts revolving around the Boyles—I've trained myself to have this nightmare. A pepperoni pizza and two cans of Bud didn't help. I peel the curtain away from the window. It's raining. Fragile, misting rain that I can't really hear, so seeing everything wet in the parking lot surprises me; pallid, chilly light shines from the lot's four corners; 3 A.M., bleak as can be.

I shower. Pack my bag. Move to switch on the television, then re-member its previous malfunction. I should ask for money taken off my bill. I won't, but I'd like to.

The phone rings, and I'm trekking across the cheap carpet. Find my-self stepping over a grimy mothlike stain. Seized with a crazy premoni-tion that stepping on it will bring me bad luck.

"Hello?"

"Jase?"

"Yes?"

"It's Fennessy. Sorry to bother you. Woke you up, did I?"

"No."

"You left me this number . . ."

"Is Robyn okay?"

"Not to worry. This isn't that kind of call. The Boyles, Shane and Liam—we found them. And before you ask—they're fine."

"Where were they?"

"Long story, but everything's getting sorted out."

"I've got time. Was it revenge? Did Tad hide them? Because the mother didn't strike me as the kind who would—"

"I need you to do something for me. It's really important."

"Your voice . . . you don't sound like yourself."

"I've got the flu. Listen, Jase, can you do this thing for me or what?"

"Tell me about the Boyles—"

"Jase, go across the street."

"What?"

"Go across the street and you'll understand everything."

"Across the street from my motel? I'm in New Jersey. I don't get it."

"Okay, how about this? Look out your window."

I try taking the phone with me, but the line between the wall jack and the base is tangled. "The phone cord doesn't reach. Hold on." I undo the knot. "You really want me across the street?"

"Are you at the window?"

"Yes."

"Now look out."

So I do.

And I don't see anything, not right away.

Then I see everything.

ires spinning. The rain, the wet pavement—they saved my life. Because the tires are spinning and water sprays behind the van. I notice my rental, parked where I left it, at an angle to my door. Staring out the window, I have a clear view of the motel parking lot, the highway, and the playground. I'm watching two headlights burn on the side street fronting the playground. They are set high—a truck or a van. And behind them, water is spraying because the van's tires are spinning . . .

The headlights go bouncing up and down.

The van jumps the curb. Sparks. The front end hits and pitches up again. Through the rain-beaded windshield, a black blob fighting with the steering wheel. Gunning the motor. No face. I don't see a face. I let go of the curtain and dive back into the room, back to the bathroom, and I'm scrambling, on my hands and knees, I'm crawling like a beast caught in tar, but I get into the bathroom, fall into the tub.

The van explodes through the room.

I don't hear the window shattering.

The air conditioner bashed like a piñata.

Or the wall buckling inward.

The bed flipping sideways, its frame snapped.

And the table, the lamp, the nightstand, the crap television—everything bulldozed.

The tires don't stop. They rip up the carpet. Spit the thin foam padding underneath. They find new purchase on the plywood flooring. Rubber shredded away, hubcaps flying, rims grinding out.

I don't hear that.

My arms are folded over my head.

I smell gasoline.

I smell heat and oil and sawdust and rain.

Somewhere out there, a woman screams. She saw it happening.

I don't hear her.

The sirens.

Cops, ambulances, fire trucks.

Nothing makes it through to me.

The tires have stopped spinning. They are silent. Do I hear anything, lying flat at the bottom of the motel bathtub?

Yes.

I hear children singing in a language I don't understand.

Chapter 10

They have to coax me out, this broad-shouldered cop wearing a bulletproof vest—his sidearm provocative and oily, threatening me in 3-D—and a female paramedic. It's the woman I listen to, finally. She seems less likely to harm me. I'm probably in shock. She puts a blanket over my shoulders. Says her name is Lin. The cop tells me to watch my step coming out.

The remnants of my room. Yellow tufts of insulation and shattered two by-fours disarranged in a postmodern jigsaw. Glass crunches underfoot. A blue van slumps where my bed stood less than an hour ago.

They've removed the occupant.

His remains, I should say.

"Looks like a drunk driver," the cop tells me.

I stare at the wreckage.

"We found an empty tequila bottle under the seat." He makes a drinking motion.

"Is he dead?"

"You bet. He suffered major trauma." The cop taps himself on the forehead. "That's why we always encourage proper seat-belt use." He emphasizes his point by grabbing my elbow and pulling me forward to view the bloodied front seat.

I can't tell if he's kidding or community-liaising.

I notice a book on the passenger floor. Thick, pebbly black leather, the title etched in dull gold. It's a Spanish translation. I know the author. But seeing his name sends a ripple through my belly.

The van door is open. I reach for the book.

"Easy there, bud, you can't remove evidence from the scene."

I draw my hand away. "Sorry."

"Hey, this is your jacket, right?"

And it is. Hanging from a wall hook where I left it last night after returning with my beer and pizza. I nod.

"That's yours to take," he says. "If you had any bags, I think they're pulverized."

I give the blanket back to Lin. Slip into my jacket. This takes a minute. My hands aren't too steady. I keep missing the sleeve holes.

My brain starts thawing. "Officer, just because you found a liquor bottle, that doesn't mean the guy was drunk."

"What're you, an attorney?"

"No, I'm a journalist."

"Journalize this. The lady who's staying over at the end there? She had an early flight. She was looking out the window for her taxi. Saw the van swerve off the highway, plow into your unit."

"I happened to be looking too. The van came from the street by the playground. He aimed for my room. It appeared intentional."

"Was raining, right? Kind of makes it hard to see details."

"For me or your other witness?"

The cop rolls his eyes. He turns his back to appraise the first orange sliver of dawn.

I grab the book and stuff it under my arm.

Diners are good places to read about the underworld; timeless, claustrophobic—as if the clock on the wall were counting minutes in some slower realm. Wishing I could open a window. Fried grease smoking the air. The windows are gritty. I rub a circle. The sun's up and the night clouds have blown inland. My stolen book feels heavier than it should, heavy like guilt on a dying man's soul.

DEMONIOS.

I finger the letters below. The *A,* the *H,* the *M,* of *Aubrey Hart Morick.* No one's ever tried to kill me before.

Unless I count the fiend who grabbed Matthias from our tree house. He would've killed me. Given the chance. Or perhaps, if I'd been with my brother, he would have spared us both. Two noisy little boys within earshot of family, we might've been altogether too risky.

But Matthias was alone in his time of need, and so am I.

From a 7-Eleven pay phone, I rang Chicago.

Nobody called me.

The Boyle boys aren't being welcomed home.

Whoever placed the call to my room knew I was there, and why.

I order pancakes, hash browns, a pot of coffee. I'm hoping to starch up. I've never felt this tired. But the food won't go down. I prolong my shakes with caffeine and cigarettes. My old friends—they're planning to kill me too.

The book's pages are thin, worn, and crackly as a fire. Morick the Elder's first line:

Los demonios estan con nosotros siempre.

The demons are with us always.

I should be calling Robyn. But I'm not. She'll hear my voice and know how I'm feeling. I don't want to frighten her.

You'd think I'd grown accustomed to fear. That I was born to it, or converted, a long time ago, up in the Michigan woods.

I can't sit here any longer.

Food untouched, I pay the check and leave.

B eautiful Newark.
    Braking at a stoplight, I'm contemplating evil.

Newark, Chicago, London—I don't care which, take your pick—squeeze any number of people together, and nastiness bubbles up. People get trapped in those bubbles. You see them staggering around, hanging on corners, riding around and around in cars.

I drive by the prison where Bag Martinez lives. Looking at a prison tells me a lot.

It tells me I never ever want to go to prison.

If I've marked my map correctly, then I'm almost . . .

Here's the YMCA.

I'm early by a few hours.

Slip into a patch of weedy shade tucked up against the fence. You know, it's a rental I'm driving and I could be dead right now, so I'm not exactly worried about scratched paint.

Shut my eyes again (imagine it's night—the shushing of the traffic lulls me—my body calling for sleep, but I know the coffee won't let me go).

I'm out.

Wake up panicked but with time to spare. Bag's lawyer told me Bag is born-again, surprise, surprise, and I don't know what to expect. The worst would be a line of nonstop Jesus talk and a stonewall job when I ask about Morick. What I'm not going to tell him is that a tequila-swilling demon lover tried to off me a couple hours ago. I don't know if Bag has friends. I figure he does. Bikers are tight on both sides of the bars. The less that Bag knows about me, the more I like it.

I step out of the car for a quick smoke.

This is one shitty, decrepit YMCA.

The asphalt's busted up. The building is flat, institutional, and made of aqua bricks. My throat lining feels scraped. I heel-crush the butt and head for the door. Don't need to worry about my paperwork, my tape recorder, my notes . . . everything that got knocked sideways and buried at the Sandcastle.

This is an old-fashioned talk we're going to have today. Or not. If Bag is anything less than forthcoming, I'm gone.

Head up, and I don't pause at the info desk. Don't even make eye contact.

I read the signs. I find the locker room without breaking my stride. Descend a red stairwell with nonskid decals glued to the concrete steps. Narrow corridor, bleachy doorways where the mops hit every night for a thousand years.

Sweaty-gym-shorts aura, that cheesy, unwashed stink the chlorine can't cover up.

I pop through the Men's door.

Empty.

A showerhead running and steam tendrils floating ghostly.

Another door marked Pool.

The pool area is crowded, understaffed, and overheated. I can taste the water, sense it burning up my nose. Should've left my jacket in the car. Then again, maybe not in this neighborhood. I'm feeling possessive about my stuff, so I'll suffer through.

The prison guards are easy to pick out. Two burly black guys in uniform, they're moving slowly and looking bored but alert.

I'm not five steps onto the tiles and they've got me pegged.

The pool must be slotted for rehab this hour. I survey the variety of disabilities afflicting those rolling along in chairs, on crutches, or using canes to keep from tumbling to the ground. It's a slick world in here. I slow down. The thought of falling on my ass in front of this crowd, when I've got full use of my limbs, is too easy to picture.

Bag says something to his guards. They bust a gut.

A woman in a red one-piece gives them instructions and they turn mockingly serious. The guards transfer Bag from his chair to another made of PVC pipes.

Bag is still talking and I notice his eyes following the woman. She's walked back into an office. Through the office window, I watch her flipping sheets on a clipboard.

I'm willing to bet that Bag is not her favorite patient.

But he fancies her.

The guards move off, one glancing at his watch as the other fishes a pack of cigarettes from his pocket. Neither acknowledges me. I suppose I am a secret, a privilege best kept quiet.

Bag's unblinking punk stare sizes me up, as I do him in kind.

His ventilator scar might've been made with a putty knife; the starburst of keloid tissue shines beneath a Fu Manchu mustache tied with white beads on either side. I wonder who shaves him.

"You the reporter man?" he asks by way of greeting.

And he knows the answer, so he's lucid enough to play games and I'd better be careful with this guy, I remind myself. He and his buddies killed people for entertainment.

I show him one of my cards. He can't take it from me. I hold it in front of his nose and listen to him prove he can read.

"Thanks for granting me this interview," I say. Psychopaths love gratefulness.

"My lawyer didn't think it was wise to be talking to you. But I said, man, what are they going to take from me ain't been ripped away already?"

Scratchy, sandpapery voice. His 'stache droops below his chin. He's hairy all over. I don't know about his head because he's wearing a bandanna. But his legs look like furry broomsticks. He can't maneuver by himself now that's he's out of his motorized chair. We're alone in a corner, our only companions a stack of kickboards. Bag tells me I look like Clark Kent, which I don't. It's the hero/reporter thing he's putting a dig into. I let it go. I'm not here to argue. I'm here to get a story. Bag's giving me the goods. He's reminiscing about the old days with the Blood Hogz and the gang's leader, Denis Defrancesco.

"Sick shit. We'd cut up rabbits. They scream. You know that? Out at Denis's farm, we ran this thing we called Porky's Drag Racing. Heh heh. We'd wire three, four pigs' rear legs together, spray gasoline on their backs, and then . . . whoosh! Drop a tiki torch on their asses. This shit was hilarious to us. Hell, we drank hairspray. Mounted anything felt damp. But we were a crew, man. Down there in the swamp of life, we learned brotherhood, you know?"

"Graham Morick? Was he part of your brotherhood?"

Bag doesn't hesitate. Doesn't ask me where I got the name. Just answers, "No way. Graham was clean-cut, an egghead. He didn't belong with us."

"But he associated with the Hogz?"

"You could say that."

"Maybe you could explain it to me."

"That's not an easy thing to do, Clark. Let's see. What can I say? With Graham around things were totally different. Altered states, right? Graham talked apocalypse. Hell on earth. He wasn't playing either. The boy had visions. Pure goddamn energy! And charm. Smooth as honey from the comb. Let me tell you, somebody *taught* that boy charm. They schooled him in it. Now strictly from a business standpoint, he kept outside the operations. The nuts and bolts didn't hold his interest anyway. But we consulted him for . . . shall we call it proper guidance? On the macro level, partner, Bonny Prince Graham was calling the shots. We became like children under his spell."

Red One-Piece comes out of her office.

"I'm afraid Mr. Martinez needs to get started now."

I smile at her. "Give us two minutes." Showing her my fingers. One. Two.

She's scanning around for the guards. Waltzes into her office again, clipboard goes down, and lifting the phone. Her free hand twirls a whistle on a string.

"Tell me about that night at Plucky's," I say.

"My last night upright I call it. Denis ate a tab on the ride over. He's loosey-goosey. Talking under his breath about tarantulas and collapsing stars. General blotter shit. We're not even through the door. He launches the first copper jacket of the evening without looking. Into my neck. C-3. I drop like a sandbag. Can't move. If I'm breathing, I don't know it. But I fall in a good spot. I can watch the whole shooting gallery. Once it gets hopping, I pretty much go deaf. The gunfire washes you out. Everything is part of the noise, you included. Plucky's was this shore roadside establishment. You know the type, man. Fish-fry Fridays. Longnecks. Four-dollar pitchers. When the tide was rolling right, this guy would come around. Back his pickup straight to the door. The bed's all sparkly with ice and oysters. They had a pool table. One of them bubble hockey games. I used to love to play that shit when I was a kid. We'd been barred. We wore colors. They had a no-colors policy. Some bullcrap."

103

He pauses to suck in breath. His cheeks turn scarlet.

"This happens to you sometimes? You'll be okay?"

He nods and his breathing falls into a rhythm. Says, "We decided to go in there and kill everybody. That's all there was to it."

"How did Graham Morick first approach the club? I mean no offense, but he had to be crazy walking up to you guys. You were strangers."

"Stranger than you know, partner. Nobody could remember how he got inside. He wasn't there at the Farm. No, sir. Then he was. That's the sort of talent he had by the bushel. Miraculous were his deeds, amen. One day. He spreads his wings. Takes me aside. In close. I'm not ashamed to say it. I thought about love. Not the stick-it-in-me variety. Eternity. Something bigger than a single person, a whole lot bigger, and he's letting me . . . partake. Here comes the pain. I feel it. Oooo . . . it's sweet black and hollowed-out like a bad tooth you suck on all night. Only it ain't a tooth. It's him. And whoever I was, whoever you were . . . it's gone in a flash. You're his mind bitch. And you don't re-member shit anymore. You're weak. You're done, finished, and . . . just nothing. A lamb. And you're scared of him like you were of your daddy when you still messed your drawers. But you don't know why. He told the gang we were soft. Made us feel like that's a verdict issued from the mountaintop. Treated us like we were kids or, you know what's more accurate? Like retards. Because kids got potential at least, don't they? Bunch of sorry-ass retards. Guess he was right about me. Take a look around, Clark."

Bag's eyes sweep the poolside, the assorted wheelchairs and their oc-cupants. Faces like crumpled lunch sacks.

"That's how we felt after he took control. He put a stop to all the stuff we enjoyed. Everything got momentous. And fast."

"He became your leader?"

"No. Denis was always top dog in our pack. I guess you'd say Graham took on the role of spiritual adviser. But it was like he was our de facto leader. He steered us along."

"De facto?"

"Hey, Clark, I ain't got nothing but time here. You think being a quad is limiting? Try being a quad in the can. It's boring, dude. I educated myself. Praise unto the Lord and the state of New Jersey."

"The state's paying to give you aquatic therapy?"

"You look that term up before our visit? It ain't about me, man. This cripple over at Rahway died of sepsis last year. His family sued because he'd been vegging in the pen infirmary for a couple three years. I'm a show pony. If the system grants mercy to scum like me, blah blah . . . you know the routine. Keeps the bleeding-heart pussies off everybody's back, and I get to go swimming."

"Why are you still . . . ?"

"Locked up?"

"Yeah."

"My lawyer tried for a hardship release. Transfer to a halfway house. Said the government was wasting tax dollars keeping me under key. But basically, citizens remember that bucket of blood we turned over at Plucky's and no politician is going to touch my case. Don't squirt any tears for me, Clark. I did the shit. I can rot for it. Denis didn't slip me that .38 slug, I would've gone in there and whipped the lightning around and good. God's truth is I wish I had a taste. If my legs came back, that's what I'd be into. Looking for a taste of what I missed that night."

I watched his lips curl back, his yellow-corn teeth.

"Was Plucky's the worse thing you guys did?"

"Fuck no. We carried out human sacrifices before that. People we picked up on the highway, at rest stops mostly. A few simpletons we knew. Tweakers who couldn't pay anymore, were looking for any way to get amped. We'd get them out there to the Farm and butcher them."

"How did you lure the people from the rest stops?"

"We used sympathy. One of our gals—Miriam usually, she was good to look at and seemed a lot younger than she was, which wasn't old, maybe twenty—she'd come on and tell them a sob story, how she was lost, some guy beat her, whatever, and she'd pull this long, pitiful face. Couple of us would sneak up behind the parties and thump them. We had an old pickup, a U-Haul hitched to it. They'd wake up bolted to a table at the Farm."

"And you killed them?"

"Eventually, yeah."

I'd read about a rash of people missing from interstate rest areas on the Eastern seaboard. I've interviewed a thousand liars. Bag isn't lying.

"Graham convinced you to do these things?"

"I don't recall exactly. But, yeah, he was egging us on. Said it would be righteous."

"Why do you think he did that?"

"Testing his power, I guess."

"But you didn't tell the cops about his involvement?"

"What's there to tell?"

"He was part of the planning. That's conspiracy."

"No way, man. We did it alone."

"But you just told me they were his ideas."

"Our conversation's at an end here, Clark. I've got to swim my laps." This is a joke, of course. Bag can't swim. I doubt if he can float. He's the definition of vulnerable. Yet strength emanates from him. He possesses a long-term survivor's calm. If he's learned to live with his fate, to make peace with it, still there's the unspoken issue of a bogey-man under the stairs.

"Are you afraid of Graham Morick?"

"Adios, reporter man."

"Did he ever talk about children? About kidnapping children?"

Red One-Piece has returned. She's taking charge.

"Time's up," she says.

She lifts Bag's limp hand and waves good-bye to me. Then she wheels him around, pushes his PVC chair to the top of a concrete ramp sloping into the water. Bag tips his head forward so the therapist can remove his bandanna and stretch a pair of goggles over the ex-biker's shaved skull. Bag's head lolls. The therapist straightens him. The goggles, I notice, are placed crookedly. A quizzical expression crosses the therapist's face. Her gaze aims over my right shoulder. I hear shouting. She sweeps around Bag's chair. Bumps it with her hip. Not knowing why, I get out of the way. In time to see the source of the commotion: another patient tumbling from a chairlift. Smacking the floor. The fallen man bucks with a seizure. There's blood—stark red in this realm of fractured turquoise—speeding along the tiles.

An attendant gasping *Oh shit* boosts herself out of the pool to help.

Bag's capped insectile eyes find me.

"Watch your back, Mr. Kent," he says.

His needling rasp unnerves. I exit the pool room. Any faster and I'd be running. Don't turn around, I tell myself. Hit the door. Navigate the lockers, the hallway, up the stairs, shove through a second, then a third set of doors. The air from the parking lot is chemically tinged. Antifreeze scorched on a hot engine block. I'm filling my lungs with bad air. The Y's parking lot is full of cheap compacts and sedans. I pick mine out, the row by the fence.

Walk.

Breathe.

Feeling I have only now emerged from the deep.

Chapter 11

After Plucky's, the principals of the Blood Hogz saga were dead, or in Bag's case, permanently immobilized. Associate members, maybe as many as fifty, splintered and joined up with other clubs. DeFrancesco's home base—the Farm, located in rural Monmouth County—was put on the market and remained unsold, the grounds standing vacant for the past five years. I planned on visiting. But when Bag's lawyer set the meeting at the Y, I postponed my drive in the country.

Driving is what I'm doing now, and if I want to save time, I'll need to pass the Sandcastle again. That's why I picked it in the first place, a midpoint between the prison and the Farm.

They've towed the van from my room. That much I can tell without slowing down. A couple of guys wearing tank tops are nailgunning plywood over the new drive-through. No crowd. No emergency vehicles. No skid marks either, because the van driver never touched his brakes.

I'm past it. Concentrating on the views and trying to keep my head from coming apart. My mouth feels full of salt, my jaw aching like it's been pried open—the queer stiffness that comes after a visit to the dentist. I roll the glass down. Drink up the wind.

My route leads me back into America, away from her shores. Through expensive beachfront real estate, through cheap summer cottages converted into yearlong dwellings. Suburbia crops up. Then Highwayland USA, which resembles nothing but itself and carries a whiff of desperation, of wanting to pass by, never pause for long, to get away to a place more settled and less trucked over.

I'd drawn a map and put it in my wallet. The unfolded paper flaps in my hand as I steer with the other. Following my own directions. Making the turns. Not screwing up. I find the next road, searching for the last left-hand turn that will take me to the Farm. Everything appears as it should: spreading out, little houses pushed back under shade trees, trailers, cars, and wire fences. Evidence of life becomes scarcer: a black dog drinking ditch water, a kid tooling on his motorbike, a ponytailed man—no, it's a girl—dressed head to toe in denim and thumb out, shouldering an army rucksack. I don't stop.

The Farm road isn't marked. But I'm counting miles, keeping track on the odometer. A thatch of black-eyed Susans grows up around a rusty, topless pole, unprotected from the sun. I pull over. Get out. Run my fingers along the upper rim of the pole—a sharp edge. Sure, the Hogz would cut the sign down. Makes sense. Or a souvenir hunter got what he wanted, a piece of history.

I point the car and give it some gas.

The house is the color of sewage. It appears to be caving in, left of center, as if a great suction underneath were pulling the entire two-story down a drain. I touch the rough shingles, break off a chip. Asbestos. I wrote a story about cancer and substandard housing a few years ago. Saw piles of this stuff.

Junk bikes and a truck chassis in the side yard. Burn barrels.

A rail line gleams in the distance. No path venturing out.

Hog pen. And a barn, painted black and not well, the scabrous wood peeling in long curlicues. The weeds are littered with beer cans. I am not learning anything by standing here. The barn doors are padlocked with a stout length of chain.

Look up.

A white pigeon is spiked with a screwdriver over the entrance to the barn. I roll one of the burn barrels through the gravel and flip it. Climb on top. The bird's decayed, eyeless. He doesn't really even stink. I work the screwdriver loose. Then notice vermin moving through his feathers. He has a moon-shaped hole in his belly. I let him fall in the dust. I've never fed pigeons in the park. My mother called them feathered rats. I drop the screwdriver into a Ziploc and shut it in my trunk. I climb the porch stairs. The screen door is slashed, a big Z. A second ragged rip sneers above the handle, and tucked inside it—a card.

I snatch it away.

Tarot.

Later I'll learn that it comes from the popular Crowley Thoth deck. Oh, a thrill seeker might have left it here to be cute and mysterious. I tell myself that. Assure myself too that tarot cards, all the various and infamous decks, are widely available. People living on your block probably have one, forgotten in a musty drawer. But this card is not weathered; the edges are clean. Blue and gold, it depicts the god Mercury. He's juggling. Behind him, raising his fist, crouches a cynocephalus—the Egyptian glyph of a dog-headed ape; guardian of the bottomless pit and also a symbol for writing. Mercury is messenger of the gods. The card names him otherwise.

The magus.

I slip the card into another baggie.

I'm going home.

Chapter 12

I t's good to be driving my own car again. My wrappers litter the floor, my half-drunk coffee from the doughnut shop hosts bacteria in the cup holder. Chicago, city of my birth, lends a sense of protection, a double shielding. The street grid hints at order, the horrible traffic disagrees; and the slow, cold drizzle of rain taps on my windshield—it's nice to be back. Because here, in this town, I know where I am and where I'm going.

Which is to Unimaginable Vortices.

Father Byron. He knew about me, about the note at the Chaucer Arms (because it came from his very hand), and about the Morick–Blood Hogz link. Maybe, filed away in his knowledge bank, I'll find the name of the man who tried to kill me at the Sandcastle.

More important, I want to know the reason why.

Robyn's not expecting me home for another day or more. She's probably worried I haven't called to check in, but I can be that way—so involved in the task at hand that I block out the world. Forge ahead. She'll be concerned but otherwise occupied. I've got a little gap to operate in, wiggle room. Later tonight, I'm thinking, I'll surprise her and we'll both get a special treat.

I park the car a block away and walk. The fluorescent tubes inside the bookstore are lit. I pull open the door and enter.

Father Byron dressed in a charcoal suit. His hair combed and gelled down like a shower cap. He is smartly shaved, ruddy, and redolent of a pine grove.

"Jase, I'm so glad you've come." His eyes flicker down over his shoulder.

He's behind the counter, standing upright at the bulky register. I have to take two steps before I see what he's looking at.

It's an ax.

With a long, pale blond handle that's been taped partway like a hockey stick. Leaning there, balanced, its heavy blade chocked against a bundle of *Fortean Times* magazines. Byron attempts to hide it with his trouser leg. He's counting money into, or out of, the cash drawer. A pink rubber band strangles his wrist.

"Expecting me?" I've stopped in my tracks. Outside of striking distance, I think. I take a step back to be sure.

"You've learned a thing or two," he says. "I can see it in your eyes."

"I took your suggestion."

"Mine?"

"I went to see Martinez. He told me how Morick enticed the gang into action."

"What ugly actions they were."

"You admit leaving the note?"

"Yes."

"Why didn't you just tell me yourself?"

"Would you have gone?"

"I don't know."

"You like to hunt for it, Jase. Nothing wrong in admitting that. Some of us are destined to be gatherers." He waves at his papered surroundings. "Others are born to the hunt."

"They tried to kill me at my motel."

They? What am I saying? Have I succumbed to the conspiracy theorists?

He fidgets. "I'm shocked. But I'm not surprised. I could've prepared you better for the risks. My fault entirely. I'll take full blame. Scaring you off was the concern. I wanted you to understand how dire circumstances had become. His true malevolence and the power he exerts over those under his sway, it's progressed far beyond—"

"Why would they try to kill me?"

"We've reached a critical juncture. Now that Morick has the boys. The *right* boys. They've been with him for nearly a year. That's too long. If he failed, we should have discovered the bodies. He discards failures. There's no telling . . ."

"The man who tried to kill me, he had this book." I slip *Demonios* from the inner folds of my jacket. Turn the cover around, so Father Byron can inspect it. I move forward to place the book on the counter.

"Stay away from me."

Father Byron grabs the ax, rears back with it. The bills he was counting flutter to the ground.

"Are you serious?" I'm almost laughing. Imagine if someone passes by and looks in the window. What will the person see? A disheveled man in a leather coat holding up a book. A book! Another man wearing a suit threatening to strike him dead with an ax. I do laugh.

"Back off. I don't know what you're up to."

"What I'm up to? What are you up to? Achieving the status of madman?"

"Am I mad to defend myself? Regina is missing. You must know that. The police think she ran away from her husband."

"Did you tell her to run?"

"Ridiculous. You know what happened? Morick took her. One way or another, she's with him now. It must bring him great joy to spoil her life. To turn her to his purposes . . . things are changing quickly. The hour of the ritual is at hand. How do I know you aren't lost as well?"

"Look, Father. I'm setting the book on the counter and—"

"Jase, I warned you. I did." His grip tightens and his fingers go white as candles.

He might swing. He just might . . .

"I am setting the book on the counter. Steady there. Now I am retreating."

The ex-priest puffs. He is wide-eyed, lips parted. Slowly, the ax falls to his shoulder. He returns it to its resting place, within reach. He takes his pipe and lighter from his pocket. Tries to fire up. Can't. No spark, his hands palsied. He drops the lighter into the trash can at his feet. He studies the tome I've put before him. Dead pipe in hand, using it to point.

"You found this on the killer's person?"

"Nearby."

"He knew he was about to cross."

"To die, you mean."

"There can be no death, not if you interpret death as an ending."

"For the sake of argument, he crosses over to where exactly?"

"To the Flipside."

"You're saying the afterlife? Heaven and hell, that sort of thing?"

"Another level of existence as real as our own."

"Does Graham Morick subscribe to these crossings?"

"He depends on them."

"But if his followers die . . ."

"He's begun to gather his thralls."

"Thralls?"

"His slaves. Those Who Follow. That's what he calls them. He's building an army for himself. In this realm, yes, and outside of time, to carry out his will."

"How many are there?"

Father Byron shrugs, raises his eyebrows, and drops the corners of his mouth. "When I attempted a census, years ago, an impossible task really, for these people are concealing their identities—as far as I got, which wasn't far at all, but I cared to go no further—I encountered a few dozen, heard mention of many more, but today—"

A loud snap signals he's broken his pipe in two—stem and bowl. He sets the pieces beside the register.

"You're paranoid," I say, thinking there can be no rudeness, not when the discussion involves a man who's brandished an ax at you. "My partner talked to him, and she said—"

"She talked to Morick?"

"Yes."

"Go on."

I shrug. "He's harmless."

Father Byron rocks back, smiles, his hookish thumbnail tracing cruciforms on the black book. "Don't converse with him again. It may already be too late for your partner."

"I can't talk to him?"

"You're ill-equipped. Talking would jeopardize your soul."

"Thanks for the warning. But I plan to interview Morick. As soon as possible."

"Do not. Even a single conversation with him is incredibly dangerous. He plants his seeds. To approach him is to invite him into your spiritual core. You think he tried to kill you? I wouldn't doubt it. No, I wouldn't. Your life is inconsequential. Morick is a supreme manipulator. He thirsts for Power."

"I can handle him."

"In these matters you cannot."

"What matters? Can't you speak about them? Or is it there's nothing to say?"

"There are avenues available to one of his experience. He'll distort your sense of self and reality. He'll impose control. Willing or not, you will submit."

"Oh, that's crap."

"Your doubt makes you weak."

"He'll put a spell on me?" I wiggle my fingers in Father Byron's direction.

"Call it what you will."

"So this card?" I toss the Ziploc to him. He catches it.

He smoothes the baggie, turns the card over. He doesn't break the seal. "The magician," he says.

"Does Morick put stock in that avenue?"

"He does not. Parlor tricks. Gypsy traveling show." Father Byron pinches the corner of the baggie and drops it next to the book.

I am frustrated. With Father Byron's oblique commentary and with the fact, if Byron is to be believed, this card points away from Morick. "The card was left there with a purpose. You're telling me that Morick wouldn't do that. Morick's not involved."

"I never said that."

I throw my hands up. Take back my things. Start for the door.

Father Byron slides to the end of the counter. "Listen. That card being there? It's exactly the kind of thing Morick might do. Just because. He'd drop a thing to confuse you. Pump smoke. He isn't going to walk up to you and say, 'I can control demons. I can order them to devour your mind.' His acts aren't foolish. Quite the contrary."

"Then what should I expect?"

Head shake. "You won't get any more information from me. I don't feel safe now that Morick is on the attack. Possessing those boys has made him bold. I'm afraid he might be using you already. What you told me about your partner is troubling."

"But I haven't even met him yet."

"That would not be necessary."

"Enough bullshit. If I find out that you are in any way responsible for Regina Hoffman's disappearance or for the Boyle boys' abduction, I will make it my mission to see you exposed and jailed. You're a liar. For all I know, you may be a kidnapper and murderer as well."

A red aisle carpet leads out of the bookstore—a dirty thing, threadbare, without a discernible pattern. I'm following it.

My back to Father Byron, my arm stretching out for the door—

Voice in my brain says, *Do we remember that this fellow has an ax? That he seemed, a moment ago, quite capable of using it on our skull?*

A second voice—it's Byron and he's close behind me—causes me to spin around.

"Mr. Deering? If there's a trail of bread crumbs leading into the dark wood, my caution to you would be simple."

"What?"

"Don't follow."

Chapter 13

I let myself into the condo. I crack the door, my key embedded in the lock, and the living room greets me darkly. The sky's a black box. Night divided by four. I see my ghostly face in the window. Neighboring lights glow across the river. A smudge disfigures the third rectangle of glass. Robyn sits there mornings, on the velvet bench, sipping tea in her dressing gown and bumping her knees against the cool pane. The curtains are pulled open, corded. Kitchen's in perfect order. But these factors don't necessarily add up to Robyn not being home. She doesn't burn lights unless she needs them. It's when I call out, checking every room, I realize she's not here.

Gone out.

Not like my Robyn.

Her answering-machine tape is blank. I rewind and listen to the hissing playback. Erased? I won't go that far in my suspicions. Though I get a little pang of guilt knowing I should've called from New Jersey.

Where is she?

I'm starving. Maybe Robyn was too. I'm standing in the kitchen trying to decide what I want to eat when the front door opens. Robyn, bundled up like a Russian princess, rushes inside. She immediately senses me.

"Jase, you're home!"

"I just walked in the door."

We embrace. Robyn puts a lot of torque into her kisses. Her mouth is cold. Her lips, her tongue—it's like she's been chewing ice.

"Where were you?"

"Up on the roof," she says.

This news alarms me. I have no fear of heights. Neither does Robyn. But our rooftop isn't exactly square. It has weird angles, each of them guarded by a flimsy, low fence. That fence isn't going to save anyone. When we're up there together, I'm constantly watching Robyn's feet. Her depth perception is practically nonexistent. The far-off lights are deceptive and too mesmerizing. One false step and she's free-falling. Usually, when I'm with her, I slip my arm around her waist, hug her tight.

"You went up to the roof alone?"

"Uh-huh."

"Why?"

"I don't know. I wanted to think."

"Think about what?"

"Nothing special . . ."

"You went to the roof to think about nothing?"

"If you must know, I was thinking about you."

"Well, that I can understand."

"I was thinking that you need to meet Graham."

Graham. Why is the sound of his name starting to set my teeth on edge? Maybe I have the wrong idea. He might be a great guy, right? He might be someone I might actually enjoy talking to. Robyn isn't attracted to losers. She isn't, as far as I know, attracted to kidnappers and child murderers either. I decide to open up, as Father Byron might say, an *avenue.*

"I'd like to meet him sometime."

"What about tonight?"

"You can't just call the man on a minute's notice."

"I can do anything I want to do," she says. Her hips press into mine. "Call him."

The Mexican restaurant is my choice. Great moles. Tortillas cooked unapologetically in lard. Margaritas, not that frozen, iridescent crap, but real-live tequila, Cointreau, and lime concoctions they mix tableside in shakers resembling silver bombshells. Taxis are scarce in a cold snap. We're proceeding on foot. Rounding the corner in the cold, stomping blood down into my calves—I almost hallucinate the sound of ice chiming as a glass fills with tart bliss and then the sharp aftertaste of salt dissolving on my tongue.

Robyn squeezes my arm.

"Promise me something," she says.

"Sure."

"No questions. Not about his past, not about this horrible Boyle business. No hard-hitting Jase Deering interview. Not tonight, okay?"

"C'mon. Don't tell me how to do my job."

"This isn't your job. We're going out as friends."

"Graham is your friend?"

"What kind of a question is that?"

"A simple one."

"I just met him." She takes two steps, then adds, "He could be."

The interior design of the restaurant favors rough-hewn woods, primary colors, and stone idols. Potted tropical plants surround the tables. From my vantage point, I spy the entrance between the leaves. We are seated opposite the bar. Cozy leather booth fronting a wall painted lemon. A Mesoamerican mask hangs over us, leering through the eyes of a red-faced dog.

Robyn has her back to the door. She's lost in thought. I wouldn't say she's anxious, but she isn't acting normally. I can't figure her out. That's one reason I love her. I'm about to ask her why she's so edgy when the door opens—we're engulfed in autum chill. I pull my arms in at my sides.

Morick.

My first look at him isn't a clean one.

I can't exactly lean into the plants for a better view. Instead, I watch Robyn. She knows he's here. She's touching her hair, straightening her long back. I may be putting into words for the first time something I've known from the minute I considered Robyn my romantic match—I am excited by the fact she can't really see me.

I crouch deeper into the booth. The door stands open. Morick's filling the frame, swiveling his head around looking for us. The cold is like a shovel blade whacked upside my spine. He is tall. Men are always measuring up one another; we know size at a glance. Six foot six, I'd guess.

I wish I could see his face.

He shucks his overcoat and strips off a pair of green-black leather gloves. Morick has spotted her, my Robyn. He hangs the coat on a peg near the door and strides over to our table.

What shape of man do I see when I look up?

Wide at the shoulder, narrow hips. No fat, but not heavily muscled either. Lithe. A swimmer's build. His skin is pale; he would burn easily in the sun. He has dark semicircles etched under his eyes. I'd bet he sleeps no more than four hours a night. His hair stands in untamed chestnut licks around his head. His smile is boyish, a cad's. His smell hints of the sea. He wears a fisherman's sweater, black jeans, and scuffed Italian loafers. On his right hand: a signet ring. His handshake is warm.

His smile shines.

I stare at him, our hands clasped.

The slightest tickle of a sore throat nags me, an indigestive bubbling up below the beltline disturbs. Can meeting someone cause sickness? Trick of the mind, no doubt. Nerves.

"You must be the famous Jase."

"I'm famous only in my own mind."

"Ha! That's great. I know the feeling. Fame is such a fickle lady, isn't she?"

"*Fickle* is the rejected man's word for *discerning,*" Robyn says.

"Great line," he says. He scoots into the booth with Robyn. I'm not sure if he and I would fit next to each other. "Have we ordered yet?"

The dinner is fabulous. I can't recall eating a better meal in my life. Yet strangely, I don't remember what dishes we've chosen from the menu. Every course is a surprise. It must be all those margaritas. Our waiter is a portly, bald man with orange sideburns. Perhaps he makes the selections for us. He's wearing a white shirt, matching white slacks. He whisks away our emptied plates with one hand as he deposits a bouquet of clean, freshly salted glasses with the other. His whole body shakes as he mixes our drinks. Then he fills each glass precisely to the rim. He doesn't waste a drop.

I've followed Robyn's rules for the evening. No interviewing, nothing but the friendliest form of banter leaves my lips.

Graham is an old friend. That's what you'd think if you passed by the table. We're in easy company. The conversation never lags. No topics cause tension. Graham broaches the first forbidden subject. I almost miss it. So casual is his introduction of Aubrey.

"I want to show you something my father taught me. Who'll let me have a coin?"

I reach into my pocket. "Any particular . . ."

He peeks at my hand. "Give me the quarter, if you don't mind."

Graham clears a space in the middle of our table. He takes a salt shaker and wraps his napkin around it, makes a little white tent. He places my quarter faceup on the tablecloth. "All right, boys and girls, here we go. I will now make this coin disappear."

He covers the quarter with the shaker and polishes the air above it with his hand.

"Concentrate. Okay, ready?"

He lifts the shaker. But the quarter's still there. He looks disappointed. "Let's try this again." He sets the tent back in place. Then he raises his arm and slams his hand down on it. Robyn jumps. Only the shaker's gone. No broken glass and no spilled salt grains. The napkin collapses. He sweeps it, and the coin, off the table.

Robyn claps. "That was great. Where'd the salt go?"

Graham leans back, lifts the glass shaker from his lap. He drops the napkin on the table. Robyn picks it up.

"Sleight of hand," he says. "That's what it is. Not magic. The only thing that's magic is the way I made you feel. That's how my father did business. He made people feel magical. And they were more than happy to pay for it."

I hold out my palm. I want my quarter back.

"Jase, I said you pay for it."

"What if I don't want to pay?"

"That's never a choice." He smiles and reaches into his pocket. My quarter is hot as I take it back from him. The coin sticks to my damp skin.

"I wish there were more to it," he says.

"Talking about the trick or your father?"

"My father was the trick. I'm not talking about him though."

"You're talking about magic," Robyn says.

"Magic, yes. I absolutely wish magic was real."

"Well, isn't it?" Me—I'm blurting out the question. Thinking about my trip to the Farm and tarot cards, about strange voices, books about demons, and Father Byron's sermonizing. *Cast off your baggage.* "You'd be hard-pressed to find a person who doesn't believe in some kind of magic. They may not call it by that name. But what drives people's lives, I mean, it's not logic. That's for sure."

"Don't confuse bad logic with magic," says Graham, wagging a finger.

"They're inseparable," I insist. "We humans haven't come far from the days of peering out of the cave into the . . . whatever's out there . . . asking ourselves, 'Does it want to kill me, to eat me? Can I kill it and eat it?' We're scared. *As a species.* That's why we survive. Fear's the motor. But not fear alone. Fear coupled with an irrational belief that we can beat the toothy beast hiding in the dark. We don't stay in the cave. We go out. Why? What's pushing us? Where does the need to conquer come from? We're magicians. That's what I'm beginning to think. In our hearts we believe the unbelievable. We seek to master the natural world. It's crazy, but it's gotten us this far. Why give it up?"

"I couldn't agree with you more." Graham leans back in the booth and stretches his arm along the top of the upholstered seat behind Robyn's head. "Women are usually much too practical for this nonsense. How about you, Robyn? Where do your sympathies lie?"

She has pinched a corner of the napkin between her knuckles and is mercilessly twisting the free end. "I'd trade anything to have no fear."

"You're missing the point—," I start in, but Graham cuts me off.

"So would I," he says, as he reaches down and stills her hand.

R ight now, I'm too jet-lagged for philosophy," I say.

"Been traveling?" Graham asks.

"I had business on the West Coast."

Robyn frowns. Does she want me to break her rules? I doubt it. I'll avoid the question easily enough. Nicotine nags. Robyn hates it when I light up after meals. Says it chokes her. I excuse myself.

"Ducking out on the check?" Graham asks.

"He won't get far," Robyn says.

She flags down the waiter, begs him for a coffee.

I find the restroom. Splash water on my cheeks. Pull a couple of paper towels from the dispenser and dry off. Finger-comb my hair. Take out my cigarettes. Stab one from the pack. I'm not clouding up the toilets like a student. Out into the hall. A guy with his necktie in his hand jabbers on the telephone. Behind him there's a fire door that leads to the alley. I go out. Stuff a matchbox in the lock so I don't get trapped. I've got a bit of shelter here—a little cutout in the brick wall and a Dumpster blocking the wind. A pile of butts scattered around the Dumpster wheels—I'm not the only one who's used this alcove. The night's even colder. Change of wind. Or maybe it's me.

No, it's colder.

My pager vibrates as if it hates the idea of my taking a break.

I read Fennessy's callback digits in the gloom.

M r. Necktie has his address book open. He's squinting and pecking out numbers. I loathe waiting. I'll drink my coffee and come back.

A busboy clears the table. He spreads out a new tablecloth.

Where's my dinner party?

Outside, through the wet glass—raindrops tapping into Graham's outstretched glove. Robyn, at his side, flips her collar. The two of them converse. He peers up the street.

I join them on the sidewalk. "Hey, guys."

"Where were you?" Robyn backs herself under the awning.

We link arms.

"Feeling all right?" Graham buttons up. His leather overcoat is vintage World War II era. It creaks when he bends his arms. "We thought you might've disappeared."

"Somebody's trying to reach me." I hold up the pager. It goes off again and I almost drop it in the gutter.

We're walking. The rain's turning icy.

Robyn slows down, raises her chin from the flaps of her coat. "Didn't they have a phone inside the restaurant?"

"I dial while you two ditch me?" Ribbing them, that's all.

"I took a lap around the restrooms," Graham says. "But I couldn't spot you."

"The phone was broken," I say. I'm scoping the block. Furniture boutiques and dress shops. Not much open at this hour. Neon glows at the upcoming intersection.

"Could've sworn I saw a guy talking on the phone, but I must be wrong," Graham says. He's not wrong. I saw the guy too. Graham's wondering why I'm lying. Maybe it's spitefulness. I want Graham off-balance. Deal him a verbal sleight of hand. I like the idea of his doubting me. Gamesmanship—and we're playing games tonight. Aren't we?

"Look, I need to return this call."

"Jase, the weather's shit. Can't it wait until we're home?"

"It'll only take me five minutes."

"I'll walk her home," Graham offers.

Now. I have a choice to make. I don't have a lot of time to make it, a few seconds at most, or the pause will act as my answer. And so here it is—me thinking on my feet in this cutting rain. The night's been going along hunky-dory. But wrong choices ruin everything. A bad ending leaves an aftertaste. If I say no, then I blow it. *No* means more than no. It means I'm feeling a bit threatened. Graham, maybe, gives me the creeps. But he doesn't. I don't feel he'll harm me. Not physically. *No* means maybe I don't buy his nice-guy routine. He's not going to try anything on the street. What's his motive? None I can deduce. He wouldn't hurt Robyn. That would be glaringly stupid. He's not stupid. So maybe my answer isn't about what I expect from Graham. It's about Robyn. *No* means I don't trust Robyn. I look at her face and see she's beaten me to the same conclusion. She's waiting for an answer. She wants it. Now.

"Maybe you can catch a cab?"

"What cab?"

I see her point. The lanes are empty of traffic. This part of downtown quiets at night. A police car slows as it passes, the lone officer scanning storefronts. He never glances our way.

"Go on then," I say. "I'll catch up to you."

Robyn is satisfied. She releases me. Graham crooks his elbow and she threads her small fist through the gap.

GENIE'S PIANO BAR. MUSIC NIGHTLY!!! The sign buzzes over the archway.

Meet up with a garish door: orange fingers rubbing a lamp—Ali Baba smoke coaxed into forming a baby grand. I rush in. The strains of "Paint It Black" on solo piano tangible in a hall bereft of light. I ask the barman to turn my dollar bill into quarters. I pump them into the pay phone near the entrance.

Fennessy answers on the first ring.

"It's Deering." I crane my neck, trying to glimpse the street. The windows are curtained—plush velveteen folds. No matter. Graham and Robyn are already out of sight. Rejoin them? I'd have to run.

"Guess you missed your opportunity with Bag Martinez," the detective says.

"No, I talked to him this morning."

"When?"

"Noon." The van, Newark, the Y, the Farm . . . could it really have been today? "I flew straight home."

"Oh, buddy. You haven't heard."

"What happened?"

"Martinez is dead."

He accidentally drowned. That's what the official report is going to say. When his attendant left him to aid another patient who'd seizured, slipped, and cracked open his head (I was there, I was there . . .), Alejandro "Bag" Martinez rolled down the pool ramp in his chair made of PVC pipes. The pipes floated. But somehow, without a cry for help or a splash, without a single person noticing until the damage was done—his head slid underwater and his lungs filled like two chlorinated pink balloons.

I lean against the wall.

"Jase?"

"Yeah, I'm here."

"What happened out there?"

The van crashing into my motel room . . . I never told Robyn. The shock hadn't worn off. I hardly believe it myself. Fennessy's call brings it back in 3-D. My New Jersey calamity wasn't a dream. Those children singing through the wall . . . it happened. Somebody tried to run me down. A voice on the phone, a man, told me to go to the window. What man? Bag and I talk poolside. You have a conversation with a person. You don't expect that minutes later, out of the blue, Death is going to cancel him. It's like communing with ghosts. The exchange takes on added weight. Reality stands on its head. The impossible becomes slightly more possible. Do you ignore it?

I'm on the sidewalk. Chicago trapped in a blur. I don't want to follow in the footsteps of Graham and Robyn. I'm not about to stalk them. That's too pitiful. I go the other way. Turn east. Here's a street I've never been down. All your life you live in a city. Can you ever know it? This street is posh. Snazzy walk-ups. The lit windows show me interiors of affluence. I watch my shoes slapping the pavement.

The first sawhorse—I ignore it. The sidewalk ends. Chunks of broken concrete mount on either side of me. The path narrows. I'm treading on gravel. Gravel changes to mud. Into the street then, I look both ways. The tequila in those margaritas—my coordination takes a hit. I clamber over the rubble.

A half dozen more barriers block the street. Orange headlights flash. The roadway drops six inches. Sand piles emerge. I gaze into the freezing rain. Pick my way forward. A metal sign—Road Closed.

I locate no passage through the demolition.

Turn around.

I will follow Graham's and Robyn's footsteps.

Follow them home.

A fter the sluiced streets, the lobby of our building feels overly hushed—like dropping below surface, transit from one state of matter to another. I hold my breath.

Let it go.

Breathe in the floor polish and discount aftershave.

Johnny, ensconced behind his reception desk. He looks up, waves.

"Good evening, Mr. Deering."

Riding the elevator up.

I use my key.

I'm careful not to scrape the lock.

Silence. The bedroom illuminated; a fan of clear light, more noticeable because of the darkness in the other rooms, cuts across the hallway. The blood in my chest percolates, reacting to the rumble of Afro-Cuban drumbeats I hear playing—*that* would be coming from the stereo beside the bed—a nightly ritual of Robyn's, of ours.

"Jesus, you scared me!"

Robyn, crying out as she rounds the door, empty glass in her hand. Two Tylenols spilling to the carpet. Pip, plop. Preventative measures: she doesn't like waking with a tequila-induced headache.

"I thought you might be asleep," I say.

"Sleeping with the light on?"

"I thought—"

"Well, I'm glad you're here." She kisses me.

I taste only Robyn's toothpaste.

"Was Graham a gentleman?"

"I thought so. Didn't you? He was charming."

"You know what I mean. After he walked you home . . ."

"I don't know what you mean."

"Was he a gentleman?"

"Jase, I'm flattered. But jealousy is so tiresome."

W e're in bed. I'm showered.
Robyn joined me in the stall, just for the company, to warm up she says. She hogs the showerhead, cranks on the handle, and the enclosure packs with steam.

"You never said how your interview with the scary biker went."

I have soap in my eyes. I reach for the spray of water.

"Unproductive."

"I told you he was a dead end."

N ow she's climbing on top of me. Her excitement is a statement, not a question. We neck like we're home from the prom. She pins me. One hand disappears behind her. Then I pass through an unforgiving circle she makes with her thumb and forefinger into a deeper second gloving. I'd swear I'm about to touch flame.

My body cannot judge this woman. I will not resist.

"What did you think of Graham?"

"I liked him," I say.

Her smile spreads against the crook of my neck. She sits back, and that's when I notice the necklace. Braided leather cord around her neck, and suspended from it—a smooth, dark green stone resting in the hollow of her throat. About the size of a man's fingertip, I'd say.

"Where did you get that?"

She doesn't ask me what. She caresses the pendant. She lies. Tells me she went out to lunch yesterday with a college friend—a *girl* friend. They gabbed. Drank too much. Ate too much. They had a gorgeous Latino waiter, her friend informed her. They flirted. He was *muy bueno*. Dark-skinned—her friend said that you could tell he had Indian blood by his strong, flat features and shiny blacker-than-black hair—a bittersweet chocolate man she called him.

"Do you love it?"

"I don't know."

"My girlfriend gave it to me."

"Did she?"

"It's bloodstone. See the bright red specks? That's the *blood*. She told me it's called the martyr's stone. I had no choice but to fall in love with it. The weight feels nice."

Leaning over, her hair veils us. The stone swings above my face. Pendulous, a small extracted eye watches us.

Robyn isn't talking. She's too busy conserving her strength.

Applying it downward without remorse.

Chapter 14

I research our new friend Graham Morick. No information maven like my partner, I don't have her contacts or her patience. But I am a professional journalist. I know how to find things out. I camp at the library.

Graham is a puzzler. Trying to solve him is a frustrating exercise. In the parlance of background checks—he's clean. Amazingly clean.

He does, indeed, illustrate books for children.

If he has a secret, it's that he publishes under a pen name.

Having a father who's a renowned satanist might make anyone shy about tagging his John Hancock on dust jackets across America. Graham donates a portion of the profits to underprivileged children. I dig up a photo of him handing out books to kids. There's no caption. But the environment is clearly impoverished, and the children have brown skin. Could it be Mexico? So many children are in the photo it's hard to make out the man in the middle. It's Graham. He's seated on a rock and wearing a woven cap, a gift, I'm guessing, from his hosts. A girl, no more than six years old, rides his shoulders. Her tiny fingers latch onto his ears.

I call the local Barbara's Bookstore. They have Graham's latest title on the shelf. They offer to hold it for me. Barbara's is a short walk across town. The fresh air will do me good.

The salesclerk has my book shelved behind the register. She's courteous; she wields no ax.

"Ring it up? Or would you like a look first?"

"A quick look wouldn't hurt."

"The author is local. He comes in the store, from time to time," she says.

"Have you met?"

"Oh, yes. Very nice guy. You'd never suspect him."

"Suspect him of what?"

"Being famous among certain circles, but it's all relative, of course."

"Of course."

I leaf through the pages. A children's book—I sit down on the edge of a window display and read it, cover to cover.

Slippy Goes for a Slide, an animal story by Graham Rick.

A snake is born. Then orphaned. He lives in an overturned pirogue. He ventures out into the world of his swamp. He makes friends with a crocodile and a snowy egret. Together they fix a hole in the pirogue and drift around, meeting fellow swamp creatures. The pirogue fills up like a miniature Noah's Ark. They're a happy mismatched family. The story ends with a voyage to the sea.

I buy the book. And I ask the clerk to gift wrap it.

Is that a package with a ribbon you're holding?"

"It might be."

"I like packages." Robyn loops her arms around my neck.

"Presents, you mean?"

"Well, yes. Presents are so exciting."

"Be excited, then."

She uses her fingernail to slit the paper. "Not a set of cutlery I see."

"Might be very thin cutlery, you never know."

The way she opens gifts—the girl in her really steps out. She knows it's a book. She can figure what kind of book by the shape and size. But still there's a frenzy to get at the thing.

"Aha." She tosses the wrapper on the countertop and scrounges in the drawer for her loupe.

"You don't have it already, do you?"

I'm joking. But there's a moment's hesitation on her part.

"No, no. Shush . . . let me read." She snaps on the desk lamp, curls her hair behind her ears, and presses the magnifier to her eye.

"Stylistically, I'd say he owes a debt to Hemingway."

"You're ruining it. Now be quiet."

I have a favor to ask. I'm willing to wait. I want Robyn to be receptive to my request. She pours over the pages. Taking in the words and as much of the drawings as she's able. I feel sorry. Her viewable world is closing down, the aperture shrinking. One day she'll need me to read to her.

"I'm finished," she says.

"The book's not half-bad," I admit. "Sara would've liked it when she was younger. Maybe even Syd. Though she might've asked, 'Daddy, what does Slippy eat for dinner?' "

"I think the idea behind the story is sweet. Friends are family. A bad start at birth doesn't predestine you to a painful life."

"That's heavy-duty analysis for a tale of talking animals."

"You're a talking animal."

"Please, my ego's big enough."

Robyn walks over to where we keep our books. We use an antique barrister's bookcase. The front is mostly glass. The overhead doors are horizontal; they swing out and retract into the cabinet. She opens the top door. I hear the hinges squeak. Good luck fitting anything on those shelves. I never throw a book away. But she isn't looking to fit it in. She faces the book out and closes the cabinet.

"I'm being serious, Jase. If what you told me about Graham's father is true, then he must have had a confusing childhood. I think he's trying to work his way out of it. And he's helping other unfortunate children do the same thing. It's heroic."

"I'd like to hear more about his childhood myself."

Robyn cocks her head to the left. She's considering. I've ruffled her suspicions, and she's correct to be wary. Graham has talked to her more than he has to me. That much was obvious at the restaurant. More than the first phone call and brief encounter in front of the fire. They've had a chance to warm up to each other. I want to pry, but I'm afraid of what might crawl out into the light. Perhaps they've covered the damaged-childhood ground already.

I don't like to ponder what else they've covered and uncovered while I was away.

"It would be illuminating," she says. "That is, *if* he's willing to talk in depth."

"I'll come right out and say it. Graham is a suspect in this Boyle business. The police have questioned him. I think if we learn more about his father's—I'll call them his occult experiments—then we'll adjust our view of Graham accordingly. Case closed."

"You think he did it?"

It's an honest question.

"I don't have enough information."

She'd like to protest. But doesn't.

"You want your interview?"

"He could come here. A chat is all I want."

Robyn leaves the room. The door closes quietly at the end of the hallway.

"Explain it to him. The worst he can do is refuse." I'm calling out to her. "Don't be angry with me."

"I'm not angry."

She stands beside me. Robyn has put on her coat, accessorized with a pair of Moroccan red boots, and a hairy angora beret that matches perfectly. She achieves coquettish and exotic in a single swoop. Ridiculously, my first thought is that I wish she were my girlfriend. And she is.

"Where are you going?"

"I'll need to persuade him in person, I think."

"Oh. I hadn't meant . . ."

Robyn is on her knees at the closet door. By the sound of it, she's rummaging around in a laundry basket she keeps there. It's full of purses. She rises up. In her hand, a beaded clutch I've never even seen before. She transfers her wallet, keys, lipstick . . .

"Let me get my jacket," I say.

Pause.

It takes me a second.

Robyn has her hand on the doorknob, and twisting her torso around to face me, she says, "Graham is a sensitive person. I'm only thinking what's best. He won't respond to pressure. That's what you do, Jase. You pressure people."

She wears her Versace sunglasses. I gaze into polarized ovals.

"How will you—"

"It's around the corner. I'll manage. Give me some credit, please."

I don't want to treat her like an invalid.

"What if he isn't there?"

"I'll turn around and come home *tout de suite.*"

"Look both ways and cross with the light," I say, half-convinced she's going to change her mind and ask me to join her. The jealous boyfriend in me wants her to stay. The reporter in me wants the story, whatever the cost.

How many women are inside Robyn?

Have I met them all?

"I shouldn't be away long," she says, heading out the door.

I let her go.

Chapter 15

R obyn brings me the good news.

Two days later, we are seated in the living room. Sunset bronzes the windows. Robyn has poured a round of beers. The bottles set out like munitions. She's slicing Irish oat bread she's baked for the occasion. I've never known Robyn to bake. There's a cold bowl of butter. The long, serrated knife she uses diligently. I'm watching Robyn's fingers. She's being careful. She's so eager for the evening to progress smoothly.

"Your father," I say to our guest.

"My father, yes, well . . . no dancing around the subject I see. Good. It should be easier this way. Quicker at least." Graham smiles, cups his chin with one hand. "My father was notorious."

Serpent of the Plains, I think.

"They called him the Serpent of the Plains," he says. He fixes me with his haggard boyish gaze. The hairs at the base of my skull bristle

Graham rolls up his sleeve, shows us a blurry black mark running like a sine wave from his wrist to his elbow. Robyn can't make it out. I notice her attention divert toward the drawer containing her loupe. But she holds back. To inspect him under magnification would be impolite.

"My father's work. He tattooed me. I was six. A magical age, he said. This is what we did at bedtime instead of reading fairy tales."

Robyn clucks her tongue. "That's awful. It must have been confusing. Not to mention the pain. And to have it be your father . . ."

"He was a fool. A public fool, at that. Embarrassment stung the worst. I was picked on at school. My whole life, really. It continues, as you know. Persecution of witches, I guess, being a proud American tradition. Trials from Salem so forth down the line. My father did everything to bring it upon himself, and his family suffered disproportionately. His reputation proves hard to shake."

"What do you think of your father's beliefs?" I ask.

"I don't know if he had any. Other than making money—that was his true deity. He was an actor. A shill to the devil. He knew it was nonsense. But the profits were real. Tomas Maltz, of the Maltz family—the big brewers from Milwaukee—willed us his mansion. We lived like barons for a time. It was huge fun. Despite the fakery and the abuse, I remember joyfulness. That house was a wonderful place to be a boy, a veritable museum of oddities. People showered Aubrey with unusual artifacts. If you only saw how they yearned for his approval. We had a lot of toys. Half the year, it seemed, was taken up with extravagant trips to strange lands. We were make-believe aristocracy. Then it gradually fell apart."

I am always interested in how things fall apart.

"Couldn't Aubrey depend on his followers?"

"Those adults prowling our woods in robes? Please. Most of them were cash poor. And incompetent. My father attracted two kinds of personalities—the strong and the very weak. They would literally trip over their feet, come running up to our kitchen door with nosebleeds. Far more circus than coven. My father installed as ringmaster. Any excuse for screwing themselves silly—that part they perfected. Pardon me," he says to Robyn.

She fails to acknowledge the apology.

"My father's legacy was a ruined name and a modest fortune squandered."

"What's the Cloven Print?"

He sighs and crosses his long legs. "A bit of mystical magical malarkey. It was supposed to link souls, if I remember correctly. There were incantations and rituals. I can't keep them straight. No one could. Not even Aubrey himself. He goofed up on occasion. It was amusing to watch. His audiences chewing the sides of their mouths as they earnestly tried to grasp him. They wanted to believe him so."

"And the mirrorrorrim?"

"That's a new one on me." Morick frowns, points a finger. "Where'd you hear of it? Timmerman and his ilk? I'll wager it was them. Was it?"

I try a different path. "How do you know Bag Martinez?"

"What's the name again?"

He denies knowing Bag or anything about the Blood Hogz. Says he's never lived on the East Coast. He's visited Manhattan, not New Jersey. He wants to know who this Martinez is. What's his connection? Is he with Father Byron? They are the lowest vermin. Demon seekers. Zealots. Crazies. He ought to sue. They plague him. But he's reluctant to engage them head-on. "They would love nothing more," he says, "than to drag me down to their level."

"Shane and Liam Boyle," I say.

He spread his hands out on his thighs—large bony hands, spatulate fingers. He's trembling. "Timmerman, Father Byron as they call him, will sink to any depth. He's incorporated this tragedy to his cause. It sounds terrible, I'm aware of that, but if you ask me—and you did—I'd say search closer to home. It's usually in the family. People don't want to accept that. But it's true. What about their dad? I saw his photo in the paper and he looks like a first-class jerk."

No sweet talk about the Boyles, which throws me. I dismiss it. Because here's a golden chance to see him under pressure. He just made an error.

"You met Tad Boyle at a university gathering on July Fourth, the year the boys went missing."

"Impossible." He sips his beer.

"You wouldn't forget his face?"

Long bottle pull, a silent belch. "No, I spent that particular July in Spain."

What I have—all I have, I realize—is Una's recollection. That's a thin rope bridge connecting me to the past. I am detecting its sway. Will it snap?

"Here, doubting Mr. Deering." Graham sticks two fingers into the pocket of his jeans, comes out with a passport. "Check the dates."

I'm a bluff caller. The stamps are in perfect order. Entering Madrid on July the first, returning to New York on August the second. He wasn't even in the country.

"Always carry your passport?"

"I don't drive. It's my ID."

"What were you doing in Spain?"

"Research." He butters a wedge of bread. "You're a pretty suspicious guy."

"What kind of research?"

"Sketches for a new book I'm working on. It's about a church gargoyle that comes to life and meets his counterpart."

"I love Spain." Robyn startles us.

I'd almost forgotten she was in the room.

We eat our bread in silence. This could be church. Morick's handled my questions (the ones that sound too conspiracy-laden I keep to myself, and I mention nothing about the van at the motel), but I've learned next to nothing.

So I stop probing.

I've had my doubts confirmed. I'm thinking Byron and his brethren, if there are any, are wrong. Morick's not a necromancer. He's miscast. They've constructed a fantasy around him. Taken a smart, sensitive guy with a skewed view of the world—a talkative traveler with a traveler's way of making other people feel small and parochial—and built him to meet their needs. He's not totally sympathetic. Bit of an ego. Prissy and impatient, add a whiff of privilege. He might inspire jealousy.

But I don't suspect him of being, well, *evil*.

Despite my reluctance, I'm left with the sprouting seeds of admiration.

Our conversation lapses into a discussion of real estate. He envies ours.

"It's wonderful how quiet it is."

Robyn says, "Too quiet if you sit here for hours alone."

The three of us rise and stretch.

Robyn gathers plates and bottles. Graham surveys our modest row of windows, enjoying the view, and humming. I join him for a look.

"What's that song?"

"Sorry, bad habit. I'm accustomed to my own company."

I recognize the song. The lopsided chant I had searched for at the Sandcastle—he knows the melody. Is he taunting me with it?

Robyn pulls my attention away. "Jase, could you lend a hand in here. The damned disposal has sprung a leak."

"Excuse me," I say.

Bemused, glancing out the window again, Graham nods. His vocal cords settle back on the tune, like an interrupted bird returning—hop, hop—to its feed.

Here in the kitchen, a wall separates us, but I hear, faintly, children's lilting singsong in the distance. It's not Graham's voice. Not this time. I crank open the small window over the sink. On tiptoes, I put my ear to the screen. Can't tell if it's in my head, if I'm remembering or imagining.

"You hear those kids singing?"

"No," Robyn says. "Listen, there's nothing wrong with the disposal."

I peer into the drain.

"I think we should tell him now," she says.

"Tell him what?" Little, darkened holes—is the singing coming from the pipes?

"That you're not going to pursue the story."

"But I am."

"Not in his direction, I mean. You'll steer away from him." She touches my arm, applies gentle pressure. I take it to be an encouragement.

"That would ease his mind," I say.

"It would."

"Do you hear that singing? It's children."

"Like a group of them?"

"I'd say a chorus."

"There are no children living on this floor. I suppose you might be hearing them from down below somewhere. Maybe it's an echo in the elevator shaft. What's it matter?"

"But you hear them?"

Robyn shakes her head.

Now, Robyn's hearing is a well-tuned instrument, far superior to mine. I move nearer, to her side. Perhaps it's all where you situate yourself?

Thinking I'm about to leave the room, she places her hand on my chest. "Wait. What are you going to do?"

Her interference begins to irritate me. That plus the damned singing. My nerves are stripped. Somewhere during the evening Robyn has switched from being my partner to playing Graham's advocate. I don't appreciate her changing teams. "How about I resume dissecting our guest? Any objections?"

"Stop it. You know what I mean. He's been forthcoming. Don't spoil things."

"On the surface, he's peachy as pie."

"You are a child sometimes."

"But I'm really starting to wonder what lurks below. Aren't you? You can't be as oblivious as you pretend. He's a little too perfect. Perfect the way liars are all perfect. I think if we poke harder, all sorts of wonders may spill out."

From the living room comes the soft hiss of water dripping on hot coals.

Robyn turns to face it.

I push my head around the corner.

To be engulfed in a wave of nausea. Ringing ears. Clamminess. Vertigo. I'm suddenly at sea. Observing ripples, like heat floating up off a sun-beaten road. Morick sits on our love seat. One foot bouncing jauntily. A tight smile. I feel panic approaching. The surge hasn't hit me yet. But a dark crest blots the sky.

He asks, "Everything all right in there?"

"Yes." I fake a cough, poorly. "The disposal is, ah, clogged."

"Thought I might've smelled something burning?"

I smell it.

Air defiled. Like a scorched teakettle. Smoldering wool.

Robyn and I search the condo. We open oven doors and sniff at electrical outlets. Find nothing out of order. My sense of control has slipped. I need to get it back.

I need answers.

I want to ask one last question."

Graham returns to the window. I see two Grahams. One sitting on the inner ledge, and the other reflected in the glass. His back is to us. We're standing, Robyn and I, and there's no mistaking the adversarial shift in mood.

"Go ahead," he says.

"How did your twin brother die?"

"An accident."

"Was your father responsible?"

"Indirectly, yes."

"Tell us what happened."

He props his foot on the bench where Robyn sits in the mornings. He is talking, not to us, but to his reflection.

"Griffin had no fear. He loved to shock my parents. He used to climb everywhere, over fences, up gates, trees, the sides of houses. He'd grab the gutter spout and go.

"We had, outside of our playroom at the Maltz house, a balcony. It was an old, old house—much of it was rickety. My father never allocated funds for repairs. One afternoon, my parents had guests out in the yard, a cookout. Children were not welcome. Griffin was eager to gain some attention. He stepped out on the balcony, maneuvered himself onto the rails; he took hold of the overhanging shingles and hoisted himself up to the rooftop. The roof leaked. Right inside the playroom we had buckets to catch the drips. I told Griffin he'd fall through. He didn't listen. I couldn't see him making his ascent. But I heard his scrambling feet. He wanted to touch the weather vane. To shout down into the garden party and show them how brave he was.

"A shingle came loose, then another. He didn't fall through. He slid. I watched him come somersaulting right over me. The shingles fell first.

141

They almost hit me in the head. But I could've reached out and put my arms around my brother. He was right there. I stood, transfixed. His momentum carried him past the edge of the balcony. It was a great height, thirty feet or more. No matter where he landed, he'd have broken a few bones. He ended up without the slightest sprain. It was miraculous. But, as it happened, he dropped onto a garden wall. Topping the wall were these stubby spikes. I looked down. Griffin waved to me. Very slowly. I thought it might all be a joke. But the shaft of the spike was stained bright red, the point sticking through his neck. He died in the ambulance riding to the hospital. The doctors knew. They knew the minute they saw him. Nothing was ever the same. The accident changed our family. Wrecked us. We turned grotesque. To each other, we were absolute monsters."

I have no follow-up.

Graham sits, unmoving.

"I would never hurt a child," he says. "It's not in me."

I ask him to leave.

Robyn says, "But, Jase, you had a brother who died violently. Tell Graham. Tell him. You share this bond. Why would you ask him to go?"

The idea of sharing my experience with Graham repulses me. I don't want him to know what's inside me. He knows enough already. He's become a player in my private life. I've earned my history. And Robyn has no right to drag my pain out for this fraud's perusal. I'm ready to rage at the two of them.

He says, "We both know a secret, don't we?"

I say nothing. I'm bent over, picking at carpet threads.

"Brothers can't be replaced."

No more of this.

I shut myself in the bedroom. Lie there on top of the covers. I will my mind to empty, empty, empty . . .

Robyn enters, shimmering. Her face lighted from within.

"Graham's gone. He apologized for upsetting you. Jase, I hear them. The kids. They're singing in some other language."

Sweat drips behind my ears.

"It's beautiful," she says. Her eyes tear up. Lips tremble. She begins laughing, can't help herself, and she sucks a knuckle between her teeth to stopper the noise.

And I know she *does* hear them.

I sit at the edge of our bed. My enraptured lover can barely keep on her feet.

The singing stops.

Robyn bows her head. She steps aside to let the voices pass.

The sudden silence—it's even worse.

"You'll drop it then?" she asks me.

Gently, I pull her down. We're sitting side by side. I place my hands on her shoulders. "We should be more determined than we were before."

"Determined to do what?"

"Expose him."

"Why?"

"He lied out there. That story about his brother . . . I felt the lies in my gut. It was a trick to get me on his side. But I won't go. There's something missing in that man. He's incomplete. And he scares me."

Removing my hands, she says, "You're such an arrogant prick."

"This isn't arrogance. It's about finding the truth."

"Find it alone."

"Robyn, listen. Graham tried to have me killed. At the motel in New Jersey, a van crashed into my room. The driver had a copy of Aubrey Morick's book. I heard those same singing children. Graham makes the voices. I don't know how. Listen to me. He's doing something to both of us."

"A van crashed? What are you talking about? Are you insane?"

Hostile jab. Made worse by the possibility she may be right. Crazies never claim their craziness. I don't let that stop me. But I do pause.

She fills the gap quickly with poison.

"I can't be in love with an insane person," she says.

She's up. Arms folded, and her back rests against the opened door.

"Meaning what? You'll cut and run?"

"If you don't change your mind and quit attacking Graham, then . . . yes."

"You're sleeping with him?" I ask the question without thinking.

She doesn't respond. The color climbs from her neckline to her forehead—a big red V, but not for victory. For betrayal, yes, and for loss—hers and mine.

"I think you had better leave," she says. Her face turns to the wall.

I grab my jacket from the hall closet.

No turning back.

No last words from either of us.

Leave.

That's what I do.

I leave.

A week passes without a phone call.

Two weeks.

I vacillate between anger and worry.

Typically the job of reconciliation falls to me. I am a born confessor, chronic transgressor too, and therefore a person experienced at making amends. Like most long-term couples, Robyn and I have broken and repaired our relationship many times. This break feels different. I run my palm across the cracks. They have the touch of permanence. I flash on a future without Robyn. I'm not in the picture either. Our strengths and weaknesses correspond too much. Take away Robyn and my structure fails. I'll never get over her.

So I am ready to forgive. That much I've decided.

What I'm waiting for is contact.

Contact never comes.

Here, I think, is a new beginning.

The destructive blow has landed. Fissures and fractures appear. They creep like spiders into the corners of my life.

And, with every such beginning, one can pinpoint the arrival of an end.

Chapter 16

The Boyles are gone. By now they've put their prized belongings in storage. I drive past their residence and notice a placard in the window. Small, tasteful—the agency's name written in cursive gold script, and below it, a local phone number for inquiries. They're offering the house for rent. Call me curious. I buzz the property-management company. Inquiring, that's all.

"How much is the rent?" I ask.

Tidy sum quoted.

"Whoa, that's a lot."

We are talking about a truly exceptional dwelling, the agent insists.

Not so much a lie as an inadvertent truth.

"For how long will the house be available?"

Six months to a year. Possibly longer. The owners are unsettled regarding dates.

Really?

I ask if I can have a tour.

How about later this afternoon?

Yes, that will do.

In a matter of hours . . . impulsive, not thinking sequences through to their logical conclusions . . . oh, I know what I should have done.

Should've, should've. Snooped a bit. Indulged in vicarious, ghoulish fantasies. Mental reenactments. Played out my little theatrical adventure with the unwitting agent as my partner.

But no.

The good angel on my shoulder screaming at me the whole time, *You're not thinking! Not thinking!* I could barely hear the agent run through her list of amenities. I fought the urge to ask about home security, locks on the doors, etc. About, maybe, ghosts.

You're not thinking, Jase!!!

My good angel needs to quiet itself.

The agent turns to me at the bottom of the stairs. Keys twirling. *What do you think?*

I rent it.

Sign a month-to-month tenancy agreement. Sure, it's sick. But it's more intriguing than sick. No? Want better reasons?

One: I've needed an excuse to move out of the Chaucer Arms anyway.

Two: It will be good to have the extra space for my daughters on weekend visits. The Chaucer has made overnight stays prohibitive. This factor, I'll grant you, is edging toward the morbid and unwisely tempting fate. So it is.

Three: Here's a way to win Robyn back. She'd never set foot in my studio. I'll send her a postcard from my new address. She won't be able to resist this temptation.

Would the arrangement be okay if the Boyles knew?

No, it wouldn't. But I'm not going to tell them. My guess is that if Una reads the contract *and* if she's sober, then she still won't remember my names, Christian or sur-. Robyn made the contact. Una met me with eyes glazed and a pickled, pharmaceutically reactive brain. The management agency doesn't seem to care. Not as long as the security deposit is good and a check arrives every month.

The first time I'm inside all by myself . . . the Boyles' spare keys in my humid hands, heart booming, the signed papers are God knows where in transit to processing, stuffed in a folder, shoved in a zippered satchel, and the ink tacky on the dotted lines . . . alone with my secret, my possession, obtained with a degree of falseness . . . inhabiting this my new residence . . .

I shut the front door. Turn the two dead bolts. Noticing the higher lock is fashioned of cast iron and brass—an antique, and not keyed, therefore unable to be opened from the outside; nonetheless it has recently been added, the locksmith's pencil marks evident in outline and the sticky mechanism engaging only after a fuss—when the panic swiftly, ever so swiftly, slams home.

What have I done?

I invite the girls over for the weekend. First big visit to their daddy's new city domicile. Surprising how quickly I pack up and move out of the Chaucer Arms. Four car trips to convey everything I own. The girls are excited. But they're always excited. Their stepfather drops them off with their luggage and shopping bags. I can tell he's wondering if I've had a sudden windfall. He knows the price of things. His handshake is a little firmer than usual. I'd like to be there when he tells Isabella I may finally have come into my own. Bustle on the pavement—the girls oohing and aahing as they ferry their assorted travel cargo from curb to house; you'd think they were embarking for Africa.

Have I said very much about the girls? Probably not. I curtain off that happy corner of my universe to stay sane. To compartmentalize is to go on living. My girls, my bewitching preteen daughters, Sydney and Sara, are fraternal twins.

They don't even look like distant cousins.

Sara is, without a doubt, a Deering. She has my color, my hair and eyes. That's where the similarities stop. Inside she's a little Isabella. Yet, somehow the traits that drove me from her mother endear me to her. Absent are Isabella's cool calculations. My wife's arrogance is my daughter's healthy confidence. Sara lacks polish. She's a diamond that should never be cut. Her motives are pure and I hope they stay that way.

Syd looks like her mother. But she's all me. Seeing your personality transplanted into the body of a child is disconcerting. The faults are there, more apparent than ever, as if nature wants to show you a quick summary of yourself. But what good is that? I love knowing that my curiosity, my taste for the macabre, and my skewed view of the world—they'll all go on. She even eats her rice the way I do: always last, always with a spoon, and only after a blood-racing dose of soy sauce. Her temper is mine. So are her constant questions sprung from explorations into who knows what about whom and how and why, always *why*. If I die today, a piece of me stays and moves forward through time. It's a kind of immortality. Perhaps it's the only earthly immortality we're afforded. I pity Syd's future boyfriends. I pity them and I smile.

The Boyle case puts too many hooks into me. Missing-child barb, twin barb, unsolved-mystery barb . . . I'm too invested. Shouldn't have taken the bait. I can't say that honestly. Because I did take the bait.

And I would again.

I t's Halloween.

The girls' favorite holiday, and mine too, little pagans that we are. Love of chocolate, of costumes, of being scary and scared in the same instant.

Love of visiting strangers in the dark.

Calling them out.

I like to read aloud to my children. They're getting too old for it. *Too mature.* They always correct me when I say *old.* I don't know if my reading makes them smarter or any more appreciative. Maybe, long run, this exposure to literature will backfire and they'll eschew books in favor of junk entertainment. Or they'll be rendered pretentious, afflicted with a lifelong flair for the overdramatic.

Who knows? I like it so I do it. They put up with me.

Tonight's selection is as traditional as it is clichéd.

"The Raven." *A poem by Edgar Allan Poe.*

I've been busy settling in, juggling the work assignments on my own.

Handling everything Robyn used to and then having to explain why I'm placing the calls.

The girls are invited to a chaperoned shindig in Lincoln Park. I'll give them cab money. Make sure they have my number memorized. They're going as dead cheerleaders. Syd's idea. She cajoled Sara into joining her. Sara secretly wants to be a cheerleader. She told me so. Made me swear I wouldn't tell Syd. The secret's safe. *Hey, you want to cheer? Then cheer.* Don't let stereotypes stop you from enjoying yourself. I told Sara to stand up to her sister. Syd *will* skewer her if she finds out. But she'll respect her too.

The girls. *My* girls. Check out their costumes.

The two-piece uniforms—crop tops and three-pleat skirts—are constructed of stretchy material that's lighter than I'm comfortable with. Fake bloodstains drizzled right over the heart. Syd's the artist, I'm sure. I like the social commentary even as I deplore the navel-baring. Nothing indecent, but still I prefer body armor. Their black-and-orange pom-poms are a nice touch. I miss being a part of my daughters' daily lives—I've lost out on that. Having them at home, under a roof with me, only sweetens the pain. It's almost as it should be, as it might've been in an alternative universe where time stops and their parents are in love. I set a curfew. Level my gaze to show them I mean it. I like playing the heavy for a change.

Prior to tonight my role has been as a kind of chauffer and guide about town. I pick up Syd and Sara. We go out. Have a blast, or not. I don't do the major disciplining. Fact is, I sometimes blow through their mother's rule book with insouciance. At the end of the day, they get dropped off on the doorstep, and I'm zipping into the city lights. We only get so much time. I want it to be pleasant. It's simpler being a pal than a dad. But it's not necessarily better—not by a long shot.

Kids are scrutinized these days. Their leashes get shortened. Free time is blocked out and filled up. I don't know why. Probably so they don't end up like Matthias. Stolen away. Erased. Lost in the world. Although it's silly to make a one-to-one connection. Freedom doesn't always equal danger. If Matthias hadn't been playing in the woods, then what? Another kid gets whisked off in his place. I was in the woods too. I made it out alive. If harm wants to find you, it finds you.

Halloween—the hour when creatures show their true selves. In my case, it's girls wearing skeletal white foundation, Keds, and seaweedy wigs.

I kiss them going out the door.

N ightfall, I'm kept busy answering the Boyle door for those kids who don't know what happened here, or the others who are brave enough to test the neighborhood's only real haunted house. The doorbell rings trickle off. Fennessy pages me. I'm calling him back. I miss the girls' returning home. No time to talk! They fly past without a word. They are giggling and rambunctious. Their energy is contagious. Syd has her wig stuffed down the front of her sweater. I shoo them inside. The detective distracts me. He's acting coy. Needs to see me urgently. Won't divulge details over the phone. *Have I been keeping up with the papers?* Not today, I haven't. My girls are preferable to newsprint. I say tomorrow, let's conduct our business tomorrow.

He persists. I relent.

He's understandably baffled when I give him my new address. Thinks I'm joking. Then he gives this weak gasp and tells me he's stopping by for a face-to-face.

See you soon. Come around the back when you get here. I'll leave a light on.

I hang the phone up in its cradle.

I've been dipping into the Boyles' liquor cabinet (they really should've locked it). Cognac. I'm unfamiliar with this spirit and it's gone to my head. That explains why I feel drowsy, heavy-lidded, and puffy as an old owl. I open up the back door for a breeze. The air carries the dislocated, country smell of a smoldering leaf pile.

Poe.

I forgot to read my poem.

Glide down the hall. Kick off my shoes. Lift the book from the sideboard. My thumb marks the place.

Too late now; well, maybe it's not. The girls were running around, feet pounding above my head, for the longest time while I talked to Fennessy. I heard the toilet flush and flush again. The bathtub filling thunderously. The sink tap disgorges full bore.

They've gone silent.

I call up the stairs.

"Are you two asleep already?"

Thump my way to the first landing.

"Care for a scary story to tuck you in? We should read it now. I've got a visitor coming. He's on his way."

Wooden stairs are slippery when you're in socks. Crooked, narrow architecture—I'm ducking beneath each passage because I haven't grown accustomed yet. The staircase takes a hard left-handed twist and my head sloshes as I go around. Grip the banister.

Look in on my daughters. Bags of candy spilled on their beds. Their childhood has nearly ended. Next year, the year after—they won't go for these fun and games. Side by side they lie sleeping. The whites of their eyes turned-up fish bellies in the dark. Lazy mouths hanging open. Breath is the sole reassurance they are at rest. Witness, as I have, bodies flung with regularity into vacant lots, eased to the floors of tumbledown shacks, or arranged just so on the banks of reedy backwater ponds.

Unsound sleep, indeed.

How have we arrived here? As a society, I mean. Violent death trolls the waters of our consciousness. Tragedies served up daily for our perusal—our (admit it) entertainment—and processed with all the care given a factory widget. We market our collective horror. Rake in the profits without shame. This feels like an old American pastime to me.

Give us what we really love. Blood and guts. I am no better.

Nevermore.

Poe nailed that part, didn't he?

The word throws an ice-cream chill into my spine. I creep downstairs. Head for the porch to try to shake it loose. I'll meet the good detective outside, under the pinpricked stars. The girls are knocked cold. We won't be bothering them. I uncork the cognac. Poe was a lover of this stuff. It goes down hard, like swallowing hot ribbons. But the warmth pooling in my gut has charm. Glass in hand, I grab the newspaper off the kitchen counter and take it with me. Unlock the screen door. I'm careful not to let it slam and wake anyone inside.

F ront page.

Below the fold. A photo of the four Boyles in happier times. This house, the backyard snapshot of summer lushness; I recognize the porch steps, the buckled siding on the garage. Their tanned faces creased with smiles. It's almost too much to bear. The newspaper spread across my knees. I'm leaning into it under a dim yellow porch light. Moths tap to get at the bulb.

Headline:

"Kidnap Father's Dublin Death, a Suicide."

Tad Boyle hanged himself. Using a printer cable fashioned into a hangman's noose, he leapt out a window at Trinity. We know what's happened to the boys now. We can surmise. He killed them and hid their bones. Silencing himself is part of the bargain. Good as a confession, then. What a coward. Leaving behind no note, no map. What a heartless bastard. I wish I could've interviewed him though. We might have talked. Then again, I'm glad I never did.

Let others feast on his remains. Robyn gets her wish. I'm not going to write about any of them. God grant peace to the innocents—Shane, Liam, and poor abandoned Una. Graham hit the nail on the head. Search closer to home. Look at the father. I'm happy to have cut my ties with a cursed family.

Realize, I'm thinking this as I sit in Tad's lawn chair, on Tad's porch.

Tomorrow is the anniversary of the abduction. It's the boys' birthday. I wonder if the approaching date is what pushed Tad to suicide. The guilt must have gotten to him finally. Knowing his sons would celebrate no more birthdays.

His cognac has lost its fervid effect. Though I gulp the last drops, watery chills race through me, pumped up from an inner glacial spring.

I wonder if Una's coming home. I understand why she'd want to be away. On some instinctual level, she must've known what befell her children.

Return to this house?

How could she?

I hear the gate creak, the bitter clang of a falling latch. Leather soles scuffling in the gangway. The halo of porch light inscribes a circle. Beyond, I'm blinded. The detective emerges only to be pulled back into obscurity. His coat sleeve has snagged on a dogwood bush. He pauses to disengage himself. I witness minor frustration. He continues along the garden path until, with a visible start, he notices me motionless in my webbed chair.

"What are you doing there, pal?"

"Waiting for you," I say, and raise my glass.

Up the steps treads one tired policeman. He's seen the world, seen it turning to shit before his eyes, and all the people with it too.

"You're living here?"

"Sure, why not?"

He sees the newspaper. Knows what I know. "Because you shouldn't be. Nobody should. I'm worried about you."

"Where's the raven-haired Detective Maria San Filippo?"

Fennessy cocks one hip against the porch rail. He waves his hand in front of his face. "You've been drinking."

"Officer, honestly, I only had a couple. By the way, is she available?"

"Maria?"

I nod.

He shakes his head.

"I'm suddenly on the market again. That's why I ask. But pardon my intrusion."

"You're not intruding."

"I thought they had rules about cops dating."

"Dating?" He gives me a strange appraisal. I watch his expression soften, then flatten out like a board. He's looking up at the house. "A light went on. Are your daughters here?"

"They are." I haul myself down into the yard. An uncomfortable sponginess afflicts my knees. "But they're not in the attic."

"And that light is?"

I nod. "You'd better come inside."

ober up, man, and do it quickly. I check on Syd and Sara. They're sleeping. Whoever's in the attic hasn't touched them. I don't want an intruder even thinking about my kids.

The Boyle house has an attic access in the hallway between the bedrooms. It's a trapdoor. Cut into the ceiling. There's a pull. Give it a hard tug and down drops a ladder. The apparatus unfolds squeakily. Musty odors of enclosed rooms exhale in your face. Fennessy puts his foot on the lowest step, no gun out, but it's there if he needs it, under the flap of his jacket. I appreciate this cautionary use of firepower around my children.

Fennessy sticks out his thumb. He's going up.

Palm to me—*Jase, you wait here.*

I'm not arguing.

He takes his time going up those last steps. He's listening. I'm listening too, and all I hear is the two of us trying to be quiet.

The only way to enter the attic is headfirst. I'm no cop, but headfirst seems like a bad option.

I can't see him anymore. A light is on up there, as he said, shining left of the cutout. His weight transfers along the floorboards over my head—I know where he's standing, that's he's walking around, checking the whole area. I hear his footsteps. He's above the girls' room—the boys' old room. I guess if something bad was going to happen, it would've happened by now.

Fennessy pokes his face down through the opening.

I jump back and hit the wall.

"Come up," he says. "You'll want a look at this."

brass table lamp with a broken shade sits atop a chest of drawers with no drawers. I don't see the missing drawers. But junk crowds the attic; it's hard to figure what's what. When the agent showed me the house, she said as much. I was a prospective temporary leaser. I expressed no interest. We didn't bother going up. She demonstrated how the ladder worked, then she shut the trapdoor.

I hadn't explored.

Fennessy stands in the corner, ducking his head. He bends at the waist to touch his knuckles against the back of a television that lies bizarrely, screen facedown, on the floor. I don't see any shattered glass or evidence of damage. The lamp illuminates the corner, and the corner alone. The design suggests intention. Boxes are stacked shoulder high like mini-ramparts. This nook once had a purpose.

I'm hesitating on the ladder.

"It's safe," Fennessy says. "Nothing here, except for maybe this." He gestures at the odd furniture arrangement.

"Who turned on the light?" I'm considering heading downstairs, waking the girls, and marching them out of this place.

"No one did."

"What?"

"The lamp's plugged into a timer."

I enter the boxed-off area. The containers are marked TAD'S BOOKS. And, yes, now that I've moved closer, I see the timer's clock face.

Fennessy crouches and studies it. "You never noticed the light going on before?"

"I don't sleep in the rafters." The television power cord leads to the outlet, but it isn't plugged in. I notice another grouping of wires running from the rear panel of the set. Where do they go? "Who puts a timer in their attic?"

"It's pretty weird. Set to switch on at one a.m., off at six a.m."

"That television—you think it fell?"

"Fell from where?"

There's nothing nearby. More likely, somebody tipped it over and left it there. The outline in the dust suggests it's been like that for a while.

"Look, this old lamp is plugged into the timer. But the television is right next to it."

"Uh-huh."

I'm nodding, sorting the jigsaw of this tableau. My eyes follow the other wires. I stoop. Claustrophobia, alive and well, back here. The dark lending a hand. I peer into the gap where the wires go. It reminds me of when I looked for the birthday tape at Robyn's. Except this time I see something.

Orange coils? Glint of metal?

Fennessy says, "I think the television used to be on the timer. Tad or Una probably unplugged it. Somebody from the property agency stuck the lamp plug in without thinking. They didn't know how long the house would be unoccupied and assumed the owner left the timer as a security measure."

"When the Boyles lived here, the attic TV snapped on every night at one?"

I shove the chest of drawers with my shoulder. Reach into the unseen. I feel a sharp edge, four panels coming together at right angles. Buttons and knobs. A radio receiver? I learn by touching. Shadows chop my arm off at the wrist. I banish the thought of rats. Try to. Walk my fingers lower, on the floor, where the orange swirl appeared—a chunky nub of plastic and prongs—I put my hand around it.

"Exactly," Fennessy says.

"And they leave the TV lying facedown?"

"Hey, man, what can I tell you? People are strange."

I pull out an orange extension cord. It's stuck. I am reminded how Tad Boyle died. Cords, cables, nooses. Pause. Above me, I find a small rectangular window. During the day, this window allows light into the attic. It is night. The glass is pitted, opaque. No help. A thick layer of dust furs the ledge. The roof slopes steeply on two sides. I'd need to be standing in the middle if I wanted to use my legs for leverage. I'm at the edge. I swallow hard and yank on the cord. Metal scrapes wood.

"Do you have a flashlight?"

Fennessy hands me a fat pen. "Twist it," he says. Then: "What did you find?"

Ah, pen*light*.

"Move that chest away from the wall, please."

"What's under there?"

I shine the penlight.

Push myself deep into the corner. To reach it, Tad had to go down on his knees and crawl—the same way I am crawling right now.

It's a videocassette recorder—a VCR—hooked to the TV and the extension cord.

I finger the buttons.

One of them is gummed up with electrical tape.

"Plug this in." I pass him the end of the extension cord.

Fennessy assists.

A minute green eye signals current flowing to the unit.

I hit Eject.

The machine has no tape inside.

I didn't expect any.

Slip my hand into the empty slot. I've gotten close to something here, but I'm left wondering exactly what.

Take up the light again. Flash it into the catacombs of cartons.

There, against the wall. Something small. Shining. A rough stone. Lift it with my fingers. My light flickers on the wall behind. I see strange symbols. Marked in crayon. A child might've drawn them. To the right of them: slits and the clock face.

I say, "Here's a second outlet, another timer."

The rock's extra heavy, secreted away in my pocket, and I'm not telling.

Decide to ask questions instead.

"You told me Tad was taping the nanny, Regina. He used motion detectors hooked into his cameras?"

"That's correct. He showed us where they were. We confiscated them and took the tapes he'd made—the ones he handed over."

"He gave them to you freely?"

"Tad was cooperative. His boys were a higher priority than his voyeurism."

Fennessy rummages around, peeking into boxes. He's bored now that the drama of discovery has passed.

The rock buzzes. No, it doesn't. It radiates cold, lumpy iciness against my hip and alternately burns hot as a briquette. I don't share my find. I don't know why. Only that it is mine. Mine to have. Mine to figure out.

I plant the VCR next to the lamp. Dust motes everywhere. I sneeze. Hope the girls don't hear and get scared.

Who's up there, over our heads, causing such a racket?

There's a strip of electrician's tape over the Play button. A folded wad of the same tape falls out from under the strip as I peel it back. The wad kept the button pressed. I test with my thumb. The strip has lost much of its adhesive. I see residue around the button, where the strip has been pulled and put back many times.

"How does the recording process work? Considering the VCR was synchronized with the TV. Both of them were switched off most of the day. They were turned on only at night."

Fennessy doesn't answer. He looks confused, frowning.

"Was he spying on her with this machine?" I ask. Want the answer to be yes.

Fennessy indicates no. "Jase, that's not a camcorder. A VCR can only tape broadcasts or playback something that's been prerecorded."

Okay, I'm no technological wizard. I drive a stick shift and still prefer my typewriter to my keyboard.

"He didn't use these things to monitor Regina?"

Fennessy shakes his head. "Tad Boyle rigged his house with state-of-the-art surveillance equipment. This stuff you dragged out is basic retail, intended for home entertainment. TV shows, video rentals, et cetera."

"Where are Tad's cameras and tapes now?"

"He wanted them back. We caved. Thousands of dollars' worth of electronics—they weren't relevant, other than the tape of the abduction. That, obviously, was a key piece of evidence. Tad wanted us to keep it. But the others . . . you know, things go missing in evidence rooms. I understood his concern. These recordings were private and embarrassing. He was already in danger of losing his job. Tad begged us to remain silent. Said he didn't need more negative exposure. After that effort, he's not going to leave his high-tech toys lying around in an attic."

If Tad was watching Regina with sophisticated gadgetry, why would he bother tinkering with sticky taped buttons and extension cords?

Why put this setup here in the attic?

"You're saying all he could do with this is play tape all night long?"

"I can't see any other function."

Tad, what were you doing? Why did you tip over the television?

Unless it wasn't Tad.

I force Fennessy to drink a beer. He asks for a glass. I oblige. He wipes the bottle mouth with his handkerchief. He's cautious. He hates germs. He doesn't want any trace of the Boyles entering his body. I supply the glass. Repayment for checking out the attic bogeyman, delivered courtesy of the Boyles' fridge.

"Regina Hoffman came home," he says.

"She did?"

"Her husband called me this morning."

"She's okay?"

Nod. "She told him she went away to think."

"And you believe that? If Morick snatched her . . . if he was able to convert her to his cause . . . she's dangerous."

"Listen to yourself. You sound like Father Byron. She went to visit some friends. They talked her into coming home. I have enough trouble figuring out why people do what they do when there's a crime committed. There's no crime here. She's an adult. Everybody needs to screw their heads on straight now and again. She didn't realize he'd go to the police. I spoke to her."

"You spoke to Regina? How did she seem?"

"She was sorry for all the trouble she caused."

Maybe Fennessy's right. Father Byron's paranoia is infectious. I'd like a second opinion. "What did your partner think?"

"Maria's been preoccupied."

"With?"

"Personal matters."

"Like what?"

"She's pregnant."

"Who's the father?"

"You're a rude man."

"I'm only curious about the lives of my friends." I light a cigarette; toss the dead match into the garden.

"Curious?"

I arch my eyebrows, devilish. "It's not you, is it?"

"Rude and classless," he says, though he's smiling. "This lawyer she's been living with for the past year. He wants to get married. His firm has been dangling a private-sector job under Maria's nose. Six figures, chic high-rise office, and the guarantee of no street dealers popping shots over her head. I don't think she can resist."

"Good for her."

"That's what I said. Grab the gold ring. Have your baby and make a decent life for yourself. Leave the gutter behind."

I catch it then, in his tone, the way he puts his lips around the words. He doesn't mean them. See, I was right from the get-go. The sad sack, the poor bastard, he's pining for San Filippo. She is his partner. I ought to understand this. And I do. Maybe the job brought them together *and* it keeps them apart. The vibration I'd picked up on, the way they keyed into each other, how San Filippo beamed in his presence . . . it was a one-way vibe. Apparently, I had it backward.

Fennessy loves San Filippo.

Whatever she feels back, it isn't enough.

Unrequited love: it's the vilest kind.

"Don't bad-mouth the gutter," I say. "The gutter provides me with a living."

"Hear, hear!" And he claps me on the back.

The house quiets. I'm numb, but the postponed jitters have subsided. The girls—I check them once again—are asleep and unperturbed, as they should be, as I would have them remain, if given a choice.

I go back into the attic to retrieve the VCR. I carry it downstairs. The trapdoor closes without making a sound. Why am I feeling guilty? As if I've entered a conspiracy without knowing.

The folded piece over the play button—taped and retaped. Why? I take the stone from my pocket. The dense weight bobs in my hand, angular and sparkly as fool's gold; it's practically jumping with energy. Hold it out at arm's length. Zoom it to the tip of my nose for a close-up. Top view, bottom view. Side view: there's something familiar here. This rock is the flying asteroid from the Boyle videotape. The object that showed up at the end of the abduction recording—*this* is it. But I knew that, of course. Didn't I? From the moment I spotted it under the . . . who can say what a man knows? Why he acts the way he does, in private, when he knows full well he's unobserved?

I run to the refrigerator. Try an experiment.

Pull off a magnet that's glued to the property management's phone numbers.

Yes, it repulses the rock. The rock is a magnet too.

And whoever used this magnetic stone knew exactly what it was, and where to find it. He, or she, attempted to disrupt the tape, just as San Filippo theorized. This stone sent the recording into frenzy. And it belongs to the Boyles.

The Boyles own a set of encyclopedias. Purchased, I'm guessing, for the boys' future. I page through the entries. Here's what I want. The picture is a close match.

Magnetite: also known also as lodestone. Some ancient cultures believed lodestone to have magical properties, including the power to give its bearer invisibility.

Isn't that what the deliveryman wanted? He knew about the camera and the stone. But his attempt at erasure failed.

I'm going to bed. First I need to check the locks on the doors.

Did the Boyles want to be invisible too?

I think they did.

My hand fondles the dead bolt.

What were they so worried about keeping out?

I am dreaming in the Boyles' bed. Of a man running through the woods with a boy slung over his shoulder; the boy in question is Matthias, my brother. I have these dreams. I hate them. Like old enemies, they seem to return under the worst circumstances. Joy and vigor evidenced at each new arrival.

In this version, the man has no face.

His head is white. Nosferatu white. Stone bald, varicose. His skull pulses; the rear view—my view, the follower's perspective—is of a crinkled fruit, an appearance suggestive of softness, rot. He smells of bandages. His unbuttoned hunter's jacket flares wide at the bottom, like a cape. He is ridiculously tall and wide and beastly. A phantasm carved from my psyche. Black, red, yellow, orange leaves somersault through his wake.

He knows I pursue him.

He glances over his empty shoulder.

Shadows roost in his eye sockets.

He stops.

His body revolves, like he's standing on a turntable. He faces me.

My brother is dead. He shows me this. His style of display has a vaudevillian theatricality. Hairs grow suddenly over the beastly man's white head. Black, matted hairs. He weeps. He holds my brother. Holds on to him and will not give him up.

The man pleads with me: "Forget what you're seeing here. Lies, all lies. Go home."

His glasses are taped at the nose. Lenses speckled with paint. He's coughing.

I am trying hard to wake up from this nightmare.

He is my father.

Later, not yet legitimate morning, but I'm unable to get back to sleep; I eat a breakfast of leftover Szechwan noodles and hot coffee. The kitchen frosts blue with the dawn. Chewing and staring. My head full of debris; I'm slowly clearing a trail back into the realm of the living.

Did I see my father that day in the woods? Did I see him?

I saw no one.

My father was home in Chicago with a case of influenza. He loved Matthias. He was our dad.

Who then?

The jagged end of that question blows through my mind. Gouges me. I scratch my grizzled jaw. Toss the emptied carton in the sink. I'll never know who's responsible. Matthias won't be avenged. This reality feels like a new crime.

I've got an hour until my ex and her husband are scheduled to pick up. Early birds. Joggers. They check their stocks in *The Wall Street Journal*. They sip orange juice and crunch a bowl of bran flakes. Healthy, beautiful people, movers and shakers—they're taking my children home. I need to shower, shave, and look presentable.

The girls must already be awake. I hear their voices mumbling through the floor.

I look up.

Voices through the floor . . .

Chapter 17

How long does it take for a man's life to reassemble? After love is lost, a partnership abandoned, and a career jeopardized?

I don't know the answer.

I'm not there yet. I can function, sure. Fake it just fine. But the dead can sometimes walk. Have you seen them?

I have.

Filmed (or videoed) like the Boyle twins.

Only the dead don't need artificial resurrection. They walk when we dream and in our memories.

Because I've seen them; and I've been one too.

In my case, the zombie life did me some psychological good. Patched me well enough I can pretend I'm healed. *Time's necessary for these repairs*, I assure myself, *considering the amount of turbulence you had to ride out.*

I scar up fast.

Forward being the only direction I know.

Oh, I have bad days. Days where I wander the streets and guess what? I end up in front of our old building. I see Johnny through the thick plate glass. Watching his TV. I'm like some heartsick teenage kid from a television program—an old show, black-and-white, everyone's hairstyle dating him or her—I'm the kid who throws pebbles up at his girl's window. The girl who jilted him and he's trying to win her back.

One evening, I'm standing there. Johnny comes outside. He motions me over.

"Hiya, Mr. Deering."

"Johnny."

"So how's life treating you these days?"

"Can't complain."

He nods. First time since he's come out, he meets my eyes dead on.

"You know she ain't here?"

"Is that right?"

"Sold both units." He nods stoically. "New occupants arrived last week. Lousy tippers. I never saw Ms. Matchfrost. Three guys from a moving company showed up with paperwork, signatures. They boxed her stuff. Took the furniture. Strange, I thought, Ms. Matchfrost always being a hands-on lady. But it's been a long time since I've seen her."

"Same here."

"I thought you might want to know that."

"Right, okay."

"I notice you stand here sometimes." His eyes avoiding mine again, then he smiles and shakes my hand. "You take care, Mr. Deering."

"Thanks, Johnny, for telling me. I appreciate that."

I do something I've never done before: I call Robyn's family. They are a cold and Waspy bunch. It's like talking to a Scandinavian law firm. Robyn limits her contact with them to two formal phone calls a year, so I'm not expecting much, and the only news fit for any Matchfrost exchange is the good kind. I'm sure this must be a law.

Her mother answers.

The conversation is awkward, but mercifully short.

She hasn't heard from Robyn.

Is there a problem?

I lie. Say I've been out of town. Robyn must be traveling too. We have both been so busy. We're busy people.

Traveling? Well, I hope she enjoys her time away.
We say good-bye.

I look up Graham Morick in the phone book. No phone listed. I don't know how Robyn found a number to call. I search her papers. Find a slip with his name and a street address. I have her large, blocky handwriting on a scrap of paper. Swallow any pride. I trudge through the rain. Find the handsome brownstone. Robyn's right—it's around the corner. I knock on the door. An elderly black man in cocoa pinstripes answers.

"Good afternoon," he says. He watches judiciously as the torrent blows across his stoop. The door closes slightly.

"Good afternoon. I'm looking for Graham Morick."

"There's no one here by that name. Are you certain you have the correct address?"

I consult my tattered slip. The rain smears the ink. I'm wet as a rat. How must I look? The grizzled jaw, the cheap raincoat: a man who is on a mission, or just out of one.

"Are you selling a product?"

"Pardon me," I say, backing down the neat steps. "My mistake."

"You're a salesman?"

"No, it's nothing like that. I must have received bad information. I'm sorry for disturbing you."

"You have not disturbed me."

"Have you lived here long?"

"Forty years."

"Thank you for your time. It's a lovely area, this block. You're lucky."

"Get off the drugs, son. Go home. And pray to the Lord for strength."

"That's good advice. Thanks."

"It's never too late."

He raises his hand, as if in pity, and shuts the door.

———

Now I've reached equilibrium. Every day I step out on the Boyles' front stoop to retrieve my *Tribune*. I look both ways down the block. Do I expect to see her?

Why else would I look?

Robyn has vanished. Boxed up her life, with a few items of mine, and lit out. Not a call, not a letter. Four years we were together. *Vanish* is putting it too mildly. It sounds blameless. She's chosen him over me. They've probably forbidden each other from mentioning my name. I'm still shocked.

I stroke my chin like a man growing his first beard, which I am.

Work anchors me. I drop the Boyle story, run fast and far in the other direction. Case closed, anyway. Force myself to forget about Morick and his alleged thralls, who may or may not count Robyn among their fold. Do my best to ignore the wound I suffered. I turn my back. Take a few easy assignments. Whip the articles out on autopilot: urban blight, river contamination, guns in schools . . . these things pay the bills. Almost pay them. I'm slowly going broke. Well, I've never been the richest boy in the neighborhood. But I can't even afford the roof over my head. The Chaucer Arms is sadly more to my level. This house becomes the trap where I've caught my proverbial fox's leg.

I am not ready to start chewing yet.

Instead of swearing off debts, I swear off women. Like hell I do. But I'm in no shape for them. Pursuit requires energy, and mine is spent. Directed toward basic survival. Besides, I don't look good at present—baggy eyes, gray showing up in my beard; and my hands . . . aren't so easy to keep steady. I lie low. Stick to what I'm best suited for, given my current incarnation:

Writing and boozing.

Both exercises best achieved alone.

I miss her. I thought it would be the sex. It's not. I miss Robyn, her essence. Sounds corny, but I miss her soul. That's why it hurts. Morick took the best part of her. He beat me where I thought I was strongest. And, to be honest, I miss the sex too.

The Boyles' house clamps down—my refuge, my cabin in the woods. I snug in, not fighting it. If I'm going to pieces, this is where I want the disintegration to happen. Let them break down the door and find me spilled across the floor like a puzzle.

I give the phone number to almost no one. So no one calls.

Hardly eat, but when I do, I order in the cheapest grub—egg rolls, mostly. Looking back on this spell of isolation, hovering over my past self like a spirit, I see a scruffier me hunched over his keyboard, drinking coffee laced with Scotch, and taking bites out of a cold shrimp egg roll. He—I—we're not unhappy.

We aren't anything.

At my leisure, reclining in the Boyles' marriage bed, I listen to the loud whir of the ceiling-fan blades slashing the air over me. I am willfully ignoring the rules of my lease and common sense, chain-smoking between the sheets while I read Aubrey Hart Morick's complete oeuvre. I don't learn much. He's a terrible writer, a rambler—a convolutionist injecting ink into the ocean of other men's thoughts. His philosophy boils down to this: we are, each of us, all of us—asleep. Mankind has been lulled.

We can be awakened, however. There are three ways.

Defile the Flesh. This tenet espouses the mind-freeing potential of tattooing, ritual scarification, and self-inflicted pain. Aubrey himself never went "under the gun" and died with no tattoos or body modification of any sort. But, like many gurus, he said he had developed beyond the rules required of his followers. He also makes the outlandish claim of having gouged his own eye, from the root, with a tablespoon. Father Byron's story of Aubrey losing his left orb in a childhood episode of abuse seems more plausible, and three secondary sources I consulted repeat the "pencil encounter" almost verbatim. I don't know which story is true, if either. Aubrey Morick said whatever popped into his mind in front of crowds. His speeches were frequent and interminable. He spoke without notes, and often without sense. He wrote in the same fashion. The foremost goal was to shock the audience and shore up any slippage his waning notoriety may have suffered between gigs.

Outwardly, he directs disciples toward sadism, torture, and disfigurement of enemies. He cites ancient tribal customs and warrior ethics, employing an unsystematic hodgepodge of contorted historical facts. Facts are not important to him. Spirit is. And in the spirit of defining supremacy of the Self, a little bloodletting never hurts.

Feast on the Living. Here he promotes parasitic living as the finest aspiration of Man. In the figurative sense, one is urged to live off the labor of others. Sweat not, except in pleasure. I like that line despite myself. Most of the Morick aphorisms, which are incidentally collected and available in pocket form, lack wit and flee from memory as quickly as the eye passes over them. Morick believed that any work done but solely for the perfection and gratification of the Self and the Self's desires was waste. This waste naturally led to the depletion of Spirit and was deemed reprehensible. Cons, street rip-offs, purse-snatching, thieving, marrying for position and money, embezzlement, the duping of friends in securement of loans—were suitable career moves, as long as they were played for maximum advantage and terminated when the advantage itself ended. Above all else, he recommended the seduction of benefactors.

In the more literal sense, he avowed experimentation with cannibalism.

Love the Dead. The Serpent of the Plains illustrates, in various reiterations throughout his texts, an obsessive preoccupation with dying and the dead. Nothing new as far as religion goes. But Aubrey Morick asserts that Death is not simply transitional. It is vital. Utmost in importance is the method or active mode of death. Suicide becomes celebratory. Murder is a gift. For page after page, he revels in oppositions and reversals. Worship the death's head as life force. The grave is the marriage bed. To be a man of bones is to be a truly fleshed-out man. And so on. A smart thrall, he writes, will find his opportunities, and thus his joy, in hospitals, sanitariums, rooms of execution, morgues, mortuaries, cemeteries, etc. For as much ink and paper as Morick devotes to this concept, it remains—to me at least—the vaguest of the trio. The more elaborative his efforts, the more obscured his subject proves.

Sex with the dying or those about to die—condemned prisoners are given as an example—is heartily encouraged. Yet literally and physically "loving" the dead never enters the discussion. I find this omission strange. Was Morick prudish in his deviltry?

Cannibalism, yes, by all means. But necrophilia is a no-no?

I glean these philosophical tidbits from the volumes. Death is not an end. It is not the culmination of a life. It is a means to exercise certain otherwise unobtainable magical freedoms. And Power. Death reshuffles the deck and puts the aces and kings on top.

Taken as a whole, A. H. Morick's is not an organized religion; *dis*organized makes a better, if charitable, fit. He's practicing sorcery, here and there, but it's his own personal brand of hocus-pocus. He holds back on particulars, rituals such as the Cloven Print are alluded to but never laid bare. They are too dangerous for novices. The Serpent doesn't offer his thralls empowerment. He's a stingy demigod. Slavery in the service of the most fearsome master appears to be the most a lowly thrall can afford.

Aubrey Morick was a madman. I don't believe, even if he were acting a role at the outset, that he could have sustained his sanity for long. There's too much crazy energy alive in his words. Dips, turns, flights of dark fantasy, abound. He was a true believer, if only in his twisted self.

An interesting anecdote, found in the appendix to one of the tomes, leads me to believe I might have been wrong about the necrophilia. The lack of explication was, perhaps, a mere oversight on Morick's part. In the mid-seventies, a group of six people—the youngest was a schoolteacher in her thirties—broke into a funeral home in Pittsburgh, Pennsylvania. They stole a dozen bodies and would've gotten away with them if their truck hadn't thrown a tire outside Titusville. A highway patrolman stopped to help. The truck had expired plates, and the group appeared to be heading for a destination across the state line. But when questioned, none of them could say where. The patrolman became suspicious and began checking their licenses. The odor of their cargo soon drew the patrolman's attention. Once in custody, the perpetrators identified themselves as "thralls of the Black Blood Druid" and stated their intention in stealing the bodies was "to have an orgy."

Now, it might have been a promotional stunt. Aubrey Morick paid for their defense attorney and appeared every day in the gallery at their trial. He was easy to pick out in the crowd. Tall, gaunt, he wore a deep red turban and matching cloak. During the court recesses, he stood alone in the corridor and smoked cigars, shunning reporters and, when goaded, flicking ash on their shoes.

The ceiling fan thrums. I put down my papers. My feet on the floor, my head dizzily fumed with tobacco and too many words—I switch the fan off. Silence. Then on again.

Off.

On.

The white noise, the whirring . . .

I venture down to the neighborhood video store. Open an account and rent the first thing I lay my hands on.

Poltergeist.

I'm not planning to watch the movie. A film about suburbia, television, ghosts.

I'm in the ghost business these days. Maybe I've always been . . . Matthias, my father, the Boyle twins, Tad, my missing Robyn . . . now the Morick clan.

I reconnect the VCR in the attic.

Leave the TV's volume setting where it is.

The movie plays. I'm down the steps. Close the trapdoor.

My eyes are shut. The score, the actors—music and voices transfer through the floor audibly. I can hear it in the boys' room and everywhere else on the second floor. There's no way Tad and Una wouldn't know something was up there blaring in the attic.

Enter the parents' bedroom and push the door until it clicks.

Switch the fan on.

I can't hear the tape playing.

But my heart pounding comes through loud and clear.

Chapter 18

Make a pilgrimage, as I did. Outside Milwaukee, in the woods, you will find a lake. Next to it a mansion stands. Stroll around the back to the Maltz graveyard. They charge a fee to tour the mansion and its grounds. Beer aristocracy, the Maltzes were always smart about their money.

I pay my fee to the smiling attendant in the Maltz's former vestibule. The paneling was chosen for its darkness and strong grains; the home, what I see of it, purports a nautical theme. I exit the mansion.

The weather has turned nasty. The sky is raw, clouds torn. I huddle inside my jacket. But the blustery winds don't spare me. It's an edgy chill bearing from the north.

Aubrey's buried here, rubbing shoulders with four generations of the Maltz family and a veritable pack of their beloved pet dogs. If the engravings are accurate, they favored Doberman pinschers.

Release the hounds.

A hillock. Yew trees. Climbing vines on the gravestones. I think this one entangled at my feet is called a running rose.

Aubrey Hart Morick's tomb protrudes above the ground. They've erected a statue. Of a skeletal being. Arms extended, a mockery of Christ imagery, yet only the knowing would detect the implicit irony.

Two red marble serpents writhe around the legs of this pale, chiseled specter. The cap over the grave is a foot thick. As I expected, there's a spattering of graffiti. All in praise of the man whose bones rest underneath. Some visitors are like me, they've traveled here for a reason.

Red lichen and moss cling to the damp-to-the-touch stone. A spider's web bibs the skeleton, and I have to assume, on these well-kept premises, that the web has intentionally been left undisturbed. It's a macabre tribute. I'm aware, because of my research, that the snakes—I squat to inspect them—represent black blood pythons; Sumatran short-tails with huge girth, relative to length, and orange bejeweled eyes.

I want to stroke them. They are the only shining parts in the configuration.

Instead, I read the tomb's epitaph. Short, concise—name, birth and death dates, followed by a single line of remembrance.

Here lies one who knew the Secrets

I drive to Milwaukee's main public library and dig into archival news files, scan about for items related to Morick family traumas. Aubrey Hart's consumptive father in Belfast, the cruel, dipsomaniacal stepfather in Milwaukee, the dead twin, Griffin . . .

I discover, to my astonishment, that Aubrey's wife, Iris Morick, is alive. I find a reference to her on a *Milwaukee Sentinel* microfiche, an international story lifted from the AP. She was Irish. Aubrey married a girl from the island. But she left the United States. Went back home; where she was confined to live in a mental hospital. How did she find herself inhabiting such a place? Nearly thirty years ago, she tried to commit suicide while in police custody. The courts judged her of unsound mind.

Her crime?

She had attempted murder.

Last heard of, she was living voluntarily at a Catholic-run facility; she'd been deemed fit for release but had chosen to stay for further treatment. Far, far away from where I sit.

I jot the facts.

Whom did she try to murder?

Not Aubrey, her husband.

Graham. She tried to drown her son. And she didn't do it in the bathtub or a secluded garden pond or in Lake Michigan for that matter. On a windless summer afternoon, she rowed—just two in the boat, mother and son—out into a glassy oceanic bay with a little picnic basket resting between them like a treasure. They ate tea cakes and lemonade. She slipped him a sedative, probably in his lemonade bottle. Then she cuffed a stone to his leg and cast him overboard.

Fishermen saw her struggling. She was a small woman, he a large boy. They saved Graham from certain death at sea. The harbor police took custody of Iris.

In Ireland.

That's what gets to me.

The Moricks were living there then. After Griffin's death, they moved across the Atlantic. Then Iris turns murderous and tries to kill her remaining son.

Una Boyle lives there now. Her sons are still missing. Husband and wife pick up, leave America. And then Tad loses his life.

In Ireland.

Chapter 19

I fly into Dublin. The airport is like any metro airport. The city is big and dirty. Where does all the paper come from? The crushed lager cans I understand. But the paper? I rent a car. Other-side-of-the-road driving. Everything narrower than I'd prefer. I make three directional mistakes. Finally solve the riddle of Dublin traffic. Get out. Into the countryside. It's green. I pass many sheep. Travelers' caravans parked on the outskirts of crumbly, tilted places. The paper follows me. I'm smoking more. Must be the cold sea climate, the soft rain. I feel like a million bucks. Stop for cigarettes. Buy a scratch ticket.

Lose.

The hallway is poorly ventilated, stuffy with a tincture of varnish. They seat me in a green chair that exhales softly as I stretch my legs. I'm expecting a priest or a nun. You can't walk five steps in this place without passing a crucifix. Iris may find comfort in that. I don't. My presence doesn't merit a priest or a nun. I get a sexless person, wearing gold spectacles, black pants, white shirt, who tells me it will be a few minutes before I'm seen.

Therefore, I remain, for the moment, unseen. I'll give the sisters this much credit: the housekeeping is spiffy. I'm tempted to say immaculate. Religious language, unanchored, floats to the top of my brain. Sexless pops around the corner. He/she smells like baby powder. I start to rise up but am signaled to keep my place and then reassured my turn is coming. Instead, I'm offered water. Surprised to see it arrive in a real glass, heavy, quality stuff etched with use. I drink and taste disgorged bilge. Seaweed and gull droppings, a school of slimed, dead mullet. Couldn't be, right? I'm polite about it. This place wrings the politeness out of you. Swallow what's in my mouth. Deposit my glass on the side-board, slip it around the back of a framed photo—a black-and-white, girls on a lawn walking in procession with their hands folded. Little temples. Those damned Catholic schoolgirls in their blazers and skirts.

I'm enjoying the thready birth of my first Irish headache.

"If you'll follow me, please," says Sexless.

I ris Morick and I are seated in a conversation room. Two chairs, a table, and a lamp. The door closes. We are alone. Iris Morick appears lucid. A tall woman with sloping shoulders, she has gray hair that's pinned back, and slate eyes. Her complexion is a bit sallow, which I first attribute to the lighting and her circumstances. She presents as well-groomed, dressed in slacks, a blouse, and cardigan—all shades of blue and a size too large. I notice no makeup or perfume. Her mood seems relaxed. She lights a cigarette and asks if I'd like one. I decline. Mrs. Morick has given me permission to tape our conversation. A transcript excerpt from my taping follows.

Iris Morick:	You here about Aubrey?
Jase Deering:	Not Aubrey . . . I'm visiting to ask about your son.
IM:	(She nods.) I had two sons.
JD:	I want to talk about Graham.
IM:	(She pulls at her lip.) I did my best.
JD:	To be a good mother?
IM:	(Laughs.) I did my best to murder the bugger. What do you think they locked me away for?

JD: Did you think he was evil?

IM: No.

JD: Then why did you try . . .

IM: Let me ask you a question. A person needs a soul to be evil, doesn't he? (She places her hand over mine.) You look like an honest young man. Tell you a story. One day Aubrey killed my Griffin. He slashed his throat with a razor. It was Aubrey's stepfather's blade. We had a whole box. The old man did a bit of barbering over in Prussia, I think it was. Stepdad used to take nips out of little Aubrey's backside when the mood struck. No excuse, of course. Not for cutting the throat of your own. I witnessed it. Graham did as well. It was during a ritual. Aubrey went overboard. He didn't expect the boy to die, not spiritually. Irrational, but that was Aubrey at the time. Both of us were mad.

JD: The Cloven Print? Graham told me it was a sham.

IM: It's real. But the thing hadn't worked. At least Aubrey thought it hadn't. I helped my husband lug Griffin's body to the top of the wall. The three of us did the dreadful business together. Graham jumped on him, made himself a sweaty spectacle pouncing on Griffin's body. To drive the spike through his neck, you see? We had to make quite a mess to throw off the police. I didn't want my husband to be arrested. But Graham enjoyed it, right? It was like playing games to him. He took great pleasure. (She shakes her head.) I make no claims to my own innocence. I'm going to hell. The good sisters will concur. Their project to redeem me has failed. I can't be saved. Go on. Ask them on your way out. I'd love to hear what they tell you.

JD: Are you mentally ill?

IM: Insane? Does it show? I'm being sarcastic. You asked politely. No, I feel all right these days. Though I've got the bone cancer. When they told me I'd be having a visitor, I thought it might be one of the children come to say good-bye . . .

JD: Your children?

IM: I had another child. Nobody knows. I mean, the sisters knew.
      They took her from me. A daughter, but she was off-the-books.
      Graham knows about her, that's for sure. He used to visit me.
      Years ago, he did. I was labeled a catatonic, but I knew when
      he came into my room. The doctors thought it might be
      therapeutic. (Unintelligible.) I was no threat to him, was I?
      Him a young adult now, big, mature lad, and me all withered
      in my sickbed. (Laughter again.) And I know he was aware of
      my, my . . . my cognition. The way he talked to his mother. The
      things he said to me . . . (unintelligible sound, coughing). He's
      keeping an eye on my daughter these days. He wouldn't let her
      go unattended. (Nodding.) That's a worry. I think about him
      lying in my bed. Tall like Aubrey in his prime, a spitting image
      of the old Serpent. (Dry laughter.) Nights are hardest. Even
      with the pills and prayers.

JD: When was she born?

IM: She's twenty-five. Doesn't she look like a beauty queen though?
      (Smiles. Iris is missing an incisor.)

JD: You've seen her?

IM: She's come around for a visit, just like you. I was telling you
      about that. How I got confused. When you rang the office and
      asked for a visit? I thought you might be her. I don't have
      visitors, not for decades I didn't. Now she drops in. "Hi, Mum."
      Then, when you called, they said it was a man, a man coming.
      It's him, I thought. Horrid Graham. But I said my prayers. God
      told me it would be someone else. And God was right. He
      hasn't been here. I worry about that. What's he doing? I don't
      think I would see him this time. After everything, I would have
      a right not to. Soon I'll be dead. He'd get a thrill at that. But a
      mother wants to know.

JD: Know what?

IM: How did they all turn out? The lovelies, my little lovelies . . .

After, always after the fact.
My mind races with things I should've said, chances blown.

178

I park the car. Leave it on the street and start searching. St. Stephen's Green. I wander the paths. The Moricks tag along in my head. I emerge on the other side, aching for a drink. Harcourt Street to Hatch Street Upper. Down the hatch is what I need. Go on. This pub's called the Bleeding Horse and sounds about right. Dark enough inside. But big glass windows combat my claustrophobia. Caves lend us an ancient mammalian comfort. I'm sheltered inside this place. I can see out. Watch for my enemies. From the looks of the crowd, I fit okay, maybe a little too grizzled. Higher mileage on me, but the chassis hasn't fallen apart. There are a fair number of students. Laughing at one another as they should be. I'm not looking for company.

I luck out and get a stool by the taps. Order a Bulmers and a shot of Jameson. Cold cider and a straight whiskey—lovely. When I look up again, I've had three more of the same. Feeling better. A woman pries between me and the cornered wall.

Bumps me in the kneecaps.

Hard.

My fault? I'm turned sideways to minimize distractions. Grooving for good and hammered. Now I swing around.

It's Una Boyle.

She's looking for a refill, empty pint in her slender, ring-heavy hand, but she's looking for more than that too. Maybe I flatter myself.

"Tinker's drink," she says, referring to my three-quarters-down cider.

I nod back. The shock of seeing her muzzles me.

She's tottering a bit, nothing that says she's blasted. In Ireland, she doesn't seem so broken. A tarnished majesty is hung on her sorrow. And she's striking too; more noticeable than when I saw her last—the unpleasantness in the garage—and I do my best to dismiss thoughts of that disastrous exchange. I'm in the moment and drunk. The lighting helps. Jet hair tumbling around a pale face. Una's cheeks are ruddy with the booze. Under the sweater, her limber body seriously at work. She moves that way—a bendy girl. Half-pack of Silk Cut Purples clutched in her fist. Her jeans are snug but not overly. They fall nicely on her, I'll admit. Pale blue moons rising in the corner of my down-turned eye.

Devil in my ear.

Tad's buried in the cold ground. The woman is grieving, yearning. Iris's daughter? Morick's sister? Shall we find out? How to do that? Can't ask outright, not if you want the kind of attention you crave. Not if you want answers either. You like them damaged. Well, here's your perfect ten. Make your move.

"Let me get this," I say. The bartender, quite familiar by now with my cash pile, chooses the proper bills. Takes her empty glass.

"Guinness," she says to him. To me: "You're writing about us?"

"Among other things, yes."

"What sort of other things?"

"Investigative. You live around here, right? You must have seen me walking through the park. Is that it? Did you follow me here?"

"I may have."

"That's sneaky."

"Is that woman with you?"

"My partner? Robyn? No. We're not together anymore."

"Just as well."

"I've been to visit Iris."

"Who is she?"

We're in her flat. She's lit some candles, found a bottle of Bushmills in the cupboard. She keeps her sweater on and shucks off everything else without a warning.

Why is that such a turn-on? I'm out like a shepherd's hook.

Pared to the bone, not an extra ounce of flesh on her. Thighs like cemetery marble. They won't warm despite my busy hands and the peat fire glowing in the fireplace.

Riding me.

Talking nonsense filth at my request.

The talking-filth part, not the nonsense part.

"Go fuck yourself," she says.

Her eyes are mischievous slashes.

I'm ready to break out laughing. Only she's locked on like a chimp's fist.

Jesus.

I adore a woman with a bit of hair downstairs, taps into the Garden of Eden of my slithery reptilian brain. Una is a jackpot. The Mighty Sin is unmistakable. If you're doing it right, there will be hell to pay. And you don't care. You're a split-second god. I'd sell out for that any day. She mixes in these little side-to-side hitches. Wicked really, the effect they have. I'm shifting dimensions.

"Go fuck yourself," she says again.

I reach for the whiskey bottle.

Second thoughts. Afraid I might chip a tooth. Guilt's on the way and I haven't even finished. I need something to bat it aside.

Una lays her palms over my eyes. Presses down.

"What're you doing?"

Her mouth in my ear. I expect a kiss, an amorous bite perhaps.

"Shhhh. What do you see?"

"Nothing."

"What do you see?"

I feel her rhythm speeding up. She's loose. Wet.

Tight.

"I see stars."

"Stars?"

"No, it's darkness, nothing but darkness."

"Come on. Give it to me."

That does the trick. I'm quivering like some poor slob getting the paddles in an ER because he's flatlined. Electrocuted by sex. I arch. Buck out the aftershocks. Robyn flashing before my eyes. Una takes her hands away. They both lean close to paint me with whiskey kisses.

Later, the candles gutter as they die. Two left. Their flames lengthen and turn twisty. Una opens the shutters to let the moon inside. She's bathed in nocturnal light. Some must be coming from the streetlamps. Doesn't matter. She sways, dancing flat-footed—backlit, silvery, sad, beautiful. Every object in the room decides whether to be black or white, outline or shadow. My mind fogs over. Clicks back.

"Are you Graham Morick's little sister?"

"Don't be silly. That stooped old hag lied to you."

"Iris told me about her daughter. But she wouldn't tell me her name." Tumblers spin in my drunken brain. "How do you know what she looks like?"

"I only know that men think all women are hags in the end."

"You're no hag. Though, you might be a Morick."

"You honestly think it's me?"

I nod like an imbecile.

Una shows me her hands, doing this weird gesture. Like sign language, but odder, almost Masonic. Index fingers scissoring under her middle fingers, pinkies tucked below ring fingers—a big forked split down the middle, and her thumbs hidden against her palms. Contortions out in front of her, arms stiff, wrists folded down, as if she's offering me a choice of which set of knuckles to kiss.

"Don't do that," I say.

"Know what this means?"

"No, but you're frightening me." I'm only half-serious. I lie there, drifting. Sinking into a drunk's coma, shaking my numb head.

"Haven't gotten that far yet?" She paws the arm of the couch. But they don't exactly resemble paws; the action isn't pawing. Better to say hooves—a pair of prancing hooves. She laughs. I notice her overbite and dental fillings.

I attempt to get up.

She pushes me down. "All right, I'll stop. I don't want you leaving."

Una pours a stiff whiskey. She sits upright at my feet, wedged into the corner of the couch, a look of determination crossing her face. Even with my senses dulled, I have to wonder, *Is she waiting for me to fall asleep?*

"Waiting for me to fall asleep?" I ask, slurring, yet knowing I'm slurring—that's about where I am in terms of consciousness.

She strokes my shins. Her nose buries deep in the glass, cupping her words.

"Worry I'll set you on fire?"

At least I think she says that. It's a joke. I don't believe she'd hurt me.

I believe very much in sleep.

Couches and sleep.

Sleep.

Una talks in another room. Is she on the phone?

I should be going. I'm sandbagged, alcohol and exhaustion. In a few minutes, I'll be off. But, wait. Here she comes. Feel her coil next to me.

Her hand closes over mine. I never even open my eyes. The red lids tell me it's a bloody new day. I'm aware of the cold nibbling of her rings on my skin.

Her harsh breath blows past me. She had another whiskey while talking on the phone. She's a tougher customer than I ever was.

Una slides to the floor, kneeling. I'm prone on the couch. She's pushing a heavy object—it has a handle—into my hand; it's more a grip than a handle. There's a curve to it. I don't blink. Try, instead, to roll on my side, away from her, whatever it is she's doing.

We're having a lethargic struggle. I want to win. *Give me my hand back*, I'm thinking. I want to sleep a little more. I jerk my arm to shrug her off.

The gunshot wakes me.

At once, I am fully awake.

Bolt upright.

Afraid.

My eyes wide, looking down on . . .

Una's body.

A great tongue of gore hangs from the hole in the back of her skull. By her face, you'd never know it. Blood, shapeless and primitive, pools on the boards. Her expression is beatific. More of the blood had whipped out behind her, hitting things, the wall for example, and it's running down. Red tears. Pieces—grit and gobs. Her life voided. Yet she looks plain stoned.

The pistol.

My God. I've been squeezing it for dear life. Now I wipe its entirety with the tail of my shirt, lay it gently on the cushions, because I don't really know about guns. I don't want accidents . . . I don't want it to go off *again.*

I find my socks. My shoes. I put them on without sitting down. Hop on one foot to keep my balance. My breathing is loud. I've never heard it so loud.

Hyperventilating, that's what this must be.

Even with the gunshot still ringing in my ears and . . .

Where are my things?

Am I leaving any evidence?

Fingerprints, of course. Hair, fibers. My sweat, my dried saliva. No time to do anything about it. But I'm a foreigner, I've never been printed. I look down at the body again. Dead Una in her sweater and nothing else. I want to cover her up.

She has my semen inside her.

I go back and lift the gun—using my shirttail again—and I leave it next to her.

As if she shot herself.

She did.

She absolutely did shoot herself.

Una appears to have been living alone. Little or no evidence of Tad—he's been erased. As far as I know, no one saw me entering her building. But I can't say for certain. It was late. I was staggering drunk. I absolutely don't want anyone seeing me leave now that it's morning. The street looks placid enough. But that only makes me consider how loud the gunshot was.

So I need another way out. Before I go, I decide to have a look around the flat. I'm on an adrenaline high. Fear circuits are overloaded. My mind turns cold. I will never get another opportunity like this. Being careful not to touch anything unless I plan to keep it—I start my search in the bedroom. I'm no burglar. No lawman either. I don't know how to toss an apartment.

Do my best.

The unit is small, perhaps not by European standards, and I manage a thorough job. My sense of time has shattered. Feels like a month since I slept with Una, a fraction of a second since she died.

The only bedroom—it could belong to a hotel. Nothing personalized: a bed, a mirror, an empty wardrobe.

Fasting bachelors have better-outfitted kitchens.

In the bathroom, I learn that Una owns a single towel and takes quite a number of prescription pills. I dry swallow two Valiums. Pocket the bottle.

She's in the sitting room.

Grate my teeth as I step around her corpse.

Come up with zero.

Where are her clothes?

losets.

Her luggage—I kick the bags out into the room. The large bags fall open and are stuffed with women's clothing. Not very clean, or very incriminating. Her carry-on feels light. It rattles. Covering my hand with my sleeve, I release the latch.

Videotape.

Jam it back into the bag—mine now. Ball up my leather coat and force it inside. I'm sweating like a pig. My mouth tastes bittersweet from last night's alcohol, and I'd better not be sick because there's no time for . . .

I hear the two-tone siren of a European police car.

ang out the rear window.

The fall won't kill me. Drop onto a garden shed, dent the roof, and slide off into a patch of dewy grass littered with cigarette butts. My right leg soaked.

Leap a stone wall.

Here come the gardai.

I rush to a taxi stand, thankful there are no cabs to be had. Gazing at my wristwatch, I'm just a businessman off to the airport. The police car speeds by, makes the turn, and stops in front of Una's building. I'm walking away, wondering where I left the rental. Positive I'll never make it that far.

Yet I do.

Chapter 20

I don't sleep.

Not on the airplane, or on the el train.

Convinced I'll be arrested at any moment.

Through the doorway, I lose everything but the video. Hurry to the attic. Turn the television upright and insert the tape.

I've scored a victory.

But I'm not prepared to celebrate.

What have I won?

It tastes like my own descent.

I wouldn't call it a snuff film. It's more a log. You could stretch and call it a confession. I would resist the temptation for multiple reasons. Not least of which is I don't think Aubrey Hart Morick was confessing. I think he was archiving his grab at immortality.

The tape reveals the Cloven Print in action. Morick the Elder caught murdering his own son. It's a home movie, of amateur film stock; someone's gone to the trouble of transferring it to a video format. Scratches and flecks of dust show throughout. The sound quality warbles muddy at best, and at worst, it drops out completely; you might be watching a silent picture. The view is too dark, hazy, obscured. The watcher gets the sense of a large room, not a typical American family dwelling. I know, because Graham told me when we met at the condo that what I'm about to see happened inside the Maltz mansion.

Which room, I have no idea. I never completed the tour.

Aubery Hart Morick fiddling with his camera. With the lighting. His twins, Graham and Griffin, bounce a soccer ball back and forth in the barren hall. The boom-boom-boom of the ball overloads the microphone. The boys are clumsy, tripping over each other. They sprawl on the floor and giggle. Aubrey grows impatient. The undraped archway leading outdoors glows harsh white.

"This will have to do," Aubrey mutters.

Begin the chant. As I taught you, remember?" He leads them the first few phrases, but they sing it strong. I know their chant by now. I've heard it twice before. Once at the Sandcastle, again when Graham visited the condo. Aubrey is overjoyed. There is a muffled sound—his voice swallowed by velvet as he cloaks himself, dons his cowl.

The boys lie like two edges of an arrow.

Their heads touch at his feet.

Aubrey climbs onto a three-legged stool. He slips a noose over his head. Snugs the knot up, nice and tight. Slackness apparent in the rope as the Serpent steps down off the stool. He hovers over the boys. His voice is impossible to decipher. A continuous, barely detectable mumble, like the buzzing of a beehive.

You never see the blade.

One of the boys, Griffin it is—it has to be (given what I know at the start)—the sleeve of Aubrey's robe covers his face. He stiffens for a moment. They must've drugged him beforehand. Because that's all.

Aubrey climbs on his stool again. The slack disappears. He kicks the stool away.

He hangs by his neck.

For a minute or two, as long as it takes him to run out of oxygen, for the panic to hit, he's simply floating there like an angel. He set up the camera poorly, in a bad position. I don't think it was intentional. The viewer can't see the length of rope tauten or any of the gallows mechanism. You see the noose. It's white. His cowl pulls aside during the struggle. You glimpse Aubrey's grimacing face and the noose as he twists. The other end of the rope is tied somewhere off-camera. His neck doesn't break. But he's strangling. He sways like a slow pendulum. All that's visible for the record are his cloaked body, the knocked-over stool, and the prostrate boys—maybe there's a puddle around Griffin, hard to say, could be shadows.

Aubrey starts to fuss.

Then he's kicking wildly. His pale legs move apart, together again, apart, like a pair of gigantic shears snapping under his cloak.

He takes the barber's razor—here you see it, clearly, the long, black handle decorated with a silver pin through the end—and flips it open. He's sawing at the rope.

Two thralls and Iris rush in. They lift him, the thralls do, and Iris gravitates to her son. She's not angry. Inquisitive. I'd call her attitude inquisitive.

She never looks at the camera.

None of them look.

The screen fills with electric snow. End tape.

Then it begins again.

Replaying the ritual. The videotape is full of back-to-back copies of the Cloven Print film. This is the tape that played over the boys' room every night. They listened to it through the floor. Una—their mother— set it up. Her sons dreamed to the chants. They heard a failed rehearsal of their own murders, while they slept below in innocence.

Chapter 21

Watching the Cloven Print video has me thinking about the other tapes—the vanished birthday and Tad's inadvertent recording of the twins' abduction.

I want to see them again.

My memory is fuzzy. As fuzzy as the image of the man playing pinball in the birthday video. It was Graham. He was watching the boys. And Una knew it.

Something else.

What part did Una play in the kidnapping of her children? If she and Graham were working together, she could've handed the boys over to him. Tad was the only obstacle. His knowledge might have been his death warrant. What did I know about Una?

She lied to me the night she died.

She knew what Iris looked like because she was Iris's daughter. She had been to visit her mother days before I did.

As an infant, she was put up for adoption. The nuns took her from Iris in the asylum. Graham had to have found out. He located her. I don't know when. He informed her of her lineage, her legacy. He convinced her to prepare her sons for sacrifice.

She married young.

Her husband played around with his students.

She was a good enough actress to fool me when we interviewed her. I thought she was bereaved. She fooled me again in Dublin. She brought a loaded gun to me while I slept. Was she going to kill me or set me up as a murderer?

I don't have the answer.

But she was a good actress.

I find the background file Robyn made summarizing the principals associated with the kidnapping. Leaf through the binder.

Payoff.

In college, Una joined an all-female theater troupe. They called themselves the Black Mollies. She played a few lead roles.

Yes, I want to see the abduction tape again.

I'm withholding evidence—the rock from the Boyles' attic and now Aubrey Morick's recording of Griffin's ritualized slaying. Implicated in a murder overseas, on the run, if only in my mind, but here I am walking upright into a police station; worried that my guilt will be as obvious and crude as if I wore a dress. But no one blinks. I meet Brendan Fennessy and we go into the same room where I watched the Boyle tape the first time. Fennessy looks ragged. His mind is elsewhere. Like most cops, he has a full caseload of other people's misdeeds and tragedies. His life has not been absorbed by the Boyles the way mine has. He handles the tape. He leaves me alone.

Pen in hand, I open my notebook. These habits provide a small comfort.

I tap the remote keys. The tape plays. I locate the buttons I'll need to halt the action, and to advance it frame by frame.

The boys are tussling with cushions on the couch.

Block them out. I'm looking for someone else.

The deliveryman.

Freeze him. In his crouch, with his gray gloves, his bushy mustache, sunglasses, and crow-black hair winging out stiffly from either side of his milkman's cap. His uniform bags at the knees, the legs are cuffed. His shirt is too big, it hangs. His shoes look small, not working boots, but narrow and pointed with a tall, blocky heel—the image isn't that sharp, I might be guessing, filling in the details I hope to see. The walkie-talkie— he plays with it to show the boys, like it's a toy—or a prop.

Unfreeze.

His body language. The gestures. Posture.

When you've been on intimate terms with a person, you would think you'd recognize certain qualities. Maybe not.

He's in the shot, but he isn't grabbing the boys.

He lures them.

They aren't interested—shy with a stranger. Kids are that way. Cautious and slow to warm up to new faces.

The deliveryman knows about Tad's camera, doesn't want to get too close to the lens. But he's unafraid of being seen.

He wants to be seen.

Only not too well.

The boys don't cooperate. They hold their ground.

The deliveryman leaves the shot.

Then the arm . . . it's slender. The fingers . . .

I can't be sure.

But the boys have changed. The trick revealed to them.

They're animated, happy, gravitating where they hesitated before.

Freeze.

Quite a fix she'd gotten herself into.

She couldn't call to them, not using her normal voice, because Regina's chained in the kitchen. Right where Fennessy showed me on the last viewing—yeah, right there—her foot shakes.

Una was the deliveryman. I'm positive.

She had to lose her disguise to attract the boys.

She's kidnapping her own children.

Why?

That I haven't figured out yet.

Didn't Tad see the tape? Couldn't he recognize her?

I don't know how many times Tad even watched his secret tape before he turned it over to the police. He didn't see his wife acting a role. He saw an intruder. He saw his future stolen away. He didn't notice his wife because he wasn't looking for her. Perhaps the purpose of the ruse was to fool Tad. But why?

Duped, he gave the tape over to the authorities. He admitted to his surreptitious voyeurism, his affairs, and the underbelly of his marriage. He called his character into question. Una played no part in that. People felt sorry for her. I felt sorry. Tad was a fall guy, a delaying tactic. His purpose timed out. The Chicago police had no longer considered him a suspect. Until the news of his suicide. Their investigation suffered a serious loss of momentum.

There must be simpler ways of absconding with a pair of boys.

And yet, Una never left.

The boys were gone. Dead? I don't think so. Gone away. With Graham? Was he her accomplice? It made the most sense in an apparently motiveless crime. Una and Graham kidnap her sons to perform the Cloven Print. Why would she go along with Graham? Are the ravings of a discovered brother enough reason to kill your offspring?

It's more than that. Iris told me as much, if I'd been listening.

L ater, back at the Boyles', I replay our interview.
This time I'm listening.

Grant that Iris Morick's surviving son is a magician, a man of unusual influence. To Una he's a triple threat. And it's not because he's her brother. What did Iris tell me?

He used to visit me. Years ago, he did. I was labeled a catatonic, but I knew when he came into my room. The doctors thought it might be therapeutic

The way he talked to his mother. The things he said to me. . . .

I think about him lying in my bed. Tall like Aubrey in his prime, a spitting image of the old Serpent. Nights are hardest.

A daughter, but she was off the books. Graham knows about her, that's for sure.

Who was Una's father? I'd assumed Aubrey or a fellow patient. But Iris had been locked away for five years when she became pregnant. Iris never mentioned Aubrey calling on her.

He used to visit me. Years ago, he did.

I think about him lying in my bed.

He's keeping an eye on my daughter these days.

My daughter.

Our daughter.

A magician, a brother, and her father too.

Graham is Una's father.

Chapter 22

Opening the back door for a splash of sunshine on my face, even if it is November sun, I find a square blotting the light, a note pinned to the screen.

Meet me at Funspot Bumper Cars 7PM tonite. Much to tell re: Una &, like the song says, where the Boys are
Regina

I try calling her. Resetting our meeting place. Her number is disconnected. Regina's more paranoid than I am. I don't want her to run again.

She's guessed it or put it together over time. Una's ploy: posing as the deliveryman. I have a stranglehold on this story, or vice versa. I need a person to testify to the fact of a delusional Una capable of kidnapping her sons, perhaps killing her husband, and trying to frame me for her own murder. I need to know the extent of Graham Morick's—her father's—involvement. I need a witness.

Funspot.

Not a location I'd choose. An indoor amusement park and arcade situated on the northwestern outskirts of the city. I'd spent afternoons eating corn dogs and feeding quarters to carny barkers at Funspot when the girls were younger. When Sydney and I rode the Octopus together, I pointed out how close we were to smacking the roof of the place. We jolted around in circles. Syd threw up on my shoes.

I'm going to stick out in an amusement park, especially alone.

Not riding the Octopus, but standing at the edge of the bumper cars with my hands in my pockets. A singular, middle-aged man looking around for, I don't know, maybe someone special? Hey, kid, you want a piece of candy? Not good. Figure I'd draw attention and quick. Maybe even get security to ask me my name. The last thing I want is attention. All I'm doing is meeting a young woman for a conversation. Public venue. Full of hyper kids and bored-to-tears parents. Security guard on the door. The whole enterprise likely under electronic surveillance. Where's the danger?

I'm not expecting any.

I tell Syd and Sara that I'm picking them up at five. We'll grab some burgers and fries and hit the arcade attractions afterward.

The bumper car operator is a mouth-breather.

From afar you might guess he had a deformity. His eyes are tiny, widely spaced apart. Slits in a mask of latex. Simian, mashed nose and deviated septum therein dominates from the middle. He breathes audibly, though not well, and if you are privileged enough to hear his speaking voice, the pinched-off quality isn't soon forgotten. Today, he's sleepy at the control panel. Lids blink open, once, to reveal buttery whites, irises of impassive green. From afar, as I started to say, you might think he'd been born with no eyeballs, skin pockets where the eyes should be. Despite this, if you approach him closely, you'll notice they twinkle. I notice. It does not make me feel any kinship. I desperately want to leave.

His hands are permanently red, arthritic claws. They flake. I watch him manipulate the controls. I do not want him laying hands on my girls. But he's lifting the chain. Waving children through as they race to the cars. He checks their straps. Back behind his console, he punches a big green button, adjusts a lever.

The cars are rolling, banging. Van Halen blares from the speakers. The sound is mostly static. I have no camera to photograph my daughters. I am not here to record the event for posterity. I am here to pretend. To play a normal man enjoying life.

"Mirrorrorrim."

The operator has spoken. It had to be him. No one else around.

"Pardon me. Did you say something?"

"You heard me."

He holds the door with a claw. It's a storage closet, deep and filled with bumper-car parts. The lighting filters through, dingy yellow; makes it so the space actually feels darker. *No*, I'm thinking, *I'm not going in there with you.*

"C'mon. Hurry up. They'll fire me for leaving my post."

I see a small woman in the shadows. My heart skips.

She steps under the soiled bulb.

Regina Hoffman.

She's holding out her arms to me, as if to embrace.

I move toward her. Pass the threshold. Lift my own arms.

But she doesn't want a hug. Her hands are out front like hooves. She's twisted her fingers the way Una did back in Dublin.

It's a sign. An identifier. She shows me whom I'm up against. The Cloven Print. Morick and his cult of believers—she's now one of them. *Don't even trust me.* She said that when we'd parted at the museum. She knew they were following her. Knew she wouldn't be able to resist them once they took possession.

"Long time, Jase," she says.

Hit from behind with a rubber mallet, the hammerhead blasts me like a powder keg. On my knees among cables, peanut shells, greasy food wrappers, a push broom. Vision scrambled. Hit again. Walloped into a nova of pain.

The two of them lay their hands on me. Man and woman. Nathan and Regina. Struggling with my dead weight. Dragging me farther into the gloom. I lose a shoe. Ears ringing. I'm fighting.

"Get his shirt open," Nathan says.

Regina rips at my collar. Buttons pop. She scratches my throat with one of her nails. I swing my arms. Shoving her. Hit again.

"Now," she says. "Let me have it."

Nathan produces a syringe. She stings my neck, jams the plunger home.

I twist.

Feel seeping warmth invade my chest.

"I've got to go," the operator says to them. "The ride should be over."

Regina throws the emptied needle away. Grips my head. Stares into my eyes.

"The light," she says.

Her husband shines a flashlight in my face. The light hurts. But I can't blink.

"The boss sees me missing, I have to explain why," says the operator.

"Go, maggot." Regina's voice warps.

"Syd and Sara . . . please, don't hurt them." I'm begging to what part remains human inside Regina.

She gives me a sweetheart smile, kisses my forehead. "Don't worry, Jase. It's not your girls that the Black Blood Druid wants."

In the spiral down, I sense relief.

Hear her say, "It's you."

Chapter 23

First realization: I am naked.

Second: I've been stuffed into some sort of sack.

Sleeping bag. In a vehicle moving at high speed over uneven terrain. I poke my fingers through the cinched-up hole. Spread the opening. Not much. Replace the fingers with my eye. We're in a hatchback. The rear seat folded down. I'm laid out like a bag of dirty laundry. Try yanking the zipper apart, but it won't budge. Fingers out again, searching, and then I feel why. Touch the knot. The drawstring fed through the zipper pull. I bring the knot into the bag. Voices from the front.

"Slow down," Regina says.

"I'm going to use the headlights," says Nathan.

"Druid warned us not to."

"I can't see in this rain."

"Go the same way as the last time," she tells him. "When I brought you to meet Druid and his other thralls at the lodge."

"That was daylight. Not this blinding—"

"Slow down! I don't want to end up in the ditch. We can't blow this."

"You want to dump him here and leave?"

"Druid would kill us."

"Maybe we could run."

Silence. Regina's words, when they finally come, are tremulous. "I've seen him do things. Walk into a restaurant and eat off other people's plates. Drink their beers. Steal their wallets. They didn't bat an eyelash. Because no one saw him. No one he didn't want to see. He'll pay us a visit. Maybe while we're sleeping. Slit us open. You want to wake up with his arm inside your chest?"

I've got the knot whittled down. Pick at it with my teeth.

Nathan stays quiet. I hear him light a cigarette. Those French Gitanes and their heavy fumes. I'd better not cough. They think I'm unconscious. The windshield wipers are lashing. The roadway is noisy. Branches slap at the doors. A torrent washes under the car. We must be following an unpaved access. Hills, we're definitely driving over hills. We change directions. Nathan cranks the wheel. I have no idea where we are. Or how long I've been out. We hit rocks. Then something larger. Tree limb? The front end goes up. I hear scraping underneath. The sound of—the muffler, or tailpipe, a loose section of the exhaust system—metal tearing away.

Regina says, "We don't have any choice. He told us what we had to do."

The car slides. I feel us lean right. We're losing the battle. Nathan cuts his speed. Keeps us on the road. Moving forward.

"Why are you depressed?" he asks. "The boys were happy to see you. Weren't they?"

"Yes, I know."

"Is it because you're worried about the new mother?"

"I'm sick of her."

"That's disrespectful. We are all together in this process. Druid told you how important you are to the Cloven Print. They all adore you."

"Whatever."

"I think you're jealous of the new mother."

"The turn is around here somewhere. I don't want to talk about her right now."

"We haven't passed the Fistula camp mark. You keep an eye out for the tree. The turn comes after."

"Genius, we passed the mark five minutes ago."

I'm working my way out of the bag.

Nathan says, "How could I miss . . . oh, no, shit—"

I grab the wheel.

Off to the left—a field of empty blackness. A large body of water, a lake, the low night sky hovers over its waves. Climbing between Regina and Nathan, I get both hands on the steering wheel. Aim for the water. Push with all my strength. Nathan's big. Even through his raincoat, I feel his thick upper arm pummel my ribs. He's fighting me for control. But I've surprised him. And I don't care where we go as long as it's off this road.

The trees thrash around us. A gap opens.

Locked on, I will us through.

Windshield cracking, cracks wider, gives. We're showered in glass. Rain.

Regina says, "No."

The car goes over and down.

Nathan brakes.

But nothing can stop us now. Faster and faster. Silent. Airborne. Hard bodyslam into water and rocks. We land nose-down in a white froth. Slick boulders chunked up on either side. We're not sinking, not yet. I'm knocked into the backseat again. The hatch has burst. I have my way out. Look at them. Nathan, unresponsive—maybe he's dead—slumps against the dashboard. Regina straining, attempts to unbuckle his seat belt

Grinding.

The hatchback's hood slips under black water.

Water pours in the back. We're filling up, getting heavier. More grinding.

I try to save her.

She won't take my hand.

I help her rip off Nathan's coat. Wrap my arms around his chest. His legs are trapped. He outweighs us both. The water is freezing.

"Regina," I say, "he's not alive. We need to get out."

She doesn't listen. The water's at her waist. So cold I can't hold my arm in it for longer than a few seconds without pain.

I feel a bump. Hear a steady sawlike bite of steel on stone.

Scrambling out the hatch, I take Nathan's coat and the sleeping bag. Naked, stumbling to the shore, I carry the coat and bag over my head. Sit on the grass. Turn back in time to watch the hatchback submerge. Chains of bubbles break on the surface.

Then nothing but a dark, impenetrable lake. The lapping of waves, the wind . . .

I slip into Nathan's huge coat.

L ights.

Lights playing on the water.

And car engines roar above me, from the road's edge.

Morick and his thralls.

They're coming.

They're using spotlights.

"She's there. Look," I hear a voice say.

I look too. Regina treads water on the surface, under her arm— Nathan. Somehow she freed him. She's crying, screaming.

"We see you, Regina. We're throwing a rope."

Regina yells to them, "He's getting away."

"What?"

"Over by the rocks," she calls out. "Deering. He's on the shore."

The spotlight on Regina never wavers. But the others are swiveling around, flashing over the water, and popping from rock to rock.

I pull the coat high and cover my head.

Step between the boulders. The lights shine behind me. Catching up.

I'm looking for a path up the slope. But it's a sheer drop. I go farther, my feet cutting on rocks, then crunching sand—slick weeds, roots . . .

The lights hit my back.

"Here he is," a man shouts.

I hook my hands on the top of a boulder. Pull myself higher. The light fixes on me, is joined by another, then a third. I see a possible path.

"He's going for the road."

"Got him. Keep those lights steady."

I feel a heavy object in Nathan's pocket, bouncing against me as I climb.

Take the coat down off my head. They've seen me. There's no hiding. I reach into the pocket. Regina's gun. I don't know anything about guns.

But how much do I need to know?

I spin around. One-handed, I point the gun at the lights and pull the trigger.

The gun fires.

Once.

Twice.

"He's shooting. Kill the lights. Kill the lights."

I hear barking. Dogs.

On the third pull, the gun jumps from my wet hand. I hear it clatter on the rocks. I'm in the dark again. The gun is gone. In the water.

But I have a chance.

Make the road.

Hug the sleeping bag to my chest, bend low, and run.

They're coming.

I dive into the underbrush. Zigzag. Cross a clearing. To be swallowed by vegetation. Total darkness. I'm slowly working my way, but the brush is denser. I can't see. Nathan's coat snags at every step. I decide to lose it. Naked and pursued. But they don't know I've dropped the gun. Take my time. Burrow through the bushes like a rabbit. Where are the lights? The dogs?

I walk until I can't anymore.

Here's a fallen tree.

Next to it, I unroll the bag. Cover the bag with dead leaves.

Crawl inside.

Hide and wait.

I don't know what Regina injected into me. What it was that filled the syringe. But it's morning in the woods, and I'm seeing things. Things that can't be. Trees move. Yet I don't feel wind. And the animals. They might exist in books. Mythology, folklore, fairy tales. I spot a deer walking upright on two legs. I see reptiles. The forest floor is undulant with snakes. In the distance, an alligator passes—an alligator's head married with a hog's body. I'd climb the trees for a better view. But the trees are frightening. The branches feel soft as flesh and that warm. If I knew a cave, I'd wall myself inside. But there are no caves. Mounds. Valleys. People's voices from just over the thicket—they might be real. I touch the bump in my neck where the needle drove home. My neck is stiff. The muscle lumped.

The forest grows warm and sunny. I'm lucky. A tough November freeze might've killed me during the night. But it's morning. I'm dry and alive.

I backtrack. Find Nathan's coat. Put it on. Leave my bag rolled up under a dead brown bush.

I'm afraid of the road.

But the road is the only route I have.

I stick to the margins.

Eyes peeled open. Cautious. Stop to check my flank. I'm north. I can taste it in the air. The trees are northern trees. The sky is a crisp, unbroken blue.

Last night, we were close to them. To their camp, to the Fistula.

I'm walking the other way.

How far will I have to go down this road?

Are they looking for me?

I find the marked tree that Nathan and Regina talked about. The Fistula mark carved into the trunk—it's a snake. I would've never found it on my own. I'm not smart enough in my current shape. I'm too desperate. Too fucked-up.

I couldn't miss this.

A nude body hangs from the lower limbs.

The body belongs to a man.

I see something in the grass that looks like beef jerky. Pick it up. It's the end of a thick leather belt—chewed through, blackened, blood stiffened, and kissed with metal hornets. They scourged him.

I approach. See him struggling. He can't possibly be alive. I pick up a branch from the ground. I nudge him.

Crows fly out of Nathan. He's strung up by his ankles with a filthy chain. The links loop through the treetop. Strung up and gutted: his body cavity transformed into an alcove for scavengers. Did he drown first? Was he dead when this happened? Is this his punishment? I don't know. Arms flung outward—he's a man falling. His fingertips graze the grass. He's been burned. Maimed. They used a torch and knife. The tools aren't here. Neither are his sex organs. Whoever did this to him took them. There's a bloody imprint on the ground, near his head, where a receptacle—maybe a bucket?—was set down and later dragged away. The stain blazes in the dirt.

The windless grove smells like a barbecue pit.

I run a few yards and throw up.

They did this. They have them . . .

Robyn.

And the boys.

I head for the Fistula.

Chapter 24

Matthias is walking beside me. I don't mean his spirit, not a conjured memory. My flesh-and-blood brother is here. Psychiatrists will say he's a stress-induced phenomenon. He's me hallucinating *him*. I'll take what I can get. It's my brother. His skin, his eyes, his hair, and I notice, in my ear, the stir of sweet child's breath. I sense him first. See him next. Out of the corner of my eye—this kid, my brother, is kicking up dirt on the road. If I turn, he's gone. So I stop turning. I want him there beside me.

I don't want to die without him.

We locate the turn that eluded us last night in the rain. Enter the brush. I'm not afraid of the trees, not with Matthias covering my back. The dogs are whining. They must smell us coming. We make a big circle around the outskirts of the camp. I'm not being stupid. Even with my brother, I don't earn invincibility.

I position myself downwind. No fence but the trees.

I'm getting glimpses of what lies behind.

The guard dogs are Doberman/German-shepherd mixes; chesty and huge paws, long in the snout; their faces are hairy nozzles jammed with fangs. They hate us.

The lodge house is old, sunken, constructed of logs. Lakeside, there's the spine of a pier decaying into the water. No neighbors in sight. The camp is isolated. Nailed above the lodge's main door, a logger's crosscut saw streaks rusty orange. The cabins—I count a half dozen—are built like smaller versions of the lodge. The thralls must have boarded over the windows. I don't see a square inch of glass. Which is good, because nobody can see what I'm about to do.

I take off Nathan's coat. Climb up into the crotch of a tree.

Matthias isn't with me.

I'm alone.

Bark nips at my sweaty face. The lodge opens. I see a drunken man, pale and shirtless, stumble out of the house. Beer gut. His rock-star-length red hair is flat and slicked, reaching to his shoulder blades. Others are standing in the shadows. Partial faces, the white blur of an arm, a pair of legs. The man falls. No one emerges to help him. He stands and, jerkily like a puppet, retraces his steps. He runs square into a tree.

Sits.

He is not drunk with alcohol, but fear. I am wrong about his hair. He has none. Neither does he have a scalp. His wet, vesseled skull sugared with sand from his second fall, and dust halos around him.

It's Father Byron. He has less than a minute to live.

Graham Morick walks down the lodge steps.

Thralls follow.

My stomach revolts against me, and I am trying for a silent vomit. Stick my fingers in my mouth to muffle the noise of my retching.

Morick will hear me.

Will kill me.

Morick lays a hand on the ex-priest's back. Comforting him. He reaches under Father Byron's chin with his other hand. Makes a fist. Blood shoots in a fine spray: a garden hose when it's first turned on. Morick opens Father Byron's throat. Not a speedy movement—he's being gentle, effortless.

The leakage changes to a steady pouring, dark as used oil. Father Byron sitting on his haunches. Morick stands. The slightest motion made, hardly a shrug. The thralls—more of them from inside the doorway—come forward.

207

Father Byron, poor Father Byron. At least it's almost over. They're forming a ring. Holding one another's hands. Morick says a few words I can't quite hear.

Father Byron attempts to rise. But he can't walk on rubbery legs.

They fall on him.

The dogs see me. They're trotting over to my tree. I need to get down. The branches snap like firecrackers.

I fall.

I don't remember falling. I'm kneeling beside the trunk. My mouth fills with blood. The forest wheels around like it's attached to a giant spinning drum. I hear them. They crash through the brush. Shouting at me. They know my name.

Run.

I rise and move forward.

The forest floor tilts. Drops me. I touch my forehead; my skin has split.

Stand.

They surround me.

Their sloppy crimson faces—*they were biting him,* I think.

I'm next. My fear enlarged, I'm teetering on the brink of hysteria. I choke on my blood. Spit. Wipe my lips on my arm. Notice the sticky, red smear, the dirt in it. I look around me. Giddy. *You people,* I think, *we speak the same language.*

The language of blood.

Morick appears outside their ring.

"Bind him," he says. "Then take him to the cabins."

Chapter 25

They tie me with a thick, white rope. My arms are down at my sides. I don't resist. I wouldn't have a chance running. There are too many of them. Men and women in equal numbers, twenty strong or more. Morick's slaves—some dressed in street clothes, others in simple hooded shifts of white, black, or red. I suppose the choice of shifts or no shifts, of colors, signals a kind of hierarchy. Graham wears a sweater and jeans. His appearance is no different from the first time I met him at the Mexican restaurant.

Now that I've been apprehended, now that Father Byron lies bled out and bitten in the courtyard, Graham has other business to attend to. He disappears inside the lodge.

The rope pulls tight. They leave a few feet hanging in front, and this they use to lead me to the cabins.

Number 4.

The numeration painted with a stencil.

Three cabins between mine and the lodge.

I stop at the door. They prod me forward harshly. My balance is tested.

Camp odors—the stink of mice and wet logs, of moldy wool and bug spray.

Inside: an army cot, a chair.

One of the women—she's wearing a red shift, hood up—I see her profile (she's seventy at least, gray-haired); she tells me to lie down on the cot.

I lie down on the cot.

They back away from me.

The door closes.

I'm alone.

I hear a bolt sliding.

My eyes flick to the doorway. The dead bolt has been installed backward—locks from the outside. I have a keyhole, no key.

I think they're gone, but then the woman's voice speaks through the wood barrier.

"You have no idea how long it really takes to die," she says. A dry cackle that diminishes and tells me she's finally walking away.

They didn't bother to turn the light on. There's a fixture over the cot, a switch plate screwed on the wall beside the entrance. I don't even know if the camp has electricity. But I'm sealed up in cabin number 4. The single window boarded like all the rest. The door shut. A sword of sunlight thrusts underneath. My room, above and around me, is a cup overturned and trapping the dark. Quiet except for the mice. They must be numerous and bold. I feel a furry contact on my calf. I kick my legs.

I count back from one hundred. Breathe in through my nose and out through my mouth. My head aches where I bashed the tree trunk coming down during my fall. It's cold lying here so still.

The door opens.

I don't even hear the lock disengage. It's a man, an enormous, bear-sized man, and he has his hands full. He leaves something in the chair. I notice a Harley-Davidson tattooed on his triceps. An Iron Cross on his sunburned neck.

He approaches the cot. Looks down on me.

Hairs show from every opening of his leather vest. His chest pumps and his nostrils flare. I smell onions, beer, sweat.

He presses his thumb into the muscle of my thigh.

"You're soft, bro."

His hand doesn't move. But I hear an unsnapping, the rasp of steel dragging against leather. His other hand—the knife catches the sun.

I'm going to scream.

I try rolling off the cot. He jams his thumb down, and pain shoots in two directions along my leg.

"Don't you move a muscle," he says.

He cuts my ropes.

I say nothing.

"Druid told me to tell you—get dressed."

He goes out, slamming the door behind him.

I run over. Twist the knob and push.

Locked.

Flip the switch. The light, at least, works.

Bear-man left me something folded in the chair—a pair of boxer shorts, a white shift. Sandals placed on top. I sniff the clothes. They smell like detergent. I put them on.

I survey my quarters.

Washbasin. Sink. The hot water spigot coughs dry. I turn and turn the handle. Nothing. The cold side rumbles, spews brown, then yellow water. It clears up. I smell rotten eggs, sulfur and iron. I drink. The toilet doesn't flush. The bowl clogged with cigarette butts, beer cans, and an army of black ants. Tank lid cracked, duct-taped. I take the tape off. Heft the lid. I could use this bigger piece as a weapon.

It's heavy, the broken edge feels sharp.

Mice droppings sprinkled along the floor like chocolate jimmies. I'm smashing them with my sandals as I pace.

Under the cot, I discover a small boat fashioned from aluminum foil, a box of incense sticks, and a book of matches. Open the book. Tuck it into the waistband of my boxers. I'm dying for a smoke. Waiting and smoking go well together. I make due with waiting alone.

I see my sword of sunlight turn into a gold bar. The bar gradually disappears.

Hours, half a day passes. What's keeping them?

The bottom of the door is my new window.

They're doing something out there. Footsteps. Words, whispers.

Quickly, I wedge the desk chair under the doorknob.

I watch, amazed, as they insert an elastic tube under the door. I'm so surprised, I almost shout. A soft hiss emanates from the tube mouth. I place the flat of my palm above it. Feel the air disturbed: a constant pressurized flow. The taste on my lips is medicinal. Taps deep memories of clinical settings—dentist chairs, operating rooms . . .

My eyes start to burn. I squeeze them closed. My throat tickles. My brain goes sluggish, woozy. Are they gassing me? Cover my face with my sleeve.

I pinch the tube.

The hissing stops.

More whispers. A tug on the elastic.

I hold. Clamp my finger and thumb and *hold.*

Someone outside the door touches my hand.

I jump back.

See the person's—a man's—fingers wriggle under the door. Impossibly long, they're clawing up, higher and higher, on my side of the wood. Gouging great curled strips out of the door plank. A twitch of gold: the oval signet—Graham Morick's ring, his hand.

The crack under the door gapes. Spreading. Pink light floods underneath, and irrational as it may be, I know that Morick—he's coming through that space.

I grab the broken tank lid. Kneel. Fix my eyes on those wriggling fingers.

Rear back with everything I have and . . .

Chop.

I hear a shriek.

Grab for the bloody damaged hand, the mangled fingertips. Before he can pull back, I pin the meat of his hand with my own.

The sharpest edge of the tank lid—I press it down, put all my weight, my anger, my fear, on the first joint of his two broken fingertips. And I carve. Until the porcelain edge breaks and the lid snaps apart in my hands.

Many voices are screaming curses. Fists thump the wall. Kicks.

The chair I wedged under the doorknob.

It won't stop them. It may slow them down.

They try to swing inward, but the chair blocks their immediate entry. I lean my shoulder next to the lock, dig in my heels.

A chair leg falls away. Spindles splinter.

Banging.

They surge against the door and me.

The door will split from its hinges. I know this.

It's splitting now.

Screws drop like bullets.

I hold my ground. Legs and back muscles tensed.

The destruction of the door halts.

The voices go away.

They must've drugged me. Anesthetized—I'm both nauseated and silly. That gas from the tube was my poison. Forget everything I've ever known about time. Time, my ability to judge its passage, has liquefied. Fast slow. Slow fast. My brain fumbles, unable to adjust and find the rhythm of what I've called reality.

But the blood is real.

Sticky, black pudding pools between my knees. The two fingertips I see in the middle of the pudding are real. Under the chair, yes. Two of them.

One.

Two.

I admit that I am unable to suppress a childish giggle in the sea of this awful nightmare, because, upon first sight of the severed digits, I recall the children's song "Where Is Thumbkin?" I laugh from my belly.

Here are Pointer and Tallman.

How are you today, sir?

I have something dreadful I need to do.

Feast on the living.

I put the smaller one in my mouth. The fingernail is no different from a fish scale—bad liar in me trying to fool myself—it's a broken crab shell, an unpeeled shrimp, a remnant of exoskeleton scratching my tongue. I gag. Spit it out on the floor. I'm hyperventilating. Sweating gobs. My face greasy. I'm in need of a shower, a good soapy wash that drains the hot water, if there is any, from the camp. Press my palm firmly against my sternum and feel quaking. Pick the finger up. Pop it in my mouth. Run to the sink tap. Scoop water past my lips. Drink, drink. The tip swirls, logrolls, will not go down. Spit. I catch my reflection in the mirror.

Madman.

It's all right, okay. A madman can do this. I throw it back. Horse pill. Hoodoo vitamin. Black magic vs. black magic.

Fight Morick.

Big swallow.

Don't stick in my throat. Pray. No choking.

I've done it.

Where is Tallman?

I spin around, hunch over.

Here I am, here I am. There on the floor. He's a bigger meal, of course. Swear finger. But I'm hungry for him.

They kick in the door. The chair shatters.

Morick standing in the middle. Ashen. His hand wrapped in a towel. I see him pull back sharply after taking one look at my eyes. A thrall bends to retrieve the severed digit.

"Where's the other one?" the thrall asks me. He's freckled, bearded, tonsured.

I rub big circles over my stomach.

How are you today, sir?

Very well, I thank you.

Run away.

Run away.

The thrall steps forward. I'm not budging. From the folds of his cassock, he produces a huge, blocky plastic gun. Die? I'm prepared to die. Try and kill me. Loud click and an electric chattering. The Taser fishhooks drill me in the right pectoral. I scream as I fall over.

Morick above me . . .

Laughing.

Chapter 26

A basketball backboard mounted on a pole, they've removed the hoop and net. One of the thralls must be an artist. The backboard is painted. Depicting a snake's head, but it's Graham's face—looks just like him too. Two followers hold me in place, as a third straps me to the pole. I face outward. My feet balance on the sand-filled base. Once I'm secured—and they've done a fine job, I can hardly breathe under the straps—they lean me back and push me, pole and all, up a ramp into the lodge.

They aren't taking any chances. I have two guards: Bear-man and a young Hispanic with cornrows, his cheeks hatched with scar tissue. I hear singing outside the lodge. Through the open doorway—smoke billows, torches pass, the chants of the thralls begin. The lodge room is spacious. Their song echoes.

My guards have acolyte duty.

The room is studded with candles. One by one, they light them. No folding chairs to set out. But crates upended and a ring of large stones—these are the seats for the ceremony. I focus on the altar. Misshapen, cobbled together, it's a dome of broken slabs. Takes me a minute to realize they are gravestones. The thralls—they stole them and brought them here.

I'm next to the altar.

I'll have an unobstructed view of the proceedings.

The chants grow faster, more insistent.

raham Morick leads them inside.

The room fills. An iron bar crosses the door. Thralls organize themselves by shift color. Those who wore street clothes now don robes. Graham cloaks himself in black velvet. It is his father's old vestment. I recognize it as the dressing Aubrey wore to perform the Cloven Print.

Graham steps right up to me.

He says, in a hushed voice only he and I can hear, "You're a trained observer. Eager to look. Yet you are unprepared to see. I am going to give you the gift of sight." He punches me in the stomach. His lips fasten to my ear. "I meant to ask you something. How did I taste?"

I couldn't answer him if I wanted to.

Graham positions himself at the altar. Hidden behind the unearthed cemetery markers, he bends and lifts something from the floor. He hikes his robe. He's wearing a tool belt. He slides the object from the floor into a holster on the belt. Adjusting his wardrobe, smiling, he raises both arms. I notice his bandaged hand, a white paw.

The thralls quiet. They bow.

A new song—much slower, deeper—reverberates around us.

I hear a second sound under it, originating from outside the lodge—a gas-powered engine. Someone has switched on a generator. Graham doesn't react. He's expecting it.

"Come, my dung beetle," he says, motioning to the crowd.

He moves around to the front of the altar.

Trailing him are two spiral cords.

"I am calling you forward," he says.

A thrall moves up from a stone seat on the floor.

"Nearer to me, come now." Morick retrieves a candle stand from the corner. He sets it down. He hikes his vestments. His cock twitches above the candle flame. Thrall eyes rivet to his every move. The flame gutters, fizzles as he rubs saliva with rapid splitting fingers around his uncircumcised phallus. His groin is shaven. He peels back his foreskin.

Firelight: he is magenta.

He speaks directly to the risen thrall. "You are a death hole, putrid soulless larva, an endless grave into which I will pour my nothingness. Show yourself."

It's Regina Hoffman. She pulls her shift off. The woman in the red hood who spoke to me takes it from her.

Regina's legs quiver. She's aroused, in terror. Her skin shines.

Graham places his wounded paw on her head.

"Are you to be gathered?"

"I am," she says.

The singing stops.

So we can listen.

I watch the thralls. They ready themselves like sprinters at the starting blocks.

Graham, in a three-part flourish, draws his weapon, shows the congregation, and places the weapon in contact with Regina's head.

I close my eyes.

Hearing and not seeing may be worse, because I do see them even without looking.

Graham fulfills his promise to me—the gift of sight.

The thralls greet their debasement open-armed,

He orchestrates them, instructing them as they frenzy.

And the whole time, like punctuation to his orders—I hear and see it—the nail gun going off.

ear-man wheels me from the lodge. The smell of blood hangs in our wake. He leaves me in the courtyard. The others divide up. I hear cabin doors close. Vehicles drive away, headlights killed, down the blackened road. They do not return. The night is frigid and tangy with smoldering fires. It rains. The rain stops.

I watch the forest.

The next day comes and goes. The camp appears abandoned.

I scream and scream . . .

This may be their method—to have me die of thirst and exposure.

The sun sets. I don't even see the dogs around.

he weather report says frost tonight."

Graham stands in front of me, drinking orange juice from a glass.

"What happened to Robyn?" I ask.

He ignores me. He sips.

He's walking away. I turn my head and try to follow.

"No, wait," I say.

I'm tipping backward on my pole. His bandaged hand resting on my shoulder, he pushes me past the cabins. We enter a path leading into the woods.

"Are you taking me to see her? Where are we going?"

We haven't gone far. I see a shed with a padlocked door.

"Is she here?" I ask.

He brings me upright. The jingle of keys. He opens the lock, pulls the chain free.

Graham steers me into the shed.

From the darkness outdoors, he's taken me to the confinement of this shed. My eyes won't adjust. There isn't enough available light. He stands the pole straight.

"Tell me what you did to her," I say.

He walks out.

I see a light erratically swinging along the path.

Graham—he has a lantern hanging from the wrist of his good hand. The glass of orange juice refilled to the brim.

He puts the glass to my mouth.

I clamp my lips shut.

"Really," he says. "If I wanted to kill you, I would, you know." He puts the lantern and the glass on a workbench. The shed holds a few lawn tools, cardboard boxes full of empty cans and bottles, and a pallet of bagged dog food. In the dirt, a grouping of loose rocks set out in a pattern a child might arrange.

Nothing more.

Graham's hair is messed. He stinks of incense, sex, and beer. His eyes are tired. He hangs the lantern. He rubs his good hand on his jeans, blows on it. I see his breath. He picks up the juice and drinks half.

"Do you want any juice or don't you?" he asks.

I nod.

He gently tilts the glass until I've drained its contents. The juice tastes fine—cool and sweet. I want more.

After I've finished, he exits the shed. He props the shed door open with a shovel.

Then he's gone.

He's away for a long time. I wonder if he's coming back or if he went to bed.

Soon after I have that thought, Graham visits me again. He's carrying a burlap sack. He opens the neck of the sack and lays it on the shed's dirt floor.

When I look down, I see a burnt stick lying on the ground. The end of the stick remains concealed in the bag.

"What is that?"

He closes the door. I hear the chain sliding against the wood. Links passing through the iron latch. There is a bright metallic snick as Graham locks the padlock and a thud as he lets it go from his hand.

The burnt stick on the floor moves.

Drawing itself out of the bag.

I see it is a live snake. Perhaps nine feet long, slender. Its charcoal body slips mercurially through the grouping of stones. I want to pull my feet up but can't. The straps at my knees are too tight. I try to keep still. Stillness may save me.

The snake flicks his tongue to test the air. It is a long, thin tongue, deeply forked, and the snake whips it out, sucks it back into his mouth like a noodle. Over and over.

Graham's voice: "That's a black mamba, Jase. One of the most venomous snakes in the world. Very long fangs. Even if I had a stockpile of antivenin, and I don't, it would be ineffective in saving your life. Mambas can kill with a drop or two. But he's swollen with venom. They tend to inflict multiple bites. Death by mamba isn't supposed to be all bad. Feels placid, I'm told. Toxins attack the heart and brain simultaneously. He's South African. This cold weather will kill him. He can't be happy about that. You aren't, are you? Knowing you'll be dead soon."

I don't answer. I'm afraid to make a sound.

"Lysergic acid diethylamide. Old-fashioned LSD. I put it in our juice. I've given the snake some too."

The top of my head feels rubbery, as if it's inflating.

"Good night," Morick says. "It should be an interesting one."

He is fast. Faster than my eyes. One second he's in the corner, and the next he's near the door. I can't tell the difference between the snake and the snake's shadow. Which is closer to me? He knocks along the wallboard. I'm praying for him to find a hole, a cranny he can disappear into. He lashes into a stack of empty soup cans. They tumble. I hear scraping, scratching, and then a sound like rubble pouring. A cloud of dirt stirs. The grouping of rocks lying in the dirt—he weaves between them. Angry.

He pauses.

Is he *thinking*? Am I? Are the drugs taking effect?

He slips silently to my right. Under my field of vision.

I wait for him. Is the acid working on me? I don't know. But this is happening. The snake and I share this space. I don't want to lose control of myself. I don't want to provoke him. My body grows hot. I am fighting to stay focused. Keep still. Every object appears clearly to me as if I'm staring through a just-washed window.

There he is.

The snake raises the front of his body. He levitates off the dirt floor. His head floating, bobbing slightly, angled toward my left shoulder—level with my throat.

Our eyes meet.

How can I not look at him?

Shaking, the both of us. His hood flaring as he opens his mouth to show me.

I'm expecting the inside to be pink.

I stare into a cavity of wet and inky blackness.

Behold, Man, why I am given this name. Black mamba.

I think if I yell, he will strike. If I breathe, he will strike. If I blink, he will strike.

Not my face. I'm bargaining with him, mind to mind. *Not my eyes, please.*

He is turning like a monstrous marionette.

He strikes.

I do not feel it.

I am not his victim.

Chapter 27

It takes hours, most of the night, and I watch it go down. The snake swallows the field mouse. The dying mouse progresses through the narrow chamber of his killer's digestive tract. I wonder when exactly he dies, when his fear and perceptions turn off. The snake retreats to the farthest corner of our room; curls upon himself—himself.

I continue to be in great danger.

But the snake and I are biding our time.

I wasn't given any acid. I doubt my South African companion was either.

Fear is our drug.

Exhaustion. I let the straps hold my weight.

Morick enters the shed, going slowly, carrying a hook and long-handled bag. His eyes move. His head does not. He finds the snake. Without hesitation, he drops him into the bag and closes it.

"You look rested," he says.

I can feel the flesh hanging off my skull like melted wax. My mouth, tongue, throat—dried out. Speech is unobtainable.

"You are a special man, Jase." He opens his palm. Two capsules.

I gobble them.

"That should keep you going. We've got a long day ahead of us."

He carries me out. My limbs are floppy. I cannot fight. I go along. He drops me beside him in a Jeep. A bottle of Gatorade is between the seats. He opens it for me, and I gulp it down. I see the bandage on his hand is fresh, snowy. I want to crush those stumps in my fist and hear him scream. Instead, I watch the trees hunching over us as we drive underneath them. The forest is dense, kaleidoscopic at this speed. I can't run. My unbound muscles burn and cramp. My head lolls against the seat.

"Please don't vomit in my Jeep," he says.

We veer off the road onto a lesser passage cut into the forest. The Jeep settles into two ruts. Our progress slows. The tires throw dirt. I could leap out here. Make my break for the heavy timber.

One thing stops me: a rifle in a scabbard, mounted next to the driver's seat. If Graham can shoot, and I have no reason to think he can't, he'd put a slug between my shoulders before I reach a hundred yards. My head is clearing, but I'm uncertain my legs are up to functioning.

"I was with Una when she died," I say.

"Oh, I know that," he says.

"She was your daughter?"

"Daughter and sister. I can't believe she told you."

"Your mother told me."

"That figures. She's always hated me, hated my power."

"I've seen the film of the Cloven Print."

"Excellent. That saves me from giving you a tutorial."

"Why did Una kidnap her own children?"

"Good question, Jase. The pills must be kicking in."

The ruts lead down into a valley. I notice a pile of animal scat ahead, steaming between the ruts.

"That's bear shit," Graham says. "These woods are full of bears. It's why I keep the rifle handy. Black bears. They're not as cuddly as they look. Tad always reminded me of a dumb bear. Una wasn't trying to fool Tad. No challenge in that. She was trying to fool me. Tad's perversion, his cameras . . . Una's stunt wearing that amateurish disguise . . . She wanted me to believe Father Byron had snatched my progeny. To keep them from achieving their destiny. As if he and his gaggle were capable of executing something of that magnitude. All talk that priest. All priests as a matter of fact."

I spot an outcropping of gray rock.

We slow.

Graham says, "Tad was chosen. By us. Me, I should say. I sent them the snake wine as a wedding present. Go and make me some babies. Tad was a glorified sperm donor, not a speck more. The boys were bred for this. Tad was disposable. I planned to gather him when the time came."

"Did you?"

"No, it was Una who talked him out that particular window."

I put the pieces he's given me together. "Una prepped the boys for their part in the Cloven Print. But she changed her mind. They were her children. She couldn't go through with it. Regina was innocent. You got to her later. Brainwashed her into thinking she stood to gain more with you than not. She brought along Nathan, lured Father Byron. Am I right?"

"Close enough."

He turns off the Jeep's engine. We sit there, listening to birdsong.

"Una's mind broke," he continues. "Mother's genes—she's mad as a March hare. Una forgot why she loved the boys. It was because of what they would become someday, I reminded her. Yet she became confused and thought it was for what they are now. They're only boys."

"How did you get them back?"

"I took them; that's how. Una could never stand up to me. After all, I am her *father*. She called me that night in Dublin. You were passed out on her couch. She wanted me to tell her what to do. I told her. 'Shoot him. Then shoot yourself.' It didn't work out though. Not exactly."

"I didn't kill her."

"I would admire you more if you had. Una was no longer useful. Her boys are her legacy. I'll make them significant. In and through the Cloven Print, we shall be Eternal."

He believes. This is no act of showmanship. Morick has a dark faith. I study the terrain. There's a large, boarded mouth in the gray rock.

"What is this place?"

As if he didn't hear me: "The boys are ready. I am ready. You were kind enough to supply a replacement for Una. We are closer than ever. Robyn Matchfrost will usher in the new epoch at my left side. I adore her."

Graham swings out of his seat. He takes the rifle and points the barrel at the boards in the rock. "That, Jase, is a gold mine."

He said her name. It's true then. Not my delusion. Robyn's here. She's with the boys, and with Graham, in every aspect.

"Let's go for a walk," he says.

We'll do the Cloven Print down there. Tonight. I built the gallows. No margin for error. The thralls are coming back to the roost. High spirits. We are all in high spirits." He shakes his rifle in the air. "The Maltzes owned this gold mine, the Fistula camp used to be theirs. They sold. The new owners turned it into a fishing camp. They used to dump their garbage down in this mine. We need to watch for bears."

"Are the camp owners thralls?"

"No. I had to convince them to give me the property."

I'm sure he did.

"Sleep, but we must wake ourselves," he says.

I follow him to the head of the mineshaft.

In the shade, I feel the cold of the surrounding rock. Graham sits on an overturned wheelbarrow. He aims his gaze down the shaft. When he speaks, his voice booms into the chasm.

"I envy you and Robyn. Truly, I do. You'll stand witness to the Cloven Print. Think about it—the most significant magical feat of the last thousand years. I'd like you to look after me, Jase. Once the ritual has taken place, I'll be inside one of the boys, Shane, Liam—whichever boy. But he will be me. I won't be inside forever, mind you. Transformations take time. You and Robyn will be my caretakers. Small families are the best. How does that sound?"

He's a liar. I've watched him kill two people. He'll kill me too.

Finished making his pitch, his brow twists into furrows. As if I've been the one trying to sell him on this concept of partnership. But I've got nothing to sell. I am silent. He wants something more, a sign of agreement.

"Living is better than dying, no?" he asks me.

"Yes, it is."

"Good man. Now back to the Jeep. I'll take you to visit Robyn and the boys."

We're driving to the camp. The same ruts, the same road. I don't understand. I thought Graham and I were alone here after the thralls dispersed.

He parks in front of the lodge.

"Cabin number one," he says.

"Robyn and the boys are in cabin number one?"

He nods. "I'll wait here. Don't worry, I won't rush you. But my slaves are coming. We need to make the last preparations. Robyn will be glad to see you. Go on. Talk to her. Say hello to the boys. I don't want them to see me right before the ritual. Bad luck."

The door to cabin 1. This dead bolt has been installed correctly. Robyn, if she's inside, is no prisoner. I knock.

Robyn says, "Come in."

Chapter 28

Shane and Liam are the first to greet me. Big eyes filled with expectation. I open the door to a roomful of toys. Many more, in boxes, stacked against the wall. Children's books crammed into a bookshelf, crayons, blocks . . . two child-sized beds, equipped with guardrails. A single bed beside them—Robyn's—I see her nightgown and slippers. I smell her. Hear the sound of water running. She's washing her hands. Shane and Liam are drinking from sippy cups. Eating crackers. The floor is carpeted and covered in crumbs.

"I tried to get the boys to sleep. But they're so excited."

Robyn walks out of the bathroom.

She looks good. Her face scrubbed clean, her hair in a braid. She's smiling. Her eyesight is weak, but she knows my shape, my smell.

"Jase, you're here!"

She runs to me.

Graham's voice behind me—he lied about staying out—says, "I told you I'd fetch him. I promised, and I delivered."

I feel Robyn's tears against my cheek, and my own.

"I didn't think you'd actually do it, Graham. Not actually bring Jase . . ."

She's squeezing me.

The boys tug at her legs.

"Shane and Liam, this is Jase. I told you about him. He's been looking for you."

I pull Robyn close, whisper to her, "You have to help me. He's crazy. He's going to kill the boys."

Robyn releases me.

Says nothing.

"Jase has agreed to help us," Graham says.

"He has?" Robyn asks. "Well, I knew he would."

"Everyone will be arriving soon. Don't want to break up this reunion but . . ."

Robyn stares at me. I wonder what she sees. The foggy configuration of a man. Not long ago, I was her lover. Her partner. Now am I a friend or an enemy?

Once the boys see Graham, they forget about me.

"A book! A book!" one of the boys shouts.

Graham crouches and the boys climb on him.

"Kiss Papa, Liam."

The boy on Graham's right knee kisses him.

"A book, Papa," Shane says. He rubs his head into the crook of Graham's elbow.

Graham reaches to the bookshelf, chooses a volume he wrote.

"You want to hear about the snaky?"

Liam and Shane settle in his lap. He has no trouble telling them apart, I realize. Quick study: Liam is the fairer of the two. He has a small dimple in his chin. Otherwise the boys are identical. Has he already chosen one for sacrifice?

After he's finished their story, he tickles them.

I'm looking at Robyn, searching her response for a clue, when Graham says, "Hey, Jase, will you look at this?"

Liam and Shane hold their arms out in front of their chests. Their stubby fingers don't have the dexterity, but it's the effort that excites Graham.

They're making little cloven hooves. Showing me who they are, what he has destined them to be. It is obscene.

"Time for you two to take a nap," he says.

G raham shows me to cabin 6. He tells me, "You'll find food in the refrigerator. Hot water. You can freshen up. I'm counting on you. Robyn, the boys, and I, we all are hoping for the best. No one yearns for disappointment. I know your strength. And, later this evening I want you to share in the power. The thralls will accept you as one of their own. Don't be afraid. We are together."

"Together," I say.

"I have to lock you in."

"I understand."

"Thank you for cooperating." He makes the hand sign, the presentation of hooves.

I do my best to reciprocate.

D espite the upgraded accommodations, I am caged. I don't touch any of the food. If Robyn helps me, we can make it. If she doesn't, we will die.

Morick's slaves arrive in a flood.

They are loud, bristling. Laughter volleys throughout the camp like gunfire. Their exuberance cannot be contained.

How many will be *gathered* in honor of the Cloven Print?

I don't fear for them.

And I don't fear them either.

T he chanting commences. On this night, Morick gives the thralls a surprise: the last Cloven Print recording of him and Griffin singing with their father. Broadcast through loudspeakers.

I press my hands over my ears.

The crowd moves past my cabin.

They walk to the gold mine.

Robyn.

I am lost.

A quiet knock.

"Jase," Robyn says. "Do you hear me?"

On my feet, ear flush to the door. "I'm locked in."

"I have a key." She asks me first to listen. "Down by the pier. There's a boat waiting for you. The motor is gassed. Follow along the bay. When you make it to open water, turn south. Go directly across the main lake. You'll find houses. Make it that far and you're safe. You don't have much time. They'll be coming for us."

"Please open the door."

"Promise me you'll do as I say."

"All right, let's go."

"I'm not going."

"What?"

"I'm staying here with the boys."

"No."

"They need me."

"We're taking them with us."

"That would be wrong. This night is for them, not only for Graham."

I pound on the door. "You can't stay. They'll slaughter you. All of you."

"I'm their new mother. I see the situation differently."

"You're murdering them."

"No one's murdering these boys. Graham and I have talked to no end—"

"I've watched Aubrey's tape."

She doesn't deny what the tape reveals. She's watched it too. The particulars of the Cloven Print are no secret. She is well acquainted with the Morick legacy. "Graham isn't Aubrey," she says. "Shane and Liam are the mirrorrorrim. They will bridge two realities. Aubrey's ego undervalued the importance of the mirrorrorrim to the ritual's success. The splitting of the mage is essential to his reorganization. Power emerges from the new dualism and destroying one fundamental entity—" She cuts herself off, sighs, as if her exegesis is all too much for me to comprehend. As if she's argued this point before and lost. Exasperated, she says, "I will never let Graham hurt these boys."

"He will."

"We can't go with you."

I see a key slide under the door.

Pick it up. Plug it into the lock and turn.

I'm out.

The remnants of the thralls' bonfire—a dome of heat, the closest treetops are singed black. Ashes, flakes like snow, whirl around me.

She's gone.

R obyn's told me the truth. I find a rowboat tied to the end of the dilapidated pier. Carefully, I inch my way to it. Maneuver inside. There's an outboard motor, ten-horse Mercury, and a heavy-duty portable gas tank. I lift the tank. At least five gallons—it's enough to get me as far as I need to go, with extra fuel to spare.

I disengage the tank.

The matches I found under the cot—they're still tucked in my waistband, damp, but I only need one to light.

Burn the camp. It's the only choice I have.

The houses—those people living on the other side of the lake—they will see the flames and smoke. They'll call for help. Graham can't have his ritual.

Not with a crowd of rescuers speeding down the Fistula road.

The tank bangs heavily against my knee. I begin my way uphill to the cabins.

A boat shack nestled beside the pier—I passed it once and never noticed it. I set down my flammables and push the door—it's open. More gasoline. Notice the smell instantly. This must be where they stored the former outfitter's supplies. I see splintered oars, bait buckets, fishing nets, tackle, life vests . . .

Grab four vests and the tank. Run back to the boat. Shuffle along the slick, warped boards until I'm near the motor. Toss the vests between the seats. Reach in with the tank. Kneeling in the dark, I reattach by feel the outboard's fuel line to the tank clamp. Robyn and the boys are coming with me. If I can find them, I'll force her aboard. Knock her unconscious, if it comes to that.

Back outside the shack, I'm dragging two metal cans filled with gas. Up we go.

It's easier walking with a can in each hand. But my shoulder sockets are ripping loose. My legs tremble.

To the top of the hill where . . .

All's quiet.

Cabin 1. Locked. I bang on the door. Silence on the other side. Not Robyn begging me to go away. Not the startled boys crying out. They aren't here. She could've taken them to the gold mine. The boys might've been at the mine when Robyn slipped me the key. I don't know. I don't have time to figure it out.

Start my pouring at the lodge. Soak the steps, the outer walls. I make a circle and let the foundation be my guide. Use up the first can. Throw it away. Unscrew the second can. Stumble. Drench my feet and the bottom of my shift. Going slower now, I don't want to waste a drop. Ring around each cabin. Measure my splashes so I don't run thin, not before I've finished dripping perimeters of soon-to-be fire.

All done except for cabin 1. If Robyn and the boys are in there, hiding from me, keeping their silence . . . I can't bring myself to torch it.

For the rest of this place I want an inferno.

Strike a match for the Druid's lodge. The first few paper matches fall apart in my fingers. Feel the panic creep across my chest. If I can't light this, then what?

No need to worry.

A bud of flame—I cup it. Hold my breath so I don't blow the thing out.

I light the lodge steps.

Weathered wood catches fast, and the entire camp is a tinderbox. No alarms. No extinguishers. Nothing to stop what I've started.

Steal an unburned stake from the thrall's bonfire pit. I tap it on the steps and the fire walks up like a trained dog. Now it's almost easy.

I transform the grounds into a circus of oranges, yellows, reds.

Crackling heat.

I wait for Robyn.

She knows I'm down here in the boat. Knows I want her and the boys.

If she sees the blaze . . . she's smart. She'll come with me.

I hear cries.

Someone running . . . not Robyn . . . one of the thralls, in red . . . the old woman.

Robyn can overpower her. She'll make it.

My last can, a tiny pool of gas swishes at the bottom, I trail its stain down the length of the pier. I don't want any followers . . .

Dry my fingers on my shift.

The matches ready in my hand.

I've waited too long. The thralls are scattered in the camp. Trying to control the fire. They won't be able to do anything. They need buckets and hoses. Water. They'll come down to the lake to get water.

The best I can do for Robyn and the boys is to leave. Bring others back to the camp with me. Police. Fire. Ambulances. Witnesses.

I pull the starter cord on the motor. Nothing happens. Pull again. A sputter, a dry cough that promises nothing. I pull again. The engine starts. Dies. I check the throttle. Repeat the same rhythm of failure. Cough. Sputter. Die out. The motor has been sitting too long in the shack. The gas is old, the oil mix wrong. I pull. Nothing. Check the throttle. The oil-mix knob pops off, rolls under my seat. I run my hand until I touch the fuel line. Test the connections. I pump the bulb in the fuel line. Yes. The fuel line has air in it. I squeeze the bulb until it turns hard.

Pull.

The engine belches smoke. But it's running. Chugging. I adjust the throttle. Smooth out the idle.

A rock sails over my head. Eyes up, on the shore, the camp engulfed. Bear-man throwing rocks at me. He yells out. He lumbers downhill and calls other to join him.

I light the last of the matches, set the book on fire. I drop it on the spill along the pier. The pier burns.

I open the throttle and gun it.

The boat kicks.

I almost pitch out into the cold lake. The boat swings hard into the side of the pier. My aluminum hull slaps the pilings. Smoke in my face, in my throat. Gun it. A guttural roar but no progress made.

Untie the rope, fool. The bow, you're tied to the pier.

I put the motor in neutral. Crawl over a bench seat. Throw the life vests out of my way. Get my hands on the rope. It's tight, wet, stiff as cable. I need slack.

I take hold of a piling.

The pier burns. Thralls jump into the water now, wading.

I unwind the rope. Heat on my hands. The rope burns. I drop it.

Reach backward, fall backward, grab for the throttle.

D eeper water under me—I follow the main channel of the bay. The sky lit. The forest in flames, and the Fistula camp succumbs, crashes in on itself. Smoke pumps gray cotton into the night sky.

Entering the main lake, I lose sight of the rocky shore. I trust Robyn and turn south. Rectangles of lamplight nestled among the trees. A red dot blinks on the horizon, a tower. I make that light my beacon.

The stink of gas clings to me.

I'm gliding over water, the air filling the shell of my boat, but still the harsh throat-grapple of melting rubber thickens against my chest.

The heat.

My fuel line is melting—the rubber burning underneath my seat, at my ankles. The rope tied to the bow has burned down like a fuse. I see it too late. Flames leap around my shift.

My legs grilled. I stand and the fire stands.

I jump overboard. Flip the boat, my mind says. The water is too cold for survival. But I'm hurt and wet and the motor's gunning and the boat flies away from me.

The boat burns. I freeze. I'm choking on lake water and oil. I perish by fire. I die by water. I'm dying.

I paw at something—a vest bobbing on the waves.

Do I swim for it?

No, I don't.

See a grave opening up for me. Leave the vest. Dive in. Dive deep. Dive.

In, then out.

Chapter 29

O *ut.*
    The rescuers fish me out. The cold did as much to save me as to kill me. I'm alive. But barely, a Lazarus compelled from the tomb. Taken by helicopter. Through clouds. To a burn unit in St. Paul, Minnesota. Where I spend six weeks screaming. Where my skin comes off. Where I wish they'd left me to my quiet death under the lake. Hatred is enough to keep some men alive. Not me. I want to end it. But here I am. Pushed through and carried along.

    Reborn.

I am a sheet of blistering pain.
    After a while, I'm transferred closer to home. Treated to a long ambulance ride. I remember the ride Matthias's body took in Michigan. I haven't enjoyed his presence since the Fistula road. I have a rear view out the ambulance doors. The streets of Chicago. If the ambulance driver were to take two turns, we could drive past Robyn's condo, the office.

    But he stays on course.

    A new planet, but it's the same universe of hospitals. The ceaseless racket of machines and people as they carry out the business of living, recovering, dying.

The girls—my Syd and Sara—don't visit me. I get served an envelope of papers, their mother has initiative. She's seeking sole custody. I'm a danger. Negligent. Reckless. A bad father. When I was kidnapped at the Funspot, the girls were abandoned. They suffered trauma. My ex-wife's lawyers assert I'm involved with a cult. I am an unsuitable parent.

Fennessy visits. We don't talk. He talks. I lie there and listen.

The bodies at the lodge numbered more than a dozen; they have been autopsied. None of the men were over six feet. They had ten full fingers each. None of the women were natural blondes. Graham and Robyn escaped. I want to tell him they hid in the gold mine. They waited for the authorities to vacate. No children among the dead either.

Shane and Liam—they took the boys with them.

Imprisoned in my body, I fall into a torrid affair with morphine. Then the docs take my morphine away. I bounce around with prescription narcotics. Poor substitutes for the pleasure I've known. Find Percodan. I'm out of the hospital. My lower half resembles burnt plastic. I'm learning pain management. The pills mix nicely with Scotch. I can't afford the single malts: those sophisticated bottles the liquor store owners keep locked behind glass. My thirst requires quantity. One day I realize that I haven't talked to anyone, haven't had a real conversation, in months. I'm an addict and a drunk. I lie in bed. Spend my time wisely, though. Write the book in my head, the Boyles' story. I dictate it into a handheld tape recorder. Hire a typist. I start missing my appointments at the hospital. The drugs ferry me along. I meet a generous doctor who doesn't ask too many questions. He writes scripts. He gives me the names of two colleagues who'll do the same. I thank him for being humane, for supplying me with a new expensive habit I need to pay for. But I have formulated a plan.

And I execute.

Finish the book in a white-hot month. Write a teaser article, culled from the book. Sell both immediately. Buy a commando knife. Liquidate everything into cash. I need wheels, so I keep my car. My other possessions fit in a single carry-on bag. Destroy my credit cards. Spare one for emergencies. Burn the Rolodex. Break my lease. Open a numbered bank account. Buy a gun. Learn to shoot. I'm ready to die. The future is blank. Buy a box of razor blades. Clear my desk and existence has a Zen-like clarity. My life reduces to a hard kernel of truth. I have one final task.

It's twofold.

Find Graham Morick.

Kill him.

Chapter 30

All the best stories are about time. The horrible ones are too. I don't mark days passing or even seasons. Throw away my calendars. I keep a list of cities. False leads. Dead ends. The crossed-off places are a jumble in my head.

Barcelona. Bucharest. Wichita.

Miami. Dakar.

I break down in Chicago. Regroup. My funds are low. Book a room in a residence hotel. Here I don't seem out of place. We're wanderers housed under the same roof. No one pays us any attention, and that suits my needs. When people start to notice me, my comings and goings, I check out. I write a few serviceable pieces for my old employer, the *Chi-Town Monthly*. These are pity assignments, doled out like charity. The sad-eyed editors want to remember our old times together.

Then one day, Free Ray calls.

Free Ray is a huffer. He gets high sniffing various inhalants. I wrote an article about him once, before I ever the heard the name Boyle. I cared about Ray and wondered how he'd turned out. But that was a long time ago. I don't have room for him now. I try to cut him off. His words stop me cold.

He says, "Those missing kids you wrote a book about? Hey, man, check this out. I found those missing kids' graves."

I ask him where.

"Meet me," he says. "I'll show you."

On my drive, I'm trying to remember everything I ever knew about Free Ray. He has this dream. In it, he's always stoned. Ray wants to live his dream. He does this in the cheapest way possible. He digs up cans from the Dumpsters behind hardware stores, any place that carries paints or glues or solvents. Auto-body shops and service stations are on his milk run. He'll sniff a boosted gasoline container for days. Hide the thing and pour off the fuel into Pepsi cans. Rationing. If he's feeling energetic, he might even scratch together a few cents to add a quick trigger pull of unleaded. Carburetor cleaner. Octane boosters. Whatever. If it's in a can, he'll sample.

But it's paint supplies he prefers.

"As you may know, metallics are the class of the field." He educates me. "More toluene, which is what gets you fucked-up." Ray's personal favorite color, simple Krylon gold, is getting harder to come by. He is a connoisseur of Krylon. "Let the skater kids make fun of me. I'm an ancient. Been doing this shit for*ever*." The marble rattling inside the cylinder gives him comfort.

Free Ray's hair is greasy maple taffy. Caught up in one of his reveries, he touched his head with bleach-dampened fingers. "Sometime, somewhere, man. Can't really be sure." But where he wiped, the hair color has gone away in streaks. Skunk-white racing stripes weave into his scalp. He wears a crocheted wool beanie on his head. Not to hide the dye job, because he's proud of that accident. The hat keeps Free Ray's ears toasty when the wind blows, and cool under a sunny blaze. But that's not its sole function. "Double duty," he says. Flashing me a bottle of nasal spray he's secreted away. Stowed up under the wool hat. Free Ray slides the sprayer out, plugs his vacant nostril with a filth-encrusted thumb, and squeezes while in he sucks a tremendous geyser of medicated vapor. He repeats this process hourly.

There's a constant rash lingering around his mouth. He attempts

with a narrow goatee. Doesn't work. Probably makes the
rse. Of course it itches. He can't stop himself from rub-
problem. Or it was.

interviews, the area of infection on Free Ray's face con-
. Scaly alterations multiply. He applies a thin layer of
ral puffy lesions. I look away as he does this.

s passed for both of us. I know it has for me. Yet I'm
another October's crisp, purpling dusk. Shane and
y dead. That's what brings me here. I need to be their
incensed with burning logs from unseen fires.
rest preserve's north parking lot.
rve isn't exactly a park, with swing sets and baseball
ooded valley near the airport that the county set
abitat and refuge from the city. A strip of prairie is
nce. Deer and squirrels live around here. Ignoring
ople feed and photograph the animals. They let

tly what you notice are the trees. A dense patch of
y pedestrian paths, a bike trail, and a serpentine
the grounds. Beyond the woods strip malls exist.
al estate. Low-rise apartments finish a close sec-
eserve, there isn't much green happening to the
erhead.
ome to hang chains across the entrance in an-
oing the opposite direction, finding their way
tched on their low beams. It's not yet dark, but
rancy gets tamped down. Everything blends.
r feels, somehow, closer. Gray time. I begin to
there, parking beside the picnic shelters, trail
frog ponds. I'm not alone.

ck to it. I slow-ride the curves all the way to
ement pillars keep me—if I had the sudden

241

urge—from demolishing a grove of junk trees and then launching ove
a steep embankment into the bottom of the valley. I pull the hand brak
Free Ray steps into my headlights, years evaporate, and, almost immed
ately, I notice the rash—thick, tomato red—contracted down to
oval. Like a lamprey's kiss on his dry, chewed lips.

Free Ray lives in the forest preserve woods. He used to sleep in an
Honda CRX. The car didn't run. But he could push it. You had to be
of the parking lot before nightfall. He'd cross the street and sleep u
dawn at a twenty-four-hour fast-food chicken place. Then he hurt
knee doing something. He's not certain. "Wonder what it was, du
Doesn't matter in the end, I guess," he philosophizes. But the CRX
towed. Free Ray scrounged a pup tent. Discovering the gift of mob
and feeling both blessed and paranoid, he moves his camp every ni
This way, he reasons, the preserve cops can't find him. They *can*
him of course, but that would mean effort and a couple extra gu
chase him down while they hauled off his shit from the campsite.
Ray never bothers regular citizens. Therefore, the cops leave him
Everyone's happy.

Until he finds the graves.

W hat took so long? You look old. Grew a beard, huh? It'll b
soon," Ray says. "We gotta move. I'm not playing around
there after sundown."

I hold out my freshly ripped-into pack of Marlboro Lights. F
can't say no. I offer the cupped flame from my lighter. He le
Glows orange. Those facial hollows deepen—he's a jack-o'-lant

He backs away. "Who's that?"

Furtive eyes. Ray's shoulders juke left, right, and left again.
ping invisible punches. Fists rise. Chin drops. Leaning way bac
the ropes.

"Easy," I say.

"C'mon. Pulling this shit on me."

I throw a glance behind me, but that's playacting. I know wh
sitting in the passenger seat of my beat-up car. I didn't bring

This is a graveyard search. I brought something better. The sun disappears below the horizon. Pink sky blushes through the park trees.

My passenger is gloomy. He's unwrapping a stick of Wrigley's spearmint, but before he's finished, he's up and on his feet walking over to us. Cop walk. We've all seen it, right? Well, maybe not if you're Joe Clean, living la vida oblivious, safely tucked away in the suburbs. But even then you've probably had a glimpse that instantly connects with your inner criminal. An angry flare vomits hot, jagged gold into your skull. Hands clamp to the steering wheel as your eyes cut sideways. You mark the approach in your wing mirror.

Fucking cops, you think.

His specter is upon us.

"No way," says Free Ray.

"He's worked this case from the beginning."

"No, no, no, no, nooooooo . . ." Free Ray starts a backward jog into the tree line.

Brendan Fennessy takes a long step forward, arm out, and snags Ray's elbow.

"Jase tells me you found the Boyle boys? That's big-time reward money heading your way, Ray-o."

Free Ray perks at this consideration. He shakes his arm. Fennessy cuts him loose.

"I'm doin' my part. Be a good citizen."

"Sure you are, Ray-o. I wouldn't have guessed otherwise. What charity you going to sign the check over to?"

"Check?"

I say, "The *reward* check. Detective Fennessy wants to know where you'll make your donation."

"The Help Ray Get High Fund," he says.

We're all laughing. It's not a happy sound. We're walking now. Strolling over to the woods. You spot us, you might imagine three buddies cracking a brew at the park, meeting up for an after-the-whistle bitch session. Arguing sports. Talking women. Or it could be simpler. We're only selling each other drugs.

Who would guess what we're really about to do?

To verify if Free Ray found the skeletons of two little boys snatched from their home. We're men on the brink. Fennessy's involvement in the Boyle case cost him dearly. Like me, his career of late is a series of gutter balls. And also like me, he's lost a partner. Free Ray? Free Ray lives on the brink.

We've entered the shade of trees.

I ask, "What have you got for us?"

On the glide, moving at a brisk pace, he says, "Little way to go before we're there. Isn't far. Closer than you'd think for burying a body."

Two bodies, I think. And I'm right about the body count. But I'm wrong about everything else.

Free Ray hunches his shoulders and dodges overhanging branches. He's guiding us along a deer path. I'm tucked close behind. Fennessy draws the flank. The detective is tense, quiet. The surroundings are doing a number on him. Given my history, you might think I'd hesitate. I should've adopted a new personal rule. Something along the lines of *Stay out of the woods.* But there's no rule. I go anywhere this story leads me. I can't deny my antenna. There's a vibe about this place. A hum. I'm onto it, same as Fennessy. But the vibe isn't saying danger.

Death.

I'm sensing we're in the proximity of death.

"Look out. Next bit is steep," Free Ray says.

He drops.

His hands grapple roots excavated by summer rains. He's sliding down on the seat of his jeans, controlling his progress with fingers latched to the root system, and avoiding the rocks that claw up from the dirt.

Free Ray is nimble. I understand for the first time that he's a forest dweller, a kind of homegrown aborigine of these parts.

Fennessy and I are having trouble with the slope. I've resigned myself to getting filthy and I'm moving faster. When I hit bottom, I look up. Fennessy's sweating and flushed. He's mumbling under his breath. He contorts to prevent his sports jacket from rubbing into the grime. Strikes the pose of a man who's taken an arrow freshly in the back. I hear a distinct rip. The fabric under his arm opens like a white mouth. Fennessy stares. Shoots me the bird. He has long, slender fingers.

I've always admired him as a cop and as a man.

We're experienced suckers. The detective and the writer—we've been chasing the same ghosts together. Acting separately, though often in parallel, we've employed our various skills and come up empty. We've both taken it in the neck too. Had our integrity questioned. Our credibility trashed. Past the tipping point, well, we are clearly there. Clearly. To our peers and maybe to ourselves—we're off the map.

Mudflat.

Valley floor. The land rises again a few yards beyond where we're standing.

Fallen leaves the colors of mice litter the ground, clenching as they undergo a preliminary stage of rot. Free Ray's found his mark. He crouches and beckons. I'm looking down as we approach him. My grandfather taught me how to read animal tracks up in Michigan. I've never put my knowledge to good use. The dried surface of the flat is a record. Ignoring the Reeboks Free Ray's wearing, I count dog, deer, and raccoon prints. If Fennessy thought Ray's claim was legit, he would have called in a forensics unit. They'd hang tape. Set a grid. We wouldn't be mucking around the scene. Erasing evidence with our feet.

But Fennessy didn't tell anybody where he was going this evening. He's off duty. Coming out here on the sly. Using personal time. Taking the necessary precautions against humiliation. This way he could be anywhere. Doing anything.

No one will ever know.

I don't call him on it. I'm following the same plan. Don't want the attention.

Let's just go and see.

We can stop and have a drink afterward. Heading to the forest preserve to meet Free Ray, Fennessy and I talked about the best places to get drunk around the airport. We were distracting each other. Helping.

That's why I called him. Why he came.

Free Ray's hopping up and down.

Toad, I think. He's found something. Then, *I hope it's them. The Boyles. I hope this phase is finally ending.* He kneels beside two large, irregular shapes sunken into the earth.

Free Ray shouts, "He stuck 'em in these old wells."

Concrete. Two slabs about the size of house doors. Mud-frosted. Cockeyed. A ridge of dark, almost purple, stuff is squeezing up between them. Their surfaces are deeply scored and cracked. The corner nearest Free Ray juts in upheaval.

"Wells?" Fennessy asks, his voice rising. He's circling the slabs. Staying outside. Not drawing too close.

I hear his heart beating. No, it's my heart. Superloud. The adrenaline gives me a twitchy body shake. I'm dry. Skittery. Holding my breath.

Fennessy shuffles in for a better look. Bends at the waist and inspects. The muscles in his face relax. He says, "These aren't wells. They're pit toilets. Look at the outline. These were the shitholes." He points. "Here? That's where the wall went, separating girls and boys. Outhouses. Okay? The county must've filled them with concrete. So kids wouldn't fall in."

Free Ray acts angry. He licks his palm and wipes saliva into the pitted block.

"Whadayacallit? Engraved? He engraved them. You're so smart, then explain the words. Do it, Inspector Gadget. Explain what it says right here in fucking stone."

The tension has left me. It's as if I've broken a fever. I feel renewed. I'm happy it isn't the Boyle boys dumped underground. I want them to get out of this alive. I watch Fennessy squat alongside our addict companion. The detective—he's about to put his arm around Ray but then changes his mind—silently pats the ground. He is relieved. We wasted time here, but that's not the worst thing in the world, is it?

Fennessy's attitude kicks in again. He adjusts his glasses to read Free Ray's spit-polished scripture. I'm there too, interested, peering over Fennessy's shoulder. The concrete is badly cratered. Pieces removed or pulverized back to sand. What remains is forked with fissures. A cone of burnt twigs is off to the side, and the scorches of blown fireworks. Serious damage has come by way of iron. Someone struck with great force. Testing a crowbar or a sledgehammer—whatever it was, whoever it was, possessed a goal of simple destruction. I'm guessing probably kids on a lark. It's fun to smash things, to burn them. I've done it. Ray's not lying about the engraving. The words are small and legible, not a stamp in the wet, original pour but a recent message painstakingly chiseled into the southern quadrant of these old toilets.

Fennessy intones the pulpit: "Reign in chaos eternal, O Great Deceiver, and bring us the darkness triumph . . . triumphant."

Heavy-metal prolixity. This blend of bombast and portentousness is gothic teenage stock-in-trade. Gobbledygook. You know the types: their uniform of overpriced concert T-shirts and dusters, fingernail polish and eyeliner. The only color is black. Verbal tics. Dirty hair falling over their eyes. They're riding a freight train of hormones and psychotropic drugs. Bored, lathered up, you know . . . sledgehammering kids. Easy to dismiss. Easy to forget. Cryptic is where they excel.

"*Triumphant* is spelled wrong." Fennessy taps the offending letter. "Should be an *a*, not an *e*."

"So what?" Free Ray asks.

"How far did you make it in school, Ray-o?" Fennessy asks.

"Eighth grade. Why?"

The detective raises an eyebrow.

"Aw, screw you, man." Free Ray throws a clod of dirt into the distance, toward the deer path. "There's more writing under the mud. I didn't scrape it clean 'cause I thought it might be, like, evidentiary."

"Evidentiary? Hear that, Mr. Deering?"

I light a cigarette. No need to worry about contaminating any crime scene. If we keep ruling out these avenues, all the dead ends, then maybe eventually we'll catch a break. Tonight, after we settle on a bar, I'll buy the first couple rounds. That'll put Fennessy in a better mood.

"This is really excellent police work, Ray-o. You missed your calling."

Free Ray gives the cop his space.

I join Fennessy over by the slabs.

How exactly does Ray know there's writing *under* the mud?

Sparrows land and flutter back to the trees.

Land and flutter.

Higher in the trees.

Safety.

Fennessy is holding his right hand in his lap as if he's been bitten.

"You okay?"

His hands are dirty. The moons of his nails are black. He's staring at the uncovered section of slab. He's blinking. Lips parted.

He grabs my wrist and pulls me down.

I see the slab.

MIRRORRORRIM

Every crime has secrets. For something to be a secret, all you need is a person who knows and everybody else. Cops work around secrets. They find them. They crack them. Some they keep. I am the only member of the press who knows about *mirrorrorrim*.

Under the inscription, a flap of green tarp is showing. A corner. Fennessy elbows me aside. He grabs the tarp and hauls it up. Loose dirt is falling away, crumbling under him. The top layer of soil disappears and we see a sheet of cheap plywood, the kind used to board up vacant businesses. Ray was standing on it the whole time. Fennessy tosses the tarp. He and I take opposite sides. We flip the board over. Standing astride a hole in the ground. A grave. It's empty. We're getting close to the water table way down here in this mud valley. The bottom of the grave is filled with leaves, swamped with mocha water. Smells like coins.

"Where's Free Ray?" Fennessy asks. He unsnaps the holster on his belt.

Ray picked a tree to hide behind.

It's a special tree. Hollow. He needs this tree. He put something up inside it.

We're turning.

Turning.

Free Ray comes at us.

He has a Louisville Slugger. He's gripping the tapered handle. The bat was shattered long ago. Shattered low, right above the missing knob. The bottom is a jagged stake. Ray swings. Connects with the back of Fennessy's skull. The detective goes down. Before I can move, Ray stuffs the broken end of the bat into my stomach. I expect to see it sticking there. I'm impaled. But no. Ray still has the bat. He whams the barrel against the side of my head. I'm sprawling. I almost go headfirst into the grave. And it is *my grave,* I realize. Fennessy kneeling. Ray has another clean shot. It is a sick, wet smacking sound.

I get up.

I would like to run away. But I can't breathe. I'm bleeding. I try walking and my own blood warms my face and soaks my shirt. I stumble over the slabs. Behind me, Ray is hitting Fennessy.

I see a man in the forest with us.

"Help."

The man watches me. He's looking down the steep drop-off. I can only see his head and some upper body.

"Go get . . . police. He's killing him."

The man is coming down to where we are. Slowly. Wordlessly. He's being careful not to slip on the roots.

"Please."

The man is dressed casually for business. He wears a jacket, like Fennessy. It is soft gray with purple accenting threads.

"Stay back and call the police for help."

The man must be an idiot. He walks past me. He carries something in his hand.

"I didn't know he'd bring anyone," Free Ray says to the man.

The man does not respond. His eyes are amber. Flecked. I noticed them as he passed. He's clean-shaven but has a heavy five-o'clock shadow. I try to move faster and I'm sprawling for the second time.

"*That* cocksucker"—Free Ray points the bat at Fennessy—"is a cop."

The man holds a chisel.

Iron chisel. Black leaves. Ravine. Dry mudflat. Stumps.

The man has bluish dust on his trousers.

He cut the stones.

Free Ray sees me looking around. He comes over and kicks me in the face.

Fennessy must be dead. I get a flash through the red-black spots. Blurry motion. Ray is whaling on him. Straddling Fennessy's unresponsive body and swinging the bat down from high up over his head. Two-handed. Grunting with each blow.

The man thumps the chisel against his thigh.

I crawl. I'm not looking. My fingers snag the web of roots.

"I got him." Free Ray's squeaky croak. I hear his footfalls. He's not even running. I hear him slapping the fat part of the bat against his palm.

Gunshot.

I spin and Free Ray falls into me.

He opens his red-rimmed mouth. Nothing. I hear a clicking from somewhere deep in his throat. I push him away. The tumbling bat seems dipped in blood. I pick it up.

I look for the man. Was he one of Morick's thralls? Yes. Maybe. From the Fistula camp—there were so many, and with their hoods, I didn't always see faces. But he's one of them. He is a servant of Graham Morick. Sent to set this trap for me.

He's nowhere.

Fennessy's gun is still in Fennessy's hand. I smell the gunshot on the air. He saved my life. I make it over to him.

"Mirrorrorrim," he says.

I'm cradling his massacred head. Saying, "I know . . . I know . . ."

He's gone.

Chapter 31

aracas. Quebec City. Singapore.

Place names, not years. But it's been a decade since the boys were stolen. Brendan Fennessy's grave is covered with grass now. The ambush at the forest preserve has given me a strange hope. If Morick's clan wants me dead, then Robyn and the boys might still be alive. The thralls have not forgotten me. I continue to search.

Cairo.

I came to Egypt to find them.

To find Graham.

And, once more, I am returning home empty-handed.

I slide the blind open on my portal.

Vertigo as I stare down into the murky lime Jell-O of Lake Michigan. My stomach is flopping.

I'll stow my pages. Buckle my bag. Wipe sweat. I don't know what to do when I'm not writing, not searching for them, swallowing pills and chasing with booze and seeing him, them, her, Robyn, but Morick mostly. The boys are lost and Robyn too and I need to put my pen down but it gets harder afterward to sort time out, the reality from the fiction from the nightmare and any day could be the one I'll have my shot or put that sturdy little double-edge razor to his throat, reminds me I need to tape up a new blade because the Egyptians kept mine—

We've landed.

J ase? Jase!"

Maria San Filippo meets me at the airport. The last time I saw her was at Fennessy's wake. She was devastated, silent. I pleaded with her to talk to her former colleagues in the department. They'd decided the murders had drugs at the core. I saw the Morick stamp; literally it was there on the stone. I spoke old crimes, kidnappings, and rituals in the woods. I told them about patterns. Got back the same treatment Father Byron had when the Boyles were snatched. No one bought what I was selling.

Her hair's shorter, sexier, if that's possible. She's made an upgrade in attire too. Her suit must cost in the four-figure range. And *her* figure? Is curvaceous, decidedly rounded. She's pregnant. I'd say about to drop.

"You're a hard man to find these days," she says.

"No address. No phone. No friends."

"A few friends."

"How did you know I was walking off that plane?"

"Credit-card activity. You changed your ticket and there was a fee. The Egyptian police filed a report. You caused problems."

"Nice to know one's privacy's protected."

"If privacy were protected, I wouldn't have anything to tell you."

"What do you have?"

"Al and Jeanie Westphal. Heard of them?"

"Never."

"They are very wealthy, and retired. No dependents. No heirs. Until last week. A long-lost daughter—they've reunited. And now they have grandchildren to consider. My law firm rewrote the Westphal wills. I think you will find their beneficiaries as interesting as I did. Let's go someplace more private."

We walk through the terminal. Maria's condition dictates our pace. I'm unused to making small talk, but I make an attempt. "You must have quite a big family by now."

She shakes her head. Tough ex-cop, she gives up so little. "We lost three babies. The doctors aren't able to explain it. They want to be comforting but end up being vague. I have trouble internally. That seems to suffice. Well, we're trying again. I'm a month from the due date, and the doctors . . . we're on schedule." The gold cross around her neck brightens as we pass a sunny window.

I have never actually been inside the Admiral's Lounge. San Filippo has a manila envelope. Paper copies. I can look, she tells me, but I cannot have. The will filings, documents legal and extralegal—I scan them.

San Filippo says, "The Westphals lied. They don't have a daughter, or any grandchildren. Their *daughter* is blind. She has two children. Boys. Twins. Their birth certificates are fakes. Good fakes, which makes them more troubling. The daughter/mother's name is Daria Jillette. Fake papers on her too. They told us the children's father is deceased. The Westphals bought them a house. The boys are homeschooled. The grandparents visit often. They're with them now."

"Where?"

"New Mexico. Out in the desert."

"Lovely. The pieces fit, except one's missing."

"Graham. Maybe he's hidden himself better."

"Or maybe these people aren't who we think they are."

"Here's a ticket. You might enjoy the desert air. It's the red-eye. I hope you don't mind. Jet lag is probably the least of your problems. So, no harm done." She smiles.

"Why are you doing this?"

The smile evaporates. "They murdered Brendan."

I nod. "I need to go to my safety-deposit box. I'm out of cash."

San Filippo passes me another envelope. Smaller, discreet. Stuffed with bills. She hands me a cell phone. "You find them? Don't do anything. Call me. I'll have FBI agents swarming the homestead within an hour. Promise me?"

"I promise."

Some promises are meant not to keep.

My flight to New Mexico—the attendant is calling us to board. I go to the men's room. Avoid looking in the mirror. Wash my face. Dry off with a paper towel. There's a man, an airport employee, emptying the trash. When he turns his back, I wrap the wet paper around the cell phone and toss it into his gray bin.

Another plane ride. Land and hail a taxi. I take a minute to size up my driver. He's perfect. I open the stuffed envelope and pass him a bill. "Show me where I can buy a gun."

"What kind of gun?"

I hand him a stack of green paper. "You know what kind."

He counts the cash.

"I can do that," he says.

The air-conditioning blasts over the seatback. From the radio, Tejano tunes. He drives to a small house. He parks in the street. Eyes flash in the rearview mirror.

"How much bang you looking for, mister?"

"I want a pistol, a revolver. It has to be in excellent condition. Nothing smaller than a .32, and I need to carry it under my shirt."

"Not a cannon?"

"And not a popgun either."

"Wait here a minute," he says. I give him money. He comes out a few minutes later with a paper bag.

I look in the bag. "That will work. Thank you."

"It ain't loaded. I got them to throw in a box of shells, gratis. If you're looking for a party, something like that, I know a couple spots."

"Is there a firing range around here?"

"I can do that too."

I understand why prophets love the desert. You push out of time. Despite my sunglasses, the dazzle spikes my head. I touch my crown. The hairs feel like straw. The scars on my legs don't register the temperature. They're dead meat.

Mountains at my back, the sun going down. This is where rich people go to get skin cancer. A neat real estate development of adobe-style ranches, one road in, then culs-de-sac. Each house has plenty of space, a couple of manicured acres. Graham must feel safe here. No fence, no security, no dogs.

I'm standing in his backyard.

The windows are covered with heavy shades. I can't see through. When I get closer, as my back skims against the rough adobe wall, I discover that the windows are painted, coat upon coat, with white paint. I touch the cold glass with my palm. I'll break it, reach for the window locks, and climb over the ledge. I can be inside in less than thirty seconds. I'll start shooting. It should all be over in two minutes.

I hear voices.

They're home.

I draw my gun and move toward the noise—electronic bleeps and buzzes.

Someone shouts. I crouch behind a pot of flowers.

The shout came from inside.

I draw my gun. The sliding patio door; vertical blinds hang on the other side. I test the handle. It moves.

Graham and Griffin Morick are sitting on the sofa, playing a video game. They look fine, strong, and clear-eyed. But it's *Shane and Liam*, not Graham and Griffin. They're alive. They've grown older. Older than I was when Mathias died. Twelve years under their belts. Their resemblance to their predecessors unnerves.

Jaws drop as they watch me invade their home.

I aim the revolver at them. Press a finger to my lips to urge their silence.

They're afraid of me. Good.

A woman works in the kitchen, frying chicken. She's a redhead; her short, bobbed cut, a mom's hairstyle, shows off her long, graceful neck.

She turns around and doesn't see me. My Red Robyn. Her eyes are like marbles set into her face. They don't follow me as I rush past the boys and step around the counter. I stand behind her and listen to the grease popping in the pan. She's lived with Graham much longer than she lived with me. She's a stranger. My enemy.

She senses a human presence. Turns off the gas. Dinner's ready.

A moment of near-recognition—I am not one of the boys. Her eyes are fixed and unblinking. They've obviously gotten worse. She can't pick me out of the shadows. But who forgets the way someone feels, someone loved?

I point the gun at her head.

"Where's Graham?" I ask.

The bloodstone he gave her sways on its tether around her neck.

Confusion in her look, asking, "How . . . ?"

I grab her elbow. "Tell me."

"Down the hall. The second bedroom. But, Jase, you don't have to . . ."

I hold the barrel of the gun inches from her face.

I can't do this.

Need to find another way.

Do it now.

I think too much about killing. I can't. I leave her. Shane and Liam wait for me to walk out of the kitchen. They go to her side.

The hallway is narrow, cool. The walls are clean. No pictures. Indian rugs spread on the tile floors like islands.

The click-clack of my heels resounds as I walk between them.

I open the bedroom door.

Raise the gun. Finger the trigger. I've got six bullets and I'll use them all.

Graham's last trick plays out.

The room is empty.

I lower the gun. The room has only one decoration. My brain tries to comprehend it.

Black wings—a frozen ascension.

Robyn and her sons join me. Robyn's talking. The black wings—she tells me how she tacked Graham's robe to the wall. How she opened its folds and spread them. Under the robe is a low altar, a ghastly jumble of glue and rope and peeled sticks.

They aren't sticks.

She tells me her sons built the table from Graham's bones. Yes, I see that now. Here's the Druid's skull wrapped like a great precious egg in velvet; the fabric dyed black on one side, red on the reverse. She holds up his head like a chalice. *Put it down.* She does and covers it again, so I don't have to look.

"You're amazed, right?" she asks, beaming. "Graham really did it, Jase."

The hangman's rope Graham used during the Cloven Print—they've coiled that round and round his skeleton. Robyn's palm hovers over the altar. She finds the frayed end of the rope. Beside it is a straight razor, closed into its handle, black and old; adorned with a silver pin. Even so, the length of the weapon quickens my heartbeat. I raise the gun. But it's the severed rope she chooses.

"We cut his body down when it was finished."

Graham Morick is dead.

He cheated me and I can't believe it. The years I've wasted, my sanity—

But Robyn and the boys are alive. I've found them and that's enough. It has to be or else I'll . . . Robyn and the *boys*—plural.

Shane *and* Liam—what happened? If Graham performed the ritual, then one of them should be as dead as Graham.

"Why are both boys still alive?"

Robyn says, "Shane, Liam, come here. It's all right. Jase is a friend."

They approach and she holds them close.

"Aubrey never understood the true power of the mirrorrorrim. Graham grasped at it. He *needed* my help. I convinced him neither boy had to die. It wasn't going to work that way. Graham's soul was at stake. To make the wrong choice during the ritual would be doubly fatal. He should pick later, I told him. Once he crossed over, he would see what to do. He would have his power."

"You never could have convinced him."

"I did," she says.

She crouches and reaches under the altar. She's holding a silver disk—it's a film can. The kind I haven't seen since projectors wheeled around the back rows of my eighth-grade science class. There's a label stuck to the front that says, simply, *The Print*. Robyn pops it open and shows me the 16mm reel inside.

"It's all here," she says. "We used Aubrey's old Bolex camera and tripod, the same one he shot Graham and Griffin with at the Maltzes. Graham kept everything in storage. He was meticulous. He had such a strong belief in tradition."

"You filmed Graham's hanging?"

"His transformation," she says. "Oh, you have to watch it."

If she saved the boys, then why are we here? It's because Robyn believes. She has convinced the thralls to wait. Graham left them, but they have him in spirit. They have him dwelling inside these boys. All while they anticipate his evil return.

I touch her red hair. Let the strands fall through my fingers.

"Why didn't you tell me where you were? I would've taken you home."

She shakes her head, grabs my hand, squeezes. "My home is with the boys. I'm keeping them safe until Graham emerges. We're his family."

Morick's bloody doctrine addles her brain. I cannot listen to her. It's sickness. That weight drops heavy on my heart. What Robyn needs is help. She needs me to save her from this madness.

We have to get out of here.

"You have phony papers? You and the boys have passports?"

"The Cloven family provided everything. Graham watches over us. I feel him. Sometimes I swear he's here in the house."

I decide, in that moment, what we'll do.

"Pack a bag. We're leaving—the four of us together. Run now. That's the only way. Before any of the thralls know I found you. Hurry, we must move quickly."

She's confused. But she doesn't argue. I usher Robyn, Shane, and

Liam into the bedroom she tells me they share. There's a noise in the distance. A rumble.

"We don't have much time," I say.

Robyn opens her mouth, but she says nothing.

A truck turns into the adobe's driveway. The big engine idles and switches off.

Al and Jeanie Westphal.

I shut Robyn and her sons in the bedroom.

I spy around the corner of an adobe wall. I'm not even breathing. The Westphals walk in their front door. They're carrying groceries. I don't recognize them from the Fistula. I've never seen them before in my life. It's like they stepped out of an AARP brochure. Ma and Pa Retired America.

"We're home," Mrs. Westphal calls into the silent house. "And we have ice cream sandwiches."

I meet them in the kitchen.

They look like grandparents. My grandparents, yours.

"Who are you?" Al asks me. He sounds like he really cares about my answer.

The head.

God help me.

I shoot them both in the head.

Chapter 32

Robyn doesn't resist my plan for fleeing the country. She has a lot of cash stuffed in her duffel bag. I don't ask where it came from. I'm grateful to have it. Money makes everything easier. She even helps me chart our course. We'll fly south. Hire a small plane. Buy a sailboat. We pick through countries the way other couples sort paint chips for their living room. This one's too dark. That one's too busy.

I want ocean access and few tourists. A place to disappear into. Lack of development and instability are not detractors.

Robyn and I talk as we leaf through an atlas of the lower Americas. *How about here?*

We make the decision together. That's how it feels. But it's Robyn's suggestion. I'm excited to be making choices with her again. I've missed having a partner. Robyn can be so persuasive. We tear the page from the atlas. Our final destination is set.

Spend a few hectic days in the Exumas, Bahamas. I'm eager to track down a projector. I want to see the film. I need to know Graham's dead. I keep searching for him. Out of habit, and in perpetual fear. I've taught myself to believe in him. Yes, I believe in ghosts. One ghost.

Other necessities push to the front of the line. Remnants of Morick's thralldom will follow us. They're real enough. They've got serious motivation to do me harm. After all, I've stolen their legacy. And San Filippo won't take long to piece together events as they went down fatally in the desert. I broke a promise. Deep down she's still a cop. She'll make that call to the FBI.

We are pursued. I can't take time thumbing the Bahamian yellow pages to locate A/V equipment. Instead, I'm haggling and paying cash for a wooden live-aboard cruiser. Not much to look at, but she's seaworthy. I like it better that way. We won't draw attention. Despite everything, I'm thrilled to be heading out on the water. Pick up supplies next. The cash makes our trail harder to follow. I thought I might have to watch Robyn. But she's with me at every step.

It's like slipping back in time. But too much has changed. It's more like visiting the past in a dream. And I like my past, love this dream I'm having of it. No time for nostalgia. This trip goes *forward*.

Maps.

We'll need good maps.

Waterborne, we drop south.

We sail through the gauze of tropical heat. Coastlines are fickle places, speaking the language of horizons, always promising departure.

Where do you want to go?

Somewhere we'll never be heard from again.

Fugitives—kidnapping and multiple murders are among our crimes. Do I see us going to the law? Could we explain our way out of jail time? Instead of answers, I get an image— Bag Martinez turning blue at the bottom of a swimming pool. That won't be me. No going back, no homecoming in our future. I will never see Syd or Sara again. And that is almost too much to ask. But I have Shane and Liam.

I have Robyn.

We haven't slept together. An avalanche of booze and bad nerves— my desire's underneath the mountain. It's going to take a bit of tunneling. Robyn was Graham's lover. This she confirms in detail. She talks of him as a widow would. Grieves for him, telling me she still loves him. She awaits his return.

I would be lying if I said I'd lost all hope. I'm able to do something I thought impossible weeks ago. I put my hand out and clasp Robyn's. The ember of passion burns.

Robyn is totally blind. The Westphals sent her to three respected doctors for examination. There will be no recovery. She must continue to live as she is. We do our best to help her adapt. That is the only course of treatment left.

Chapter 33

After days at sea, we've grown silent with each other. We four are pensive. Sight of our destination revives us. We pull into port. Clear customs; our papers are good. The inspections run smoothly. We have clearance to travel inland.

Hunting for the passage that will deliver us.

The sun, climbing the horizon, strikes fierce. Jewels ride the waves. Ripples writhe sluggish beneath the hull. We churn a path of molten silver bubbles. Water and air become one element, indistinguishable. Breathing is drinking. We immerse. I clean the smudges off my sunglasses. They slide down my nose. Use the same rag to mop my face. I am drenched in my own juices. Sweat dribbles down my cheeks.

A village, our village, lies up a river of garbage. Junk floating in dark-roasted water. Daylight, but the rats are out. A girl with a long pole is doing her best to drown one. On both shorelines and in top-heavy boats of dubious construction, people are busy working, cooking over steamy kettles, attending to myriad chubby-faced children, young and old conversing, sitting, crouching, climbing every surface of raft and land.

People everywhere.

One by one, we silence them.

They stare at us.

We're foreigners in the truest sense.

Shane, Liam, even Robyn—it's like they're enjoying a holiday. I am not. White man trespassing in a brown world. I check the view of the ocean over my shoulder. When it vanishes, I feel cut off. A trapdoor slams. Apprehension and history precede me. White people mean bad news. We glow like phosphorus.

Docked and tied off. It feels funny to walk on solid ground. The earth undulates beneath my feet. We move in a cluster, the boys, suddenly shy, wedge in between Robyn and me. The villagers part to clear a path.

Are they more frightened than I am?

I think so.

Buggy eyes follow us with trepidation. Ahead—a courtyard, and, at the far side, an official building bakes through the midday. Palms stand sentry. Dogs are snoring on the steps. It may be a post office, or a bank.

We go inside.

Fans turn above us, but the heat doesn't falter. We find a man in a suit. Robyn converses with him in broken Spanish. He answers in broken English. The look in his eyes is universal. Money. He smells money. I clutch the duffel against my chest.

Robyn pulls me aside. "He says there's a house we can rent. A large island, beaches, all down the coast. Tourists have stayed there in the past. It sounds simple."

"How do we get there?"

She leans over to the man. She speaks to him. He sits behind a desk. He is watching my bag.

"There's a road with a bridge," she says.

"I'm not leaving the boat here. Ask if we can go by sea."

Robyn learned Spanish in college. I didn't. But the man smiles and nods.

"Yes," Robyn tells me. "He wants to know if you have a map."

I dig the map from my pocket. He slips a pencil from his jacket and begins drawing. He turns the map upside down and pushes it to me. He traced a line, back out the river mouth, and along the islands. The largest island fits like a jigsaw cutoff about to slide into place. His mark hugs the coast. It is a crooked line, not very long.

"Tell him, okay. We will meet him there."

"Yes, sir," the banker says, not waiting for a translation. "No problem. I will be there at sunset. Very nice house. You will see."

It's more a glorified hut. We step off onto a rickety pier. Fun-house grade, it torques left then right. A third of the boards are missing. In the gaps, through a lens of shallow hazel water, bright fish dart from piling to piling. I take Robyn's arm. We make it. Broken shells mash underfoot. Shane is running. Liam chases. He picks up a stick. Boys are like dogs, they can make a game of anything. Robyn rests her head against my shoulder. Her hair blows loose rusty streaks across her sunglasses. This place is remote. No signs of neighbors. You feel the lack of human presence. Desertion. But we are bringing new life. We can hide here. We can be ambushed too. I wish I'd somehow brought along the gun.

"Let's have a look," she says.

I call out, "You guys stick close to the pier."

The boys nod in unison.

"Right, let's go," I say. Robyn, chin high, regards the hut. Her aim's dead-on. We walk. If I didn't know better, I'd swear she can see it.

The hut logs are plum-colored, peeling badly, eaten by beach, wind, sun. The tin roof shimmers. Heat rises off it like a griddle pan. Quivers in the afternoon swelter. The door blazes yellow and has no lock. I go in first. Opening the huge shutters that are facing the beach, unhinging them, it is like removing a wall. No glass or screens. A framed 3-D portrait of paradise you can fall into.

The entering wind billows my shirt.

I turn to face the interior.

Table, chairs. Cookstove and pantry shelves. A fingerling-pale lizard—he is almost translucent—skitters into the path of sunlight slashing the floorboards. I find a broom and sweep him through the door. I whisk the shells of dead bugs from the corners; a sprinkling of glassy sand grits under my sandals. The room smells—hot metal.

Robyn fans herself with the map.

The living quarters need sprucing, but they are manageable. We've

265

got ice chests in the cruiser, electricity too. We'll get by for now. The main room is for eating and living; the two at the back divide for sleeping. I duck in. Utilitarian bunk spaces complete with pairs of musty olive, army cots.

Thinking again, this isn't so bad.

It's like a cheap summer camp.

Up to this point, we've slept like a wolf pack. Now there are two separate bedrooms, and a choice has to be made.

"Given any thought to the sleeping arrangements?" I ask.

Robyn tilts her head, considering. "I'd assumed the boys would stay together. You and I would share a room. Are there enough beds?"

"Not beds, cots. We have four."

"That works."

Robyn ventures forward, nudging one of the cots with her knee. She bends and tests the canvas with her fingers. She lies down, stretches out, hands laced behind her head. "There's another cot in here?"

"It's right across from you."

"Push them together," she says.

"Maybe it's easier if you and I . . ."

"Lie with me, Jase."

Robyn reaches out, crooks a finger. I step closer. I hadn't expected anything to happen between us so soon. I'm caught off guard. I feel something break loose and melt in my chest. I'm first-date nervous. My heart gallops. Her hand finds the leg of my khaki shorts. "I've missed you," she says. She pulls at the fabric, her hand kneading, then freeing me. "I've missed us doing this."

Despite the open window, the bedrooms are dark and close. Sweat glistens on her skin. She spits into her hand.

"The boys are right outside," I say.

I lower myself onto the cot. The metal feet scratch the floor.

"Then we'll have to be quick, won't we?"

Robyn takes her sunglasses off. She lifts her hips off the cot and bunches her sundress up around her waist. Underneath, she is naked. I remember this body. Her hand thrums a slow rhythm between her legs. We kiss. Her tongue is twisty, combative. She grabs a fistful of hair at the back of my head. Our mouths seal. She's sucking air from my lungs. I break. Our faces, so close. After everything lost, here we are. Found again. Here she is. Robyn.

"Your beard," she says, rubbing her knuckles under my chin. "It's rough. You feel different than you used to."

She can't see me. We touch foreheads.

"It's been a long time," I say.

She turns around and pushes backward.

"Go hard," she says.

S hane, silhouetted in the doorway, says, "There's a truck coming."

I am somewhere between sleep and wakefulness. I traverse that fuzzy gray edge, abandoning my dreams for this waking world. I am aware of Robyn. Her curves spooned into mine. I drape an arm across her waist. A draft of air has finally reached us. It is cool, like a third skin caressing ours. Alive in my body, my senses cleansed. I enjoy a physicality I haven't experienced in years. Blink in the pleasant half-light. Hear the sea crashing in the cove. Inhale the pungent jungle aromas.

I breathe Robyn too. Taste her sweetness and her salt.

Shane fidgets. He shifts his body weight and bangs an elbow into the door. Softly he swears. Is he really worried about the truck?

Or is it me, lying next to Robyn, who bothers him?

"The man from this morning," I whisper, "he's coming to help us. That'll be his truck." Robyn is snoozing on. A lick of damp hair clings to her neck. I study the rise and fall of her chest. Attempt to disengage without disturbing her.

When I look up, Shane has vanished.

I go outside to meet our visitor.

A way from the village, the banker's English grows more fluent. The sunset is a bloody host dissolving in the ocean mists. Volcanic colors wipe the horizon.

He sighs. "It is a lovely view of the sea. I forget sometimes how lovely.

I don't drive back here often enough. We used to have more tourists, you know."

"Not anymore?"

The banker shakes his head. He is baby-faced, though in his tailored suit, he does not appear fat. His features are the color of dark honey. When he is not speaking, he is smiling. "I have some things for you in my truck."

He gives us a lantern, a gallon of mineral water, and matches for the stove. "There is a latrine over there by the bushes." He points to a wood structure at the back of the hut. I hadn't noticed it. We have a shower and a toilet aboard ship. "Keep the door latched. Use a light if you go out after dark. There are big cats in the jungle. Don't be scared. But watch for them. You have a torch?" I tell him yes. He shows me the generator. It should work, he says. He adds that someone will come in the morning with fuel. If we want any food, water, sundries—we must take the road into the village.

"Okay, that should do it," he says. He slips out of his jacket and lays it across the front seat of his truck. He rolls his sleeves. In his fingers, he has a thin, black cigar. I give him a match.

As he smokes, he watches the boys still playing on the beach.

"Your sons, already they like it here."

My sons.

"We need a film projector," I say.

"Cinema?" He frowns, shakes his head.

"Not a cinema. Come with me to the boat."

"Sure, no problem."

We step along the pier. The banker is nimble. I board the cruiser. He waits for me. I return with the duffel bag and the canister of film. I show him the reel. Explain the importance of having a projector. I stress that we will pay top dollar if he is speedy.

"If I can locate such a thing, I will send it with the fuel. I cannot guarantee this."

"I appreciate your effort."

We shake hands. I pay him from the duffel. I want him to know this will be a fruitful relationship. So he will do his best.

Chapter 34

I n the morning, no one comes. No diesel fuel, no projector.

We walk. Take a shopping trip. There's a farmer's market some-where between us and the village. The road is deserted. It winds through a canopy of trees. Our course is rugged. The walk home, carrying sup-plies, will be tougher. At least we're traveling through shade. We see children playing. But before we reach them, they disappear. Here and there, dotting the brush, are rooftops. Colorful walls of azure and ver-milion. We cross a bridge made of hand-cut planks. Vines dangle into an emerald abyss. You can hear water burbling. Look down. The ravine stuffed with fog.

Pretend we're a real family, no better or worse than any you see in the less popular vacation spots south of the border. Maybe we look grubbier—it's all the energy devoted to wondering if our journey is fi-nally over. You'd see us and pass right by. If you're observant, you peer up from the pages of your novel to notice a couple of tall, good-looking twin boys. You may feel a tug of curiosity or even sympathy, noticing the way they link their arms with a woman you assume to be their mother. You judge from her subtle movements that she must be blind.

Where's the father?

There, looking harried, sleepless, but lean like the cigarette he's stopped to light or the beer bottle he's buying from the shop merchant as he scans the faces of strangers with more than casual interest. Maybe if you locked eyes with him, you'd feel his suspicion or perhaps his plea. You'd see us and read the surface facts, but you'd miss the story.

The market is a one-man shop on wheels—a handsome thatched awning, and a red Coca-Cola cooler packed with iced fruit. We load up.

Back home, Shane and Liam transfer our supplies to the hut. Robyn organizes. We eat rice and beans. Mangoes and chili powder. Crash out through the hot afternoon, stomachs filled and tongues stinging. I'm worried about this sanctuary. I don't see us staying long. That road at the top of the hill is our lifeline. I take another walk. Reaching the summit, I spin around and view the hut, the cove, our cruiser bobbing. It's a perfect snapshot of tropical ease. I am uneasy.

I can't lay my finger on why.

The road runs two ways. Run a short jog in the direction opposite the village. It's not so different from the Fistula's road. I don't wander far. There's a lagoon jammed with birds, snakes, and God knows what else. Monkeys. We have monkeys. Chattering brown ones and black ones with tufts of hair growing pointed over their ears. The sun dips below the trees. Eighty-plus degrees and I'm chilled.

I hear a small engine approaching.

A motorbike—and driving it hard through ribs of mud, a teenaged boy. Strapped to the back are two jerricans. Our fuel.

I help the teenager carry the cans down to the generator. After some effort, we get the thing started. It smokes, but it works.

"You have something else for me?" I ask.

Sí, sí.

He brings me a cardboard box. The stamps on the side say infant formula. But they are faded. The blue lettering has worn gray. I tear open the flaps.

The projector.

I pay him in American dollars.

The sky above us is bruised. A storm's blowing in. Miles out to sea, making a slow crawl inland, but it is approaching. Thunderclouds, like huge smoky brains tearing themselves apart, throw javelins of lightning. The ocean itself seems lit from below. I can't hear the thunder. Not yet.

I assemble the projector.

No instructions come with our equipment. I am not mechanical. I find too many parts in the box. I stop to polish the lens. Screw it into place. Reabsorb myself in the puzzle of connecting the rest of the pieces. The work is soothing. I have a purpose. I want to watch Graham's demise. Working, I fill a conch with dead cigarettes.

The storm rips at the night.

We're hiding inside a drum. Each boom trembles the hut walls, and the constant thrash of rain bleeds the joints. Tight rooms, low ceilings. Reverberations buzz in my bones. The word *catacomb* jumps into my head. At the windows, doorjambs, even the cracks in the walls—water begins to creep in.

I pry the window an inch. My face instantly doused. Witness an enormous tail of sand that spiraled out into our cove—erased in seconds. The buoys marking the channel are Clorox bottles anchored to the bottom with chains. They've torn loose. I spot one hurled up on the sand, tumbling sideways. The waves hiss. Foamy heads rear above the beach. Explode. Bowing trees are soon shredded. And the moon is buried away. I haven't seen its light since we docked.

The galaxy looks different down here.

I shut the window.

I pull the chain on the only bulb in the hut. Forty watts of light; in other words, near darkness. But we have electricity and an open socket growing like a tumor in the wall. The prongs don't match the plug. But I borrowed an adapter from the boat. I reach into the infant-formula box and find it empty. I'm finished. Run the thick black cord into the wall. Switch on, and the motor whirs, the fan spins, we have light. But we have no screen. I pick the blankest wall. I crack open the canister. Thread the film.

We're ready.

I latch the shutters. I don't want them bursting open, followed by electrocution in a deluge. Robyn and I take chairs. Shane and Liam lounge atop each other under the table. I extinguish the lonely bulb.

The home movie begins.

A bit of preliminary film rolls, numbers and such, then the wall changes, dims, to a view of a large, open room. Graham used black-and-white stock, in keeping with Aubrey's other recordings.

A large, open room . . .

Silent movie.

I find a volume knob and twist.

Background noise, but at least there's audio.

Wooden beams are visible in the ceiling. Candlelit. Iron stands surround the boys and dark gray candles—I can only guess their color, and my guess is red—are burning.

Hundreds of candles. The room dances in flames. We see two figures. The boys are already lying on the floor, on either side of a three-legged stool. A hangman's noose suspends, to the left, above the stool.

"I don't recognize this place," I say. "Where did you perform the ritual?"

"We could've gone anywhere. Those Who Follow span the globe. Graham did so much to prepare. He brought many into the family."

"Those Who Follow? You mean his thralls?"

"I don't like that word. *Thrall* implies slavery, don't you think? We all made a decision, Jase. We chose to follow. Those Who Follow is much more appropriate."

"And where did you follow Graham?"

"Everywhere he asked me."

"The ritual happened in the States?"

Robyn nods her head. "New York City. It was a judge's loft. Graham told me the views were lovely. It was expensive and quiet. So perfect. We couldn't even hear the traffic from the streets below. The judge gave us the keys."

"Was the judge present?"

"Graham insisted we do the Print alone. He wanted no interference. Graham was exhausted. You made real problems for us. After the fiasco at the Fistula, Graham grew paranoid. Those Who Follow were in chaos. Some panicked and fled. Others expressed doubts. Graham worried you'd find a way to stop us."

I wish I had.

"But I told him he was wrong," she says. "You'd never hurt us. You loved me. I think you convinced him of that. I said you had the safety of the boys in mind. I did too."

On the film, the boys are inert. Two heaps.

"They look lethargic. Hardly breathing."

"Graham gave Shane and Liam a sedative. He used too much. He gave me some too, in a cup of tea. He didn't want us to be afraid."

"We weren't afraid," Shane says.

"Be quiet now," Robyn points at the wall. "And watch."

Graham enters the frame. To see him, celluloid or not, is a shock. He gathers his robes in his hands. "The Black Blood Druid walks between the mirrors . . ."

Robyn's head drops to her chest. She recites the next words with him: "Between the mirrors. And into Eternity."

"And into Eternity," Graham says as he kneels.

He kisses the boys on their foreheads. They look asleep.

Robyn presses into me.

Graham invokes his father. He lays his hands on the boys' chests. He speaks of serpents, of moons, of the dark heart of human destiny. His hood is down. He looks haggard, not the vital charmer I first met.

"At this point, you knew he wouldn't kill the boys?"

Robyn says, "I told him there was no need to sacrifice a boy. The mirrorrorim were sacred. His spirit needed to pass this realm. When the day came for his Emergence, one boy would be transformed and the other would live as his strongest ally. Graham was so anxious. The Cloven family was unraveling. He said his thralls lost confidence. It was going to be expensive to hide us. He thought the money might dry up. We'd end up in jail. Or worse. Public humiliation was his biggest fear. That and betrayal."

"His followers needed a sign."

"The Cloven family needed the ritual performed. To see him take action."

"Was he afraid he'd lose his nerve? Fail like Aubrey?"

"If Graham had any doubts about his magical power, he kept them private."

Graham steps out of the frame.

There's a final adjustment to the camera. I hear the rustle of his robes. Moments later, he strides into the picture again. Hood up. Purpose to his step. He appears rushed, ready to get it over with. Prepared to claim his magical godhood.

Soft cry of wood on wood as a cloaked Graham drags the stool and centers it under the noose.

From under his robe, he retrieves a bundle.

He unbinds it.

He crouches on the stool. He unrolls the bundle on the floor. I can't see what's inside. The snout of his hood aims down at the ritual tools. Though his face is hidden, Graham's movements look unsteady. It's strange to see him so unsure. He touches the objects in the bundle. He picks one—the barber's razor he inherited from his father, who inherited it from his stepfather. He bares the steel.

Blade in hand, his arm sweeps once, symbolically, over Liam. He lifts the razor again, passing it brightly over Shane.

Robyn is chanting.

He stands and reaches up for the noose. The rope hangs too high.

He grabs the loop and yanks downward. Not enough slack. He climbs from his perch and goes to a hook protruding from the wall. He uncoils the rope. The noose drops. He secures it once more.

Graham is tall. But regaining his position on the stool, captured nearly a decade ago on film, he looks smaller. Mortal.

Standing tiptoe, he slips the lowered rope around his neck. Draws the knot snug over his left shoulder. I see his chest heaving under his vestments. Knees trembling. His life depends on balance.

He is about to die.

In his wicked philosophy, to be reborn.

The time for words is ended.

Robyn's chant stops.

A quick jerk of the rope changes everything. The stool tips. Fallen, it turns a slow circle underneath his suspended body. An awful tension begins.

Graham Morick is strangling.

Dying.

He has the razor in his hand. Plucked from the bundle spread on the floor—the instrument of the Cloven Print. Does he regret not using it?

He slashes the air. Slashes in the direction of Robyn. But she's several feet away, this blind woman who convinced him to alter his plans. If she were closer, he could open her throat.

His body shakes.

Then he is still.

The blade clatters to the floor.

His arms drop to his sides, fingers opening.

Fingers.

I lean toward the image flickering on the wall.

I am counting fingers.

The camera is almost too far away. If you didn't know what to look for, you'd miss it. But I don't miss it. I cut off two of his fingers. I swallowed one. And now I am counting ten. Ten whole digits. The skeleton in New Mexico was a prop.

This dead man—is he the judge?

Or just another thrall obeying commands?

He is not Graham Morick.

The frame knocks sideways. Someone behind the camera bumped it. Graham was there, yes. Orchestrating. Faking his death scene. The Cloven family needed a miracle to believe and he gave them one. Without knowing it, Robyn delivered his solution. Stage his death. She'd be his blind witness. Then years later, he could reemerge. Kill one of the boys and resume his throne. The family would surrender to his power. He would be their resurrected king.

Like Aubrey, Graham was a con man. He didn't change his mind about the ritual or the boys. He changed his timetable. My eyes snap to the shuttered window, the door.

Graham is out there.

I stole his means of escape and return.

The film continues.

Robyn crawls under the hanged man, tapping on the floor.

She touches the blade.

She closes it.

She sits cross-legged beneath him.

The body swings.

She cries in rapture.

For minutes we sit and watch it—the boys and I; Robyn is turned toward me. Her vacant eyes have closed. What is she hearing? Her own ecstasy relived.

I hear the hum of the projector fan.

Bugs fly through the cone of light. A moth flutters. Spreads itself open, pressing outward like a hand on the wall.

No one moves.

We don't breathe.

In the film, on the floor of the loft, the boys are convulsing. I suppose you could say it was an effect of the overdose of sedatives. You could say that. Their eyes roll. Both boys, simultaneously, thrown into fits. They moan and drool. Their tongues hang from their mouths. Eyes spun back in their heads, faces grimacing. They begin to shout. They blaspheme.

The wall turns bright white.

The loose end of the film flaps around the reel.

I snap the projector off. The wall goes dark. The hut is dark. I can't see Robyn or the boys. I reach for the chain attached to the bulb above us. I touch Robyn's face instead. The wetness of her tears—the tears of a believer. I cup her cheek.

"He's coming back," she says to me.

"I know."

"You want to be there with us?"

"I do," I say.

I pull the light chain. Robyn's beautiful face illuminated.

"I need you to be truthful with me," I say.

"I've always been truthful," she says, pushing out her chin.

"Did you ever come to this place before? This village, this hut? Were you ever here with Graham?"

"No. Why—?"

"When I researched Graham, back in Chicago, I saw pictures of him with children. They looked like the children who live here. Did Graham visit this place? Did he?"

Her shoulders slump. Chin held not so high.

"Yes."

"And the banker? Is he a Cloven family member? Is that why he's helping us?"

She shakes her head. "I really can't say."

Chapter 35

I don't tell Robyn what I saw on the film. Confrontation would be a mistake. It would amount to my word against Graham's. My observation, which she can neither verify nor deny, versus her own deep religious experience. I wouldn't win that battle. Where Robyn goes, so go the boys. If she turns them against me, I'll never get off the beach.

It would be crazy to launch the boat in this storm. I'd kill us all in the cove. Cave the hull against those unmarked reefs. No, I won't do his dirty work. We have to wait until morning. Clear skies. For tonight, we're trapped.

The winds are dying.

I lie in my cot and speed them along with my will.

I cannot sleep.

Yet I must doze off, because I startle to find Shane on my left side, Liam fixed on the right. He's gripping the cot tubing. Bouncing. Shaking me awake. There's extra space in here. Robyn told me tonight she wanted to sleep in the boys' room. I helped cram her cot alongside theirs.

"What is it?"

"We heard a noise," says Liam.

"What kind of noise?"

Shane begins, "A scary noise like—"

"Someone walking around," finishes Liam.

I bolt up.

We stand around the kitchen table. The projector sits between us, displayed like the carved bones of a bizarre bird. We are not using our eyes.

Three males listen for a fourth stalking outside.

An earth-slurping gulp of mud—we all hear it.

"That's the sound," Shane says.

"Something is on the other side of the door," Liam decides. "It's walking around the hut. We heard footsteps."

"Stay put. I'll have a look."

I grab a spade near the back door.

The bogeyman lurking outside is a recurring theme of the boys' nightmares. Mine too. I've checked for him before. When we were sleeping out on the sailboat, he splashed like a porpoise. Tonight, he is real.

Nightfall.

If you don't have a moon over your shoulder, you're lost.

A monkey, I tell myself—or a stray dog from the village. That's what's circling our perimeter. Or it could be Graham coming to hack us to bits in our sleep.

I carry a heavy-duty flashlight that I brought in from the boat. Hearing the banker's words about the jungle cats, I kept it in the house. On a shelf above our little propane stove. Click the button. The light is weak, syrupy, like it's been burnt. The battery is dying. Salt air gets into everything. It's like acid rotting the wires. I thump the plastic housing against my thigh. The beam brightens.

Dims.

I open the door.

The storm reduced to a slow, steady downpour. My light picks at the wires of raindrops. Having the light makes the darkness heavier. A beast I stab into. Here first. Now there. Revealing little more than the night gave up.

My instincts tell me to close the door.

Don't go any farther.

"Stay with your mother," I tell the boys. "Keep her safe."

To have a nightmare, one must first be asleep. Yet I feel awakened.

I leave the house.

I'm hunting footprints in a yard of slop.

Pointless, any imprint would seal itself over. The rain pocks a pudding of sand, silt, and vegetable slime. My legs are slathered to the calves. I feel like I'm wearing diving boots. The rattle of droplets against the flashlight is the only sound I can key into. How many senses can the weather nullify?

If Graham's out here, then he's equally disadvantaged.

I decide I am alone.

Soaked and filthy, I might as well check the boat. Make certain she's moored properly, that she hasn't smashed our pier to toothpicks.

I squeegee mud from my legs with the edge of my hand.

Keep walking toward the ocean. Shouldn't be difficult. I let gravity pull me down the path. The runoff warms my ankles.

My light catches the split head of a piling, then another—the pier.

Its structure rendered haunted. My light masses shadows.

The tide is pulling out. Good thing or we'd have to worry about surge.

I scan the twisted boards. Find the pier's end.

Switch to the water.

The boat is gone.

Out there in the cove, where a hundred yards could be a hundred miles, I trace her shape. Unmoored, unanchored. The sea pilots her. Damaged. She's listing starboard. Taking on water. It won't be long now. To witness any boat sinking is a sickening event. You experience the depths below, even if your feet are planted on solid rock. Mine are on a slipshod row of boards. My stomach shrivels.

I turn away.

Unwilling to watch her slide under.

How will we ever—?

The weak beam finds him.

Crouching on the pier, between me and the house.

It's Graham.

He wears a rain poncho. He's rising up now to look at me. To let me see him. A smile plays on his lips. The black, wet cape fans out like wings. He tugs the hood away.

One pair of eyes—they're his.

No stand-in. This is the real Graham Morick.

"Your light's going out," he says, chuckling.

I have no weapon.

He steps forward, carefully avoiding a gap in the boards.

"Get back."

"Oh, I'm going to get back."

He comes forward.

My light isn't strong enough to blind him.

"You're a fraud like your father. A coward. I'm going to let the world know."

"The world will know me. However, you won't be telling the story."

"I'm not afraid."

"Then you're stupid." Two steps closer. "Thank you, Jase, for bringing them to me. My family and I are going to have a reunion. Too bad you'll miss it."

"I told Robyn what you did. She knows you tricked her."

"She knows no such thing."

One step.

The razor is long in his hand. It extends from both sides. The handle is black, the blade thin. This steel cut his brother's throat, his father's rope. It is his. I don't need a closer look to know he snatched it from the altar in the Westphals' adobe. He stood over their dead bodies. Cold rage boiled. He pieced together what I had done to him.

As he rolls his wrist, I get two alternating views.

There is nothing in his grip.

He holds a glittering violet star.

He notices the focus of my interest. He raises the blade. Smile widening, he mocks my terror and touches the edge to his jaw. The blade lowers. He presses a finger to his skin. He kisses blood from his scarred joint.

His eyes never leave me.

Never blink.

I could jump in the water. Swim for it. I might make it around the cove.

"I'm going to kill them," he says. "In case you were wondering."

His grin is so satisfied.

I hate him.

Graham's shoulders hunch forward. He tucks his arms, lifts his hands as if in benediction. The blade leading his way. He coils for a strike.

I rush into my nightmare.

The top of my head connects with his chin. We go down. I raise the light and hammer him. Collarbone. I hear a crunch. He yells as he tries to throw me off. I cock my arm back. Lose the light. Watch it fall into a gap. The yellow eye swivels around and plunges into black water.

Where is the razor?

Ice arcs across my back. Once. Twice.

Then the warmth.

I punch him in the face. Squeeze him with my knees. Don't let him get a breath. I seize an arm. But the poncho slithers through my fingers.

The blade swipes.

I pull away.

Cold bites. My ear. My cheek.

Each wound compels him.

He wants to saw into my neck.

I drop an elbow into his eye.

He screams.

I climb off and run.

This is running in a dream. My legs are too slow. I hear him growl. The razor clawing the night to ribbons.

"Robyn! Get out of the house!"

The hut door opens.

Robyn with her arms crossed, confused and frightened. Behind her—the boys.

I am over the threshold.

Graham on my heels. Shoves me. I slam into the table. The projector crashes into pieces. I can't draw any air. Roll. Slippery with my own blood. I'm tangled in the projector's cord.

Graham grabs Robyn by the hair and throws her aside.

The boys see the beast attack their mother.

They are on him.

He kicks Liam.

The boy crumples.

High against the bulb—the twinkle of steel.

Graham is bending Shane backward. I see his throat bared.

The plastic poncho crackles as Graham lashes.

Shane falls.

The red blade flutters into the light.

I sweep my leg. Graham lands on his hip.

I wrap the cord from the projector around his neck. I pin him to the floor. He whips the razor behind him. But I am out of reach. All my weight drives down. Fists tight at the top of his spine. The cord cuts my palms. For everything—I do this.

Robyn cradles Shane in her arms. They are awash with blood.

She chants to her mirrorrorrim.

Graham turns his head. A choked gurgle, then a ratcheting noise from his chest, a bone-and-meat sound. His eyes bulge. He casts away the razor. Arms propped, he wants to raise himself. I will not allow it. The floor is not dry. He cannot hold. His chest hits the wood. His hand thrusts toward them—the blind woman, the murdered boy.

Graham's fingers curl and uncurl. Silently, he is pleading with them His tongue droops, obscene.

Even after he goes limp—I do not let go.

Chapter 36

No lights but starlight.

We walk.

We three are the survivors.

In an hour, the dawn grays will begin. For now, I'm thankful for the moist exhalation of the jungle. Robyn is in shock. She's like a robot. She can hear us. She clasps Liam's hand as we walk. With each step, the wounds on my back open and close like mouths. Blood seeps through my shirt. Liam helped me. We tore strips from a towel. We taped them with duct tape. My face and ear are clotted and ugly. I need a doctor. A needle and thread to close me.

Free. For the first time in years, I'm feeling free. We won't go back to the hut. Robyn, Liam, and I will walk away. Away from Graham's body. And Shane. We leave him because we have no choice.

The village is out of the question.

There must be another one down the road, or there wouldn't be a road.

We proceed in the opposite direction. Pass the lime green lagoon.

Robyn, Liam, and I have to disappear. The FBI, the Cloven family . . . they have a body to satisfy them. Two bodies. I hope that is enough.

Maybe they will leave us in peace. Time is our ally. The longer we stay away, the more we will be forgotten.

I have trouble keeping up with my fellow travelers.

My legs quiver.

Right now, we could use a ride.

I tell them that if a vehicle comes, I'll step down into the brush. We're more likely to be picked up if a mother and child are walking alone. When the vehicle stops—if it does—I'll have to convince the driver to take us to the next village.

Late morning, the sun is upon us—a truck drives up. The driver is going fast. I don't have time to hide myself.

I don't need to.

An old man propped behind the wheel of a scabby white Chevy. He wears a rumpled straw hat. Dressed like a scarecrow. His truck bed filled with chicken cages. The birds are noisy, spraying the roadside mud with feathers and feed.

He stops.

No English. But he understands. He smiles and offers me his water bottle. I take a swallow and pass it along. Liam drinks. I press the bottle to Robyn's lips.

"Have some," I say.

She sips.

We climb over the tailgate. The partition behind the driver is open. He smells like his birds. A plastic Madonna glued to the dashboard. The windshield is fractured, two small holes, empty centers with stellar cracks raying outward. The driver puts the truck in gear and we rumble away.

"*Música?*" the old man asks.

"Sure," I say.

He switches on his radio. It's very loud. A roar of static and, beneath it, a samba.

"He must be deaf," I say to Liam.

He smiles.

We drive for hours. I'm so glad we aren't walking.

I'm falling asleep, my eyelids slit. My head tips back against a chicken cage. Down in the hollow between Liam and Robyn, something shines. It catches the afternoon sun spearing through the treetops.

A silver pin . . .

Driven through an inch of pure black handle . . .

The barber's razor sticks out of Liam's hip pocket.

Why would he take this awful souvenir?

Liam turns his face from the billows of exhaust. His gesture is one of familiarity. He reaches out and touches my arm. I close my eyes.

"Wake up," he says gently. "We're almost there."

I'm seeing nothing. The world blacked out. I'm as blind as Robyn. What lies before me lies in obscurity. Cold sweat pops on my skin.

He took the razor.

The only promise is night.

A warm hand on my shoulder shakes me. I don't want to look at him. I saved him. I saved Robyn and myself. We're alive. Alive should be good. This is a new life. *I killed Graham.*

I open my eyes.

No glittering blade greets me.

"We must wake ourselves," Liam says.

For the first time, I'm seeing him.

I sit forward and take a long, hard look. Brush his hair back from his face so we are eye to eye. Liam rests his chin against my injured palm. The sunlight bands his cheeks in gold. The driver glances over his shoulder at us.

Father and son.

Liam doesn't break from my gaze. I feel his pulse through my skin. Wearing his salt-crusted, muddy cutoffs, barefoot, an American youth in a tattered Adidas T-shirt. His hair is wild and sprinkled with sand. I comb it with my fingers. His eyes are not wild. No. They're calm. Clear. I should feel relief. I sense muscles working in Liam's face. Tightening, as the flesh gathers.

This boy I saved . . .

Yet, that smile.

The radio changes from static crackle to silence. I look at the driver. His hands haven't moved. Two o'clock and ten—the way they teach in driving school. We pass through rattling trees. Their trunks sway in the wind. Slowly, the hood of the Chevy pushes forward, and the road opens, widens as we enter the village. Dusty orange glow, the air sooty with campfire smoke, and people—the shadows of people move outside the truck.

Robyn can't see them. I don't know if I'm happy for her, or sad.

They hold out their arms.

Wrists bent, their hands mimic hooves. They're showing us who they are.

Those Who Follow.

Liam rises to his feet.

On the radio, the singing of children begins.

1950   1960   1970   1980   1990

Conservative Coalition Era
(1938–1964)

Liberal Ascendancy
(1965–1978)

"Cutback Politics"
(1979–)

New Republican Era
(1994)

Lyndon Johnson's Senate
(1955–1961)

Special caucuses grow

Speaker
Sam Rayburn
(1940–1961)

"Reform Era"
(power dispersed)
(1970–1975)

Speaker
"Tip" O'Neill
(1977–1987)

Leadership
strengthened
Jim Wright
(1987–1989)

Newt Gingrich
(1995)

National
Security Act
(1947)

Federal
Interstate
Highway Act
(1956)

"Great Society" Legislation
Civil rights; Medicare (1964);
Voting rights (1965);
National Environmental Policy Act (1969)

Ethics in
Government Act
(1978)

Brady Gun Control Act
(1993)

Americans with Disabilities Act
(1991)

Legislative Reorganization Act;
Employment Act
(1946)

"Baby Boomers"
(born 1946–1964)

Legislative
Reorganization Act of
1970

Congressional Budget Act
(1974)

Budget Enforcement Act
(1990)

Gramm-Rudman-Hollings
(1985, 1987)

Reform period
(1993–1995)

Army-McCarthy Hearings
(1954)

Kefauver Crime
Committee
(1950–1951)

Watergate
break-in
(1972)

Impeachment;
resignation
(1974)

War Powers Resolution
(1973)

Iran-contra scandal
(1986)

Clinton scandal,
impeachment
(1998–1999)

Youngstown v. Sawyer
(1952)

Watkins v. U.S.
(1957)

Brown v. Topeka
(1954)

Wesberry v. Sanders
(1964)

Buckley v. Valeo;
Roe v. Wade
(1974)

I.N.S. v. Chadha
(1983)

Shaw v. Reno
(1993)

U.S. Term Limits v.
Thornton
(1995)

"Cold War"
(1945–1991)

"McCarthyism"
(1950–1954)

Korean War
(1950–1953)

Vietnam War
(1965–1974)

Persian Gulf War
(1991)

Harry S. Truman
(1945–1953)

Dwight D. Eisenhower
(1953–1961)

Kennedy/
Johnson
(1961–1969)

Nixon
(1969–1974)

Ford
(1974–1977)

Carter
(1977–1981)

Reagan
(1981–1989)

Bush
(1989–1993)

Clinton
(1993-2001)

Transistor;
Mainframe
computer
(1946)

Laser
(1958)

Soviet space satellite
(1957)

Electronic voting,
House (1973)

Moon
landing
(1969)

Computers
on Capitol Hill
(1975)

Televised
House
(1979)

Televised
Senate sessions
(1986)

Internet
(1992)

1950   1960   1970   1980   1990

Classic moment in congressional politics. Lyndon B. Johnson, the persuasive Senate majority leader (1955–1961), gives "The Treatment" to a hapless Sen. Theodore Francis Green, D-R.I.

Congress
and Its Members

Seventh Edition

Roger H. Davidson
University of Maryland

Walter J. Oleszek
Congressional Research Service

CQ PRESS

A Division of Congressional Quarterly Inc.
Washington, D.C.

CQ Press
A Division of Congressional Quarterly Inc.
1414 22nd Street, N.W.
Washington, D.C. 20037

(202) 822-1475; (800) 638-1710

http://books.cq.com

Printed in the United States of America

Photo credits: Agence France-Presse, 380 (bottom); AP/Wide World, 162 (top); Architect of the Capitol, 226; Congressional Quarterly file photo, 42 (bottom), 126 (middle); Scott J. Ferrell, Congressional Quarterly, 162 (middle), 196 (top), 354 (bottom); Douglas Graham, Congressional Quarterly, 162 (bottom), 284 (top and middle), 334 (top left), 354 (top), 380 (top); R. Michael Jenkins, Congressional Quarterly, 196 (bottom), 310 (top), 334 (bottom); Deborah Kalb, Congressional Quarterly, 42 (top); Dave Kaplan, Congressional Quarterly, 126 (top); Library of Congress, 12; *New York Times*, frontispiece, 126 (bottom), 406; Reuters, 2 (bottom), 88 (top and bottom), 284 (bottom), 310 (bottom), 334 (top right and middle); *U.S. News & World Report*, 256; *Washington Post*, 2 (top).

Acknowledgments: Letter to Sen. William S. Cohen (p. 210) reprinted by permission of Senator Cohen. Figure 11-2 reprinted from *The Politics of Presidential Appointments* by G. Calvin Mackenzie, © 1981, with the permission of The Free Press, a division of Simon & Schuster.

Cover design: Debra Naylor

Library of Congress Cataloging-in-Publication Data

Davidson, Roger H.
    Congress and its members / Roger H. Davidson, Walter J. Oleszek.—
    7th ed.
      p. cm.
    Includes bibliographical references and index.
    ISBN 1-56802-519-X. — ISBN 1-56802-433-9 (pbk.)
    1. United States. Congress. 2. Legislators—United States.
I. Oleszek, Walter J. II. Title.
JK1021.D38 1999
328.73—dc21   99-36620

For Nancy; Douglas, Victoria, Elizabeth, and Thomas;
Chris, Theo, and Emily
R.H.D.

For Janet, Mark, and Eric
W.J.O.

Contents

Congressional Time Line: Nineteenth Century

	1790	1800	1810	1820	1830
Size of House of Representatives	65	142	186	213	242
Size of Senate	26	34	36	48	48

Parties

Federalist Era (1789–1800) — Jeffersonian Era (1800–1828) — Jacksonian Era (1828–1856)

1st Congress Antifederalists (1792) ▲

Congressional Nominating Caucus (1804–1828)

J. Q. Adams elected (1824) ▼

Presidential nominating conventions (1832) ▲

Internal

Jefferson's *Manual* (1801)

Congress convenes; Ways and Means Committee (1789) ▲▼

Procedural rules, standing committees (1790s) ▼

Speaker Henry Clay (1811) ▲

Committees control legislation (1820s)

Unlimited debate in Senate (1828) ▼ ▲ ▼

Major Court Cases

Judicial review *Marbury v. Madison* (1803)

Alien and Sedition Acts (1798) ▼▲

Marshall Court (1801–1835)

McCulloch v. Maryland (1819) ▲ ▼▼

Major Laws/ Investigations

St. Clair Investigation (1792)

Slave importation halted (1807)

Rivers and Harbors Act (1823)

Bill of Rights (1791) ▲▲

Louisiana Purchase (1803) ▲ ▲

Missouri Compromise (1820) ▲ ▲

Science/ Technology/ Communications

"National Road" (Wheeling–Cumberland) (1806)

Commercial railroads (1830s)

Lewis and Clark Expedition (1803–1806) ▼ ▼▲

Rotary printing press (1814) ▲

Telegraph demonstrated (1838) ▲ ▼

Wars/ World Events

Barbary pirates (1801–1805) ▼ ▼

War of 1812 (1812–1814) ▼ ▼

Monroe Doctrine (1823) ▲

Presidents

Washington (1789–1797) ▼ ▼

Jefferson (1801–1809) ▼ ▼▼

"Jeffersonians" (Madison; Monroe) (1809–1825) ▼

Jackson (1829–1837) ▼ ▼

	1790	1800	1810	1820	1830